MEASURE OF
DANGER

MEASURE OF DANGER

JAY KLAGES

f THOMAS & MERCER

Published by Thomas & Mercer, Seattle

www.apub.com

Amazon, the Amazon logo, and Thomas & Mercer are trademarks of Amazon.com, Inc., or its affiliates.

ISBN-13: 9781477830673
ISBN-10: 1477830677

Cover design by Cyanotype Book Architects

Library of Congress Control Number: 2014959845

Printed in the United States of America

To Elly and Emma, my light.
And Kade.

CHAPTER 1

His latest Friday after-work routine of staying in had kept him out of trouble, and that was great. But his growing tendency *not* to do things bothered him, because in his gut he knew there was no courage in safety.

Kinkade Sims, or Kade, as he was called, sat on the microsuede couch with a bottle of Corona in hand, his dark, green-hazel eyes focused on the old *FutureWeapons* episode playing on the wall TV while his mind toggled between the show and his army memories.

The narrating host, Mack Machowicz, wearing jeans, T-shirt, protective vest, and helmet, leaned forward against the sandbag wall, pressing his eye to the optical sight of the shoulder-launched multipurpose assault weapon, or SMAW. When he squeezed the trigger, the thermobaric rocket blasted out of its wide olive-green launch tube, traveled about forty yards, and punched through the exterior of the test building. As the white-orange fireball exploded out through the windows of the structure, cinder blocks separated and crumbled, roof pieces shot fifty feet into the air, and the doorbell to Kade's apartment rang. The ringing was followed by several firm knocks on the door.

Kade hit pause on the remote, set down his beer, and peeled his body off the couch. When he opened the door, a pudgy man with thinning blond hair and eager brown eyes was standing there. The guy looked like he was in his midforties and wore a navy sport coat, white oxford shirt, and red tie.

"Kade, how are you? I'm Special Agent Rob Morris." He held up his FBI badge and photo credentials.

Kade started breathing again as they shook hands. There probably wasn't any reason to worry.

"Hello, Agent Morris. How can I help you?"

"Can I come in and speak to you alone, please?"

"Yeah."

As Kade led Morris inside, he became self-conscious about his appearance. The beard he'd grown in the last few months along with his scraggy shoulder-length black hair made him look about thirty when he was twenty-five. He'd added at least twenty pounds of bad weight on his six-foot-four frame. He was wearing only a pair of cutoff sweatpants, so he slid on the frayed T-shirt he'd tossed on the nearby bar stool earlier.

"Let me give my roommate a heads-up." He walked over to Alex's bedroom and saw he was still at his desk on his iPad, brown hair shoved under a bandana. The big LED countdown clock on the wall said twelve minutes until the Wall Street closing bell.

"Hey, I've got an FBI agent here who needs to talk to me alone."

Alex rubbed his chin puff beard and stared at him for a second. "You okay, man?" he whispered.

"Yeah, I think so, thanks."

"All right, call me if you need to." Alex mouthed a few more silent words while he stood and gathered the computer cord.

As Morris took off his coat and laid it on the back of the couch, Kade walked over and scooped up the grease-stained pizza box lying open on the coffee table. He snagged the four empty Coronas in his other hand and moved the trash over to the kitchen.

"Sorry about the mess," he said.

"Sorry for my surprise visit. What's this from?"

Morris was pointing at one of the pictures on the wall behind the couch. It showed Kade standing with a small work crew in yellow hard hats, next to a young double amputee in a wheelchair and her daughter. Behind the group was the framing of a new house.

"Oh, that was a couple of years ago in Georgia. Some veteran outreach."

"That's great."

Morris sat down and took a yellow notepad and a pen out of his leather flip-over briefcase. He glanced up at the wobbly ceiling fan. "Can I get your cell phone number?"

Kade rattled off the number and drained a glass of water to keep his stomach in check. The warm room and musty smell wasn't helping his cause. Nothing he could do about it, because the AC was getting its ass kicked by the record heat outside.

Morris looked like a seasoned agent. What could this be about?

He refilled his glass and sat next to Morris on the opposite end of the couch, tapping his foot on the carpet. Morris's khaki dress pants were well creased and his square-toed black leathers had a decent shine.

"What's your roommate's name?" Morris asked.

"Alex . . . Alex Pace."

Morris wrote the name down while Alex scooted by with his backpack and waved.

"Thanks, man," Kade said. "Talk to you later."

When the door shut, there was an uncomfortable silence. He guessed this visit might take a while, whatever it was for. Should he offer Morris something to drink? No, better just stay put and listen for now.

"How long have you known Alex?" Morris asked.

"Since first grade."

"No kidding. Where did you go to school?"

"Worcester, Massachusetts."

"You two live here alone?"

"Yeah. He moved in here about a year ago."

"Both single?"

"Yeah."

"Any significant others?"

"Alex, kind of. Me, not any longer."

"Have you been working?"

"Yeah, I work at Home Depot."

"And how's that going?"

Kade shrugged. "All right. It's fun helping people out with projects."

"A big change from the army."

He knows my background.

"Yeah, I felt like I needed a break after leaving the service. It's pretty low stress."

Morris nodded and set down his pen. "Well, Kade, let me cut to the chase of why I'm here. We've identified you as a candidate who could assist us with a project we're working on. So we don't waste each other's time, I need to know if you're interested in learning more and if you think you're at a place in your life where this would make sense. It's temporary, but full-time work—about a two-to-three-month commitment—and it would be physically and mentally demanding. It would be *high* stress."

Wow. What kind of assistance could he possibly provide the FBI? Some kind of freelance opportunity? The months since his final army assignment as an intelligence analyst felt like years.

I guess it can't hurt to find out more.

"Sure, I'm interested."

"Okay." Morris glanced at his notes. "I understand after your assignment at the National Counterterrorism Center and return to your home unit, you had a mental health referral and a hypomania diagnosis. Your top secret clearance was pulled, and you were then separated with an honorable discharge. Do I have that right?"

Kade felt the skin on the back of his neck grow warmer and his stomach lurch. He wasn't expecting to hear about the end of his former career from an FBI agent today. In his role at the National Counterterrorism Center, or NCTC, he had interacted with all of the military services and national agencies, including the FBI, and had earned a good reputation. Maybe his NCTC work was the connection to Morris?

"Uh, yeah. There's more to it than that, but you're correct."

Morris nodded. "I figured there was more to it after doing my own research. Senior officers who worked with you at NCTC say you did an excellent job and your ethics were never in question. Your peers loved working with you and you're greatly missed. You just seemed to run into recurring problems off duty."

Kade took a large gulp of water. Great, Morris was digging into his background and asking people about his performance. Well, at least the feedback was encouraging. Since his separation, he had made peace with the hypomania disorder, and he would put that on display right now. He wouldn't let Morris's comments get him worked up.

"You're right," he said. "I got in trouble off duty back then and learned a very hard lesson from it. The disorder just caught up with me. When I was growing up, I was told I was hyperactive with ADD, and that turned out to be wrong. All those years I just thought I'd managed to work around it."

"It obviously didn't affect your performance. Your army experience and achievements at MIT are impressive."

"Thanks. I still dispute my discharge from the army for that diagnosis. The physician I'm seeing reviewed my records and thinks my separation was a real stretch. It's a mild case, and very manageable. But the army never gave me a chance to prove it."

"Kade, the good news is I wouldn't be here if I thought this was something you couldn't work through."

"Great."

Morris smiled again and snapped a business card down on the table.

"I'm from the FBI field office in Portland, Oregon. I've been in DC this week for some information exchange with our counterterrorism division about an urgent matter of national security, and it was during this discussion your name came to my attention."

"Really?"

"Yes, you happen to have a particular talent we're interested in. Do you remember when you volunteered for a program to test a new infrared lie-detection program during your time at NCTC?"

Kade scrunched his face. *This is random.* About a month into the NCTC job, he was asked to participate in a brief Defense Advanced Research Projects Agency (DARPA) study. DARPA funded some of the most forward-leaping technology prototypes in the world, from guided sniper bullets to robotic cheetahs.

"Yeah, I got an extra thousand bucks for testing on that IR device. That was a good day for a lieutenant."

Morris smiled. "That's right. And that technology is proving to be very accurate in trials with newer models. But you are the only person on record—in any trial—who gave the machine a big problem. You produced one hundred percent false positives, meaning the device said you lied on every question, even though you only lied on the questions you were told to lie on."

That's weird. "Why is that?"

"It's not clear. The internal notes on the study were inconclusive. We recently had an independent expert review the results again, and he connected us with you. He theorizes your hypomania condition and maybe your personality make it impossible for the machine to establish the right activity for control questions. There's a small region of the brain called the *caudate* that's active when a person's lying—the oxygen in the blood increases and lights up the IR detector. But your caudate seems to be very active all of the time."

"Huh. So on the test, when I had a red card in my hand"—Kade held up his hand, remembering how the test had worked—"and they asked me if I was holding the red card, and I answered yes—the machine *still* said I was lying?"

Morris nodded. "Red card, blue card—it didn't matter. According to the machine, every response you gave was a lie. You were even lying about your name and date of birth."

"Okay, but how is that good for anything?"

Morris rubbed the palm of one hand over the fist of the other.

"Great question. And this is where I need to pause. Kade, I believe this ability of yours, combined with your other skills, could help us in a sensitive national security operation. You seem fit enough to be a candidate, and your overall record is strong. But I can't disclose any more details unless I know you're willing to participate."

Okay, he was intrigued by the offer and the revelation of this odd talent, even though he didn't understand how it could be useful. He'd become noncommittal in recent months, even turning down some other job referrals, but this was different. *Physically and mentally demanding* sounded attractive in the FBI context. He had enjoyed the rigor and lifestyle of his army assignments. When the body and mind were working toward the same goal, and there was teamwork and commitment, there was nothing like the energy it created.

Yeah, he had burned out in his final months of the army, but maybe he just needed a new fuse.

"Wow, this is still sinking in. I think I could be up for it."

"Unfortunately, I'm going to need a more definitive answer than that to proceed."

"How long do I have to decide?"

"You have to decide right now if you're in, because we start our prep phase on Monday. And if you aren't in, I need to find another route."

Kade felt his upper lip starting to sweat, but Morris's glistening forehead was already well ahead of him. This looked like an enthusiastic recruitment attempt, not a sales job. He cracked a smile.

"You know, I'm supposed to be careful with impulsive decisions and thrill-seeking behavior, and this isn't helping."

That made Morris laugh. "Kade, I want you to make a *good* decision, one that's right for you."

"And you can't tell me more about this operation now?"

"No, it's very sensitive, and we'd have to cover the nondisclosure legalities first. I'm sure you can appreciate that."

Kade nodded and then sat silent, looking at the floor and mulling it over while Morris continued talking.

"Think about why you joined the service and the positive impact you made. Your country needs your help now, and I believe you can have that kind of impact again."

Kade tried to break it down. Even if he set aside the potential excitement of this operation, something else resonated in what Morris said. He missed his army comrades and could never get that back. He loved his family and friends now more than anything. But there was something greater out there still. Something he thought was lost for good after the army had said, "Good-bye, sorry, we don't need you anymore."

My country needs my help now, and I can do something about it. I can still make a difference.

Now it made sense why Morris had to poke around so much.

He's building some kind of team and wants me to be on it.

"So you're, in effect, ignoring the army's diagnosis with this offer."

"Yes. We would still need sign-off from your physician and for you to pass a drug test."

Kade nodded. He was getting another chance.

This opportunity will never come around again.

Morris kept going. "Kade, you can't turn back the clock now, but you can—"

"I'll do it. Yeah."

"Okay. Very good."

Kade raised his eyebrows. "Will I still be able to pay my share of the rent?"

"Yes, you sure will."

"Okay. So what's the mission?"

"Not here," Morris said. "With the verbal commitment you've given me, I'll set up a meeting for Monday morning and we'll do the legal documentation and initial discussion of the operation to get us started. Please keep our conversation here confidential."

"All right."

"Great. I'm very happy to have you on board, Kade."

"Thanks, I'm excited."

When he shook Morris's hand again, a surge of adrenaline seemed to snap him out of what he now saw had been an extended funk. Somehow he'd been ready for this moment.

I'm going to be part of an FBI operation.

Morris stood and grabbed his sport coat.

"I'll call you over the weekend with the meeting location, and I'll see you on Monday."

CHAPTER 2

Forty minutes before Dismal Nitch Coffee opened, Marshall Owens parked the black Chevy Tahoe hybrid at the curb in front of the shop and turned off the engine and lights to sit for a moment.

The rain rattled against the driver's side of the vehicle, pushed by powerful gusts that would last for the next twenty-four hours. Around him the magnificent ring of pine trees flexed, and the rain streaked horizontally, glowing under the amber light of the street lamp like a thousand tracer bullets. The rain forest had always been a key part of his life, whether it was in the Oregon evergreens or the jungles of South America.

The last big, violent storm of the season, and he might not live to see another.

But the storm's unpredictable destruction brought nourishment to the land. It restored balance and culled weakness. In its full fury, the storm was merciless, but ultimately benevolent.

And in less than three months, the Chapter's own force would strike with its own fury.

Owens was fifty-eight years old with deep wrinkles cutting across his face and watery-brown eyes that seldom blinked. Today, he wore a camouflage hunting parka, thermal shirt, loose jeans, and steel-toed work boots instead of a suit or the AgriteX company uniform. A green John Deere cap covered his shaved head.

Having grown up on the other side of the Columbia River, in Washington, he enjoyed a low profile in Oregon. He strived to avoid being a creature of habit, picking places outside any established pattern for offsite meetings like this.

While he hadn't been to Dismal Nitch in over a year, it was one of the places he felt comfortable having a sensitive conversation outside the walls of the company headquarters. When the weather was this bad, and the hour this early, it was easy to see if he was being followed.

He looked at his calendar again and reviewed the profile of Jim Currence, who owned the shop and worked mornings. He had confirmed the plate on Jim's truck with a quick drive through the waterlogged rear parking lot. Jim's profile said he'd been released from the Lost Lake Forest Camp minimum-security prison three years ago. The activity log also indicated Jim made another call yesterday he shouldn't have.

Owens stepped out into the narrow side street and jumped over the stream of water flowing into the half-clogged storm drain. In the few seconds it took him to reach the locked front door and rap his fist on the storm-proof glass, he received an invigorating spray to the face. After he knocked for the second time, Jim appeared. The smile on Jim's broad, ruddy face didn't hide the irritation.

"Hi there. What can I do for ya?"

"Hello, Jim."

Owens stepped inside and removed his cap. Jim's blue eyes widened as he gazed up and recognized him, even though they'd never met in person.

"Good morning, sir," Jim blurted.

Owens moved within inches of Jim's face and his frizzy blond hair.

"A friend of mine is meeting me here in a few minutes. Go ahead and relock the door after he arrives."

"Yes, sir."

Owens headed to the window booth farthest from the front door and took a seat. He unzipped his parka and pulled out the copy of the *Oregonian* he'd tucked inside it. Jim hurried to bring over coffee.

The steaming mug warmed his thick hands while he gazed out the blurry window into darkness. There was no stunning view of the river at this hour, but he still enjoyed looking out into the black void sprinkled with dockside lights and listening to the sounds of the storm. With each wind gust, the century-old Sitka-spruce-and-cedar building whistled, swayed, and popped. It was like a favorite song, reminding him of what his Chinook ancestors endured in this region hundreds of years ago.

His grandfather was half Chinook, and while Owens gave no outward appearance of that lineage other than a slight tan color to his skin, he'd always felt the tribe's ethos in his blood. For his *tilikum*, his people, he would beg, borrow, or *mamook solleks*—make war—to achieve his ends.

Jim turned on the wall-mounted TV to CNN. The attractive brunette anchor was interviewing some retired general about the American troops still active in Afghanistan and other armpits of the earth. Residual forces remained vulnerable. Increasing numbers of special operations troops had classified deployments in a mosaic of locations across the Middle East and Africa.

The nightmare never seemed to change. Undeclared wars and abuses of power. Politicians becoming generals and generals becoming politicians. Tiny forces courageously taking on big missions, then finding themselves crippled by weak rules of engagement. Inadequate equipment for soldiers on the ground, yet billions spent on appropriations.

Waste. Greed. The American people were *elitah*, slaves, unable to change anything. Even the ballot box was ineffective.

As the television reported another soldier killed by an Improvised Explosive Device (IED), or roadside bomb, the face of Owens's dead son, Todd, flashed in his mind. He singed his throat chugging the rest of his coffee and set the mug down hard on the table. *The TV wasn't in here before.*

"Turn the TV off."

Jim scrambled for the remote. "Yes, sir."

Owens went back to reading the paper and looking out the window. When he started on his second refill, he saw the front door open. The wiry man he recognized was dressed in a tan, hooded raincoat, black slacks, and rubber-soled dress shoes. The man nodded to Jim, walked to the back, and slid into the seat across from Owens. They shook hands.

"Good to see you, Marshall."

"Paul, thanks for coming. It must have been a hell of a drive this morning."

Paul was in his midthirties with a lean, angular face, sunken eyes, and large nostrils. His coarse black hair was parted on the side.

"Yeah, only fools like us are out in this mess," he said.

"That's for sure." He waited for Jim to bring Paul's coffee and depart before asking, "So what's the urgent news?"

"The Portland field office just moved AgriteX up near the top of their priority list, and an integrated operation has been authorized by their headquarters."

"How reliable's our source?"

"Rock solid," Paul said.

Owens set his elbows on the table and clenched his hands together.

First, cartel rumblings. Now, FBI activity to worry about.

"Do you know the timing of their next move?" he asked.

"I don't. We only know they received approval for additional funding and resources out of budget cycle. Our source doesn't have access to the operational details. The op could've already been underway and now it's just getting more support."

Owens looked back out the window. He could now see the lights of a large container ship moving up the river.

"This introduces risk to headquarters before our attack," he said. "We may have to revisit our strategy for the next couple of months, but once we launch, if the feds get in the way, they'll have a bloodbath on their hands." After a span of silence he added, "Well, your news was the kind I *didn't* want to hear, but thanks."

"I don't think anyone likes bringing you bad news, Marshall."

Owens laughed and patted him on the shoulder. "Don't worry, our plans have some flexibility. The bottom line is the Chapter is now the best-financed and most lethal private militia in U.S. history. Our training is nearly complete. We'll accomplish our mission."

"And America will wake up a much better place."

Owens nodded. "We'll finally break the cycle of cowardice and indecision. You Guardians continue to do a phenomenal job. I can't ask you for much more."

"But you will."

"Of course I will. Especially in Phase Two."

Paul nodded. "I'm looking forward to it."

Owens's smile faded when he sensed Jim hovering near the table with a fresh pot of coffee.

"Jim, my friend, did you make an unauthorized phone call yesterday you want to talk about?"

"No, sir."

Owens expected Jim to be a little nervous from a surprise visit, but he was now squinting and looking uncomfortable.

Good, his program is working properly.

"Jim, last Wednesday at 11:37 a.m., you made a call to a friend outside the network and tried talking to them about the Chapter. Am I right?"

Jim's face began to flush. Owens took the coffeepot away from him and poured another cup for Paul and himself.

"Your program is behind two full versions," Owens said. He pointed his finger at Jim's chest. "You've been ignoring our upgrade messages during your weekly login for some time. Even so, the audit trail in your Zulu protocol provided markers of your unauthorized communication. You've been warned about such violations before, correct?"

"Uh, yes, sir."

"Who did you talk to?"

"Just a fishing buddy."

"Name?"

"Ed Patterson."

"I'll check it out," Paul said after Owens looked at him.

"I expected more loyalty from you," Owens said. "We set you up here, financed the shop. Got you back on your feet. We trusted you as part of our network."

"I—I sent in all the information you wanted about Congressman Flint," Jim said. "Did you see that?"

"Yes, I did. But we also have a two-strike policy at your level for any unauthorized communication. We can't take the chance of you breaking security."

Jim looked over at Paul for his reaction.

Paul shrugged. "It's the Code of Trust, buddy. You know the rules: you break the Code, you get the Code."

"Yes, those are the rules we live by," Owens said. He tapped on the display of his smartphone and pulled out a pen to write something down on his brown paper napkin. "Here, read this number back to me."

Jim took the napkin, trying to keep his hand from trembling, and spoke the number.

"Four-nine-two, six-six-seven-three-one."

Seconds later, Jim shrieked and fell to the floor. He convulsed twice, took a final breath, then lay silent on his side, eyes open and fixed.

Owens looked at his watch and knelt down beside Jim. When he checked his neck for a pulse, there was none.

"The only punishment is here on Earth, my friend," Owens said. He looked up at Paul, who had already stood and moved to watch the front door. "Can you handle cleanup? His wife will be here in a couple hours."

"Not a problem."

"And we'll want to maintain the relationship with her, so make sure we help with the funeral expenses."

"I'll arrange it."

"Thanks, Paul. Stay vigilant."

CHAPTER 3

Kade's hands were jittery and his heart was beating faster, but he wasn't nervous. At least not in the way normal people are nervous. The muscles in his neck were tight, and a mild headache would soon come if left unchecked, but he otherwise felt confident and comfortable.

This was his unmedicated normal, and it meant he was riding a razor's edge with his hypomania symptoms.

But his razor's edge had won earlier this morning. He angled the rearview mirror to look at his neck and was happy to see the shaving cut hadn't started bleeding again.

The last three nights were short on quality sleep, but that was a good sign. It meant he cared about this meeting and understood the seriousness of the business before him.

He fiddled with the cell phone he'd bought over the weekend and slid it in the front pocket of his chinos. Then he swallowed a pink carbamazepine pill with a sip of bottled water. The drug was part of a regular prescription keeping the hypomania under control and Dr. Ross said it helped reduce abnormal electrical activity in his brain. Or something like that. All he cared about was that it seemed to work when he needed it to. He took a deep breath and checked his watch.

Time to go.

The Residence Inn lobby and adjacent breakfast areas were filled with the noise of business travelers talking too loudly into their phones and earpieces. He saw Special Agent Morris emerge from the lounge area wearing a suit and holding a folded *USA Today*.

Morris gave Kade a head-to-toe scan and nodded.

"Good to see you, Kade. Let's head on back."

Morris led the way to a large bedroom suite and introduced him to a squat man whom he identified as a consultant, retired Special Agent Jerry Lerner. Lerner looked in his midfifties with wavy gray hair and large square teeth. He wore a sage golf shirt over his rotund belly, tucked into dark jeans and wrapped in a wide black belt. He spoke with a strong Texas accent.

Both men refilled their coffee mugs and sat down on the same side of the kitchenette table. A box of assorted bagels and a tub of garlicky cream cheese were in the center. Kade declined coffee and took a seat across from them after pouring himself a glass of water. It was hard for him to remember the last time he drank anything with caffeine.

"Let's take care of your nondisclosure agreement first," Morris said. "We aren't going to discuss anything today that's classified, and for your own protection, we're going to make an effort to share only the information you'll need. But we need to have this NDA processed in case we decide we need it, going forward."

Kade was familiar with the standard nondisclosure form and filled it out.

"Now, for a quick backgrounder," Morris said. "Our focus is a corporation named AgriteX that's on our organized crime watch list. AgriteX is an agricultural biotech company located in rural Oregon with revenues in the hundreds of millions. The CEO and founder, Marshall Owens, sold his first start-up, NetStatz, for eighty-seven million in 1998, during the dot-com boom.

"We suspect AgriteX is conducting a number of illegal activities, but we've been unsuccessful in getting someone inside up to this point. The group may also have links to terrorist activity, so we're highly concerned about that as well. Our current understanding is that the company provides financing and cover for an organization called the Chapter. We believe the Chapter may be evolving into a militia movement, but we need more intelligence to confirm or deny that. Owens is former Army Special Forces and has a well-trained security team."

Kade's eyes narrowed, and he drummed his fingers on the underside of the table.

"So this militia isn't associated with any white supremacist movement?"

"No," Morris said. "They've never communicated any views to that effect, and they have a fairly diverse workforce."

"Any link to bank robberies?" Kade asked.

"None," Morris said.

"How about ecoterrorism?"

"No indication of that, but it's a possibility that could make sense," Morris said. "AgriteX has made corporate donations to the National Resources Defense Council and Sierra Club, but it's unclear if they've supported more extreme environmentalists. The challenge of this group is that it's very high-tech. We know from a former employee that the Chapter uses an IR-based lie detector as a screening tool with every new recruit to make sure they're not from law enforcement. They also use it on existing members from time to time to ensure their continued loyalty. This is where you come in. Are you following me?"

Kade nodded. "Yeah."

"With our support you will get inside their organization and help us gather evidence and intelligence."

Kade's mind clicked into greater focus.

"You want *me* to get inside?"

"Yes, you'll be our primary source."

"Does that mean I'm going in solo?"

"Yes, but you'll have a support team."

Both of Kade's feet were now tapping the floor. His time in Iraq had involved a few dangerous moments when venturing into the Red Zone, where insurgent activity was always a threat, but most of the time, he'd been part of an enormous force in the well-fortified Camp Victory located at the Baghdad Airport. This FBI mission was a completely different kind of danger.

"You know, I only did desk analysis at NCTC. No human intelligence work of any kind."

"We know."

He didn't want Morris and Lerner to think he was changing his mind or losing confidence, but he had a lot of questions and didn't know where to start.

"This is a surprise, but that's okay," he said. "I'm just trying to understand the strategy better. Why wouldn't you use your undercover agents?"

"The Chapter's screening and review using this IR lie detector would immediately expose a standard undercover agent and put them at great risk. But your brain physiology is different, so you'll be able to mess up their machine and cause useless results like you did before. No one will believe you're lying one hundred percent of the time, including on all of the control questions. They'll just think their machine is malfunctioning, and they'll spend weeks trying to figure out what's wrong with it when it's working just fine."

"Or they'll kick me out right then."

"We can't know for sure, but we don't think so. You're an honest-looking guy and a strong fit for their recruit profile. You have computer and software skills they'll want to utilize immediately, and we'll need you to brush up on those."

"Can the person who left AgriteX help you get back in?"

"That person went missing a few weeks after he spoke with us," Morris said.

Kade chewed on his tongue.

Wonderful.

"And how long is this operation planned for?"

"The goal is to get you in and out," Morris said. "Just a few weeks to see what you can dig up. We'll train you so you'll be confident in yourself and with the plan."

Kade nodded. *Holy shit.*

"Do they just hire people at AgriteX into open positions?" he asked. "I mean, could I just apply for a job and get into the Chapter like that?"

"No, I wish it were that simple," Morris said. "We know they have a very rigorous recruiting process, and they usually go after particular people. Their posted jobs are really just for show. Apparently, there's a detailed behavioral questionnaire they use with recruits, but we've never seen a copy of it."

Kade nodded and leaned his chair back far enough that Lerner looked concerned he might fall.

"What's the name of this operation?"

"It's best we don't tell you, for your own protection," Morris said. "We have to be very careful about our communications."

"Okay."

"Jerry is going to give you some customized training over the next four weeks. He's an expert who's been involved with dozens of successful operations."

Kade looked at Lerner, who had put on reading glasses and was busy scribbling notes. It was a good sign Morris had invested in this experienced resource and brought him here.

"I'm going to be your primary contact during the operation," Morris said. "Agent Chris Velasquez, who you'll meet during training, will be my alternate and will manage the tactical operations center. We'll also have DEA and ATF liaisons assigned to the operation due to the suspected cannabis and illegal weapons on the site. So while Jerry is getting you up to speed, Chris and I will be discussing the plan with you, assembling your resources and support team, and documenting our agreement."

Lerner glanced at Kade over the rims of his glasses.

"Easy as fallin' off a log, right?"

"Yeah, right." Kade smiled and got the feeling he'd like Lerner.

"Your cover is going to be very light," Morris said. "You're just going to be yourself and use your own name because that's what will work the best to get you in. The Chapter could easily figure out your real identity through a private investigator or other means, and then you'd be in danger."

"Makes sense."

"Your military record said both of your parents are deceased," Morris said. "Can you share a little more detail on that?"

Kade unbuttoned the sleeves of his dress shirt.

"Yeah, my mom died from breast cancer three years ago. It cut my tour in Iraq short and hit me hard. I lost my dad ten years ago in a hit-and-run. He was a police officer making a nighttime traffic stop when it happened."

"That's terrible," Lerner said, shaking his head.

"I'm sorry you lost your parents like this," Morris said, "and that I had to ask, but thank you. Do you have any other family members you're in touch with?"

"Yeah, my sister and aunt. My sister, Janeen, was sixteen when my mom passed, and she moved in with my aunt Whitney and my eight-year-old cousin Greg. It's worked out pretty well."

"Where do they live?"

"Up in Peabody, Massachusetts. My sister finished her first year at Amherst and is taking summer credits there. I suppose I won't be able to tell them what I'm doing?"

"No," Morris said. "But we'll get their contact information from you in the event of an emergency."

Kade nodded. What would Janeen and Aunt Whitney think when he disappeared for a number of weeks? They wouldn't get his weekly calls. No long visit later this summer. Maybe he'd tell them he was going to take a trip to Oregon with his buddies.

Yeah, that would make Janeen happy. She'd given him crap for being holed up in his apartment for too long. He loved her for that. The age difference between them meant he didn't take her advice too seriously growing up. But his baby sister suddenly became a friend when his mom was gone. She could knock him down two notches if he acted arrogant. Brighten his mood with her goofy laugh. She probably understood him better than anybody.

Morris stood and stretched.

"You'll want to remove any evidence of them from your apartment, car, et cetera, over the next several weeks. Photos, letters, stored phone numbers—anything like that. Other than your aunt, sister, roommate, and employer, would anyone notice your absence?"

There was his ex-girlfriend, Darcy. Six-month relationship before breaking up in March, and he still missed her. She resigned at a DC law firm after landing an attorney position for the state of Florida so she could be near her parents in Tallahassee. There was that chance she might call, but she wouldn't think it was unusual if he didn't respond at this point.

"No, that's it," he said, and after a pause asked, "Won't it seem suspicious for me just to show up in Oregon?"

"We have a solid plan to address that," Morris said, "and we'll share all those details once training gets started. We know the

Chapter recruits its members nationally, so we don't believe being from the East Coast will raise a red flag."

"You like camping?" Lerner asked.

"Yeah, love it."

"Perfect," Lerner said.

Morris sat back down and loosened the knot in his tie.

"Jerry and I are crafting a believable cover story with bullet-proof backstopping information that'll make you even more attractive to the Chapter as a recruit. Your trip to Oregon is going to be in the guise of a much-needed vacation, so you can stop shaving again. And let your hair grow back some. I should've told you that you didn't have to clean up for this meeting, but we appreciate the effort."

Kade smiled. "All right."

They continued talking for the next hour. Morris discussed the attorney general's guidelines pertaining to working with human intelligence sources and referred to a document he pulled from his briefcase, which said the source is never allowed to break the law under any circumstances unless given express written permission to engage in "otherwise illegal" activity. Under no circumstance could Kade participate in an act of violence.

"You're not an FBI employee," Morris said. "But I still need you to sign this affidavit saying that we reviewed and discussed the AG guidelines."

He signed the document and started reading the paper next to it on the table. Morris explained that the FBI would use him as a witness for the prosecution against anyone indicted from AgriteX as a result of the operation. He stared at the page for a minute in silence and then looked at Lerner.

"If this is an organized crime operation and I'm going in with no cover, then potentially serving as a witness, it sounds like I'll have a gigantic bull's-eye on my head if all goes according to your plan."

Lerner drank from his coffee cup and let Morris answer.

"That was the part I was getting to next. Kade, if the operation is successful, you'll be brought under the witness protection program."

"I'd like to get that in writing."

"Yes, that'll be in your final employment agreement. We'll have Brian Hutchinson from the Justice Department meet with you before you sign that."

"And even if the operation is unsuccessful, I'd still like some basic assistance with a name change and covering my moving expenses to live somewhere else."

"Agreed. We'll include a modest relocation package limited to the continental U.S. with a comparable standard of living, no matter what the outcome."

"Okay, good." Kade jolted backward, making his chair groan on the floor. This whole thing was exciting but a little unsettling.

Getting more complex by the minute.

Morris slid another agreement in front of Kade. "This document is a notice that you must claim any money received for this work when you file your taxes. You'll receive twelve thousand dollars for participating in the operation, with an additional per diem during the training month."

Kade paused. Twelve thousand before taxes. Yes, he had already committed. And it really wasn't about the money. But was the reward really fair for the risk involved?

The witness protection program!

Seeing Kade's hesitation, Morris added, "There's some leeway for an additional performance incentive based on quantity and quality of information received. But there are no guarantees and that won't be in writing."

That's better. "Okay."

"This last document," Morris said as he laid the paper down, "is your permission for us to speak to your physician about your health. If he validates that your condition is manageable as you've said, and you're capable of this kind of work, then his certification to that effect will be good enough for us."

"No problem."

After Kade finished signing, Morris said Lerner would contact him the next day to start coordinating training times and a drug test.

"We look forward to working with you, Kade," Morris said.

"I'm ready to get started."

"Super. I'll walk you out."

Morris escorted him out to the lobby and said good-bye with a handshake. Once outside, Kade strode across the parking lot to his car, got in, and turned up the volume of the iPhone lying on the passenger seat in muted speaker mode. He heard the conversation resume as he drove across the street into the parking lot of the Hometown Suites and reparked.

"Well, what do you think?" Morris asked.

"Looks like I got my work cut out for me," Lerner said, sounding like he had a mouthful of bagel and cream cheese.

Morris's voice became clearer with the sound of a chair sliding back toward the table, where Kade's second phone was stuck with adhesive to the underside.

"Jerry, I picked you because I thought you might enjoy this one."

"Take it easy now," Lerner said. "You know me—if I'm not training, I'm complaining. So what's the name of this new operation anyway?"

"CLEARCUT," Morris said.

"You think he's good enough for the job?"

"As of today, definitely not. But it's *your* job to get him ready."

"Thanks. He looks like a good kid, but kind of messed up, don't you think? He's jumpy as spit on a skillet. And the hypomania thing?"

"He tried to get help in the army when most people at his clearance level are afraid to. Then his previous conversations with his chain of command were used against him when he got in trouble."

"What kind of trouble?"

"Assault, conduct unbecoming an officer, and disrespect toward a superior commissioned officer."

It sounded like Lerner was flipping through a few pages of his scribble. "Your note says his last supervisor in the army thought he was belligerent. You worried about that as far as working with him?"

"No. I talked to that supervisor, a Major Steve Echols. He's the one Sims assaulted. While assaulting your chain of command is inexcusable, Echols seemed like a real asshole."

Lerner laughed.

Morris added, "And how many of *our* agents don't disclose PTSD or other problems?"

"That's true," Lerner said. "I'm sure losing his mom didn't help either."

"And no mentorship from his dad since high school. Look, I'm not making a list of excuses for him—if we don't think he's ready after training, then he doesn't go. It's that simple. We'll get sign-off from his physician before proceeding."

"He's going to be too busy to get in trouble," Lerner said.

"You saw his record. Summa cum laude from MIT in software engineering. ROTC distinguished military graduate. Captain of MIT's lacrosse team. He was rated 'Above Center of Mass' in his first three officer evaluation reports. I've done my due diligence and spoken to key people he worked with."

"He's smart, and he was determined back then," Lerner said, "but what about now? Is he gonna be in, whole hog?"

"I trust he's going to step up and do his best. And you're going to help him get there. Overall, I think it's a reasonable investment considering the urgency of the situation."

"What about that website he was running?" Lerner asked. "The one called Wakethehelluppeople.com. Sounds like some conspiracy theory thing. A little weird, don't you think?"

"Yeah, I know about that. He stopped posting to it three months ago, saying he was taking a break. I'm not too worried about it. In fact, it's a real strength for the type of background we need. His discussion threads seem right up the Chapter's alley as far as content they'd find supportive of their views. We know from looking at the website stats that the IP address for AgriteX viewed the website pages dozens of times. And there're even a few posted comments that also came from that IP address."

"This is a good one," Lerner said. "More stealth fighters? How about more socks and T-shirts first?" He flipped pages to another title. "Mr. President, we must change camouflage patterns again."

Morris laughed. "The next one was really popular."

"'Troops die in Afghanistan while Senator Barker plays Angry Birds.' Whew . . . ouch! Okay, you're right. This could be helpful. But lacrosse? Shoot, that's a huge red flag. What the hell kinda sorry sport is that?"

"I'm sure they didn't have lacrosse where you grew up. Probably just football. What was your team, the Armadillos or something?"

There was a silent pause before Lerner broke into a laugh. "No . . . There still ain't lacrosse at Lubbock. Soccer and golf now, though!"

They continued to talk until noon, checkout time, and Kade took some notes he planned on destroying the next day. Morris and Lerner seemed like competent and genuine people. Fair. Morris had shown empathy toward his mistakes and used common sense when referring to his separation. That was encouraging. The questions and concerns raised in the exchange were valid as well. It was clear they'd both hold him to high standards, and he couldn't argue with that.

These guys are the real deal.

He looked at his notes and stopped at Morris's observation: *No mentorship from his dad since high school.* While he had always missed his dad, he hadn't thought about the mentorship angle. His dad, Alan Kenneth Sims, had served as an army infantry rifleman in Task Force Garry Owen, the First Battalion, Seventh Cavalry Regiment, after being drafted into duty toward the end of the Vietnam War. Kade's interest in the army and ROTC came late, so his dad had died before knowing his career choice or seeing him pin on his second lieutenant gold bars.

Sometimes friends from his dad's old unit would visit and share stories. He learned about the soldiers still on the ground at the end of Vietnam, doing unheralded acts of bravery. This after President Nixon had announced there were no more ground troops in Vietnam. Not surprisingly, his dad harbored resentment for politicians after the war.

He found himself often having the same feelings about the extended war on terror.

Maybe it was genetic.

After Kade was separated from the army, he was almost thankful his dad didn't have to witness the end of his career. Sure, his dad could've provided advice and support, but would it have made a difference in the outcome?

What would his dad think now about his choice? The man who continued to be a street cop so close to retirement because he didn't want to be behind a desk.

He'd say *Go for it.*

Kade raised his pocket binoculars—Morris and Lerner were leaving the building, Morris pulling a roller bag behind him. He watched until each of their cars disappeared down Westward Center Drive.

I'll step up for them.

He pulled his car back into the parking lot of the Residence Inn and went to the front desk. A young red-haired girl asked how she could help him.

"Hi, my name's Kade Sims and I had an interview in room one-fifteen earlier this morning. I was so nervous—I left my cell phone in there and need to go get it."

The girl looked at his earnest expression and face dripping with sweat.

"Sure, I can take you back there right now."

CHAPTER 4

Thursday, June 6
3:05 p.m. (PDT)
Manzanita, Oregon

The Ocean Bakery was in a small building with the same weathered, dark-stained wood siding as most of the downtown shops in Manzanita. After Kade spotted Alex drinking coffee at one of the outside tables, he paused on the sidewalk like he was checking his phone. When Alex signaled with a long rub of the nose, Kade turned around and strolled back toward the beach.

Alex caught up a few minutes later and walked beside him. The seventy-degree temperature was refreshing and cool compared to the summer in DC and they were both dressed in shorts, T-shirts, and flip-flops. Kade wore a faded red Quicksilver ball cap the FBI had given him. Five hundred dollars in cash and a laminated topographical map of the area surrounding AgriteX were sewn inside the bill.

"I can't believe you came out to Oregon," Kade said.

Alex smiled. "Come on, man. Bus twenty-six."

The reference was to their school bus number and the seven years he and Alex had spent at the same bus stop on Harrison Street until Alex's older brother, Mark, started driving them both to school. Almost twenty years of friendship, and it all began with the shared talks, pranks, and mutual bully defense at the bus stop.

"If you'd said no, I would've understood," Kade said. "You're the best."

"You'd do the same for me, I know. So how's the campground?"

"Great. It's plush, not like we're used to. They have washing machines, showers, and Wi-Fi. I've been talking with the tourists and locals. Everyone's friendly."

As part of the FBI's plan, he had stayed at a Kampgrounds of America site in Manzanita, Oregon, since the previous Saturday to establish a verifiable short-term presence in the local area. The FBI had secured him a KOA membership backdated to the previous year.

Unknown to the FBI, Kade had asked Alex to come out to Oregon and stay nearby during the operation, and Alex accepted like a champ. He just felt like he needed personal backup from someone he'd known all of his life. Hopefully, he wouldn't need it, but like his dad said, *Sometimes the only one you can trust is your battle buddy.*

They both graduated from Doherty High School in Worcester, and Alex majored in finance at Boston College while Kade went to MIT just five miles away. Alex later became a CPA, working three years for a financial services company before becoming disgruntled. He wanted to get out of the Boston area for a while, and Kade had offered him a place to stay in DC last winter, so he decided to take a risk and morph into an independent tax advisor and day trader. The result was now he could work from anywhere as long as he had Internet and phone coverage. A pretty sweet arrangement.

"How's the RV park?" Kade asked.

"It's just fine," Alex said. "The people are super nice. Can't beat this weather. It's cold at night, though."

Kade smirked. "Sweater weather?" He was referring to Alex's thick chest and back hair.

Alex rolled his eyes. "Doesn't that one get old?"

"No."

The two had agreed it would be a bad idea for Alex to stay in the KOA campground with him, and it would've been a stretch for Alex to afford three weeks at a nearby motel—his business was stable but small. So Alex had borrowed a small Jayco RV trailer from a friend of his dad's and brought it cross-country hitched to his Toyota Tacoma.

"I saw from your e-mails you've already done a shitload of hikes and sightseeing," Alex said.

"Yeah, it's keeping me in shape."

"Don't wear yourself out, vampire."

"I have to do it this way. All part of the plan. I have to get through my vacation checklist early." Kade then stopped without further explanation.

At the end of the street, they followed a narrow path toward the beach, and as they descended the back side of the dunes, the view of the Pacific was stunning. The dark blue water formed a clear, sharp horizon while bulging clouds hustled across the sky. Seagulls and petrels streamed in the air and played at the edge of the roaring tide.

To their right, in the distance, the forest-covered Neahkahnie Mountain jutted out into the ocean. They turned and walked up the beach toward it, the breeze in their faces carrying the scent of salt and pine. Huge pieces of dark brown driftwood lay on the beach, some looking like rough sculptures.

"Tomorrow the real fun begins," Kade said.

"Are you ready?" Alex asked.

"I have no fucking clue."

Alex laughed.

"Come on, if anyone's going to be ready, you are, man. For whatever you're going up against. The way you've worked this last month—you're back, I can tell."

"Thanks."

Other than giving Alex the locations of AgriteX headquarters and the Lost Lake Recreation Area a few miles from it, he had said nothing about the operation. When Alex had asked him if the trip had been prompted by the FBI agent's visit, he said he couldn't talk about it. Alex had noticed his resurgent exercise program and the stack of pistol ammo boxes in his bedroom, which he said were just for letting off some steam at the range. That was partially true.

"I've told you as little as possible," Kade said, "for your own protection, trust me."

"I know. Sounds like all that classified stuff you couldn't tell me about when you were in the army."

"Yeah, sort of," Kade said, even though this was completely different and more dangerous. "Just remember to keep checking your e-mails and voice mails regularly in case I can figure out a way to get you a message."

"I will."

"You still good with our code words?"

"Yep."

They walked for twenty minutes until they reached the base of the mountain and turned around. They retold funny stories about teachers in high school and parties in college, and poked fun at each other. They weren't breaking much new ground because they talked all of the time. When they returned to the path from where they'd started, Kade became serious before they parted ways.

"Hey, if anything happens to me, you tell my aunt Whitney and Janeen that I believed in what I was doing and that I love them both very much."

Alex stopped in his tracks and turned, his amber eyes squinting in the sun.

"No way, man. I'm not going to hear that." He gripped Kade's shoulder. "When you get back, *you're* going to tell them all about this yourself."

CHAPTER 5

After a late, heavy breakfast at a downtown diner, Kade returned to the campground and got ready to leave. The day was overcast with light sprinkles of rain. Looking east into the Coast Range, he could see fog hanging in the valleys with thin wisps rising into the air.

He packed up his camping gear and stowed it in the back of the rented Jeep, followed by his fishing gear, a bucket of bait, a cooler of food, and two more coolers full of beer he intended to share as part of a group get-together.

His itinerary for his "vacation checklist" was to go camping in the Lost Lake Recreation Area, attempting to make as many local contacts in as little time as possible. He was specifically planning to meet up with either Michele Blanford or Tanya Hollowell, and possibly some of their friends, at Lost Lake.

The FBI had queried AgriteX tax records to compose a group of female AgriteX alumni between the ages of twenty and thirty who lived in the local area and were active on social media. Then the FBI assisted him in targeting this group through social media and striking up online correspondences. The result was these two women agreeing to visit him while he was in the area, either of whom the FBI believed would potentially refer him to a Chapter recruiter.

He knew the FBI would be tracking his vehicle's movement. Earlier in the week, on Tuesday, he had left the Jeep in a designated remote trailhead while he hiked Saddle Mountain, east of Cannon Beach. While he was gone, the FBI had installed a hidden GPS device in the dashboard.

He shut the hatchback and was ready. The FBI didn't have a "need to know" about the subcompact Glock 29 pistol and two extra clips of ten-millimeter rounds hidden inside the cargo tray cover. But Alex knew about it. Kade wasn't assigned a weapon for this operation, but no way in hell was he going in without some kind of protection. He just checked the Glock with his baggage. Cougars were occasionally sighted near camping areas of the Coast Range, so his concern about the wildlife would be his phony reason for packing it if anybody asked.

He pulled out of the campground parking lot and picked up Highway 101 as it looped around Nehalem Bay and crossed the Nehalem River. He was excited from adrenaline, but part of the energy spike was from intentionally skipping his carbamazepine for the last two days. Dr. Ross had given Agent Morris "reasonable assurance" of his stability and performance while on medication, and also said his performance would "most likely be satisfactory" even without it.

But Morris and others realized during a planning meeting that he beat the IR lie detector test in the DARPA study while *not* taking any prescribed meds. The FBI support team concluded, and he agreed with the logic, that he'd have the best chance to beat the IR test again by replicating the study conditions and not taking any medication. He would bring the prescribed pills with him, but wait until after he was tested to take any.

Using therapeutic techniques Dr. Ross had taught him, such as meditation and exercises, he could avoid the onset of a hypomania

episode that would hurt his judgment. To this end, the Jeep's ste-
reo played soft acoustic guitar music from his iPod rather than his
normal rotation of hardcore.

After crossing the bridge at the Nehalem River, he turned on
to the narrow, two-lane Route 53. It was called the Necanicum
Highway, but it was really just a winding, back-ass country road.
The route snaked through the Coast Range for twenty miles before
intersecting with Route 29, the main road running west from
Portland to Cannon Beach. He had driven the 53 once earlier in
the week on a sunny Monday, noting it was popular with motorcycle enthusiasts. But today, as the misty sprinkle turned to drizzle, the road and forested countryside had a completely different,
unfamiliar appearance in the muted daylight.

He reviewed the last few weeks of training and the plan he'd
committed to memory. The workout regimen of distance running
and sprints, hiking hills, weight training, and self-defense had
made him strong. Lerner had provided him with assistance from
a personal trainer, a former marine who called him "Flash" and
liked to razz him about his choice of army service. He appreciated
the extra push and it felt good to shock his body back in shape. It
was tough, but not exhausting.

He soaked up the information from his other crash training
courses just fine. Maintaining hours at Home Depot ensured that
his overall "story" would be tight. Lerner took him through weapons and drug recognition classes at a subcontracted office located
in Falls Church, Virginia. He had asked if they'd train him on any
of the weapons that AgriteX might have on-site, and the answer
was no. Again, not the level of protection he was expecting. So he
decided to supplement his training by going to the private indoor
firing range a few miles from his apartment. He fired his Glock and
a variety of other rental pistols and rifles on the ranges three times
a week. His first time at the range had been when he was twelve,
with his dad, and he had become an expert marksman in the army.

Morris provided a number of intelligence and predeployment briefings. AgriteX was located in a privately owned forest, a roughly triangular area of twenty thousand acres. State forest enclosed the area, with Kidders Butte, Sugarloaf Mountain, and South Sugarloaf Mountain the distinguishable features. Four private dirt-logging roads provided access from the east, joining public logging roads in the state forest before intersecting with Route 53. Two roads improved with gravel provided access from the west and south, with the south road for approved commercial traffic routed to the AgriteX main entrance. Armed AgriteX security patrolled their land in shifts, making sure potential trespassers stayed away.

They discussed the profile of AgriteX, aka the Chapter, in detail. Senior leadership. Known operations. Recent activities. AgriteX was suspected of various organized and white-collar crimes. The company was known for seedlings that produced fast-growing timber for tree farms, but it was also suspected of selling genetically enhanced cannabis seed to Mexican drug cartels and laundering profits back through the business lines. The company's tacit relationship with the Sonora cartel in particular seemed to have recently started deteriorating for some unknown reason.

Interviews with the former AgriteX employee who went missing indicated the company was financing its own upstart militia. The FBI didn't have any evidence that AgriteX was providing direct financial support to terrorist organizations or that it had active terror plans of its own. At least no evidence they were going to share with him. Kade wouldn't have access to the FBI's more highly classified intelligence and analysis either.

Part of his briefing included law enforcement chain-of-custody procedures when dealing with evidence. The last thing the FBI wanted was for him to gather information and have it be inadmissible in court. Wearing a wire was out of the question, since he'd be inside AgriteX for weeks with no contact and no opportunity to get out. Instead, he'd use a small digital-camera-and-voice-recorder combo to collect information. The device was smaller than a matchbook and embedded inside the tongue of his left hiking boot.

Inside the tongue of the other boot was a burst transmitter that could send a one-time signal to a more powerful relay box on Kidders Butte, a mile and a half away. The relayed signal would alert a two-agent team located in an RV just outside the tiny nearby town of Alderville that his life was in imminent danger and he needed immediate emergency support. That was the backup plan.

The main plan was for him to self-extract, at the appropriate time, to Kidders Butte. The underside of a bogus historical marker would contain a touch-pad that unlocked a small cache of supplies. He would first use the satellite phone to contact the tactical operations center, and then Morris and Velasquez would arrange for helicopter extraction. Food, water, a first-aid kit, and a Gore-Tex jacket would also be in the cache.

The planning was by the book, as he expected from Morris. But unlike some by-the-book officers Kade had worked for in the army, Morris was clearly taking risks with this operation, knowing he was fully responsible.

Now that the risks were detailed, the whole plan seemed pretty damn dangerous. He'd had a conversation with Lerner on that topic right at the end of training.

"This operation's going to require some real courage," Lerner said. "But I think you knew that. You know what General William Tecumseh Sherman said, don't ya?"

"Yeah—'War is hell.'"

Lerner laughed. "Yeah, Sherman said that. But I'm talking about courage. Sherman said, 'Courage is a perfect sensibility of the measure of danger, and a mental willingness to endure it.' I *know* you have the sensibility and the mental willingness. And if you believe it, you'll do just fine."

Kade's attention moved back to the windshield and the steady rain that now glistened on it as he drove to higher elevation. He couldn't remember the last time he'd seen a place so dark in the daytime. Today the towering firs and spruces seemed to reach even farther toward the road with their beautiful, menacing branches. He kept track of the green mile markers when he could see them and began to count down the next eleven miles.

A kernel of worry grew somewhere in the back of his mind. It wasn't from the measure of danger at this moment. Was he dwelling on unfinished business? Maybe he was a little afraid the FBI wouldn't have his back if the shit hit the fan. Selfish to have signed up for a dangerous mission when his sister still needed him. He told himself to stop second-guessing his decision at this point, since there was no turning back.

He wasn't surprised when it began to rain harder. Buckets. The local weather was part of his operational briefing—the rain in this area was unpredictable, usually wind-blown, and often torrential. He put his wipers on the highest setting, half expecting them to fly off the windshield, and pressed on.

After feeling the Jeep hydroplane a few times, he engaged the four-wheel drive. He glanced at the odometer after passing milepost fourteen and slowed down to make sure he didn't miss the next turn in two miles. It looked like the few cars passing in the opposite direction had also reduced their speed.

He finally spotted the turnoff in the distance. As he approached, he made a slow left turn and then came to a careful stop on the wide right shoulder of the dirt logging road marking the final leg of the route.

He got out of the Jeep and confirmed it was the correct road by finding a small wooden sign that read "Little Jack Creek" near the open pole gate. His gray T-shirt and jeans were soaked in little more than a minute. He tried to scrape some of the stubborn, thick mud off his boots before getting back in the Jeep, but then gave up. A rental car cleaning surcharge was the least of his concerns.

He reset the trip odometer and headed down the road. *If you can even call it that.* It was supposed to be another 2.7 winding miles to where the Lost Lake trailhead began. The rain slowed from an absolute gush to a heavy drench with sporadic strobe-like flickers of sunlight. Maybe if the storm cleared soon, he'd be able to find a place to pitch his tent that wouldn't be a mud bog. Then his mind returned to the theme of unfinished business, and this time the face of his ex-girlfriend, Darcy, intruded. Now all of a sudden he felt like he needed some closure, a final good-bye that was never said.

Screw it, I'll call her and at least leave a quick message.

He fished the phone out of his pocket but the screen read *NO SERVICE*. That was okay, because calling her was exactly what he was *not* supposed to do. Lerner had said keeping personal numbers in the phone's call log might put someone in danger. He had left his iPhone and its contact list behind in a storage locker along with other personal effects. The support team told him to fill the new phone's call log with routine calls in the weeks leading up to the start of the operation.

Refocus.

He stuck the phone in the center console cup holder and glanced at the odometer as it ticked past two miles. Minutes later, the Jeep entered a thick curtain of fog, and the windshield clouded over in an instant. He eased off the gas and fumbled for the buttons to crack the windows. No, he needed to turn on the defroster first. Maybe both. Yes, defroster on full blast and windows open. All the way down. The odometer was now at 2.5.

He leaned forward and glanced up through a tiny patch of clearing windshield. Again he could only see fog, so he let the Jeep slow down to less than twenty miles per hour before putting his foot back on the pedal. He then stuck his head out the window to check for the side of the road, but now the road switched back hard to the left in the direction he was looking. Was this the trailhead turnoff?

No, it should be another quarter mile ... keep—

In that split second, terror in his gut told him something was wrong. The Jeep was at the road's outer edge in the middle of a sharp bend, and he was heading straight off it. To his front and right was a shallow mountain draw that dropped a hundred feet. No guardrail.

"Shit!" he shouted.

He stomped on the brake once, then on the accelerator while trying to make the sharp turn, but the tires wouldn't grip. The side of the road was like a thick mud milk shake after the heavy rain.

"No!" he shouted. The Jeep slid sideways off the edge of the embankment, hurtled down the slope, and rolled eight full times before the top side slammed into a large fir, bringing it to a jarring stop.

He didn't remember the impact, only his final thoughts before instant and complete darkness.

You blew it. You blew it. Fuck!

CHAPTER 6

The cold weight of intravenous fluid creeping from both arms to his shoulders and chest woke him. Kade shuddered and a terrible, aching pain flared in his back and neck. He lifted both arms outside the thin cotton blanket covering him and saw a splint and sling on his left arm. He saw he was dressed in hospital pajamas.

On the wall across from him hung a watercolor painting depicting a small village street lined with white houses. The trees along the streets and surrounding hills flaunted the beautiful colors of early autumn.

A vital-sign monitor stood next to the bed, indicator lights unlit and the blood pressure cuff lying on the top. The toilet and sink were in the far left corner of the room, a foldable steel chair by the closed entry door on his right. The room looked grungy.

He reached to scratch the top of his itchy head and instead felt some kind of bandage there.

What happened? I was driving, sliding, rolling.

Natural light shone through a rectangular window. He tried to sit up and take a closer look but couldn't lift his chest off the bed. When he pulled the blanket farther down his body, he saw two thick black nylon restraints running over his chest and mid-section in parallel, continuing around the sides of the bed and underneath it.

What's this? Why the straps?

The door opened toward him and he shut his eyes. Quiet foot-steps approached his bed and paused. He smelled the slightest trace of perfume. A thumb gently pulled his right and left eyelids up while a flashlight shone in each eye.

He kept his eyes open. The caregiver was an attractive woman in her late thirties with blue eyes, olive skin, and black hair pulled back in a ponytail. She was tapping notes on a tablet computer.

"Where am I?" he asked.

The woman's eyes connected with his and she took a small step back from the bed. She wore a brown, crinkly long-sleeved shirt with two flap breast pockets. A small gold patch was affixed to the right pocket. With the matching cargo pants, the outfit looked out-doorsy—not typical hospital garb.

"How are you feeling, Mr. Sims?"

She knows my name.

"Not so good. Where am I?"

"You just take it easy. You've had a long night and long day. I put eight staples in the top of your head to close a nasty laceration, but you don't appear to have a concussion. You had a dislocated elbow and your back has a large contusion. You were also very dehydrated, but you should be good with your fluids now."

"Thanks for the first aid, but I'd still like to know where I am and why I'm strapped in this bed."

"Your questions will be answered soon enough, I'm sure." She was pleasant but didn't smile. "Just rest some more and I'll check you again tomorrow."

"Tomorrow? I can't get to the toilet if I'm strapped in here."

"Oh, don't worry about that right now. I put a catheter in for you. We'll take it out before your meeting tomorrow. Now I'm going to give you something to keep the pain down so you'll get some more sleep."

"Meeting?"

"Uh-huh." She stuck him with a needle through the unbuttoned seam of his pant leg and tossed the syringe in a red plastic disposal can. She turned on her way toward the door.

"Try to sleep, Mr. Sims. You need it."

He looked at the catheter running into the urine bag and then gazed back up at the ceiling. The painkiller made his eyes begin to shut after five minutes.

As his mind relaxed, he remembered lying on the ground on his back, looking up at a beautiful blue sky filled with puffy, swirling storm clouds. Cool, wet grass cushioning his head.

The sound of flies buzzing around him broke the calm. He sat up and noticed he was bleeding from somewhere on his head. Bleeding like a leaky faucet. The blood had soaked through the top of his wet T-shirt, giving it a shiny maroon sheen.

He got up and tried to walk, but could only shuffle for a while until his boot dragged and caught an exposed root. He fell down hard and rolled on his back, wheezing and coughing. The flies were all over him. He thought he was going to die.

A large black ATV approached and a tall man wearing a black helmet and a loose gray shirt dismounted.

He couldn't see the man's face behind the dark helmet visor, but he spotted a name on his shirt as he leaned in closer.

CONSTANTINO.

CHAPTER 7

Saturday, June 8
3:30 p.m. (PDT)
Portland, Oregon

Agents Velasquez and Morris walked together down the fourth-floor hall in the main office building of the Portland FBI field office, a three-building complex on eight acres at Cascade Station, Portland PDX Airport. When they reached the briefing room, they opted for a quick stand-up meeting. Morris took a large swig from a one-liter bottle of Diet Coke and shut the door.

"So what the hell happened with Flash?" Morris asked.

Velasquez set his notebook computer down on the table along with a digital map printout with portions he'd highlighted in yellow. Velasquez was thirty-six years old, a short man with dark-brown eyes and clipped brown hair spiked in front. Even though he was 30 pounds over the 149-pound weight class of his Oregon State wrestling days, he exuded a natural athleticism and often paced around in a hunched stance like he was stalking an opponent for a takedown.

Velasquez traced the paper with his finger. "The GPS shows his vehicle stopped short of the turn to Lost Lake Campground. Hard to tell why . . . he pulled off on the border of the private land boundary—right here. He's been sitting in the same spot for over twelve hours now. No calls from the cell. There were a few bad rainstorms in the area yesterday and foggy conditions."

"Shit. Do you think he got stuck?"

Velasquez shrugged.

"Maybe. A Jeep could get stuck on a road like that after a storm even with four-wheel drive. Part of the road could have washed out. If that happened, he'd probably get to Lost Lake on foot, then try to reach out for help at the campground. Make a phone call if he could get a little coverage. Maybe even call the two women he was going to meet with. We talked through these different scenarios, including car problems."

"I don't like it," Morris said. "He's practically inside the private land. If you're far enough inside the boundary in a vehicle, a Chapter patrol is alerted and turns you around. That's what they do unless you somehow book an approved appointment at AgriteX."

"So do we try and reestablish contact? Have someone call his phone?"

"No, not yet. And I don't want anyone calling his phone. Let's have Alderville check the campground in twenty-four hours. I just want to confirm whether he's there or not. If he's not there, then most likely they've got him."

CHAPTER 8

Kade awoke when he heard the door open and footsteps follow—two men, both wearing the crinkly-shirt-and-cargo-pants getup, except in black. They unbuckled his straps and placed him in a wheelchair, handcuffing his right wrist to the chair arm. He no longer had IVs, and his catheter and urine bag had been removed.

He wiped his eyes and tried to get rid of the imaginary glue making them heavy. The man who took hold of the wheelchair was black with a lanky frame and hair in cornrows. The other guy walking in front was white and below average height, with muscles bulging through his uniform like his shirt was a size too small. They wheeled him out of the room and pushed him down the hallway. The surroundings looked kind of like a college dorm without the noise.

They passed rooms with closed doors on each side of the hall as he rolled along, and when they rounded the corner, he looked through a large window panel into what looked like a recreation room. He saw a few chairs, tables, couches, and a baby grand piano, but no occupants.

"Better put the hood on him," the escort in front of him said in a gravelly voice.

The wheelchair stopped and a moldy-smelling black canvas hood slid over his head from behind. They resumed moving again for a few more minutes, making several turns and pausing at times. Kade heard doors open and close, preceded by beeps from what sounded like access-card readers. He came to a stop for about a minute before someone pulled off the hood and he had to squint in the bright fluorescent light.

"Hood smells like ass," he said just loud enough to be heard.

The men said nothing. They positioned his wheelchair next to a table with a chair on the opposite side. Another chair was bolted to the floor beside him. He saw an opaque glass panel running across the wall on his left and heard the sound of a ventilation fan. The two men lifted him into the bolted-down chair and the black man transferred Kade's handcuff to a metal loop on the chair arm.

He heard a door open and click shut behind him. A man in his early forties with brown eyes, slicked-back dark brown hair, and the stubble of a beard dusting his face came into view and sat down on the opposite side of the table. He wore the same outdoor sportswear combo that everyone else had on, his brown in color like the nurse woman's and with the same sort of gold patch on the pocket. The logo on the patch looked like a stick-figure evergreen tree. Kade glanced under the table and noticed this guy wore nylon-and-leather-military-style black boots.

The man pulled out a spiral notepad and a pen from a thin leather case, took a brief look at Kade, fidgeted in his chair, and laid a black pistol on the tabletop about five feet away.

Sig Sauer nine millimeter.

"Good afternoon, Mr. Sims."

Kade stared at the man's hair. It didn't look like it could hold much more styling gel in it.

"Good afternoon, Mr. Sims," the man repeated louder. His mouth formed a natural frown, and now the muscles around his jaw began to tighten.

Kade thought back to mid-May and the day he'd spent with Jerry Lerner reviewing interrogation techniques he could expect. Two days later Jerry had surprised him with an all-night "training" session. Jerry forced him to stand for four hours, naked, in a cold room while being grilled by a guest interrogation expert. Smacked around a few times, then left alone in isolation. A mixture of loud music interspersed with screams and other strange, random noises ensured he got no sleep. That night just plain sucked.

The man slapped the notepad and pen down and put his elbows on the table, touching his hands to his chin. He sniffed periodically like he had allergies or a cold.

"Look, Mr. Sims, I just want to have a conversation. This doesn't have to be hard unless you want it to be."

The word *conversation* reminded him of Lerner telling him to keep his conversation light and his sense of humor intact, without being disrespectful. "Don't act like a prisoner or an obedient basic trainee," Lerner had instructed. "And try not to look like a cat in a room fulla rockin' chairs."

Stay strong. Control the situation when you can.

"Can I get a glass of water?" Kade asked.

The man nodded to someone behind him.

"And since you all know my name," Kade added, "I'd like to know who you are, please."

"My name is Joshua Pierce," the man said. "I'm the special assistant, reporting to Marshall Owens."

"That clears everything up," Kade said and yanked hard on his handcuff. "Who's Marshall Owens?"

"Mr. Owens is our chief executive officer—he leads our organization," Pierce said.

"And so where am I right now?"

"Don't you already know, Mr. Sims? We'd like to learn more about you and why you're here. Do you know why you're here?"

"No, I don't. I thought this was like the park ranger station or something."

A brownish recycled paper cup of water appeared on the table and Kade drank it down in a few gulps.

"I think you know exactly why you're here," Pierce said.

Pierce's phrase gave him a chill.

"Yeah, I'm all banged up. I think I had a car accident, but I'm not sure. It's hard to remember right now, that's all."

He thought about the planned meet-up with Michele Blanford or Tanya Hollowell. They both probably tried to contact him after he was a no-show, but with no response from him, hopefully they just thought he backed out at the last minute and weren't overly concerned.

"Where is your car?"

"I don't know. I was thinking you might be able to tell *me* what happened."

"What were you doing on our private land? How did you find us?"

Kade sighed and licked his dry lips.

"I don't know. Look, if I missed the 'No Trespassing' sign, I'm sorry. I just remember it was so foggy and rainy I couldn't tell where the hell I was."

"Our organization, our land, is private," Pierce said. "We just don't get people wandering out our way. Especially not people with your background. So I'll ask again: why are you here?"

Kade shook his head like he was trying to wake himself up.

"I was on my way to the Lost Lake camping area to hang out and do some fishing. That's it."

"You're very clever," Pierce said. "So you came all the way here to fish at Lost Lake?"

"Yeah, from Manzanita. It's really not that far."

"No, no, no." Pierce wagged his finger. "You've come from much farther away than that. From the Beltway. Do you still work for the Pentagon?"

"What?" Kade paused and shook his head again. "Uh, no, I was separated from the army about a year ago. Let's just say they didn't think I was very clever. And now I don't feel clever. I feel like shit. I'm supposed to be on vacation. Or at least I was. It doesn't look like I made it to the lake. I'd be glad to just get on my way and—"

"Vacationing out here? From Herndon, Virginia? You've got to be kidding me."

"Yeah, vacation. Some camping and fishing. Digging some of those razor clams I heard about. That was the plan."

"When did you arrive in Oregon?"

Kade took a few seconds, like he was having trouble remembering.

"Saturday. I can't tell you what day it is today, but I'm guessing I've been in Oregon about a week."

Pierce scratched down a note. "And when's your flight back?"

"It was the second Saturday after that. June fifteenth, I think."

"What airline did you take?"

"Southwest."

"What flight number was it?"

Kade shut his eyes for moment. "God, I don't remember. There were two flights—Dulles to Chicago Midway and Midway to Portland. Both on Southwest."

"Where have you been hanging out this past week?" Pierce asked.

"Uh, let's see. Oswald West, Nehalem Bay, Cannon Beach, Ecola State Park, Tillamook, Saddle Mountain, Astoria and Fort Clatsop."

"And why did you decide to go to Lost Lake, of all places?"

"I don't know. It was on my hit list like everything else. A few girls mentioned it to me online when I was planning my trip. And then someone else mentioned it to me in the campground I'm staying at, so I figured I'd check it out."

"What campground?" Pierce asked.

"The KOA in Manzanita."

"You brought camping gear with you?"

"No, I rented most of it from the REI in downtown Portland."

"And what else were you going to do while you were here?"

He gave Pierce a look like he was getting exhausted.

"Some more sightseeing. Beach time. Someone told me about surfing lessons in Seaside a while back, so I thought I might—"

"What did you do at the Pentagon?"

Kade rolled his eyes. "I was an analyst before I was separated. And now I work at Home Depot."

"What did you analyze?"

"Information."

"Intelligence?"

"Yeah, sure. Whatever you want to call it. Mostly a lot of reading. You know, world economic studies, foreign affairs, that sort of thing."

"And so your goal in coming here was to collect intelligence on our intellectual property?"

"Huh?" Kade made sure to look right at him. "Whoa. You're kidding, right?"

"Not at all. You could still work for the army, or the FBI, or maybe another company. We know your academic credentials. And since our network is very wide, I'm sure we'll figure out who you're working for. So why don't you just tell us yourself?"

"Look," Kade said, "I'm no longer getting a government paycheck, I swear. Only Home Depot. And trust me, it's not very big. Can I go now, please?"

Pierce shifted in his chair and stared at Kade like he was searching for signals in his face. He then looked at the two escorts and nodded his head once. Kade wondered what was going on behind him but didn't turn his head.

"We have a dilemma, Mr. Sims. Now that you know about us, we have to decide what we're going to do with you. It can't be a coincidence you're here. So I'll ask again, who sent you?"

Kade shook his head and flexed his arm in the sling. He thought of other words he could say but decided to sit silently and stare at the tabletop. He took a deep breath while the short, white escort, whose nametape read IGNATY, circled in front of him. Ignaty's tiny eyes looked like they were stamped right into his mean face. Skin creases and a few light scars radiated out from the sockets. He appeared neckless, like his shaved head was mounted right on his sloped shoulders and fireplug body.

Kade only had time to clench his teeth before Ignaty's fist landed hard across his jaw. The blow was followed by a hard backhand slap before Kade could raise his elbow to shield his face. Ignaty grabbed Kade's hair above the back of his neck and jerked his head back to wrap him in a chokehold.

"Mr. Sims?" Pierce asked. "Are you going to answer me?"

Kade gurgled something unintelligible until Ignaty relaxed his grip. He coughed and attempted to shout.

"Look, tell me what to say, if it gets me out of here, okay? I promise I'll forget this whole fucking thing. But if you're going to keep me here, I want to speak with the police or a lawyer. You can't just hold me hostage."

"Holding hostages is an ineffective way of doing business," Pierce said. "You're not answering the question, and you're making this difficult. Who sent you?"

Kade tasted blood running into his mouth from somewhere on his face.

"I wanted to see the Pacific . . . I've never seen it. And I heard about Oregon's awesome beaches, so I—"

Ignaty punched Kade hard in the stomach, knocking the wind out of him and doubling him over. Ignaty then shoved him upright, grabbed his hair again, and held his head in place while landing another punch to his cheek. Another hard backhand slap followed.

Kade went numb. He heard the crunch of the last punch, but it didn't seem to hurt. He saw the bandage from the top of his head fall on the floor. Ignaty drew his hand back for another blow and Kade remembered his legs were free. He slid his butt forward in his chair and kicked hard with his right leg. The shot hit Ignaty right in the balls. He turned around and staggered out of sight.

Score one for me.

Pierce smiled and spun the Sig Sauer on the table. "Who do you work for, Mr. Sims?"

Kade leaned over the side of his wheelchair and spit some blood on the floor. He was encouraged that none of his teeth were loose or chipped when he ran his tongue over them. He coughed to clear his throat and tried to relax so he could breathe. Ignaty appeared again and walked back toward him, approaching from the side. Kade glared at him and said, "You're great at hitting guys in chairs." Then he looked over at Pierce. "Like I said, I work at Home Depot. I saw there's one over in—"

Ignaty growled and put Kade in a tight headlock. He felt himself drifting out of consciousness. There was nothing he could do . . . *It's lights out.*

He heard a female voice through the warble of noise.

"Time-out, guys."

Ignaty relaxed his hold. He positioned Kade upright in the chair and stepped out of view. But seconds later, he felt Ignaty's breath in his right ear and heard him whisper.

"Keep this up, Sims, and I'll go after Janeen next. I'll fly out to Amherst and visit her myself."

Kade blinked several times. *They know where Janeen goes to school.* The blood was rushing back into his head. He kept blinking until the tears and dancing lights in his eyes began to clear. He recognized the nurse standing in front of him and rechecking his injuries. After she inspected the staples in his scalp, she shook her head.

"This session's over," she said. "Only Verax until I say otherwise."

Pierce appeared to be disappointed. He got out of his chair and stood in front of Kade.

"We'll talk more in a few hours, Mr. Sims. Crossing paths with us can be a curse or your lucky break. It's up to you. Sentries, take him to his room."

The black Sentry with the nametape HILL unlocked Kade's cuffs, stepped around the back of his chair, and lifted him back into the wheelchair. Kade knew Hill would next flip the tiny levers off the wheelchair brakes and push. Ignaty was standing a few feet away, talking to Pierce with his back to him.

Hill hadn't recuffed him to the wheelchair yet.

He leapt out of the wheelchair, took a stagger step, and brought his right elbow and forearm down as hard as he could on the back of Ignaty's massive neck. Ignaty went down on all fours. Kade kept pounding his fist anywhere he could connect. Hill and another Sentry tried to pull him off as Ignaty collapsed flat on his stomach, but Kade kept hitting the right side of his face. After another few punches, the Sentries finally pried him off and sat him back down in the wheelchair. They cuffed him to the armrest and the smelly hood slid back on his head, pulled down hard by someone behind him.

His wheelchair started to move. Above his own gasping breaths inside the hood, he heard Pierce talking in a hushed, admonishing tone until the wheelchair rolled out of the room and the door shut behind him.

He hadn't hit someone that hard since Fort Gordon, Georgia, when he was alone with his military intelligence battalion executive officer, Major Echols.

It wasn't that Echols chewed him out for violating policy during his temporary duty at the National Counterterrorism Center—Kade was going to receive an Article 15 proceeding, a non-judicial punishment process for "Failure to Report" on time for duty. He understood that. He had been late to his shift a number of times. While off-shift, he succumbed to the allure of the DC nightlife. The overstimulation made him feel invincible.

It wasn't uncommon for him to just stay out all night and then report for duty with no sleep. Or sometimes he was having so much fun, he forgot what time it was when morning rolled around.

Sometimes he would repeat it the next night just to see if he could.

But this was immature and irresponsible behavior. He wasn't as effective on the job as he could've been. It was a failure to realize his own weaknesses and manage his life around them.

At the conclusion of his grilling, the major had made one mistake when he said something within inches of Kade's face while Kade stood at attention.

"I'm sure your parents would've been very disappointed."

Kade broke his nose with a straight right.

He was then on his way to a court-martial, but ended up with a medical separation instead. It was probably easier, and possibly kinder in the long run.

Kade's breathing calmed as he tried to gather his thoughts. He visualized the organizational chart on the whiteboard where he had trained back in Falls Church. Lerner had made him draw the whole org chart at least a dozen times. He visualized picking up a blue dry-erase marker and filling in a blank box.

Special Assistant Joshua Pierce reports to Marshall Owens, the CEO of AgriteX. So Pierce is really the Chief Operating Officer. Marshall's right-hand man.

I screwed up the first part of the plan. But here I am, inside the Chapter.

Objective complete.

And they screwed up too. They should've never threatened my sister.

CHAPTER 9

The Sentry escorts wheeled Kade around for another few minutes, uncuffed him, and lifted him into a stiff twin-size bed. They pulled off the hood, and he relaxed his sweaty head on the foam pillow. The room smelled of new carpet and Febreeze.

"Take it easy now, Sims," Hill said before opening the door and exiting. Ignaty caught the door on the backswing of its self-closing hinge and gave Kade a quick, nasty look before following Hill out. Kade couldn't tell if Ignaty's face was swollen, but it had to be.

He took a number of deep breaths and gazed around the room. A window with white horizontal blinds let some broken sunlight shine through. He could see the moss-covered evergreen trees outside and noticed there were bars on the windows. Flush with the windowsill was a desk with a computer monitor, wireless keyboard, and mouse on top of it. A cheap plastic mesh chair was pushed up against the desk. Across the room was an alcove leading to the bathroom area and a tweed-upholstered easy chair.

"Kade, we hope you're feeling okay. Relax and give everything some time. We're here for you."

What the—?

He tensed up, looking for the source of the soft, resonant female voice. There was no one in his room. He looked up and around, finally focusing on a round speaker fixed high on the wall opposite him. The voice must have come from up there. He also noticed a surveillance camera positioned high in the corner closest to the window.

Looks like they're no strangers to psychological ops either.

He slid off the bed and grunted from the pain when his feet hit the floor. His body felt like one gigantic ache. He shuffled across the brown-speckled carpet toward the door. The toilet, sink, and shower area resembled a modest hotel bathroom. A plain oak-veneer dresser was crammed between the entryway and alcove, his Merrell hiking boots sitting on top of it. No ball cap anywhere.

Put the boots on? No, not yet, not with the surveillance camera.

The door was heavy wood, with a dead bolt above the knob and a flip lever on the inside. When Kade moved the lever and disengaged the bolt, he still couldn't open the door. He knocked on the wood and could tell he wasn't going to be able to kick this thing open. He'd need a battering ram to bust out if he couldn't disengage the lock.

I'm locked in. A prisoner.

He shuffled over toward the desk, saw the window, and looked to see if there was a way to open it. The lever that would allow the sill to slide sideways was fixed in place and had a small keyhole in it. It looked like he'd have to smash the glass and bend the bars. Not likely.

He sat down in the chair in front of the computer and located the single power button on the monitor. When he pressed it, the screen showed an internal network.

THE CHAPTER NETWORK
Login Status: Logged Out

He couldn't find a way to log in and the mouse didn't move any pointer. Two unlabeled peripherals he'd never seen before were plugged into the computer. He thought the black box might be a webcam, but it had a semitransparent red plastic disc facing him. Some kind of infrared communication device. The other device looked like it might be a backup hard drive or router. He wasn't sure.

He got up and sat down in the easy chair. It felt better than the stiff bed on his back, and the camera would have a harder time seeing him there. He flopped back against the headrest and looked up at the single ventilation grate on the ceiling, which looked well secured by twenty-plus Phillips-head screws. And it was too small for a person to crawl through anyway.

New age spa music began to play out of the wall speaker.

That's convenient. Interrogators use music to help achieve their desired results. So they're trying to calm me down and make me relax. And right now that's fine with me.

He shut his eyes and fell asleep for almost two hours as it became overcast outside and grayness painted the room. The music continued to play through the speaker at a low volume.

He woke up feeling hungry, with an intense burning sensation in his stomach. A few minutes later he heard the door unlock, and Sentries Ignaty and Hill entered again. He tried to avoid eye contact with Ignaty, but thought he saw two butterfly bandages and some heavy bruising on the Sentry's cheek. Maybe he'd gotten lucky and contributed another addition to Ignaty's world-class scar collection.

"Hi, guys," Kade said with excessive volume and enthusiasm.

Hill looked amused but pointed him toward the wheelchair.

"Let's go, Sims."

Ignaty said nothing and stood by the door while Kade complied. They cuffed his hands together this time and hooded him again.

"Can I get some chow?" Kade asked. "All this abuse is making me really hungry."

"Later," Ignaty said. Kade thought Ignaty had a perfect voice for narrating a horror movie trailer.

Hill pushed the wheelchair out into the hallway and moved through the complex for a few minutes before coming to a halt. Kade heard an access-card reader beep and a door open, then felt the wheelchair move for a few feet before it stopped and someone removed his hood. The Sentries lifted him into what looked like a dentist's chair, strapped him in, and immobilized his head with an additional U-shaped headrest.

The male body of some technician leaned over him and slid a wired headband device onto his head. A flexible microphone moved in front of his mouth. The room was small, maybe ten-by-ten, and illuminated by fluorescent tubes shining on undecorated white walls.

He heard Pierce's voice through a speaker in the headrest.

"Mr. Sims, can you hear me?"

Kade felt his stomach give another long growl. Pierce repeated himself a few times in increasing volume, but Kade didn't say anything.

"Sims!"

"Yeah, I hear you. But I don't think you heard me before. I'd like to speak with the police. This is a huge violation of my rights."

"The police won't help you. If anything, we'll have you arrested for trespassing. You don't have many choices here. Would you prefer to go back to the questioning room tomorrow?"

"No, that's okay."

"All right then. This is the Verax system. It's one of the most sophisticated lie-detection programs in existence. Answering the technician's questions truthfully will be your fastest ticket out of here. Your answers will be yes or no only. Understood?"

Kade was relieved he wasn't going to get his teeth drilled or some other kind of dental torture.

"Yeah."

The technician started the questioning in a deep Southern accent.

"Is your full birth name Kinkade Alan Sims?"

"Yes."

"Is your date of birth November nine, nineteen eighty-eight?"

"Yes."

There was about a thirty-second pause.

"Let's try this again. Is your date of birth November nine, nineteen eighty-eight?"

"Yes. It's right on my driver's license. Along with my address. You guys have my wallet, remember?"

"Yes or no only!" Pierce said.

There was another pause. The technician reappeared in the room, removed the headband for a moment, and repositioned it. A minute after he dropped out of view again, the questioning continued.

"Did you rent a Jeep Liberty at Portland PDX Airport?" the technician asked.

"Yes."

"Do you know where it is now?"

"No."

About a minute passed.

"Are you being paid by any government agency?"

"No."

"Have you ever heard of AgriteX Corporation before?"

"No."

"Do you work for the Home Depot?"

"Yes."

"Are both of your parents deceased?"

"Yes."

"Is your mother's maiden name Pamela Gwinn?"

Kade paused. *You're pushing it.*

"Is your mother's maiden name Pamela Gwinn?"

"Yes," Kade said in a chafed tone.

"Is your sister's name Janeen Anita Sims?"

"No, that's it. No more questions about my family. That's overkill. You guys know I'm telling the truth."

A pause.

"Are you currently working in a corporate espionage role?"

"No."

"Have you ever conducted corporate espionage?"

"No."

"Are you working for or associated with any state or local law enforcement organization?"

"No."

"Are you working for the U.S. government?"

"No."

"Did the FBI send you here?"

"No."

"Did the FBI send you here?"

"No!"

A very long pause followed, which seemed to last at least five minutes.

"Can I please get something to eat now?" Kade asked.

"Just sit tight," Pierce said.

"So how'd I do?"

"You'll find out soon enough."

CHAPTER 10

Wednesday, June 12
5:01 a.m. (PDT)
Alderville, Oregon

Agent Troy Jenkins sat down in the living area of the old Winnebago, resting his arms on the yellow plastic tabletop pocked with brown cigarette ash melt marks. Jenkins had light blue eyes and patch of curly brown hair clipped short around a receding hairline. He'd just turned forty over the weekend and had been forced to postpone a Las Vegas celebration when he learned of his assignment in CLEARCUT.

Across from him, Agent Jeff Stephenson sipped a cup of coffee and ate a peanut butter and jelly sandwich. Stephenson was thirty-seven and looked like a bear with bed-head. His muscular build suggested regular gym time and protein supplements.

Jenkins opened the window shade and the early morning light of the Pacific Northwest summer lit up the interior.

"Time to check in, right?" Stephenson asked.

"Yeah," Jenkins said. He pulled his phone from its hip holster and a can of Copenhagen from his pocket. He put a dip in his mouth before pressing the speed dial.

"This is Chris," Agent Velasquez answered.

"Hey, this is Jenkins and Stephenson at the Lost Lake Campground."

"Hey, guys, what's the status?"

"Status is we've had no contact with Flash. I checked the campground yesterday morning. Only three people there, and he wasn't one of 'em. Then by nine, I went trout fishing at the lake all day until sundown. If he'd been here, I would've seen him, easy. Stephenson just got back thirty minutes ago. He can tell you about his search."

Jenkins switched to speakerphone and placed the phone on the table. Stephenson set down his sandwich, finished chewing, and gave his update.

"Yeah, his Jeep's in a ravine inside their private property. It's right around the last GPS reading we recorded, and it's wrecked. It's going to be hard for anyone to retrieve it. I got close enough to confirm that Flash wasn't still inside. It rained enough last night that I wasn't too worried about leaving footprints."

"Shit. Hope he's okay," Velasquez said.

"There's blood in the vehicle," Stephenson continued. "Hard to say how much, since the windows were open and the rain soaked everything, but there was a fair amount of staining on the seat upholstery. It was a pretty long hike from here to the crash site, so it seems unlikely he came our way on foot. His cap was in the vehicle . . . I took it and have it here. His gear was still in the back— now all mixed up with fish bait and other stuff he packed. I left it all in there. Fuel leaked everywhere. Lucky the Jeep didn't go up in smoke. After that, I walked a small radius—maybe fifty to a hundred yards—with night-vision goggles to see if I could find him. Nothing."

Stephenson left out that he'd repeated the same area sweep with his flashlight on, calling out Sims's name. If Sims had been nearby and seen a flashlight, he might have yelled for help. This may have been risky, given possible AgriteX security patrols, but if Sims was severely injured, the operation would be over anyway.

"Damn it," Velasquez said. "Call the Nehalem Clinic, Tillamook Community, Seaside Memorial. Do another check of the campground later and give me a status at seven."

"Okay, talk to you at seven," Jenkins said, and ended the call. He looked at Stephenson. "I've got this covered right now. You go get some rest."

Stephenson didn't need to be told twice to go and recharge. These ops could be dull one moment and exciting the next. And this was feeling like it wouldn't be one of the dull ones.

CHAPTER 11

Owens was eating a late breakfast when he saw Pierce enter the executive lounge. The room was designed like a miniature pub with a short cedar bar, four round tables, and walls featuring Chinook carved-wood artifacts. A spear, hunting bow, dance rattles, and animal figurines including an eagle, bear, and elk were mounted in panels and shelves.

"Good morning," Owens said. He was halfway through an omelet and a bowl of mixed berries.

"Hi, Marshall." Pierce sat down and accepted a cup of coffee from the server. "I have an update on that guy, Sims. The one we found out at Zone Foxtrot."

"Yes, let's hear about that."

"Everything in his background checks out so far. His boss at Home Depot says he took off for a two-week vacation, and a Guardian in the area stopped by that store to make sure the boss was real. We confirmed he's been seen in the campground in Manzanita. He registered to hold a place for surfing lessons out of Seaside a month ago, paid on his MasterCard. No unusual purchases that raise any flags."

"His car?"

"We found it. A Jeep Liberty rented out of Budget at PDX. Badly damaged from taking a tumble out beyond Zone X-ray. Looks like he was packed for a fishing and camping trip. We've left everything in place for now. The distance from the crash site to the outer surveillance ring is just short of a mile. He must have crawled out of the wreck and walked a good distance."

"How about his apartment?"

"Went through the entire place," Pierce said. "We found no discrepancies. There was plenty of trip research—printouts from his desktop printer—leading up to his travel date. He consulted online communities to ask about campsites, hiking, and vacation-related stuff. He talked about this trip on his Facebook page for weeks leading up to now, and got a camping tip about Lost Lake on a travel bulletin board that seemed to spark the idea. Then he was talking to all kinds of people about it, but we didn't see any red flags. He's also got some sort of journal notebook for what looks like psychiatric treatment, which we removed from his apartment and FedExed out here."

"Good, I'd like to see that when it comes in. Did you run Verax on him?"

"We were just getting started before a problem made us take it offline, so we questioned him manually. Do you want us to put him in isolation until he's validated?"

"No, a standard Associate room is okay for now. Worst-case scenario is this kid was sent as some sort of an expendable scout, but we don't have any evidence of that. He sure as hell isn't an operative. He's too young and there's no indication of any related experience. We've monitored all the new hires at the Portland field office, and he doesn't match up with anyone we know about. We've been tracking who comes and goes from that office since March; he's never been there."

"So release him in Manzanita with the standard outbrief and monitor up to launch?"

"No. I think he might be a good asset for us," Owens said.

"For *us*?"

"Yes. Have him take the psych profile, I'll bet you'll find he's right in our sweet spot."

"Really?"

"Yes, he looks like he's just drifting without a rudder. I've stumbled upon his blog before, Wakethehelluppeople.com; he's got a hundred twenty thousand followers. He skewers politicians and bureaucrats but supports the military, even after being separated. He's a rare voice trying to awaken a disaffected public. Could be a future recruiting tool."

"So you think he's Chapter material."

"Yes. He's talented, but his leadership ability is sitting fallow. He just needs a purpose, a vehicle to make his ideas for change become reality. We can give him that."

Pierce looked down and sniffed.

"Okay, what do you have in mind?"

"We're short in our recruit pipeline for Phase Two, and we still need leadership to fill out the ranks. Let's keep him in the Associate program, but give him the Guardian protocol instead of Zulu. See how he responds from there. If he lives, we develop him further. Send him back east and try to get him working as a civilian in the Pentagon. We can get his records corrected. His skills as a software engineer would also be very useful. Did you see the analysis of his online activity?"

"What about it?" Pierce asked.

"It shows he did some freelance web work and programming. Looks like he knows the key coding languages—C#, Linux, Java, HTML, PHP, Objective C—and plays with a few others. Finding that skill set along with a cultural fit here isn't easy. Our programs have to evolve."

"Marshall, we're only twenty-four days away from Phase One launch. I know I've fallen short of the Phase Two recruitment goal, but aren't we putting the cart before the horse?"

"Are you suggesting we kill him and attract more attention with him missing?"

"It seems the safer choice this late in the game. Who's going to miss him or even know where to look?"

Owens shook his head.

"No, we keep him and just move him out with the other Associates as Phase Two. The other Associates aren't fully indoctrinated either. They'll be far away, so they can't interfere, even if they wanted to."

"Marshall, from a security perspective, I think—"

"Do it, please. We're always looking for the right kind of people. I appreciate your candor, though. "

Marshall saw Pierce sigh as if he was trying to calm himself. He knew he needed to stay below the threshold of angering his operational chief to keep him effective. His relationship with Pierce spanned fifteen years, beginning when he'd hired Pierce for executive protection while Pierce worked for the private security firm ESX. Pierce then moved to a management position at a private military company, Spectrum Defense, and Marshall returned to recruit him after starting AgriteX.

Pierce was one of the first to receive the Guardian protocol, and he'd thrived with it. Over time he had earned executive and administrative rights. He had the highest recorded scores of compliance and activity for all download communications in the Guardian and Sentry programs. Owens called this composite score the "Knowledge Index," and only executives could monitor it. While most downloads were mandatory, Owens had assigned additional, optional readings with the ability to enter comments and questions.

Guardians and Sentries also had Verax reviews and were asked loyalty questions. "Would you die for Marshall Owens?" "Would you report a fellow Guardian who had betrayed the Chapter?" The process was designed to weigh the strength of each Guardian's responses and calculate a "Loyalty Index." Pierce topped that chart too. When it came to expertise in security, surveillance, and ruthless cleanup work, Marshall doubted he could've ever found better than Pierce.

"Okay," Pierce replied. "Regarding his aunt and sister—do you want us to continue surveillance?"

"On the sister only, and keep it light. Just as a precaution up until prelaunch activities. At this point we'll need to gain his trust. Harassing his family risks pushing him away. We know where they are, and he knows that."

"Right. And if he dies from the Guardian protocol?"

"Put him back in the Jeep and notify the county there's been an accident."

CHAPTER 12

Inside one of the many one-story stucco-and-cement-tile houses packed together in the subdivision, Mateo sat shirtless, smoking a cigarette behind the folding table pushed up to the window. He was in his early thirties with a buzz cut and thin mustache curving to his jaw. Tattoos adorned his muscular body from his waist to his forearms.

Two notebook computers sat on the tabletop in front of him along with a painted ceramic ashtray and a can of Budweiser. On one computer, he was checking the evening movie times at the nearby theater. The other laptop was connected to Skype and sat idle except for a tiny graphic thermometer that showed 105 degrees for the Phoenix area. He hadn't left the house yet today, but that didn't bother him at all.

The computer interface chimed on the second laptop—the contact box popped up on the screen with the name JOHN. Mateo donned his headset, took a swig of beer, and cleared his throat. There was no picture of John as a contact, and Mateo didn't know if that was the true first name of this person he'd met only once. Most of Mateo's dispatching work was just connecting addicts with buyers and buyers with couriers, but once or twice a week he communicated with people higher in the cartel pecking order. It always made his skin a little prickly.

"Hello?"

"Mateo."

"Yeah?"

"What's the report from Oregon?"

"Not sounding good," Mateo said.

"How's that?"

"David says our deckhand thinks the catch is going to fall short."

"How short?" John asked.

"Way short. They see little activity. They think there won't be enough catch to make the quota at the end of next month. They say the processors are inactive."

"Did they say why?" John asked. "Don't they understand that we have an exclusive agreement?"

"I don't know any more than that," Mateo said. "You'll have to talk to David."

"This is bad. Did you speak with the deckhand yourself?"

"No, I only get e-mails every few weeks. No calls. I just read the e-mails to David."

John was silent for over a minute. Mateo was used to this. He knew it meant John was on mute and discussing this information with somebody.

"I'm going to have to go speak to the captain," John said.

Mateo didn't comment. He never speculated or discussed strategy. It was risky enough being a communications hub.

La vida es corta tanto como el dinero.

John added, "You make sure to let us know if the deckhand provides another update."

"Yeah, I will."

"And tell David I'm going to take a trip up there in about a week."

CHAPTER 13

Friday, June 14
12:50 p.m. (PDT)
AgriteX

Kade awoke with no idea where he was until he spotted the familiar autumn village watercolor on the opposite wall. That meant he was back in the medical treatment room.

He lifted his head off the pillow. Pain throbbed a few inches above his left ear and a general headache burrowed deep into his skull. When he relaxed back against the pillow, the pain was tolerable, but he was feverish. Sweat made his entire neck slick and his throat felt like it had been stuffed with dried leaves. He swallowed a few times and tried to push some fresh saliva around with his tongue, but the nasty taste in his mouth refused to go away.

The vital signs monitor occasionally beeped, and the blood pressure cuff wrapped around his right arm constricted every few minutes to provide a reading. The IV stand held a bag dripping a clear liquid into his left arm, which was still splinted but now without a sling. His right arm had some other kind of shunt running into it.

His memory was fuzzy. Hill had told him he could eat and drink after he filled out a "profile." The profile questionnaire was somewhere between a simple Myers-Briggs personality test and a complex evaluation like the one from his background review for a top secret security clearance. He answered the profile honestly, assuming they might put him back on the lie detector. His last memory was handing Hill the completed answer sheet.

He turned his head to the side. Weak sunlight shone through the window above the vent, and the evergreen branches swaying in the breeze outside created moving shadows on the wall. He noted the surveillance camera positioned above the bed.

Other than the dull head pain, the rest of his body felt okay. He checked to see if he was restrained again and saw the same nylon straps stretched around his chest and stomach. Even when he pushed against them with all his strength, they still held firm. He squeezed the armrests on the bed to calm himself down. Now he was really getting sick of this shit.

The nurse he'd seen before reentered the room wearing a pair of plastic protective glasses. He reached out and tried to grab her arm, but couldn't quite extend far enough. The sudden move startled her, but he didn't care about being polite anymore.

"I'm tired of being strapped in here like an animal," he said. "What's going on?"

"Mr. Sims, I know you're upset with your current situation but—"

"Upset? Yeah, I'm upset! Screw vacation! I want to get back home now. You guys can't just hold me here. I'm not a criminal. I haven't broken any laws."

"Patience, Kade."

Hearing his first name in a comforting tone made him pause. He took in her exotic appearance as she stepped closer to the bedside. They must have pumped his body full of drugs.

"Look," she said. "You're very lucky, but you just don't know it yet. We've gotten you all fixed up now because the leadership thinks you've got great potential and would be a great fit."

"What?"

"Marshall thinks that with some exposure you'll want to be a part of what we're doing here. This medical treatment is just the beginning. Most people don't end up here by chance like you did. I can't tell you more about this right now, but you'll find out some more later tonight. We'll monitor your progress through that camera, so don't feel like you're being left alone. Hopefully very soon you won't need to be restrained. Everyone's just making sure that you don't hurt yourself."

"My head hurts. I feel like I've been sleeping for a long time. Horrible dreams too."

"That's normal," she said. "You've been in a controlled coma for five days, but that ended today, and everything's looking good."

"A controlled coma? For a week? What the fuck happened?"

"You'll get more answers tonight. Now I want you to rest for a few more hours. I'm going to give you a sedative. When you come to, you'll be back in your assigned room."

Kade tried to calm down and decided to keep his mouth shut. Then he remembered again why he was here. It popped into his mind and brought immediate focus.

CLEARCUT. The operation name he wasn't supposed to know.

He knew the clock of the operation was ticking and he was wasting precious hours. Or more like precious *days*. He'd lost control of the situation and needed to get back on track. Lerner had told him to expect the unexpected. Improvise. Be creative. He'd said he would do just fine. Said that he'd have waves of doubt. Waves of fear. It was all normal in an operation like this.

The nurse stuck him in the thigh with a syringe. He wondered what Agents Morris and Velasquez were doing. The team in Alderville. Other people behind the scenes. He pictured them all sitting around, shooting the shit. Checking out and going home for the weekend. If he'd been in a coma for a week, then he'd been out of contact for almost ten days. Did anyone care? He was just a source to the FBI, or in Morris's words, an *investment*. Not a friend or a comrade in arms. They weren't thinking about him like Alex was, that's for sure. He took a deep breath.

His mind grew weary trying to sort through this state of flux. He caught himself with his eyes closed twice and fought hard to stay awake, but when he shut them for the third time, he was out.

CHAPTER 14

Kade's body jolted and he awoke. For several minutes his pulse thundered in his ears and he felt like he couldn't lie still without his heart exploding right out of his chest.

God, where am I now?

No watercolor on the wall.

The computer's here.

I'm back in my assigned Chapter cell.

He took some deep breaths as the early evening sunlight cast a soft shadow in the room. He wasn't strapped in the bed now. He felt his scalp and found the metal staples were gone. He no longer had a headache; in fact, there wasn't much pain anywhere. The splint had been removed and his left arm felt pretty normal. What he noticed most was that he stank.

He rolled out of bed and walked over to the mirror in the bathroom area. His hair was matted down in front of his bloodshot eyes, his lips chapped and covered with flaking scallops of dry skin. Some kind of bloodstained cotton-like material was stuffed into his nostrils. He started to pull the cotton out, but then left it.

There had to be a good reason it was in there. Maybe he'd had a round two with Ignaty and didn't remember.

A basic set of toiletries had been placed on the back rim of the sink. He unwrapped a soap bar and grabbed a mini shampoo bottle. After taking a ten-minute shower at near-scalding temperature, he shaved with the disposable razor and combed the tangles out of his hair with the flimsy plastic comb. He rinsed the dust out of the glass on the sink and took a big drink of water. The cabinet underneath the sink was filled with rolls of toilet paper and boxes of tissue. Nothing particularly useful.

He didn't feel like putting the ripe hospital-style pajamas back on, so he walked around naked until he realized the room was a bit too cool for that. And people were monitoring the room through the cameras, so he'd better put something on, if only a dry towel.

Inside the dresser he found a stack of white T-shirts, a few pairs of dark blue cargo pants, and matching crinkly shirts. Plenty of white cotton socks and underwear. A black nylon belt. A pair of plain Adidas tennis shoes. Everything but the shoes was still wrapped in unmarked plastic packages. He grabbed one of each item, along with the lone hoodie in the bottom drawer, and got dressed. The clothes smelled like they'd been in mothballs for a century, but they fit. He looped the belt through his new pants, and when he adjusted the length, it seemed like it had six inches of unneeded slack.

The empty pockets felt strange. No wallet, keys, or phone.

He remembered his prepaid phone—putting it in the center console of the Jeep after trying to call Darcy. It was now in the wreck somewhere. If any of the Chapter goons had found it, it wouldn't have any stored numbers of significance.

He tried on the sneakers from the drawer and they were way too tight.

Great excuse to wear my boots.

After he cleaned off the hiking boots in the sink and put them on, he stood at the window and looked outside at the tall evergreens swaying in the wind. His eyes came back to the steel bars.

It's time to play the game or I won't get out of here.

Quick knocks resonated on the door and two new Sentries entered. Their nametapes said SMITH and WOLF, and their similar brushed-up dark brown hair and pork-chop sideburns made them look like cousins. They were smaller in stature, and Kade thought he could take out one, if not both, in a fight if he had to, if only they didn't have pistols.

"Let's go, Sims," Smith said. "You're walking."

"Where're we going?"

"To see the special assistant. We need to put the hood on."

"You know I love that thing."

He heard some shuffling about and then a female voice.

"You're going to get a mild sedative now."

"Why?"

"Because Dr. Drakos said so."

They unbuttoned his top and pulled his undershirt collar over his shoulder before sticking him with a needle.

"Thanks a lot."

As they guided him down the hallway, he noticed they didn't put handcuffs on him. At first, he felt stronger and more alert as he walked, like he could run if he needed to. It took another few minutes for the sedative to kick in while Smith and Wolf escorted him down several more corridors, turns, and entryways. The floor's hard surface changed to carpet, and he heard four beeps that sounded like digits being entered into a keypad access lock. Finally, he was guided to a seat in a padded chair that felt like soft leather.

Wolf removed the hood and Kade saw a smiling Joshua Pierce sitting across from him, the Sig Sauer holstered on his side. This time he was in a comfortable office instead of an interrogation area.

The stick-figure tree design he had seen on the badges was etched in a large square piece of frosted glass mounted to the side wall.

"Mr. Sims, you're looking much better," Pierce said like they were old friends. "I was worried about you."

Okay, let's roll with some Stockholm Syndrome . . .

"Thanks," he said. "I was worried too, but I'm feeling better now. Thank you for treating my injuries, and I'm sorry to have caused a bunch of problems."

Pierce nodded.

"That's good to hear. And I think from now on you'll find us much more hospitable. We've learned a lot about you and would like it if you stayed with us for a while."

"Really? Well, I don't know," Kade said in rapid bursts. "I know I trespassed on to your grounds. Your private property. I'm sorry. You have some sensitive stuff going on here, I gather. Security is important. I understand. Corporate secrets and all. It's great that you were nice enough to take care of me. Thank you."

"You're welcome. We know you didn't learn about AgriteX in the most normal circumstances. Not in the way we would've liked. We'd like to introduce you to some of our team and have you learn more about what we're doing. But first, I need to bring you online into our network. You've been fitted with a microcomputer that's an essential part of our program."

"You mean the one in my room?"

"No, we'll get to that one in a minute. You may have noticed a small bump in the area above your left eyebrow. Can you touch that spot?"

Kade raised his hand and rubbed his index finger on his forehead until he felt a spot about the size of a pencil eraser. There was a raised bump under the skin like a small, hard cyst. He hadn't thought too much about it before, just thought it was a wound still healing.

"Yeah, I feel it."

"It's a tiny infrared port," Pierce said. "The device sits just under the skin."

"What?" Kade felt a sick feeling build in his stomach. He touched the spot again.

"That's the gateway to the microcomputer," Pierce said. "You have the ability to receive and send information to the network. The download speed isn't too shabby—two megabytes per second."

"You put a computer inside my head."

"Yes, a chipset. It's active, but now you'll get oriented to the program and the network."

Kade's mouth began filling with saliva like he was going to throw up. Pierce pointed a device at him that looked like a TV remote control and pressed a few buttons. Kade was shocked by what he saw seconds later. A number of colorful graphics appeared right in front of him in his plain view, as if they were frozen in the air.

The first graphic was a tiny stoplight in the far left side of his vision. Right of center was a white oval filled with green lettering that said *CHAPTER NETWORK*. That same tree insignia was right beside it. He raised his hand to check if he had some kind of specialized digital eyeglasses on his face, but there was nothing there.

"What you're seeing now is visible only to you, but it's a display every member of the Chapter has, myself included. Now I need you to sit in the chair over there." Pierce pointed to the chair to his right. It looked similar to the one used with the Verax machine except that it sat fully vertical instead of reclined. It faced a separate desk, positioned against two exterior windows and held about three times more computer gear on it than the one in Kade's room.

Kade obeyed. The Sentry bookends, Smith and Wolf, watched him with pistols now drawn but not aimed.

"You're going to sit very still and position the plus sign that appears in the center of your vision right on top of the plus sign in the center of the screen. The plus sign will only change position when you move your head, not when you move your eyes."

A white plus sign appeared in midair in his vision. He turned his head a fraction until it lined up flush with the one on the screen.

"Now you're going to hold as still as you can in that position for about five minutes," Pierce said.

"Okay."

There's nothing I can do. I can't run or Smith and Wolf will shoot me dead.

His next experience was like a very bad dream. A bad trip like none he'd ever imagined. Over the next five minutes, his mind was flooded with information in various forms—text, pictures, and video—at a stunning speed. His heart thundered inside him, but he didn't speak or move other than a slight shaking of his body. Finally, the words *DOWNLOAD COMPLETE* appeared just off-center right.

"Congratulations on connecting to the network and your first download," Pierce said. "You'll have at least one download per day while you're here, received at your desk in your room. It takes about five to ten minutes."

Kade sat silent.

"I know this must feel overwhelming," Pierce said. "But I'm very pleased that everything seems to be running smoothly . . . The software diagnostics checked out. You must have a lot of questions."

When Kade looked straight at Pierce, the name *JOSHUA PIERCE* now appeared in his vision. He turned and looked at the Sentries and the names *KRISTOPHER WOLF* and *PRESTON SMITH* appeared when he focused on their respective faces.

Questions? This is fucking insane.

"Sentry Smith, how are we on time?" Pierce asked.

"Thirty minutes until dinner," Smith said.

"Okay. Let's go over a few important basics," Pierce said. "Come sit back over here in front of me, please."

Kade moved back over to the black leather chair and lowered himself into it.

"Now that you're on our network," Pierce said, "you're an Associate member of our family, which we call the Chapter. When we refer to our business, we refer to it as AgriteX. You will not utter the words *the Chapter* outside this organization to anyone or it will register on your stoplight as yellow. Yellow on your stoplight will produce a painful reminder that you're doing something wrong regarding our rules and the Code. Red indicates repeated violations and will result in your being incapacitated. Green means you are good to go, of course. Make sense?"

Kade swallowed and cleared his throat. He couldn't think straight. How much of this was the sedative, he wasn't sure, but this was a helpless situation.

"Yes."

"Okay, a few quick things." Pierce stood, uncapped a dry-erase marker, and began writing on a large whiteboard on the wall. "We have our own code of behavior here, made up of what we call the Chapter Tenets. They are *Knowledge, Truth*, and *Trust*. First, members of the Chapter are not allowed to discuss the special knowledge they have gained from the Chapter outside the organization or with another member who doesn't have the proper authorization. Knowledge is compartmentalized and disobeying the Knowledge Tenet is a code violation. Offenders can be euthanized."

"Did you say—do you mean, like, euthanasia?" Kade asked.

"Yes."

Kade sat back in his chair and looked at the ceiling. He smiled for some unknown reason. Maybe it was complete disbelief. Or the drugs. This was like nothing he ever could've imagined.

But there was nothing he could do. Fighting while sedated would get him shot and killed. He needed to regroup and continue the mission. Finish it to the best of his ability.

I'm in this, whole hog.

He swiveled in place to look at Smith and Wolf, who both remained expressionless.

"Okay, I got it," Kade said. He spun the chair back, facing Pierce again.

"Next is Truth. Our lives depend on each other. If you're caught lying to another Chapter member after initiation, you may be euthanized. Use your best judgment at all times with your communications. Your program attempts to steer you in the right direction and logs your activities. But ultimately, the Guardians vote on a lying offense to determine deceit, and if you're found guilty of an offense, you'll be euthanized. Simple enough?"

"Yeah."

"Last is the Trust Tenet. The special knowledge you gain while you're here at the Chapter is a privilege you must use to further our cause of eliminating the abuse of American power and environmental atrocities. You will learn much more as an Associate. When you complete the program here, if you betray the trust of a fellow Chapter member, and it's documented, you may be paid a visit from a few Chapter alumni to make sure it never happens again."

"You mean, euthanized?"

"Possibly," Pierce said. "It depends on the breach. We have a simple saying here—if you break the Code, you get the Code."

"That's pretty clear," Kade said. "And how long would you like me to stay here to complete this program?"

Pierce snapped the cap back on the marker and tossed it into the whiteboard's bottom tray.

"As a Chapter member, you'd normally be required to stay for a year before returning to the public workforce again. In your case, we plan to accelerate the progress so we cut the time in half."

"I see. I guess I'm just concerned that my family will wonder what the hell I'm doing out here and my boss will wonder if I'm ever coming back."

"Mr. Sims, I'm a hundred-percent sure you'll be very happy you decided to take a leave of absence from your job. Your family will understand. You can tell them you met some people and networked into a very well-paying job opportunity. You can explain the great things AgriteX is doing with balancing environmental stewardship and the demands of the timber industry. Our seed technology and forestry-management software produce faster-growing evergreens for designated private farms, so we can maintain the richness of our wild forests. As part of your AgriteX employment agreement, we'll pay you in excess of a hundred thousand dollars when this training period is complete. And you'll continue to financially benefit from being part of the Chapter after you return to your subsequent occupation."

"Who are the Guardians?" Kade asked.

"The Guardians are hand selected from Chapter members for special training, treatment, and duties. Their roles and future responsibilities are somewhat different from the Sentries', such as those of Sentries Smith and Wolf."

Kade nodded.

"Ten minutes," Sentry Wolf said.

"Right," Pierce said. "Now, let's test your stoplight so you know what you're dealing with. I'm going to give you a one-second burst of the yellow light indicator so you know what it feels like. Then you're on autopilot. Ready?"

"Sure."

Pierce dialed in a code and pointed the device again, and Kade watched his stoplight turn to yellow.

This is so bizarre.

He shut his eyes and waited for whatever was coming. He expected the graphics would still be there with his eyes closed, but they weren't. It seemed they needed external light to show up. At least they wouldn't be there when he went to sleep.

"Now do you understand how this pain signal works when rules are broken?" Pierce asked.

Kade opened his eyes. Blinked them a few times. The stoplight hovered there, now unlit.

"Yeah, I understand. That doesn't feel good at all."

"Okay, we're all set," Pierce said. "Unless you have any questions, it's time to take you to dinner."

Kade sat in a daze and was slow to get up. Wolf gave him a nudge.

"Let's go, Sims."

Kade stepped toward the door and shot a glance at Pierce.

Your program must have a bug, Special A-hole.

Because I didn't feel any pain.

CHAPTER 15

Kade guessed there were over three hundred people packed into the AgriteX café. The room was noisy and the entire scene felt odd. How many companies had evening meals for its employees? On a Saturday night? Sentry Wolf and Pierce guided him to a seat at a ranch-style dining table and announced him to the group of five already there.

Two women sat next to him on his right, three men on the opposite side. He noticed his dark blue outfit seemed to match everyone's at the table. The whole café looked like an outdoor clothing convention, and now he fit right in.

"Hey, Sims, I'm Daniel." The rosy-cheeked guy with a mustache stood and offered a handshake from across the table. "Nice to meet you."

"Hi," Kade said. He shook Daniel's hand, and when he looked directly at his face, the name *DANIEL SLADE* appeared in Kade's vision. Daniel had friendly brown eyes, wavy hair, and a forehead that looked dented in the middle.

Kade wondered how the hell this facial-recognition program was working from inside his own skull, but the food and drink right in front of him stole his attention. Platters of thick steaks, baked potatoes, salad, and two pies made for a beautiful spread. Two wine bottles and two pitchers of beer sat in the midst of it. The wonderful smell of everything made him weak.

A hand gently touched his right shoulder.

"Hi, I'm Lin."

He turned his head and the woman sitting to his right was smiling at him from behind wide strands of dark brown hair. She had Asian features, and by his quick measure, she was a knockout.

"Hi, I'm Kade."

He turned forward again. Further conversation or greetings were lower priority for the moment. Even though no one else had started eating, he put food on his plate and dug in like he'd never get the chance again. Screw what anyone else might think, he couldn't remember being hungrier in his life. No one seemed to protest.

Daniel grabbed Kade's empty pint glass and the beer pitcher.

"Here, let me pour you your first Chapter light," he said.

"Thanks," Kade said with his mouth overstuffed with food.

The beer would've tasted like a cheap domestic on any other day, but today it was pure nectar.

"Where are you from?" Lin asked after he had eaten for about five minutes.

"The DC area," he said, and then reminded himself to be interactive. "How about yourself?"

"New York City."

"That's a long way from here."

"Tell me about it."

"What's your background?"

"International business sales and marketing. I help American companies make connections with business and government in China, so they can—"

Lin stopped talking when she saw Marshall Owens walk across the far end of the café and stand at the raised podium.

"Good evening, everyone," Owens said. "Please continue to eat and drink." His voice sounded confident and crisp over the PA system, like that of a college coach.

Conversation hushed. Everyone at Kade's table had their attention drawn toward the podium, so Kade followed suit by occasionally turning his head, but generally he focused on shoveling down as much food as possible.

"Welcome to our monthly dinner," Owens said. "We've reached an exciting milestone today. We mark the two-hundredth Guardian who will leave and return to government service. This force, along with the over three hundred graduates of our political action program, will help us enact tangible change in America and support our causes. With the right people in place, we will end American atrocities abroad, end our government's abuse of power, and focus on our own domestic strength. We will regain balance with the lands we live on. Some people will fear us. Some people will fight us. But everyone will respect us. We will be a powerful, unified voice that will never be ignored."

Everyone in the gathering applauded. Then a quick standing ovation grew out of the noise. Kade was the last to stand and turn toward the podium when his table rose. His stomach cramped. He was eating too much, too fast.

Owens continued. "We recognize Guardian Jeffries, who has been with us two years. He's proved to be an impassioned writer, thinker, and leader. He's had a tremendous impact with us and has assisted our continued growth and execution of our strategy."

Owens's intonation, pauses, and fluid hand gestures seemed choreographed to accentuate his points. Kade thought the overall presentation style could've made any vague generalities sound convincing. He also thought the shaved head worked well.

Owens continued. "We now expect Guardian Jeffries to be a visible leader in expanding our sphere of influence, upholding our Tenets of Knowledge, Truth, and Trust. Helping us create strong media campaigns that carry a convincing message for domestic strength and environmental protection. We've added his initials to the Chapter Founders Wall and now, Guardian Jeffries, I ask that you come to the podium."

More applause followed, accompanied by shouts and whistles. Owens shook his hand and gave him a long envelope.

"In providing your promised exit bonus, and wishing you Godspeed, we ask that at this time you turn in your badge. Following this last meal among your friends, you'll be escorted to the airport for your flight back home."

Kade glanced around and saw the smiles on people's faces. *These look like willing participants. And their loyalty is lucrative, if the bonus payment is any indication.*

After Jeffries handed over his security badge and exchanged a few inaudible personal words, Owens gave him a wink and Jeffries stepped down.

"I'd also like to introduce a new Chapter Associate today," Owens said. "Normally, we'd announce the Associate and then the Sentry who helped recruit the new candidate member. But this situation is a little different, so we're going to do the reverse. If I could have Guardian Constantino stand, please."

Kade recognized the guy who stood up. Constantino was a few inches taller than him and easy to spot with his mop of blond hair. He had a matching outfit, gray top and bottom. Everyone at Constantino's table had the same. It must be a table of Guardians. The Guardians in gray.

Owens pointed toward Kade's table, palm up.

"And if I could now have Candidate Sims stand and come to the podium please."

Kade walked over while Owens continued.

"Guardian Constantino found our new candidate near the vicinity of his wrecked car—an unfortunate accident during his summer vacation. After several rounds of discussion with our executive team, we determined that he had the skills and intelligence required to be considered for Chapter Associate. So I have officially approved him as an Associate, effective today, and look forward to monitoring his progress on this journey with us. My friends, may I introduce to you, and please welcome, Associate Sims."

Upbeat applause filled the room again. Kade stepped up to the podium and the words MARSHALL OWENS appeared in the upper-right side of his vision. He had a strong handshake. The profile photo he'd seen during the operation prep hadn't revealed the depth of Owens's intense, watery brown eyes accompanying the smile. He looked fit and right about six feet tall. Kade remembered from the briefing that Owens claimed to be part Chinook, a federally unrecognized Native American tribe that had inhabited the Pacific Northwest and now numbered fewer than two thousand.

Owens handed him a bright blue metallic badge and a small aluminum case for it.

"Congratulations, Associate Sims," he said to more applause, then moved away from the microphone and added, "I'll chat with you afterward," followed by a forceful pat on the shoulder.

A black-uniformed Sentry at the podium motioned for Kade to return to his seat. When he got there, his table clapped for him until he sat down. Owens spoke a few more words and was followed by a mix of current music, none of the stuff that Kade usually listened to.

Kade made eye contact with the guy sitting in the middle on the opposite side of the table. He had black hair and a long, angular face, milky blue eyes and a goatee on his clefted chin.

"Congratulations, Kade. I'm Walter."

"Hi, Walter." Kade gave an awkward half-wave before the words *WALTER LEFEAR* appeared in his vision-view. He then looked down at his lap. The blue badge in his hand had SIMS etched in the front with the stick-figure evergreen tree underneath it. It had to be the actual security badge, and he had to admit, it was cool looking.

Inside the badge case were two additional blue fabric tree-logo patches and two nametapes with SIMS on the front. Both had Velcro backs so they could be stuck on the front of his shirts.

"The hot rumor is," Walter said, "that since Guardian Jeffries is leaving, you're on the fast track to take his place."

Kade shook his head and exhaled in a puff.

"I really wouldn't know. Just got here and trying to sip from the fire hose."

"Yeah," Daniel added. "Whatever the secret selection process is, it looks like you've got what they're looking for. Congrats."

So it was clear that everyone at the table had been talking about him. Now an image of Jerry Lerner came to him again. Lerner had conducted a training day in which Kade watched a compilation of clips from an archive of reality TV shows, the type where contestants get voted off in one way or another. *Survivor. Big Brother. The Apprentice. The Colony.* With this content, Lerner applied some psychology and turned it into a useful seminar. Kade would need to work toward increased access to get the evidence he needed. Lerner said he should start by making as many loose alliances as possible. It wasn't a "trust no one" strategy or even a "trust but verify" approach. He was going to have to trust a few people, but trust had to be temporary, Lerner said.

Kade raised his voice a bit so the others at the table could hear.

"I don't know. I'm still trying to get my feet on the ground and understand the program better."

"Good luck," Lin said.

"It's bullshit, is what it is," the guy sitting across the table to the far right said. He had dark brown hair tinged with red and his eyes were agitated. "Sims, don't let everyone at this table fool you. They're only kissing your ass because Pierce told us all to play nice. But no one gives two shits about you. I'm just the only one who has the balls to say it to your face. And I haven't been here for a year and a half to see some slacker slide in here and butt in line in front of me."

"Easy, Hank," Daniel said.

Kade glanced up at Hank and ascertained he wasn't joking. *Ignore for now and keep eating.* He felt his mind getting a bit sharper despite the beers. At least his hunger wasn't distracting him anymore.

His mission was designed to bring down all of the people around him. With about three hundred in the room now, and another five hundred that had supposedly returned to the "outside" world, according to Owens, this wasn't a group to underestimate. Even a handful of determined people could create a ton of damage. Oklahoma City. 9/11. Suicide bombers in Africa, Iraq, Afghanistan. The Boston Marathon. So many other "near-miss" attacks along the way.

"Do you hear me, Sims?" the guy named Hank said louder. "There's no fucking way a newbie is going to make it in before me. I'll talk to the leadership myself. Or hell, maybe you'll just disappear from consideration."

Kade put down his fork, and looked straight at Hank. *HANK STANFIELD.* Red splotches marked Hank's face and the veins in his neck bulged. He looked a little sick or something. Some kind of bad allergic reaction? Or maybe he was just drunk.

"Shut the fuck up," Kade said to him, a little surprised those words came out of his mouth. He then pulled one of the pies toward him from the center of the table. Apple with cinnamon and a lattice of crust on the top. It smelled like heaven. He reached for the pie knife, but Hank grabbed it first and stood up.

"What did you say?" Hank stood up and walked behind Walter, then Daniel, around the table toward Kade's left. Kade wasn't concerned about the wide, dull pie knife in Hank's left hand. It was the steak knife he spotted in his right. Serrated with a sharp point.

Kade stood and turned left to square up with Hank, who stopped two feet away, holding the steak knife at waist level. Sized up in an instant, Hank was an inch shorter than Kade, but had a thick frame and a powerful, confident way of moving. Kade stared into his light blue eyes, keeping the knife in his peripheral vision below.

"What did you say, Sims?" Hank repeated.

Kade's heart rate jumped. He felt a twinge across his skin, his pores opening from the adrenaline. But he also felt a calm, intangible sense of certainty. He kept looking at Hank's eyes. He focused on their every movement, their dilation, their signals, like he had never observed these details before in his life. Yes, Hank's face looked like a rabid dog in this moment, but somehow his eyes said this dog wouldn't bite, at least this time. Kade was pretty damn sure of it.

"Hey, buddy, sit down and relax," Kade said.

Hank stared at him a few more seconds, then made a sudden move with his arm that made him flinch. But it was Hank's left hand, the one with the pie knife, offering it handle first. Kade took it. Hank tossed the steak knife on the table.

Hank turned and walked behind him, behind Lin, continuing a counterclockwise loop around the table, but collapsed on the floor just before making it back to his seat.

"Hank? Are you okay?" the girl sitting to Lin's right said as she got up and knelt over him. Kade just saw a dark brown ponytail and hair with a few highlights in it. Across the table, Daniel stood, wearing an expression that said he didn't know what the hell was going on either.

Two Sentries appeared within seconds, grabbing Hank under his armpits and pulling him off the ground. Then one switched to holding his ankles, and they carried him out of the area. Everyone at the table was standing up now.

"Uh, does he always act like that?" Kade asked Lin. Her name appeared in his vision-view as *LIN SOON*.

"Not really," she said. "He's kind of a hothead, but I think he's been much worse these last few weeks."

Two more Sentries appeared to the left, and the closest guy placed a hand on Kade's shoulder.

"Sims, Mr. Owens would like to meet with you now."

CHAPTER 16

Saturday, June 15
8:13 p.m. (PDT)
AgriteX

The Sentries led Kade to the executive wing, where a perky receptionist buzzed the group through a secure door and beyond another layer of access. They passed two small meeting rooms before arriving at an open door bearing the placard *Marshall Owens, Chief Executive Officer.* The receptionist asked the Sentries to wait outside while she took Kade into a large sitting room.

The decor was similar to Pierce's office but with some added luxury. A long, glass-topped conference table took up half the room, with mesh ergonomic office chairs pushed up against it. A large flat-screen TV was affixed to the wall at the far end of the table and displayed a swirl of changing, abstract color. One of the side walls featured a mural of a foggy lake with pairs of broken wood pilings extending into it. The other side of the room was informally laid out. Two black leather couches and matching chairs sat on a thick Berber-style carpet.

The receptionist left the room and Kade stood in place, looking above the mantel of the large gas fireplace made of round boulders. There was a long, crude wooden stick with a ringed end mounted up there.

"Why am I not surprised you found the lacrosse stick?" Marshall Owens said, emerging from a vault door on the opposite side of the room with a large smile on his face. Again, the *MARSHALL OWENS* notification appeared in Kade's sight. He hoped there was a program option to turn that feature off.

"Hello, Mr. Owens." Kade tried to smile naturally.

"Hello, *Associate* Sims," Owens said and shook his hand. "You know the Chinook and Clatsop tribes played the game on the lower Columbia." Owens pulled the stick off the wall and handed it to Kade. "How's that for old school?"

"That's pretty cool."

"HR informed me you were an excellent player in college."

I never talked to HR.

"Thanks. It's a Division III program, but it was an honor to play for MIT. Lots of fun."

"That's remarkable. I never played myself." Marshall replaced the stick in its mount. "Let's sit down by the fire, shall we?"

Kade wished Jerry Lerner could have heard the lacrosse comment. Owens took a seat on one of the couches and Kade sat on the other, facing him. Owens was holding a thin file folder.

"Didn't we get you some street shoes?" Owens asked while looking at Kade's hiking boots.

"Oh, those didn't fit at all—I'm a size twelve E. But it's no big deal, these are comfy."

Owens nodded like that made sense.

"Well, let me start by saying that I've been monitoring your progress to date, and I'm pleased. From both a personality and skill perspective, you have a great foundation. Now that you've been made part of the Chapter family, let me give you an idea of what to expect in the coming weeks. Do you have any initial questions or thoughts?"

"A few, yes."

He remembered Lerner's warning in case he ever had a face-to-face meeting like this. Owens had several degrees up to the PhD level in electrical engineering, computer science, and human-computer interaction. He'd been involved with DARPA contracts at the University of Washington, and it was believed, but never proven, that he stole DARPA technology, including algorithms for the IR lie detection project so he could later construct his own detector. Owens also had significant army experience in Special Forces. *So*, Lerner told him, *don't try to bullshit Owens in those areas.*

"Okay, shoot." Owens sat forward on the couch, elbows on his knees and hands clasped.

"When I was questioned, I was beaten. The guy who did it was named Ignaty. He threatened my sister. I need to know she won't be touched, ever."

Owens glanced at the fire.

"I apologize for the questioning, and Ignaty was reprimanded for his behavior. You have my personal promise she will be left alone. We take security very seriously, but that crossed the line, and I'm sorry."

Kade nodded. "Is Hank Stanfield going to be okay?"

Owens seemed surprised at this question.

"Yes, I'm sure he will be."

There was an uncomfortable silence, so Kade filled it.

"I admit I'm totally shell-shocked by this whole experience. The computer chipset, the medical procedure to put it there, and not having a choice about it."

Owens nodded. "I understand."

"But what's done is done. And now I have to go on faith. Everyone's told me this is an opportunity of a lifetime, but I need to make a couple of phone calls to a family contact and my current boss to let them know I'm committed to a new company. And maybe call a friend who can deal with my apartment and the stuff in it for me."

"Absolutely," Owens said. "We'll make sure you get your calls in tomorrow. Just know that all calls are monitored or recorded due to the sensitivity of our intellectual property. We also do random Verax reviews."

Kade nodded. "Okay. How about my rental car? I think Budget will probably start wondering where it is pretty soon, if they haven't already."

"That car has already been removed from Budget's inventory system and also from the database for the Oregon Department of Transportation. Your rented camping gear was also paid for. These are minor issues."

"Wow."

Owens smiled.

"Any other questions?"

"That's it for now."

"Good. Mr. Sims, you've responded well to what we call our G *protocol*. It's our newest process for providing select members with a dual neural chipset combined with a neuron growth stimulant. We've been refining the protocol for the last three years, but even still, we consider it a beta product. With your background, I don't need to tell you what beta means."

"A limited release, not fully functional." *And it can still have a lot of bugs.*

"Right. Our first-generation system, Z protocol, which involves a single neural chip, has been the standard for our members for over five years. I have the Z product myself, and unfortunately, anyone with the Z protocol can't upgrade to G, or I would've already done it."

Kade was now thinking about having buggy computer hardware and software inside his head. Forget the classic Microsoft Windows "blue screen of death" that could crash a computer. If the Chapter's system crashed, it sounded like it might be very hazardous to his health. He needed to learn more about what he was dealing with here.

"What's the operating system?" Kade asked.

"I developed the original firmware and operating system for the Z chip and Z program, and the initial operating system for our Chapter network, which connects all of our members securely. Since then, much more talented computer scientists than I have taken over for me in furthering the development of the G protocol and launching other projects."

"The technology is incredible."

"Thank you. We're very proud of what we've done. You're going to receive a customized curriculum at an aggressive pace, so that hopefully you'll be ready to fill a place on our software team in less than a year. Or in some other role where we can best deploy your skills."

"I can't wait to get started."

"You'll start tomorrow," Owens said. "You'll begin receiving a daily download of software code updates, instructions, and personalized initiatives. We call this the *Daily Chapter*. In parallel, you'll go to HR and be fully processed as a regular employee of AgriteX. Your job title will be senior programmer, and we'll have you working with our software that we use to track productivity in our reforestation efforts. This work is AgriteX company confidential and treated like standard business. It will occupy about a quarter of your time. The balance will be on training and other initiatives that will become evident over the next few months."

"HR processing," Kade said with a trace of concern. "I didn't think about that."

"About what?"

Kade took a good pause, crumpled his brow, and recalled a practiced line.

"The one thing I didn't like about Home Depot was the random piss tests. I mean, if I want to go smoke a bud with one of my friends on the weekend, who cares? I work hard enough. I don't know if that's a showstopper for AgriteX, as far as your policy goes."

Owens paused like he was taking a mental note.

"There's no drug testing for your job position," he said. "Common sense applies about being unimpeded for work duties."

Kade nodded and Owens moved on from there.

"In your Chapter network display, do you see the Progress tab at the far lower right?"

"Yeah."

"Okay, stare at it for a second until you see it change to blue and blink."

Kade now saw the main screen change to *ASSOCIATE PROGRAM*. There were three graphic progress indicators underneath—Knowledge, Performance, and Reward. A points total, now showing zero, was listed next to each.

"I can see it."

"This dashboard will give you daily feedback and how you're progressing through your custom-designed Associate Program. You amass points based on exercises and test scores. At certain point level thresholds, monetary rewards and other privileges are granted."

It was clearly the ultimate micromanagement tool. A carrot dangling in front of every Chapter member's eyes.

"Interesting," Kade said.

"Walter Lefear will be your primary Associate mentor. We thought that'd be useful since he's a physician, and it'll give us another means to monitor your health under the G protocol. You'll continue to have weekly medical screenings from our Chief Medical Officer, Dr. Drakos, and I'm also adding Associate Carol Reese as an additional peer mentor."

"Great," Kade said. Carol Reese had to be the other female Associate at the table he didn't meet. And Dr. Drakos had to be the one treating him, except apparently she was a doctor, not a nurse.

"A couple more things I wanted to ask you about." Owens produced a classic composition notebook with a black-and-white marbled cover and flipped to a spot in it. "You write entries in your journal, such as 'Today I feel like a happy insect.' Or on a different day, 'Today I feel like the blazing light in my life has been swapped for the dull glow of a compact fluorescent.' All of your entries are single sentences, and they sound depressing and cynical."

Kade felt his cheeks get a little warm.

"Uh, somehow you took my journal from my apartment and read it?"

"Our background check is very thorough. We had to make sure you are who you say you are." Owens pulled out a paper chart inserted between the journal pages and unfolded it. "And the mood chart—you always seem to mark your mood right in the middle, every day. That doesn't seem very likely."

Kade shrugged. "I do what the doctor tells me to do. Some parts of the treatment are good and some seem like bull. I don't waste a lot of time on the bull. I admit my life hasn't been very interesting for a good number of months. And at least in that way, the journal tells it like it is."

"I see," Owens said. "We'll try to give you some very interesting projects. And we'll try not to waste your time with bull." He tossed the journal so it landed on the coffee table and Kade took it. "As you'll find out starting tomorrow, you're going to have little time to waste. My second topic: you have a prescription for carbamazepine? Do you need these pills?"

"No, I shouldn't. I haven't taken them in a while."

"Okay, third topic: I want to ask about the website and blog that you managed."

"You mean Wakethehelluppeople?"

"Yes. What you wrote on there for a number of months looks more interesting and thoughtful than your journal, but then you suddenly stopped updating it about six months ago. Why was that?"

Kade thought about how to phrase his answer.

"I guess I shouldn't be surprised you know about the website too," he said, followed by a nervous laugh. "Uh, I don't know. I just didn't feel like doing it anymore. And people seemed to be missing the point anyway, thinking it's political when it really wasn't. I was just tired of the cover-your-ass leadership—from those in my immediate chain of command all the way to the top. But, then again, I have a patience deficiency. My girlfriend at the time thought I was obsessed with the blog, and I probably was."

Owens nodded. "Yes, we have too many armchair politician-generals with no military experience or strategic knowledge. It's all about managing political 'optics' now."

"The only optics that matter are the ones mounted on a rifle."

Owens laughed and raised a finger. "I like that. I know you sometimes made commentary on the wars. Afghanistan—you seemed quite knowledgeable on the theater of operations there."

"Yeah, I'd studied it some in my previous job. I went there once on temporary duty, just for a few weeks, but it was in a pretty safe area. I also spent a number of months in Iraq."

"What do you know about the Watapur Valley—more specifically Operation Bulldog Bite?"

That was Afghanistan. Kade took about ten seconds to put his thoughts together.

"Bulldog Bite . . . That was the First of the Three-Twenty-Seventh Infantry Regiment, Hundred and First Airborne, and the First Battalion, Seventy-Fifth Ranger Regiment. Kunar Province. They conducted air assault operations together with some Afghan troops mixed in. The enemy was a combined Taliban and Al Qaeda force. There was fierce fighting with many heroic actions on our side and over fifty of the enemy reported killed. We also suffered deaths and many casualties, not only from the fighting, but before and after—the whole area was littered with IEDs."

Owens gazed downward.

"Would you call the operation a success?"

"The brass was quick to call it a success. But some soldiers on the ground thought the op was poorly planned and coordinated. They questioned if it was really worth it. I'm not going to call it anything. Any American soldier is going to fight his hardest for his buddy next to him."

Owens sighed and shut his eyes for a few seconds.

"Yes, your summary is spot-on. It's sad our government lacks the courage to put a halt to these continuous undeclared wars. The people who chant for boots on the ground have never been on the ground in the blistering heat or freezing cold. They don't give our troops the tools, technology, and strategy to win. So they have the blood of our brave warriors on their hands. We, the people of America, need to clean house. And the Chapter needs to prosper, lead, and win."

Kade gave a slight nod. *Stay out of politics. Change the subject.*

"In hindsight, about the blog," Kade said, "some of what I wrote was clouded by my feelings when I left the service on bad terms. I also lost a colleague in Iraq. Then my mom passed away. I was just in an angry-at-life mode all around, and I think I wrote a lot of things out of that anger. So I knew I had to stop writing the blog to leave the anger behind. Maybe it was good self-therapy while it lasted. Sorry if it offended."

Owens looked back into Kade's eyes, and reconnected.

"You don't have to apologize to me," he said. "We all get angry. It's what we do with that anger that counts. In Chinook, *sollecks* means 'anger.' *Mamook* means 'to make.' When you join the words together, *mamook sollecks*, it means 'to make war.' Beautifully simple, isn't it?"

"Yeah ..." Kade's foot stopped tapping the carpet.

"Mr. Sims, people do their best, most important work when they're angry."

CHAPTER 17

Sunday, June 16
9:33 a.m. (PDT)
FBI field office, Portland, Oregon

Agents Morris and Velasquez sat waiting in the briefing room while the technician, Greg Belmont, prepped the audio. Velasquez picked a Boston cream doughnut out of the box he'd brought. Today, he wore a blue-and-white three-quarter-sleeve baseball T-shirt with jeans. Morris had arrived straight from church and was wearing a light gray suit.

"So we've got two call recordings?" Morris asked.

"Yeah," Velasquez said. "One voice mail Flash left for his boss at the Home Depot and one live discussion with us, where Agent Evans is role-playing his sister."

"Great."

"We ready, Greg?" Velasquez asked.

"Yeah. Here's the first one."

Belmont tapped a few keys on the laptop and the first call played through the speakerphone console.

"Hi, this is Julie Perkins, please leave me a message and have a great day."

After the tone, Kade's voice began the message.

"Hey, Julie. This is Kade Sims calling from vacation. I know I was supposed to be coming back on the seventeenth, but I wanted to let you know that I found another job opportunity that I'm going to take out here with an Oregon company. I, uh, really appreciate the time I had working with you and I'm really sorry about not giving you two weeks' notice. If you need to get a hold of me, shoot me an e-mail, I guess. I lost my cell phone last week. Okay, thanks again. Bye."

"All right!" Morris clapped his hands together once and it echoed in the room. Belmont recoiled in his chair at the sound.

Velasquez nodded but didn't look as happy. "He's in, but he's not in the best shape," he said. "Listen to the next one."

Belmont brought up the audio for the next conversation.

"Hello?" the female voice of Agent Evans answered.

"Hi, Janeen."

"Kade! Oh my God, I haven't heard from you in like a month."

"Yeah, I know. I'm sorry."

"I tried to call you a few times this week, and it just goes straight to voice mail."

"Yeah, I lost my cell phone. Haven't gotten a replacement."

"You sound kind of hoarse. Are you okay? Are you still in Oregon?"

"Yeah, still in Oregon. And I'm okay. Just tired. I got in a little fender-bender and had to get eight staples in my head, but it wasn't a big deal. Don't tell Aunt Whitney."

"Oh my God! Are you sure you're okay?"

"Yeah, I'm all right."

"So are you still going to visit me later this summer?"

"Uh, well, that's where I have some news."

"What? What's going on?"

"I found a job out here. A great one, in software."

"Really!"

"Yeah, I've already started their new employee orientation. Kind of like a boot camp."

"Wow. What kind of company is it? Do I know it?"

"I doubt it. The name is AgriteX. They're an agricultural biotech company. They do environmental work—forest restoration and stuff. They've got a few hundred employees and I'm in a little team with a handful of people. It was just too good of an opportunity to pass up."

"Sounds cool. Wow, that means I won't be seeing you for a while, then?"

"Yeah, that's the bad news. The initial training program and internship lasts a number of months. So I don't think I'll be getting home very much."

"Well, that sucks for me and Aunt Whitney. Maybe we can come to see you?"

"I don't know. Hey, I gotta go, Janeen. I'll call when I can."

"Okay, hope it goes well. Love you."

"Love you, bye."

Morris had a smile on his face. "Evans has the teenager cadence down pat."

Velasquez laughed. "I know. Shouldn't be hard for her—she's got two teen girls of her own."

"She was great," Morris said.

"So it sounds like Flash was pressured to end the call," Velasquez said. "But we know he's officially a Chapter recruit. He's sized up the employees he's seen at around two hundred. He's in a small group. Maybe a group of new recruits."

"But he got banged up," Morris said.

"Yeah, it could be worse than what he said on the call," Velasquez said. "In training, we told him to give us a number from one to ten to make clear what kind of shape he might be in. We asked him to weave it in so we could pick it out. So when he said eight staples, it could also mean he got hurt at an eight out of ten, from his assessment."

Morris's excitement returned to seriousness and he stood up.

"Okay, give Jenkins and Stephenson an update, and have them return to Alderville."

CHAPTER 18

The waitress brought Alex's fish and chips and another beer out to the pub's weathered deck facing the Pacific. Alex researched a few stocks on his iPad and put a plan together for this coming week of trading. A golden retriever lying on the deck looked at him with smiling eyes, enjoying the perfect mix of warm sunshine and cool wind.

He felt a buzz from his front right jeans pocket. His iPhone said he had a voice mail. It seemed like calls went straight to voice mail here on the coast. Pain in the ass.

His heart beat faster when he played the message and heard Kade's voice.

"Hey, it's me. I got a couple big favors to ask you, man. I landed a cool job in Oregon and I'm going to be staying here for a while. I only have a month left on the apartment lease, so I'll need some help when it's up. If you can just move all my junk over to your storage unit and hold on to it for now, I'll get it sooner or later. And I'll pay you if you can clean up the place for me. I owe ya big time, man. Thanks, brother, bye."

He replayed the message eight times. Kade was asking him to pick up his stuff and bring it over to his storage unit. This meant to go retrieve Kade's Glock and hold on to it. Since Kade had asked for him to clean, that meant the Glock was still in the Jeep. No mention of cleaning would have meant the Glock was with the phone somewhere else.

That's where it stopped making sense. Kade had told him he might ditch the phone and Glock together somewhere near Lost Lake so Alex could locate them later. But the Glock was still in the Jeep? Kade was at AgriteX now, but left the Jeep at Lost Lake?

Alex brought up Kade's phone account on his iPad using the information Kade had given him. The GPS in the phone was showing as "not enabled," and the phone was showing as off. The site did show the phone's last known location as a grid coordinate, time stamped JUN 08, 3:13 a.m.—over a week ago. He typed the coordinates into his Google Earth application.

It looked like Kade had ditched the phone and the Glock at the side of the road about a mile from AgriteX headquarters. So maybe Kade had been driving to AgriteX and decided to toss them out the window. Then the phone must have run out of power.

Alex had agreed to bring some of Kade's extra ammo for the Glock in a locked box but wasn't happy about it. He was nervous with the ammo in the cab of his truck as he drove cross-country over three days, even though Kade assured him it was legal. Alex couldn't be convinced to register a weapon of his own to bring west, and he suspected that Kade's unspoken idea was to have an extra weapon available. No, he wasn't a big fan of guns and there was only so far he would go.

But now getting Kade's Glock was his assigned task, and then he would wait for further instructions. He could do that. But his truck was a two-wheel-drive model, so now he had concerns about its reliability on the dirt roads weaving through the forest. He hadn't thought of that potential issue before, and now he'd have to come up with something else.

He didn't know how long this gig was going to last, but it looked like he'd be extending his stay for a while. He would support Kade for the duration. Kade had given him the shirt off his back many times. Hell, he had a veritable closetful of Kade's shirts at this point. Whether it was the free place to stay in DC while he got his business going, shared vacations and road trips, the endless dinner invites as a kid, or getting together over the holidays and picking up where they'd left off, Kade's generosity and friendship was steadfast.

The waitress made her way back to Alex's table.

"Can I get you another stout?"

Alex played with his bristly chin and glanced at his watch.

"No thanks, I've got to go."

CHAPTER 19

Lin stopped and stood at the door of Kade's room on her way out. The food on the breakfast tray she'd brought for him sat untouched on his desk. She'd tried engaging him in conversation for the last twenty minutes but mainly got one- or two-word answers.

Kade continued to stare at the computer screen with an occasional glance at the clock in the lower right corner. The best thing about being logged in was that he knew what time it was. At this moment, he thought about his door being left unlocked during the day for the last five days but then automatically locked at night. Even though he was under constant video surveillance, they were relaxing his level of physical security.

"Yeah, you're welcome, by the way," Lin said. "You might try lightening up."

"Thanks, Lin Soon, you're a sweetheart. Or a world-class pretender, according to Hank."

She shut the door and Kade heard her yell from behind it.

"Whatever, asshole!"

"Nice!" Kade yelled back.

He didn't need Lin to tell him that he was becoming more intense and irritable. This was a precursor to a possible hypomania episode, and it would have been a perfect time to take a carbamazepine, but without the pills, he had managed using the tedious methods that were part of Dr. Ross's sessions. Deep breathing, mental checklists, and mnemonics. No journaling this time.

The upside to this state of mind was he needed only three to four hours' sleep at night and he could still be highly productive. He could skip a night of sleep, even two, with very little adverse effect. This was a key difference from ADHD, one never properly noted as he was growing up. And on a normal night, he only needed five to six hours of sleep to be fully refreshed.

Yes, he was being abrupt with Lin, blowing her off while she was being pleasant and flirty. The Chapter leadership must have told her to be nice to him. Maybe she was getting paid more or something. There was an extra dash of attention thrown in for sure, and it was effective, since she was damn good looking. She could sell a Yankees jersey in Fenway Park.

She'd brought breakfast from the cafeteria the last three days. T-shirt and no bra each time, which he silently appreciated. She'd lie on his bed and say some provocative things. He felt increasingly distracted, weakening every time she showed up. But if he gave into physical impulses, it could be too risky. He could be stoked and made dysfunctional.

This was the wrong place for that.

He tried to focus on learning the underlying operating system of the Chapter in as little time as possible. A senior programmer and network administrator working on the second floor named Casey Walsh had given him four hours of training over two days. Walsh let him know where the references and documentation were located in the system and gave him access to it.

Kade wasn't permitted to go into programmer's mode, but he was permitted to view the code, and it seemed like the operating system had started as a version of Linux's open-source software that had been further developed into a proprietary version. The Chapter system was a mainframe-and-terminal setup, so his desktop was really just a user interface and monitor screen. The computer-chip hardware inside his head would most likely be programmable to some extent. But not knowing what kind of control the program was exerting on him was creepy.

He'd received the "Daily Chapter" download each morning, beamed into his skull through the infrared peripheral on his desk, in the same manner Pierce had first introduced. He recognized the download as a mix of software updates and patches, a formatted communication of Chapter propaganda, and a calendar of weekly activities.

One recent segment of Associate Knowledge instructed:

AgriteX's wind turbine produces five million kilowatt-hours per year, supplying all of our company's power and providing excess power to the Pacific Power grid. Under the Chapter's growing leadership and influence, wind and solar technology will be expanded to homes and urban centers . . .

And in the same download, another message wasn't so kumbaya:

The Department of Homeland Security and state law enforcement continue to procure and hoard weapons. Politicians fleece America, ruin the land, run up debt, and line their own pockets, while the "government" continues to put a stranglehold on our movement. They will try to seize our bounty from us. We have the God-given right to live and thrive off the earth as we choose. This is why we must be ready! We must be prepared to defend our sacred land . . .

These standard Chapter communications, by default, were spoken by an avatar of Marshall Owens's head. Thank goodness he'd explored the Options menu and found a well-buried checkbox to remove the floating-head visual in the program.

After he reviewed more downloads and completed Walsh's training, Kade noticed fifteen points awarded to the Knowledge section of his Progress tab when he synced up.

Only 985 points to go to his first reward, symbolized by a bronze coin.

He poked around in the system looking for weaknesses. He was hoping the Chapter's local area network, on which this whole system ran, was connected to the Internet, but it wasn't. He found it interesting that the computer system for AgriteX was kept separate and there was no apparent connection between the two. The AgriteX network looked like it was connected to the Internet, but despite Kade's requests, his superiors hadn't granted him access.

Other than studying and doing exercises in his room several times per day, he'd made a point to go to the regular dinner gathering with the other Associates in the last five days. It was important to accelerate these relationships, and he tried to chat with everyone.

Lin continued to sit close enough that he could pick up the pleasant smell of her hair and occasionally brush against her body. He allowed himself that small indulgence. Lin talked about how she helped set up American manufacturing deals in China and had a good number of personal contacts there in business and government.

Kade pushed his chair back from the computer and gave his eyes a vigorous rub. Last night's dinner was interesting. He thought about the conversation he'd had with Daniel Slade after everyone else had left the table.

"Where's Hank been?" he had asked.

"Apparently sick and undergoing some tests."

"That was weird last week. What happened?"

"I don't know," Daniel said. "Doc Lefear would know more. Last week was way out of control. You might be surprised to learn Hank had finished a term as the mayor for Wheeling, a suburb of Chicago, before coming to the Chapter."

"Really?"

"Yeah, pretty impressive for someone his age. He's definitely an ambitious politician, and must have been attractive to the Chapter recruiting machine."

Interesting. He was surprised Daniel spoke this freely all of a sudden.

"So, if you don't mind my asking, how were *you* recruited into the Chapter?" Kade asked.

"I came from the Philadelphia PD," Daniel said. "The short version of the story is I ran into the Baltimore Police Commissioner while I was at a law enforcement conference. He's the guy responsible for transforming the Baltimore force and lowering the crime rate in the last few years. A real leader and role model. We just ended up eating lunch together. Then it kind of grew into a mentorship. I drove down to see him a few times. And after having some great discussions, he explained to me that he knew about a private, professional development program that was extremely high-tech and had an extraordinary impact on him. When I expressed interest, a guy contacted me, I took the questionnaire, and after a couple of interviews, I was signed up."

"And that was it? You were gung-ho from the get-go?"

"No, it took some time, and I was impressed with the work they were doing. Their tax-exempt organizations support areas I care about. They donate money to the departments of first responders, military and veteran's organizations. The environmental message isn't a big one for me, but it's hard to find people who don't care about a few key 'green' issues. And who doesn't support the police, fire departments, the armed services? I don't know anyone who doesn't want to feel secure and protected."

"So being part of the Chapter, this secret brotherhood, would help you move up the ranks in the Philly PD?"

"Yeah, it would."

Kade nodded. Daniel's description of the recruiting sounded a little like a self-help scam, but maybe the fact that he was a cop before coming to the Chapter was something Kade could leverage. It sounded like Daniel could be having some doubts, but Kade wasn't going to prod further just yet.

"My dad was a police officer killed on duty, so I have the highest respect for the work."

"I'm really sorry to hear that," Daniel said.

Kade sighed. "So how do they decide who to recruit here?"

"They seem to target a particular demographic. Smart, ambitious, technologically savvy. Around twenty-five to forty years old, single, no strong family attachments. Sound familiar?"

The psych test popped into his head. It was quite a strange mix of questions, asking for responses on a scale between "Strongly Agree" and "Strongly Disagree." He remembered, "If someone hits you, it's okay to hit back" and "I like working harder so I get a bonus payment." And, "Recycling is important to me."

"Yeah, I guess they have a profile for the 'ideal member.' Well, I better get back to work. I have a lot of studying to do."

"All right. Let me know if you want to talk more. There aren't any microphones here in the café. Only cameras. It's the best place to talk. Still, be careful about what you say."

No microphones, only cameras. Unlike my room.

Kade swiveled in his chair to face the barred window in his room. The bars were the simplest reminder of his situation. He was a prisoner, constantly watched and eavesdropped on.

There was now also a crude monitoring system inside his head. Thank God it couldn't read his exact thoughts. From what he guessed, its design was somehow reliant on a combination of spoken words and an emotional response of deception being registered. Not too different from the Verax IR lie detector, except there wasn't a human interpreter.

It seemed that if the sensor in his head detected deception, and it matched up with his spoken key words through some kind of voice recognition engine, an alert was generated and the computer triggered a log of that activity. Then that log passed the activity back into the Chapter computer system during the Daily Chapter. So there had to be a simultaneous upload as well.

He decided to give his theory a simple test. He looked back at his computer like he was struggling in trying to learn something. He banged his fist on the desk.

"The Chapter sucks, but I love it!"

Sure enough, the yellow stoplight in the upper left of his vision flickered when he uttered that statement and the key word "Chapter" aloud. That information was probably stored in the chipset in his head, then passed to the main computer the next time he did the download and upload process. Too many of these logged events and there had to be an alert for some kind of review. There was supposed to be a pain accompanying the yellow signal, but he was lucky it still wasn't working.

So the key was to keep his thoughts to himself and his emotions at bay. That was a tall order. It would take practice to navigate spoken key words to avoid triggers. Someone like Daniel must have become adept at doing that over time, but the Chapter still had too many microphones and cameras around to be comfortable doing anything. *Still, be careful about what you say*, Daniel had said.

Being a software guy, Kade did marvel over the technology of the program displayed in his own vision. This admiration was tempered, though, by the unsettling knowledge of being operated on involuntarily and having no idea what had been done. It had to be serious, as Dr. Drakos, who'd been watching him since his arrival, continued to check on him on a regular basis. It didn't give him a good vibe.

There was a light knock at the door. He assumed Lin had come back.

"What now, Soon?" he yelled.

The door opened a crack.

"Hi, Kade, can we come in?" a male voice said.

It was Walter Lefear and Carol Reese. Kade now remembered they were both supposed to come by at the end of the week. He didn't see their names pop up in his vision, because he'd figured out a way to make the letter font transparent in another Options menu. The pop-up feature was driving him nuts and now he could make it go away if needed.

"Oh, hi," Kade said. "What's today, the scavenger hunt?"

"Carol and I are here for your first mentor visit," Walter said. "You'll have at least one a week from each of us, per Marshall's guidance."

"Great. Thank you both so much for taking the time out."

"Not a problem," Walter said. "It's part of the program."

Carol didn't look quite as enthused, but maybe that was just her natural look. They both could just be under orders and would rather be doing something else.

Walter put his hand on Carol's shoulder.

"Carol is going to take you to the Lost Lake Forest Camp tomorrow and orient you to that program. On Tuesday I'll take you to the clinic in Nehalem where I do some community outreach."

Carol spoke without eye contact.

"These activities will transition you toward your assigned job and will award you points. Once you start work, your performance ratings will show up in the Performance tab of your display."

"Cool, look forward to it," Kade said.

And both trips get me out of this building for the first time.

CHAPTER 20

Inside the security room, Joshua Pierce and Dr. Heather Drakos stood behind the young female technician seated at the console controlling a wall of surveillance monitors. One screen showed Kade in his room, standing in front of his own computer. He alternated typing on the keyboard for a few minutes with doing exercises—push-ups, burpees, lunges, planks, and running in place.

"Where the hell does he get this energy?" Pierce asked.

"I don't know," Drakos said. "He's been sleeping only a couple of hours a night this entire week, with occasional twenty-to-thirty-minute cat naps during the day. I'm concerned. From the way he's acting, you'd think he was on meth."

"Side effects from the protocol?"

"No, this isn't from the protocol. None of the severe potential side effects have presented while I've observed him."

"Good. It looks like we lucked out."

Drakos leaned down and mumbled something in the technician's ear. The technician then pressed a button and spoke into her headset microphone in her relaxing voice.

"You need to eat and sleep more, Kade. I'm concerned about you."

"Oh, shut *up*," Kade said.

When Kade's response came over the speaker in the control room, both the technician and Drakos couldn't help smiling a little bit. Then when Kade stuck out his tongue, turned, and mooned the camera, they both laughed. Pierce just shook his head.

"What's the prognosis on Stanfield?" Pierce asked.

"Dreadful," Drakos said. "The CT scan showed the neural growth stimulant caused an excessive reaction, and he's generated the typical glioblastoma multiforme tumor in the frontal lobe. He's got weeks left at best."

No one was more familiar with the risks of the Guardian protocol than Pierce. He was in the first group of recipients, of whom nearly half had developed the lethal tumor. Through refinement of the protocol, the risk had since been reduced to one in five—a closely guarded statistic. It wasn't clear why any given recipient might be more susceptible to developing the tumor.

Pierce motioned with a sideways jerk of his head and Drakos moved away from the technician to the other side of the room. He spoke just above a whisper.

"At what point does Stanfield become a liability?" he asked.

"He already is. We don't want to release him in his current condition. Even though he's not involved with Phase One, he still could be a general risk. He'll never make it to Phase Two."

Pierce looked disappointed and shook his head.

"Shit. Another Guardian investment gone bad. Okay, I'll coordinate turnover over to the outprocessing team. And I'll tell him he's going home just before the relocation. Are you going to give him the full diagnosis?"

"No, I'm going to continue telling him the tests were inconclusive and his symptoms are consistent with severe migraines," she said.

"Okay." Pierce sighed. "I wonder how many more people it's going to take. Marshall promised we'd start seeing a much higher success rate with this protocol. Mobilizing soldiers for Phase One was easy, but for Phase Two, he's asking me to fill a leadership bucket with a gaping hole in it. At this rate I'm going to have to institute big referral fees and signing bonuses to get more people, and we'll have to churn them out in Montana and Nevada."

She took his hand and they interlocked fingers.

"Let's go have a drink and forget about this for a few hours, all right?"

CHAPTER 21

Kade finished his assigned programming exercise for the day, and then the balding, pear-shaped Walsh reviewed his practice code in a testing environment. Walsh's "supervision" while Kade viewed the operating system code and wrote sample lines turned out to be Walsh just sitting beside him reading a *Maxim* magazine and occasionally looking up at Kade's screen to answer a question.

A knock sounded at the door and it cracked open. Carol's face poked in.

"Sorry to interrupt all this brainpower, but I've got Sims scheduled for the next few hours. They're expecting us at L-FAC shortly."

"No problem," Walsh said. "Sims, I'll review the rest of this up in my office later. You can go on ahead."

"Hey, Casey," Kade said, "before I take off—I noticed another couple of errors on the *About AgriteX* web page. Can I go ahead and fix 'em real quick while you're here?"

"Yeah, sure, go ahead." Walsh found it amusing that Kade reviewed the public website to make sure everything worked perfectly. The public website was the AgriteX Information Technology team's lowest priority. Walsh had made the case for a bare-bones website so the company would get as little web traffic and attention as possible. AgriteX customers didn't care because they had a private portal. But Kade argued that if they were looking to recruit quality people, potential employees were going to at least check the website, and it should reflect a professional web presence. Pierce agreed with Kade on that one. The site shouldn't have a bunch of errors on it.

After Walsh entered an admin password, Kade fixed the HTML code so the links weren't broken and the graphics rendered properly. Walsh left after he made sure Kade was completely logged out, and then Kade followed Carol out into the hallway. She flashed him a taut smile that said she didn't like being kept waiting another ten minutes. Carol had a pretty face, despite some light acne scarring. A cute, mousy nose softened her intense, gray-blue eyes. Her highlighted dark hair was pulled into a ponytail and wrapped in a black scrunchie. Kade figured she was in her early thirties.

A steel door in the hallway opened to a narrow cinder block passage ending at an exterior door accompanied by an access-card reader. Carol raised her badge and the reader beeped and disengaged the lock.

"So you can leave whenever you want?" Kade asked.

"No, I have to constantly check in with Security and get activities approved. And my movement is logged."

"Oh."

The service door opened to fresh, cool air outside, rich with the smell of bark mulch lining the wide dirt-and-gravel path in front of them. A black Polaris two-seater ATV was parked twenty yards away at a small turnaround. It looked like a cross between a golf cart and a dune buggy.

"It's a mile and a half to the Lost Lake Forest Camp, so we're riding this time," Carol said. "But it's a nice walk. I recommend it when you get the chance." She took the driver's seat and Kade sat to her right. There were two helmets in a mesh basket, but Carol didn't put one on, so he didn't either. The ATV was so quiet when it pulled out that he assumed it was an electric.

He twisted his head to look behind him. They'd exited on the northwest side of the two-story rectangular headquarters building. A colorful stone veneer arched over the entrances, and the building's natural wood siding was peppered with windows, all of them barred on the first floor. It looked like AgriteX had found an adequate piece of flat land amidst the hilly terrain and cleared the surrounding trees to make room for the headquarters. But all of that timber was used in the construction of the building, and trees were planted to offset the loss.

He shook his head. The particular reference information crossing his mind had to be from another Chapter download. His brain had been invaded with unwanted knowledge! How much more of this crap would he allow the Chapter to pump into his head?

The whole plug about the plantings around the building seemed to go with AgriteX's promotion of itself as an environmental steward. But AgriteX wanted it both ways. An "environmental steward" producing genetically modified crops? Die-hard environmentalists would never support that.

No, AgriteX was advocating a more populist, opportunistic brand of environmentalism. It was all about protecting the *revenue* streams.

He now imagined shoving Carol off the cart, knocking her out cold with a hard punch, and running for his life. When he looked over at her, she glanced back.

"It's wonderful to be outside," he said. "What's this Forest Camp anyway?"

"LLFC, or L-FAC, as we call it, is a private minimum-security prison, and AgriteX has a partnership with it," she said. "We employ many of the inmates, who work in a number of our business lines."

"Like what?"

"AgriteX manages some state-funded reforestation projects, and the inmates serve on the crews. Other crews maintain hiking trails or campgrounds, and assist in cleanup following floods and storms. Plenty of state funds support this work. Inmates are also contracted to do ground maintenance at the AgriteX headquarters."

"Nice."

Carol's every sentence sounded mechanical and perfectly articulated, as if she was transcribing a download. He'd have to keep initiating the conversation or there wouldn't be any.

"Sounds like a good deal for the inmates," he added, "especially on days like today. But maybe not when it's raining like crazy, huh?"

"Oh, they still take advantage of any chance to be outdoors, except during the really bad storms. They also get paid fairly and leave with some solid, transferable skills. The state likes the very low rate of recidivism from the camp. There's an optional agreement the inmates sign, allowing L-FAC to monitor their health and wellness, so they establish a healthy lifestyle."

"Seems like there should be more programs like it."

"There are—L-FAC is one of about two hundred similar private facilities across the U.S. Inmates can be moved around between them to help stop overcrowding."

"Wow."

The path turned southeast and snaked its way through the forest, up and down hills. Wooden plank bridges spanned the low areas prone to water runoff. Then the path opened up to a wide view of the Lost Lake area as it joined a trail tracing the lake's perimeter. The lake was almost black in color with the soaring evergreens encircling it.

"Hey," Kade said, "this was the lake I was trying to get to for camping. Wow, it looks awesome. But that doesn't seem to make sense if this is private land. It was listed as a park."

"You're half right," she said. "The L-FAC land is the northern side of the lake, while the public area is on the southern side. You can't access this trail from the public side, and there are some floats and signs designating the private property of L-FAC. There's a nice little beach on the public side."

"Ah."

The main LLFC building was a single-story structure with an exterior similar to AgriteX headquarters', as though the same contractor had built both. If it wasn't for the tall chain-link fencing topped with barbed wire and the full guard station behind the main gate, it would have looked like the kind of tranquil lakeside rehab center where you might find celebrities.

"How many Forest Camp counselors are there guarding this place?" he asked.

"About forty," she said. "And they're called inmate mentors, or IMs."

"I see. So are you *my* IM?"

Carol didn't answer but shot him a quick look that said *shut up*. When they stopped at the guard station, she smiled and showed her badge to the guard, who unlocked the gate. They approached the LLFC entry pavilion and its sizable cage-like door before she slowed the ATV to a halt and they both got out. A small rustic cabin sat next to the entry point.

Kade bent down to retie his boot while removing the digital camera/recorder from the tongue of it. He palmed the device and pocketed it when he stood back up. Before following Carol though the cage door, he paused and looked in the window of the cabin. Four IMs were lounging on couches next to a gas fireplace, watching a Seattle Mariners game on a large wall TV. He noticed the IMs had the same black shirts and pants as the AgriteX Sentries, but with a different insignia—a LLFC patch on the shoulder and breast pocket. With removable Velcro so they could be swapped out, he presumed.

Once inside the entry point, they passed through a mudroom containing four large sinks, a shower, boot cleaners, lockers, and storage space. Another secure door opened to a thirty-by-thirty room manned by four more IMs, where over a dozen computers blinked with various graphical status readouts. A windowed door gave a view into an adjacent room filled with rows of racked computer servers, and Kade spotted an additional IM in there.

"This is the operations room and information systems monitoring area," Carol said. "Per Mr. Pierce's instructions, Associate Sims has been granted temporary accompanied access," she announced to the IMs.

"Hello, Carol. Sure, we were notified," said the short, mustached man who stood up. He then looked at Kade. "I'm Wayne Parsons, team leader for the IMD. Nice to meet you, Sims."

Kade turned to Carol and mumbled, "IMD?"

"Inmate mentor detachment," Carol said, ensuring every "t" was pronounced clearly.

Parsons paused as if there might be further introductions or discussion, but Carol resumed walking. One of the seated IMs gave Carol an unnecessary salute.

The door chimed to signal it had been unlocked, and Kade followed Carol through. The interior didn't seem as cushy as the building's exterior had suggested, but it still seemed comfortable for a prison. At least compared to various army accommodations, dorm rooms, or budget hotels he'd slept in.

A long cement-and-cinder-block hallway, painted in yellow and lit with white fluorescent tubes, stretched in front of them. Wall placards indicated room numbers, and the rooms each had a small, square hall window reinforced with wire. The doors looked like they were made of steel. He saw an inmate approach, pushing a large cart filled with mail he was delivering to each room. At least two inmates occupied every ten-by-ten room, each with a sink, stainless-steel toilet, and bunk bed. A desk area was built into each side of the room.

"Is this an all-male facility?" Kade asked.

"No," Carol said. "Females have their own wing, but there aren't very many."

The next section contained a pair of doors marking showers, followed by a rec and fitness room and a large cafeteria. A few inmates were in each area. Next, they passed doors to the kitchen, laundry, and inmate health clinic areas.

Carol walked ahead too damn fast, as if she was trying to speed through to get back to her more important business. He kept looking at her somewhat-muscular butt, trying to decide whether it was attractive or not.

"Hey, Carol, can you hold up a sec?"

She slowed down and came to a stop in the hallway next to a door labeled "RANGE," where he could hear the popping sound of the discharges. There was a long polycarbonate window providing a view to a state-of-the-art indoor rifle range. He was taken aback by what he could see as he looked downrange at the targets lined up in the fifty-meter concrete tunnel.

"This place has the *inmates* firing rifles?"

"Yes," Carol said, as though it were no big deal. "The IMs train here, mostly, but Marshall wants every inmate to appreciate the safe use of firearms. So the inmates get some weapons training at least every ninety days. It's closely supervised, with all precautions taken. They're only using green-colored, non-lethal bullets."

"Amazing. Besides shooting guns and forest cleanup, do the inmates do anything else productive?"

"Yes, there's a telemarketing group and a data-entry group."

Kade couldn't restrain a laugh.

"That's classic. Cheap labor and good profit margin, huh?"

Carol resumed walking. "The inmates are very well taken care of."

Kade took a picture of the firing range from the camera hidden at his hip. His gut told him the whole setup wasn't kosher, but maybe it was legal. He thought again about his mission to collect evidence. It was time to get a little more aggressive. He caught up to Carol until they were walking almost shoulder to shoulder.

"So is there a reason you don't like me, Carol?"

She stopped walking and turned toward him, looking surprised.

"What?"

"I asked why you don't like me. I'm tryin' really hard here, and I get that you don't like joking around, but still . . ."

She sighed and half rolled her eyes while formulating her response.

"It's not you, Sims. It's all of this. It's everything."

Kade nodded as if he was satisfied with the answer. "Okay," he said. "So when do I get to see it? You know, the weed?" He took a drag on an imaginary joint.

Carol didn't speak and stared at him for five seconds, and Kade just started laughing.

"I don't know what you're talking about," she said, looking at her watch and starting to walk again.

"The nurseries and shit. I've heard the rumors," he said. "Come on, Carol—Oregon's a pot bonanza. When I flew into Portland, I went to a pizza joint downtown and it was literally that. Everyone there was smokin' pot right out in the open."

She continued walking. "Kade, I'm going to need you to focus on what you're doing and nothing else. Remember the guys in the front room and all of the monitors?"

"Yeah."

"We track all of the inmate interactions, progress, and overall productivity through computer monitoring. But the homegrown software isn't very effective, and the E-team wants better reports on everything. So you're going to get involved with, and hopefully lead, a software revamp and enhancement. You're going to need to know how everything works."

"Cool. I can do homegrown software. I was just curious about what else is homegrown around here."

"Yeah, well, curiosity killed the cat."

"And cats have nine lives."

"Drop it, Sims."

Okay, you've pushed it enough for now.

They exited via another guard station into a monitored outdoor recreational area of about five acres. There were all-weather picnic tables and benches, a pair of tennis courts, a basketball court, two small fields, and what looked like a corral or small dog run.

"What's your background in?" Kade asked.

"Chemistry."

"Cool."

Groups of inmates were out doing strenuous calisthenics in one of the fields, led by an IMD leader. It reminded him of army PT—physical training. He snuck a picture of that also.

"Damn, those poor guys look like they're suckin' wind," he said.

"It's voluntary, as is the whole program," she said. "It's not part of standard mandatory wellness, but the enhanced wellness program."

"Yeah, well, the enhanced wellness is making me tired just watching it."

In an adjacent area of about two acres were two gray buses parked in a column on a gravel driveway. The buses were painted with "LLFC" in white lettering on the sides and back. The wheels looked like an oversize off-road variety. Groups of IMs or Sentries, Kade couldn't tell which, were doing drills getting on and off the bus with weapons. He thought he could see two Guardians in gray standing nearby. Holding notebooks or clipboards. Hard to see, but it looked like they were evaluating the drills.

"Looks like you could go four-wheeling in those buses," he said and pointed to them. When Carol turned to look, he took another picture.

"Those are the inmate transport buses. They need some good traction to get work crews out to remote jobs. The roads can get pretty nasty around here."

"Yeah, I know."

Farther away, and somewhat difficult to see from his vantage point, was a mockup of a small building. It looked like IMs or Sentries were conducting assault drills.

"What's going on back there?" Kade asked.

"I think they're playing paintball."

Bullshit.

"Huh. Why all of the military drill shenanigans?"

"I believe they're training for various incidents, like escaping prisoners and stuff."

"No kidding. Do they use dogs at all?"

"No, no dogs."

Kade continued to watch, but the entire scene just didn't add up. If they were really worried about inmates escaping at LLFC, they wouldn't be training inmates on weapons, even minimum-security inmates. He observed how the Guardians were interacting with the IMs or Sentries in these drills. He'd seen this style of training before.

They're training their own. These are train-the-trainer drills.

"It looks like fun," Kade said. "Think I could get involved? I love paintball. Followed by drinking beer, when possible."

"I doubt it," Carol said, yawning. "Let's go, I've got to get you back."

Kade stood for a moment watching the exercises and drills. He needed to find out more about the training.

So this is Marshall's militia.
They're training for something, but what?
Defending their "sacred land"?

CHAPTER 22

Alex was back at the beachside pub, his jeans, T-shirt, and light nylon windbreaker covered with dried mud. He didn't like being this dirty in public, but the two elderly men drinking on the deck next to him didn't look at him twice. It was overcast, and the salt-perfumed breeze caressed his body in gentle gusts. When the waitress appeared outside, he ordered up a Reuben sandwich and a stout.

The knapsack next to his feet contained Kade's Glock and the ammo clips from the Jeep. Mission complete, as Kade would say. But Alex had an uneasy feeling much more was to come given what had happened earlier in the morning.

He had asked the RV park manager where he could go to rent a motorcycle, saying that he just wanted to have some fun riding off-road. The manager told him there was a rental outfit farther up the coast in Seaside, but also referred him to a guy in town who was a motorcycle enthusiast and could rent him one for less money and less fuss.

Two years ago, Alex sold the Harley Road King he'd been taking out for the occasional ride, so he wasn't used to the Honda

CRF450X off-road competition bike he ended up renting. The recommended rental owner lived in a rustic A-frame house and looked like Santa Claus wearing shorts and a sweatshirt. Apparently, Santa Claus liked motocross in the off-season.

Before leaving his hotel in Manzanita on the Honda, he had plugged his route into the Garmin GPS. The waypoints loaded in the device guided him from Route 101 and kept him on paved roads until he was about ten miles away from his target. He then transitioned to a dirt road that wasn't listed on his map for another few miles. The road was still a bit moist, with some deep ruts, but it was child's play for the bike. He would've considered it "fun" if he hadn't been so nervous. As he got closer to his target, small orange signs alerted him to the fact that he was entering private land. He encountered several closed pole gates along the way, but just rode around the outside of them and through the forest.

When he found a good stopping point about a mile from the target, he dismounted and walked the bike about twenty yards off the road into the edge of the forest. He pulled off his backpack, slid a bottle of water out of its mesh holder, and sipped from it while he checked his current location on the GPS. The smell of the forest seemed to have an additional evergreen punch compared to those he'd hiked through back east in summer. He shimmied on his backpack and hiked on toward the target location.

The up-and-down terrain would have worn out most people, but Alex ran a marathon each year, so he was usually in half-decent running shape. He planned to approach the target road where Kade's car was parked on foot from the east. He thought Kade must have left the car in one of those small parking lots you find at a trailhead, or at some kind of road pull-off.

But he was shocked when he approached a giant hill and walked right into a view of Kade's destroyed Jeep at the bottom of it. Alex looked up the rugged slope, imagined the road at the top, and visualized the car rolling all the way down to this spot.

Oh my God.

Even though Kade's recent voice mail had sounded normal and upbeat, Alex couldn't help dashing to the front and looking through the battered windshield, expecting to see Kade inside. The cabin was empty, but the bloodstains weren't a good sign. It looked like his buddy had sustained serious injuries.

It took him another few minutes to even remember why he was there and to calm down. With some strenuous effort, he was still able to open the tailgate in a left-to-right direction, as the Jeep lay on its side. Everything smelled like gasoline fumes and rotten bait, and flies swarmed around him everywhere.

While he pulled out the mix of camping gear and broken glass granules from the interior, he saw Kade's phone and put it in his pocket. After all of the gear was laid out on the ground, it took him another five minutes to find the Glock and clips inside the cargo tray cover where Kade said they might be. He stuffed them inside his backpack. God, he was nervous. He didn't like the situation and he didn't like guns. He started putting the camping gear back inside.

"Hey!" someone shouted.

Over a hundred yards away, somewhat in the direction he came from, he saw a male figure dressed in an all-black outfit walking toward him at a brisk stride.

He made a decision in two seconds. He threw on the backpack, turned, and half ran, half crawled up the hill toward the unseen road. When he heard the first gunshot, he was already moving as fast as his body would permit, trying to zigzag between the trees on the slope. The sound of the next shot sent another surge of adrenaline into his body, turbo-charging his legs. By the third shot, he was up on top of the road.

He turned left and ran down the damp dirt-and-gravel road for two to three minutes, bypassing or vaulting over puddles remaining from the recent rain. The road twisted enough that he couldn't see anyone behind him when he looked over his shoulder, but he assumed the guy was still in pursuit. He couldn't believe he'd been shot at! Were these the kind of people Kade was mixed up with?

In a few minutes, when he didn't feel like he was running for his life any longer, he realized he was headed in the wrong direction. Somehow he needed to get back to the motorcycle, but he sensed he was only getting farther away. To head back down to lower ground, he turned left again at a spot that wasn't such a steep grade. After slowing to a walk for a few minutes and collecting his thoughts, he saw and heard someone again. He didn't know whether it was the same person, but he dropped to the ground and crawled behind a fallen tree, gambling he hadn't been seen.

He thought about getting out the Glock, but knew he couldn't go there. It wasn't like he knew how to fire the gun properly anyway. He took out another water bottle from inside his pack and took a small drink. When the real or imagined human noises subsided, he sat up and powered on his Garmin again. The initial electronic chime made him cringe and look around.

Once he had a fix on his location, he got back on his feet and walked through the forest. It took him another two hours to return to the Honda, because he walked small segments of twenty to thirty yards at a time, tree to tree. Stopped, listened, continued. He didn't want to run into anyone else by accident.

When he finally reached the undisturbed motorbike, he started it up and wasted no time. He rode the fuck out of there as fast as he could without wrecking it. Two backpackers seemed to look at him with more than a casual interest when he slowed at one of the pole gates to weave around it, but they didn't say anything. The entire ordeal lasted about four hours up to the time he finally pulled up to the pub's parking lot. Longer than he thought it would.

•   •   •

Alex finished the Reuben and started on the potato salad. Despite the cooler day, he broke a sweat again while recalling the narrow escape. When he took off his windbreaker, he noticed in horror a bullet had entered and exited his jacket sleeve and torn through the slack in his T-shirt underneath. It had missed skewering his upper arm by a fraction of an inch. Or his vital organs by less than a foot.

Those motherfuckers.

He powered up his iPad and checked the Hotmail account that Kade had set up, looking in the Drafts folder to see if a message had been left in there. Kade didn't trust sending an actual e-mail, so he'd instructed Alex to check the folder first, but nothing was in there. The Inbox contained nothing except a few spam e-mails promising yet another safe, effective way to increase penis size.

He sat and zoned out for a minute. There was something else Kade had mentioned, Alex now remembered. Kade said it was possible he might not even be able to draft an e-mail, so he'd devised another means to send a message. Alex typed in the AgriteX website address, and after the main landing page loaded, he clicked on the About AgriteX link and went to that page. In the web browser, he chose to view the HTML for that page and sifted through the gobbledygook language. And there it was, inside an HTML comment tag.

```
<!-- A: go to nehalem clinic late morn 6-25; figure out a
way to give it to me; remember you dont know me. K -->
```

Alex's heart started beating faster. "It" was the Glock, and now he had to think through some sort of exchange to get Kade the gun. The twenty-fifth was tomorrow. Was Kade now a patient at the Nehalem Clinic? Maybe he should go and check out the clinic beforehand. He couldn't believe he'd gotten himself into this mess. He wasn't cut out for this kind of shit.

But I'm not going to let Kade down.

The waitress appeared again, her timing flawless.

"Another stout?"

"No, a Bombay dirty martini, up, please."

CHAPTER 23

The young male driver stepped out of the heavily tinted SUV into the adjacent visitor space, lit a cigarette, and stretched while the two other men remained inside. He was skinny and tall, wearing a green Adidas wind jacket over a black T-shirt and jeans.

The front-seat passenger, Cisneros, was in his midthirties, about three hundred pounds, and wore a short-sleeved Tommy Bahama shirt. He waited a few minutes for the backseat passenger, Messia, to finish a phone call on a borrowed prepaid cell phone. Messia was late forties, his mustache and sideburns streaked with gray. Gazing out the backseat window, he showed an intensity of thought from behind his crystal-framed eyeglasses.

"So what does Tesar think?" asked Cisneros.

"He thinks there are three possibilities," Messia said. "If the information is correct, then they've had production difficulties, or they've moved the seed to a different location. But our forest spotters haven't seen any of the trucks our source marked for seed transport moving off-site. They've seen a great deal of ATV and dirt bike traffic. There's always some, but the increase was notable enough to report. They've taken down license plates when they can."

"And what do *you* think?" Cisneros asked.

Messia pulled off his glasses and repositioned them back on his face. He said, "Owens is smart. It's possible they're moving the seed out in small quantities, to multiple buyers or competitors, for higher margin. That would be very troubling."

"What do you want me to do?"

"We've tried following some of these people on ATVs and dirt bikes, and it's very difficult. If you find one that's had clear contact with AgriteX, assign one of our affiliates to follow them. And if they attempt a transaction, our affiliate can go ahead and send a clear message. Then they can bring us the product so I have proof."

"All right."

"Okay, leave your weapons in the car," Messia said, and opened the car door. "*Vamanos.*"

• • •

Inside the entrance atrium, the stocky, gray-haired front-desk security guard watched his video screen and picked up the phone.

"They're on their way in, Mr. Owens."

"Thanks, Ken," Owens said, "I'm watching them."

The visiting group of three men walked down the moss-spotted path to the headquarters building's entrance area. The driver held one of the heavy glass doors open while the others seemed to take their time appraising the building's aesthetics.

When they stepped inside, the man with the glasses stopped and pulled what looked like a smartphone out of his pocket and stood there for a moment while the other two talked. They then walked around the rolling sphere–style fountain bearing the AgriteX company logo and arrived at the security desk. The security guard picked out the expected guest from a photo image on his screen.

"You are Mr. Messia?" the guard asked.

Messia stepped forward. "I am."

"You have a one p.m. meeting with Mr. Owens?"

"That's right."

The guard printed a visitor badge that read JOHN MESSIA. The other two signed the visitor log with fake names, the driver receiving the badge TOM MORENO and Cisneros clipping on the badge DAVID SOTO. The security guard conducted a weapons search with a wand and pat down. Messia looked unhappy about it, but he'd already been told this was a requirement.

Two AgriteX employees wearing the black company uniform with tree logos came through the secure access door.

"Right this way, please," the first escort said.

The group proceeded down the hallway, Messia and Cisneros glancing at some of the corporate awards posted on the walls as they walked. They arrived at a steel door bearing a placard labeled "EX." After the door clicked, the first escort yanked it open and held it while the second escort led everyone through.

The receptionist waved from behind the glass of the expansive reception counter. Meeting rooms flanked the reception area on the left, and several couches were in a waiting area to the right.

"Mr. Owens will meet you in room two," she said. "Please help yourselves to any refreshments in the refrigerator."

The square meeting room contained four faux-leather lounge chairs facing a low table resembling an enormous tree stump that was coated in a glassy finish and topped with a large piece of square glass.

Marshall Owens, Joshua Pierce, and two Sentries entered the room. Owens was dressed in a light blue dress shirt and khakis. Pierce and the Sentries wore their AgriteX company uniforms and had their holstered pistols visible.

"Well, you're looking good these days," Owens said.

"Not so bad yourself, Marshall," Messia said. "Good to see you." They shook hands.

Marshall had been introduced to Juan Messia three years ago when shopping around AgriteX's first strain of bioengineered cannabis seed, and the two had established a mutual regard. Owens knew Messia had been born and raised in El Paso, his parents undocumented immigrants from Mexico. He joined the U.S. Army, serving through Desert Storm as a buck sergeant and assistant team leader in an infantry scout platoon. His younger brother Raúl became involved in drug dealing in high school, later trafficking for the Sonora drug cartel before the Barrio Azteca murdered him. After that event, Juan Messia decided to not reenlist in the army and was recruited by the Sonora cartel, quickly rising in it and strengthening its armed capabilities in the U.S. He now lived in Hermosillo, Mexico, for about half the year.

"Juan, this is our Chief Operating Officer, Joshua Pierce."

"Nice to meet you," Messia said.

Messia shook hands with Pierce, and with no further introductions, they sat down. The Sentries moved to the far wall and remained standing.

Owens said, "We're happy to see you, but I admit I'm a little perplexed why you came out to AgriteX today. Something about a progress report?"

"Yes, that's right," Messia said. "Mr. Tesar is deeply concerned about the delivery of your product being delayed to July thirty-first after you had committed to a May first shipment per our agreement. So he sent me to discuss the matter further with you."

Owens and Pierce looked at each other with confused expressions before Owens responded.

"I've provided Mr. Tesar my personal assurances we'll deliver the amount of seed committed, and the seed will have the rapid growth, yield, and minimum THC percentage we specified. We also gave Mr. Tesar a sample of both the indoor and outdoor grades so he could validate our yield projections. And he communicated to me that he was very pleased that the *maribel* was the quality we'd stated. But we sometimes experience production delays, just as any company can."

Messia nodded. "Yeah, I'm aware that he was happy with the sample, but you've already delayed shipment once, and now we're halfway through the main growing season."

Owens cut his hand through the air. "You'll still yield a full harvest from our outdoor strain alone. And product from our strains will fetch four times what your Mexican product will. Listen, you're losing market share and profit margin to the mom-and-pop outfits here in the U.S. With states starting to legalize, that's going to further impact your margin. Mr. Tesar knows if he wants to compete, he needs a much better product, and he's made a wise investment in us for the future."

"Mr. Tesar is losing trust," Messia said. "He has information that your production has fallen short and you won't be able to deliver your commitment . . . That it's mathematically impossible."

Pierce jerked his head back like he'd been slapped in the face. "Mathematically impossible? What the hell is he talking about? What information?"

"Mr. Tesar monitors all of his key suppliers," Messia said.

Pierce held both palms up.

"So what the fuck does *that* mean?" He glanced over at Owens but saw that he was hunched over, grimacing, with his forehead in the palm of his hand. "Are you okay, Marshall?" Pierce asked.

"Yeah, just give me a minute," he said.

Messia continued his answer.

"It means Mr. Tesar has already made a $231 million investment to secure an exclusive deal with your organization. He has high expectations, and so defaulting on this delivery would, of course, have severe consequences."

"So you came here to threaten us," Pierce stated.

"You can call the purpose of this meeting whatever you want," Messia said.

"Gentlemen," Owens said as he straightened up and raised his hand to force a pause. He respected that Messia came to play hardball, and so now it was his turn.

"Okay, Juan. First, let me say thanks for coming to discuss this in person. I respect that. I can give you my utmost personal assurances that we're very much on track to deliver your order. Please again communicate my apologies for the delay. I can appreciate the fact you have good information, and so do we. Such as your wife's address in Hermosillo and your daughter's in Bahia de Kino. Your girlfriends' in Tucson and Phoenix. Mr. Cisneros's apartments in Portland, Tualatin, and Vancouver, and his various storage units. Locations of his numerous significant others. Names of the many people in your network of growers across Oregon whom you finance."

The room fell dead silent. Owens stared down Messia and then rattled off the cell phone numbers of the three visitors' wives without referring to any visible notes. Cisneros started to get out of his chair but Messia put a hand on his knee.

"Marshall, you don't want to start a war with us," Messia said.

"Juan, I have no intention of picking a fight with Mr. Tesar. And obviously he's invested in your assistance at a premium. But if you bring a war to my organization, we'll aggressively defend our interests. We're not worried about your *sicarios*. We've planned and trained for such contingencies, and have more than adequate manpower to follow through. I pray this doesn't escalate. I'd prefer we remain friends."

Messia broke another stretch of silence.

"Okay, so we've brought you the message, and it looks like the message is understood. You've told us you're on track with delivery of your order in full no later than July thirty-one."

"I think we understand each other," Owens said. "So this is a rather short meeting after all. Is there anything else?"

"No. We look forward to the remainder of our partnership," Messia said.

"As do we. Thank you." Owens and Messia shook hands again. No one else did.

"Mr. Bishop, if you could please escort our visitors out," Owens said to the Sentry.

Owens and Pierce stood while everyone else filed out of the room. After the visitors had exited the executive area, Owens shut the door of room 2 and he and Pierce sat back down.

"We have a leak," Owens said.

"Yes," Pierce said. "And Tesar must know that by laying this card down they're exposing that person to us. It won't be hard to narrow down who it is."

"It's someone who has been able to observe activity around the storage facility," Owens said. "They formed the wrong impression as we shuffled the inventory around. It's someone who's seen the inside of the facility in the past. Someone without total access, or otherwise they'd know we haven't produced any new seed for months."

"Yeah," Pierce said. "Maybe Tesar has it in his mind that he can seize his order by force before the delivery date."

"Then his force will be decimated, and he would legitimize our keeping his advance payment. So I doubt that's his strategy. But I may have underestimated him. It seems he *did* successfully cultivate or activate someone inside us within the last few months. Someone who's been quietly passing along information. The fact they're willing to expose that person now may mean they're ready to escalate."

"We'll find out."

"I hope that person is still around. When you narrow your possibilities down, put them on the Verax. Is it back online?"

"Almost. The technical team is still running diagnostics. We think the latest hotfixes will correct our potential issues."

"Okay, we need to resolve this situation immediately, given we're so close to launch."

"Agreed. Have the Russians or Chinese voiced any concerns?" Pierce asked.

"No, they still feel good about their own exclusives. All of their advanced payments have been moved offshore. The account access information is in the succession plan that you have access to. Really, delivery to the Chinese is all I care about, but we have to exercise great discretion."

"Okay," Pierce said. "We continue to roll over these bumps in the road. Give me forty-eight hours to dig up our mole."

"You've got twenty-four."

CHAPTER 24

Tuesday, June 25
8:05 a.m. (PDT)
FBI field office, Portland, Oregon

The speakerphone in the briefing room beeped in an undulating double tone during the conference call in progress.

"Who just joined?" Velasquez asked.

"It's Brendan Collins. Sorry I'm a few minutes late." Brendan Collins was the ATF liaison, located in the ATF's field office in nearby Maywood Park.

Morris flashed Velasquez a look of disapproval. They had discussed earlier in the break room that it would've been nice for Collins to show up to one of these meetings in person. After all, it was only a five-minute drive between field offices.

"Good morning, Brendan," Velasquez said. "We also have Neil Graves from the DEA Seattle Division on the call. With me here, I have Agent Rob Morris and Carla Singleton, an analyst from Counterterrorism."

Velasquez pressed the mute button.

"We also have Alderville and Jerry Lerner listening in," he said. After Morris nodded, Velasquez unmuted the phone.

"Okay, folks, let's get started," Velasquez said. "We're now eighteen days into the operation and it's progressed on schedule. We have about one more week of activity remaining from our source, give or take a few days, with June thirty being the target end of operation. In the meantime, we've become more concerned about the militia activity associated with AgriteX as we've further developed the profile for CEO Marshall Owens. Carla is going to summarize that for us now."

Carla Singleton slid one of the flat microphones toward herself. She had short brown hair in a pixie hairstyle, dark-brown eyes, and pale skin. Although she was lithe and petite, her speaking tone and energy seemed to multiply her stature.

"Hello, everyone," she said. "So we know from all of the available documentation we've gathered that Marshall Owens has taken a fatalistic tone in most of his public and private communications. We again reviewed the interview transcripts from Wade Rooker, the former AgriteX employee who agreed to speak with us last year. Owens had spoken in internal AgriteX meetings about how this year would be instrumental and revolutionary. It would involve some kind of new beginning, and he regularly alluded to a launch of some kind. But after checking with AgriteX and their existing customers for information on new product or service lines, we haven't been able to identify any launches within their legitimate business.

"We've been trying to track Owens's personal activity, and it's been difficult since he also resides in the AgriteX headquarters. His corporate credit card has been used for legitimate business purchases and any flights or rental cars appear to be directly related to current or prospective business activity around the country. We ran several aliases that Owens had reportedly used in the past through a number of databases and came up with one hit. A database compiling all domestic medical record numbers listed a patient visit earlier this year, on January twenty-ninth, under the name of Morgan Oliver at the Portland VA Medical Center. We confirmed from reviewing old surveillance video that it was in fact

Owens who visited the VA during that time frame. While there, a Dr. Carlton Price ordered some blood work and imaging tests for Owens."

"Any relationship between Price and Owens?" Velasquez asked.

"Not completely clear," she said. "But both were former Army Special Forces—Price a medical sergeant, Owens a former warrant officer on a B Team. They were both assigned to the Seventh Special Forces Group in the late eighties."

"Probably doing counternarcotics in South America," Graves commented.

Singleton continued. "There weren't any documentation notes on those ordered tests," she said, "but Dr. Price ordered a CT scan with contrast on Owens. We were able to obtain all of the images and have one of our physician consultants review them. The bottom line is that Owens has a grade-four glioblastoma multiforme—a malignant brain tumor."

"What's the prognosis?" Graves asked.

"Six to twelve months from the time of that test," Morris said. "So he's most likely not going to make it past the end of the year."

"We've found no indication that Owens has sought surgery, radiation, or chemo for treatments," Singleton said. "For all his love of the latest technology, he indicates a strong interest in naturopathy when it comes to his own medical treatment."

"They have an employee health clinic at AgriteX," Velasquez added. "But there's no way it would be adequate for cancer treatment."

"Carla, not to steal your thunder," Morris said, "but moving us along here . . . We're worried that the dismal prognosis for Owens might cause him to shift to a more dangerous course of action, for whatever this launch activity might be." Morris looked back to Singleton for confirmation.

"Yes," Singleton said. "That's the consensus of Behavioral Analysis."

"Who inherits the keys to his kingdom?" Collins asked.

"Maybe a VP of business development or a chief scientist," Singleton said. "We're not sure. We hope our source can fill in some gaps in the org structure very soon."

"Okay," Velasquez said. "Brendan, can you fill us in on anything you were able to find?"

"Yeah, I have two reports, one coming from just yesterday," Collins said. "We have a source inside Oeste-13, the gang controlling the largest amount of turf in the triangle west of I-5 and bordered by the Columbia and Willamette Rivers. We received word yesterday that Oeste-13 received a hit order—a subcontract passed through several layers of contacts. That order can be connected to a Juan Messia. Messia is a suspected Sonora lieutenant with U.S. citizenship who is well trusted by Sonora captain Eduardo Tesar. Messia operates primarily out of Arizona when he's in the States, but he turned up in the Portland area. We also received confirmation that he spoke into a phone that was present in the area of AgriteX yesterday. We can't draw a thick line between the two reports, but it's hard to believe they're coincidental."

"That's good," Morris said. "Neil, do you have anything else to add related to gang activity?"

"Not much at the moment," Graves said. "We've seen an increase of voice and Internet communications pertaining to gang and cartel contacts in the greater Portland area, but a seasonal increase is expected. The spike we had in arrests is also normal, but we're reviewing arrests made, including those in the state forests. We found no arrests connected to AgriteX."

"Weapons?" Morris asked.

"Yeah, I'm going there next," Collins said. "We had a gang source with access to a particular Portland storage unit facility used earlier this year as a transit point for weapons and drugs. The source claimed he saw what looked like four custom hard-shell golf travel cases passing through that storage unit, and the contents of those cases were identified to him as weapons. Since the cases were locked, he copied down the alphanumeric sequence on the outside of the cases. We know those alphanumeric sequences—the Sonora cartel uses them to track their most high-value weapons. That particular sequence is for an SA-7 Grail, a shoulder-fired surface-to-air missile."

"But no visual confirmation of an actual missile?" Velasquez asked.

"No," Collins said.

"Missiles would add a new dimension to this threat," Morris said, "but I'm not seeing a connection to AgriteX."

"When you mentioned Owens's reference to a launch," Collins said, "I just thought about it literally, like a missile launch."

Morris, Velasquez, and Singleton looked at one another.

"Carla, what do you think about that?" Morris asked.

"It's plausible," she said. "But I'd think going after commercial jets with a SAM wouldn't quite fit Owens's profile. I looked more closely at his time as founder and CEO of NetStatz, and the company had a unique culture. *Inc.* magazine did a piece on it. They called themselves the NetStatz Nation. Employees loved their big parties and stock grants. NetStatz contributed to charities benefitting veterans and deployed military service members. Quarterly, the company did local volunteer environmental work during paid company time. So Owens is more antigovernment, promilitary, and pro-environment. If he had missiles, I'd think he'd prefer a government target, like Air Force One."

Morris nodded side to side as though he was weighing everything.

"This is good information, thanks," he said. "It gives us a few more avenues to explore and only heightens our urgency. Chris and I have to run to another meeting now, but if we need to all reconvene before next week, let's do it."

·   ·   ·

Twenty minutes later, Carla Singleton sat at her cubicle reviewing her notes and updating her analysis on her computer to reflect the information just discussed. She sensed someone standing behind her, and sure enough, it was Zach Poole. The office project manager, Zach was both a beanpole and a bean counter, a tall, lanky fellow charged with monitoring current and projected operations, personnel assignments, and budget adherence in order to optimize the office's labor resources and expenses.

With budgeted headcount examined so closely these days, a greater appreciation for this role had replaced some of the grumbling about someone looking over everyone's shoulder.

But now that someone was literally looking over her shoulder.

"Hi, Zach," Carla said.

"Hey, Carla, I was afraid to interrupt you. I need to update my project matrix. You just got assigned to another op. How long is your involvement going to last?"

"Yeah, I've been on it since Monday the tenth. I'd just put down that I'll be assigned to it through mid-July, to be safe."

"Okay, thanks. Sounds like you're pretty loaded at the moment."

"No rest for the wicked," she said.

"Well, good luck with it."

"I don't need luck. I need caffeine."

CHAPTER 25

After driving more than an hour on AgriteX's private dirt roads and the Necanicum Highway, Walter finally turned on to the Oregon Coast Highway at Nehalem Bay. Kade sat in the second-row left seat with no one to his right, and Hank, who hadn't spoken during the entire ride, was riding shotgun. Sentry Cummings sat behind Kade in the third row, alone, his PPK pistol out of the holster.

Kade looked out the window toward the shimmering Pacific. His brief, pleasant thoughts admiring the scenic beauty were replaced by nervousness as he realized he could be within minutes of seeing Alex. It felt like a long shot that he'd show up. Alex was a wonderful friend, but his general reliability for being on time wasn't his strong suit.

"So why does AgriteX support the clinic?" Kade asked, to break one of the many long spans of silence.

"It's an important part of the AgriteX program, giving back to the community," Walter said.

Kade had to restrain himself from laughing out loud. That sounded like something the company must have put in Walter's download. But then Kade had a sobering thought. *He* might be due to receive the same canned phrase in a future download. It might be a requirement to reach the bronze coin reward.

This is madness.

After a few more minutes, they turned right at a blue-and-white road sign that read "NEHALEM COMMUNITY HEALTH CLINIC" and pulled into the visitor/patient parking lot. Walter turned off the engine and passed the keys back to Cummings before they all got out of the vehicle. Kade looked up at the overcast sky and felt a fine mist in the air coating his exposed skin. Hank walked over in his direction, and when Kade glanced up at him, he didn't sense any more animosity.

The clinic was a one-story red-brick building less than one-third the size of the Chapter headquarters. Kade noticed a vacant helipad beside the building and an ambulance bay.

"So what now?" Kade asked.

"Lefear does his work until the afternoon," Cummings said. "You and Stanfield park your asses in the waiting room where I can keep my eye on you. When Lefear clears out the morning rush of patients and gets some downtime, then we can go back with him."

"Awesome. Glad I can help out," Kade said.

Walter shot Cummings a pissed-off look as he popped the hatchback on the SUV and pulled out a small duffel bag. "I'm sure after you come along a few times, Cummings will loosen up and let you help more," he said to everyone.

"It all depends on Sims and his behavior," Cummings said.

The four walked through the automatic sliding doors with "URGENT CARE" stenciled on the glass and operating hours of 6:00 a.m.–10:00 p.m. listed underneath.

"So do they ever bring AgriteX patients here?" Kade asked.

"Sometimes," Walter said. "There are some really good docs at AgriteX, and decent equipment, but they're more R&D-focused up on the second floor. Still, most treatment for our own is done at the headquarters by our own. We try to keep it in-house, and it's provided free as an employment benefit."

In the waiting room, Kade scanned the patients sitting in four of the ten orange vinyl chairs. Alex was not among them. Behind the waiting area, a middle-aged woman with spiky gray hair sat behind a small window marked "PATIENTS MUST REGISTER HERE" and nodded at Walter as he opened the adjacent door.

"I'll see you guys a little later," Walter said over his shoulder. The door pulled closed behind him.

Kade sat down in one of the waiting room chairs so he had a good view of the door, and Hank sat down to his left. The smell of the room was a pungent mix of various cleaning solvents and floral fragrance. This added to the uneasiness in his stomach. Would Alex show? How would he try to deliver the Glock? If Alex just tried to hand it to him here, that could be a disaster.

Cummings sat down across from them both, picking up an *Us* magazine and flipping through the pages.

"Hey, Kade," Hank said just loud enough to get Kade's attention. "I'm sorry about what happened before. I didn't mean it."

Kade looked over at Hank, surprised to hear him speak, much less apologize. Since Hank had seemed sullen on the drive out, Kade had been hesitant to strike up a conversation with him. But Kade nodded, encouraged at the gesture. At least for today.

"That's cool, man. We're good." He offered Hank a high handshake and Hank slapped his hand in his palm and locked thumbs like they were going to arm wrestle in midair.

"Thanks," Hank said.

There was no real privacy in the room, and so Kade watched the cute young female nurse with short brown hair and blue scrubs come in and out to evaluate the patients. A teenager with a dog bite got treated first, then an obese woman with a constant hacking cough. More patients came and went. A bearded man limped in with a friend, saying his ankle was broken. A mother brought her daughter in who was throwing up. Kade's stomach was on the verge.

By the time they had been sitting there for about an hour and a half, his butt was numb from the hard plastic seat. Another woman with a dislocated shoulder was treated. A man with an asthma attack.

That's when he spotted Alex outside, recognizing his ambling walk seconds before the entrance doors slid open. He took a deep breath and tried to track Alex's movement out of his peripheral vision.

Alex was dressed in full hiking gear with a sizable backpack. Sunglasses with dark orange lenses disguised his appearance, but his favorite Stewart plaid bandana was like a flare gun signal if Kade needed one. Kade leaned back in his chair a bit and stretched his arms upward with his fingers interlocked. That was as big of a signal as he was going to broadcast back.

He saw Alex pause, scan left and right, rub his nose, then walk to the opposite side of the waiting room toward a door in the back, at the corner of the hall leading into another clinic area. It was a unisex bathroom. Kade read Alex's plan in a mental snapshot.

He's a backpacker, hiking the coast, in need of a bathroom break. Not a bad idea. Simple.

Alex pulled off the backpack and set it on the ground outside of the bathroom. Then he entered and pulled the door toward the inside, pausing for a half second before completely shutting it.

Kade was a little confused now. Was the gun in the backpack? Or was Alex going to leave the gun in the bathroom? Or still try to give it to him?

"Hey, Cummings, I've got to piss." Kade pointed to the bathroom door. He knew Cummings hadn't paid attention to Alex's entrance other than a quick glance.

"Okay, make it quick."

He got up and moved to the bathroom door. He looked at Cummings to make sure he wasn't watching at that instant, and then he ran his hands over the top flaps and pockets of the backpack sitting there. He didn't think the gun was inside. He'd used that pack a few times, and the way it was laid out, Alex would've left it near the outside for easy access.

He stood outside the bathroom door and heard the toilet flush, and in another minute the bathroom door lock flipped and the door opened. His eyes connected with Alex's for a split second and he saw Alex force a quick, polite smile as he walked by and headed toward the nearby coffee station. Kade stepped into the bathroom, shut the door, and flipped the dead-bolt latch.

•   •   •

The two Hispanic men entered the waiting room area through the sliding doors and scanned the room before being noticed by the nearby nurse. One man was in his early twenties, a gash on the top of his arm wrapped in a blood-soaked towel. The other man, in his early thirties, looked like a relative or coworker providing assistance. Both were dressed like they'd been working outside doing landscaping or maintenance. Cummings also noticed their entrance and kept his eye on them. The nurse walked up to the two men as they stood in place.

"What happened to your arm?" the nurse asked the younger Hispanic man.

"Cut with saw," he said, making a slashing gesture.

"Okay, let me have a look," she said, unwrapping the towel. "And are you okay, sir?"

"Okay," the older man replied.

The older Hispanic man's eyes searched the room and fixed on Alex, watching him pour a cup of coffee. He looked at the backpack sitting on the ground next to Alex, then he stepped away from the nurse and pulled out a pistol.

• • •

Kade scanned the inside of the bathroom. He looked in the trash can, in the small supply cabinet, the other cabinet under the sink, behind the back of the toilet. No weapon. He lifted up the toilet lid and seat. No weapon. He was lifting up the lid on the toilet tank, seeing there was nothing inside, when he heard a female yell from the waiting room, followed by two gunshots. Shocked, he hesitated a second before he clanked the tank lid back in place, turned, flipped the lock open, and burst out of the door in a crouch.

Two more gunshots fired. He heaved himself on the floor of the waiting room, trying to pick out what was happening. A couple of patients ran out the door in the chaos. While looking in the direction of the door, he spotted Alex just outside it, jogging away toward the parking lot and looking like he was partially doubled over.

"Call 9-1-1!" a female voice screamed.

"Kade, help me out!" Hank yelled.

For a split second he thought about running out the door and following Alex, but instead he crawled, scrambled to the other side of the waiting room, where Hank was pinning down the young Hispanic man with the bloody arm. A few feet away lay the second man, shot once in the head and chest, lifeless.

"Where's Cummings?" Kade asked.

"Over there—he's hit bad," Hank said.

"What happened?"

"Not sure. These two guys came in and one pulled a gun, started shooting. Cummings shot back. Then I dove on this guy."

Walter appeared with two nurses, one male and one female, the man carrying a handful of plastic zip-tie-style cuffs. He assisted

Kade and Hank in restraining the young man still struggling and squirming on the ground. They flipped him over so the nurse could secure his wrists with the cuffs, then Kade helped secure his feet with a cuff around each ankle and one binding them both together.

"I need to take Cummings in back to see if I can stabilize him," Walter said. "Kade, I'm going to need your help lifting him up. Any others with critical injuries?"

"I don't think so," Hank said.

"I saw a guy run out the door," Kade said. "He may have been hurt."

"I'll go check the parking lot," Hank said and rushed toward the exit.

CHAPTER 26

Janeen's cell phone began to ring, the Paramore ringtone barely audible inside the tiny fourth-floor dorm room of the Orchard Hill Residential Area. She was sitting at her desk in a T-shirt and running shorts, painting her toenails. Her sandy-brown hair was pulled back in a clip.

She scrambled to the bunk bed area and rooted through a pile of unfolded laundry on the lower bunk. The muffled phone lay underneath her pillow, and she grabbed it just before the call went to voice mail.

"Hello?"

"Hello, Janeen, can you hear me?"

"Yes, who's this?"

"It's Alex Pace."

"Hi, Alex! What's the matter? You sound terrible."

"Janeen, listen—I was just shot in the stomach."

"What? Did you say *shot*?" Her light brown eyes widened and she grasped her forehead. "Like with a gun?"

"Yeah."

"Oh my God, Alex! Where are you?"

"I'm in Oregon, on the coast, driving, trying to find an ER. Look, Janeen, Kade's in big trouble. He's gotten mixed up with some really bad people and I'm gonna need to tell you more about it."

"Okay, okay. Oh my God, Alex, you need to hang up now and dial 9-1-1 for an ambulance. Pull over, don't drive any more. Then stay on the phone with the operator until the ambulance gets there. Okay?"

Janeen didn't hear a response.

"Alex?"

Alex replied in a cracked voice, "Yeah."

"You need to hang up and dial 9-1-1 now! Wait, what city are you in?"

"Seaside."

"Okay, got it. Call 9-1-1, now!"

"Okay."

The call ended and Janeen noticed she was shaking. She was alone during this summer session without her regular roommate, Jill, to consult. Kade had told her he was taking an Oregon vacation, that he was meeting up with some friends there for a slew of outdoor activities. How could he be in trouble? She didn't know Alex was going on the same trip. Now Kade was mixed up with bad people? Maybe the friends he was meeting weren't the people he thought? Something drug related? He'd never mentioned any kind of drug use.

She paced around the room to untangle her thoughts before sitting at her desk in front of her pink computer.

Oh my God, I can't lose him too.

If Kade was in trouble, she was going to find a way to help. She typed "Seaside, Oregon" into her laptop to pull up a map of the town and then began Googling questions.

Over the next ten minutes, she assembled all of the answers she needed. Portland PDX was the airport to use if you were going to visit Seaside. It was about a two-hour drive from PDX to Seaside, and there was only one hospital in that town. A one-way, direct flight from Boston Logan to PDX was about six hundred dollars. She'd arrange a rental car and lodging after getting to Logan—she needed to get to Boston well before rush hour. The last flight for today left at 6:15 p.m. and arrived in Portland at 9:30 p.m.

She grabbed her duffel bag and stuffed clothes into it, followed by a box of granola bars and two Red Bulls she'd left in the fridge. And her phone charger. She'd call Aunt Whitney on the way to the airport, then Alex again.

•　　•　　•

Outside the building, Sentry Seth Robertson, a heavyset man dressed in an Under Armour T-shirt and athletic shorts exposing his enormous calves, sat in a lawn chair about thirty yards away, in the partial shade of an oak tree. He turned off the laser microphone aimed at Janeen's window and placed the microphone and small tripod inside his empty cooler. He put his e-reader and iPod filled with ambient music MP3s in the backpack and zipped it back up.

The sister of the new Associate would be going to her ninety-minute one o'clock Accounting 224 class shortly. She'd be ten to fifteen minutes late as usual. She'd just spoken with someone named Alex who had apparently been shot. This seemed an unusual development and significant enough to report, but not an emergency. He'd type up an e-mail and attach the audio file following his lunch break, since he was already too damn hungry. He wished he could've heard the city where the person named Alex said he was located.

He got up and began carrying his belongings to the car. Thank God there was only one more day of this annoying stint before driving back to Camp Walpole for final mission preparations. After months of careful planning and training, he was excited to soon receive final orders to attack the target. He knew the members of his crew were ready. He'd been worried about the other crew from Walpole after their leader had torn his ACL, but headquarters had certified a replacement, a guy named Wolf, who seemed like a more than capable backfill.

Hell, if all of the other crews were half as strong as his, the attack would be an enormous success and change would be coming soon to America.

CHAPTER 27

The whirring sound of the Medevac helicopter carrying Cummings to Emanuel Medical Center in Portland began to fade. Twenty minutes later, the police finished questioning and taking statements from all of the witnesses in the waiting room. A Tillamook County deputy took the young Hispanic man with the bandaged arm inside her police cruiser to another location.

Next, the Tillamook County medical examiner, in conjunction with the sheriff's office, removed the body of the older Hispanic man. The Oregon State Police dispatched a crime scene reconstruction unit that would arrive sometime in the afternoon, so clinic operations were shut down for the remainder of the day, except for two administrative personnel.

Walter told the clinic admins he, Hank, and Kade were stuck momentarily because their car keys were on Cummings when he was flown out.

The three gathered in the clinic's magnetic resonance imaging (MRI) suite on the opposite side of the building to privately recount what had happened and decide what to do next. Walter and Hank sat in the aluminum chairs, while Kade sat on the floor and stretched out.

Kade realized there was no longer a Sentry watching and the police were gone for the next hour or two. He debated whether to say he was going to take a break, and then just go on the run. Should he have told the police more about his situation? That he was being held captive? He could go try to find out if Alex was okay. Hank told him there was a trail of blood going out the main door into the parking lot. Alex had to have been shot or stabbed. Kade was having difficulty sorting out this jumble of thoughts when Walter spoke first.

"This was some bad violence today, guys. The big question is, why? I'd expect this maybe if I were doing shifts at an inner-city ER, but not out here on the coast."

"Did any of the authorities offer thoughts?" Kade asked.

"I heard some mention of gangbangers," Hank said. "Some kind of star tattoo on the wrist of the dead shooter meant he was gang affiliated. I'm sure there're going to be a lot of unanswered questions."

They sat in silence for a moment, and then Hank stood up.

"You know how to work this MRI machine here?" he asked Walter.

"I'm not a tech, but I can run it for a couple basic scans in a pinch, yeah."

"Cool," Hank said. "Let's talk about some more unanswered questions."

"What do you mean?" Walter asked.

"I mean, no one at the Chapter has given me a straight answer on why I feel sick. That's the real reason I volunteered to come out today. I thought I might be able to ask you for a private exam, or you might already have an idea of my condition. You seem to talk to Dr. Drakos enough. She's always running tests on me, but I don't learn shit. She's always saying the results are inconclusive. I don't believe it. Tell me what's wrong with me."

Walter hesitated, shook his head. "I can't, Hank."

Hank pointed at Walter with a finger-and-thumb pistol. "I don't think you understand. I want to know why I'm sick. Terrible headaches and blackouts. Behavior that's not me. No one's telling me anything and it's not right. I wonder if it's something wrong with the chipset they gave me. They told me the model they gave me wasn't working right, and so I've been waiting months for some kind of upgrade they promised. In the meantime, everything's getting worse. I've been forbidden to talk about it, but it doesn't look like the other Associates have this same problem."

Walter looked uncomfortable. "I think you'll get your answers pretty soon, okay?"

"So you know some of the answers, but you just can't say," Hank said.

"I think it's time to check in with headquarters and see about going back, don't you think?" Walter stood up and stretched, but when he moved toward the door, Hank stepped in front of him.

"That's what I figured," Hank said. "You *do* know more, but you're not willing to say."

Walter tried to sidestep around him, but Hank wouldn't allow it. When he attempted once more, Hank gave him a hard shove backward and Walter struggled to regain his balance.

Walter glanced over at Kade, now sitting cross-legged on the floor, tapping both feet. Kade just stared back.

"I want to know why I'm sick," Hank continued, now in a more threatening tone. "I want to know what's going on. Something very bad is happening. You better fucking tell me."

"I can't—I'm not permitted to say. That's Special Knowledge. You know what the penalty is if I violate that."

"I know what the penalty will be if you don't tell me everything right now."

Walter looked over at Kade again. "Are you going to help me out here, Sims? These are Chapter rules."

Kade gave a slight shrug. He figured Hank had about six inches in height and at least forty pounds in solid weight over Walter. Walter wasn't getting out the door without his help, and he was feeling drained at the moment. The administration office was on the opposite end of the building, and only two people remained in that office right now. They would be too far away to hear anything.

"I'd tell Hank the truth if I were you. Isn't that what we all deserve?"

Walter sighed, nodded his head, then made a dash for the door. Hank blocked him, grabbed him around the waist, and threw him down on the ground with enough force that it looked and sounded painful.

"I've got no problem killing you if you don't come clean right now," Hank said.

"Shit. Okay, Hank!" Walter put his hands up, took a minute to collect himself and push himself back to his feet. "Yes . . . I know you received the chipset, and the chipset protocol didn't work on you."

"Well, what does that mean? What happened? Do I get the upgrade?"

Something clicked inside Kade's thoughts.

"I get it now," he said. "Hank received the Guardian protocol, just like I did. They tried it on you, they just didn't tell you more about it because it didn't work. There is no upgrade. There is no current fix. Nothing. And the other Associates have the Z protocol, like the Sentries. Only with a number of the features turned off." Kade saw the yellow program light in his vision flickering throughout his statement. "How am I doing, Walter?"

Walter gave a solemn nod. "Yeah, that's about right."

"So what happens when it doesn't work?" Hank asked.

"If you don't die during the procedure itself," Walter said, "then the worst possible complication is the neural growth stimulant used in the protocol can cause a tumor."

Hank shoved Walter back farther into the room, yelled a volley of expletives, and kicked one of the nearby aluminum chairs across the floor, sending it crashing against the wall. After the sound dissipated, he walked back to the door to block it again.

"Yeah, that's what my gut was telling me," Hank said in a calm voice.

"That's just fucking great," Kade said, standing up. "Are they benign or malignant tumors?"

"Almost always malignant," Walter said.

"And what's the survival rate for these tumors when they're malignant?" Hank asked.

"Practically zero."

"Oh my God," Kade said. He felt terrible and began to worry about himself too. He'd witnessed his mom's struggle with breast cancer firsthand, first diagnosed too late and then aggressively treated with only partial and temporary success.

Hank shook his head.

"I knew something was very wrong. More than just migraines, which I've never had before in my life. Did you know I might have this tumor?" Hank asked Walter.

"I suspected you had one, but since I'm not in charge of your treatment, I haven't seen any of your test results or documentation. Dr. Drakos didn't pass on the information, and they make sure I stay in my lane." Walter blinked his eyes, grimaced, and grabbed the bridge of his nose. "I just got a yellow light."

There was silence for a good minute before Hank took a deep breath and spoke.

"Well, then. I wanted some answers, and now I have some. If I do have this tumor, it's a death sentence." Hank pointed at Walter. "And that's why the lightbulb went on when you brought me in this room, and why I asked if you knew how to work this machine. Because now you're going to scan me and find out if I have the tumor for sure. I imagine Kade would want to know the same, right, Kade?"

"Damn right."

"You can do that, right, Walter?" Hank asked.

"Yeah, I can run you through. If I do the scan without contrast and it's where I'd expect it to be, it'll take thirty minutes. It wouldn't be perfect, but that would be enough to confirm it. But I can't put Kade in the MRI—it will destroy his G-protocol chipset, which is functional. That's why they have a CT scan and not an MRI back at AgriteX. If the chipset isn't working, they'll figure it out and—" Walter winced again. "Another yellow light. That's all I can say now, guys."

"Fuck it," Kade said. "I'm *definitely* going in the MRI then." He pointed to his forehead. "I want this thing in here dead. Hank, I'll watch Walter scan you, and then you do the same for me."

"Okay," Hank said.

"Great, now we're all finished," Walter said. He looked like he was almost in tears.

"It looks like we've got our own little code of silence now, huh?" Kade said.

Following Walter's instructions, Hank stripped down to his underwear, put in soft earplugs, and climbed onto the white table of the doughnut-shaped MRI machine, his head stabilized in the headrest, with a specialized helmet placed on top of it. Walter pressed a button and the table slid Hank into the doughnut hole headfirst.

A series of loud chirping and foghorn sounds filled the room. Kade kept a close watch on Walter as he walked between the MRI machine and a separate small booth containing two computers. When several of the initial images on the screen appeared, he didn't need an interpretation or further enhancement of the images to know what the large dark blob in the front of Hank's brain meant. It didn't look good.

When Hank put his clothes back on and joined them in the booth, Walter explained that while he was no radiologist, it was clear that Hank had the cancerous tumor. He had annotated an arrow on the image to point it out, even though he didn't need to.

"I'm so sorry, Hank," Kade said.

Hank looked resigned with the information. "Yeah, me too. Now it's your turn."

"Yeah."

Kade stripped down and they repeated the same process. As he lay there with his eyes open, thinking about his full bladder, all of a sudden his vision was clear. Less than a minute into the scan, the stoplight and program readout had disappeared.

Wow, everything's gone. Thank God.

But then the scanner stopped, and the table began to slide him out of the MRI. He saw Hank's face first.

"What's going on? We done?"

"No," Walter said, "we're out of time. One of the admin assistants who's still here stopped by and said that a Jon Constantino is at the door asking about us."

"As in Guardian Constantino?"

"Yeah. The admin didn't give him entry. She met him outside and told him the authorities said the front area is still considered a crime scene. But he communicated that we three need to return to AgriteX with him now and he's waiting for us."

Kade put his clothes on.

"So what now?" Walter asked. "You guys are going back, right?"

"Yeah, I'm going back," Hank said. "Now I have some business I want to take care of."

"I'm with you, Hank," Kade said. "Walter, you say a word about what we discussed here to anyone and you're a dead man."

"I won't."

"Good." Kade walked up close to Walter and looked down into his face. "Because you have one strike against you—you already checked in with headquarters and told them to come here, didn't you?"

Walter broke eye contact. "Yeah."

"Thought so," Kade said. "Do something like that again and you're dead. And now, I never got to finish my bathroom break. I'll meet you guys at the side door."

The three exited the MRI suite and walked down the hall toward the waiting room area. They could see Constantino and three other uniformed Guardians standing outside the side door at the end of the hall. The clinic administrative assistant stood inside with the keys in her hand.

"Tell 'em I've got to use the john real quick before I go," Kade said.

Kade walked along the hall at the back of the waiting room, short of the yellow crime scene tape, and saw that Alex's backpack was no longer at the coffee station.

The police removed it. Damn.

He returned to the bathroom, and scanned the inside again while he was finishing up at the toilet. He had checked everywhere. *No, not everywhere.* There was a red plastic medical waste can. He picked it up in both hands but there was nothing in it. Nothing in the paper towel dispenser either.

He looked at the baby changing station mounted on the wall and pulled the folding table down. The Glock and two extra clips were there in separate Ziploc bags. He removed the Glock from its bag, jammed it just inside the rear of his pants, and pulled his crinkly AgriteX shirt down past his butt. He stuffed the other bag in his right cargo pocket.

After he washed up and splashed some cold water on his face, he headed back out and down to the side door where the admin lady was waiting.

Constantino and another Guardian, Lloyd, were waiting for him outside with another Tahoe pulled up to the front. Hank and Walter were in the other vehicle with a new pair of Guardians sitting inside.

"What's up?" Kade asked.

Constantino said, "Marshall's ordered everyone on restriction until further notice, and there's going to be a Verax review on everyone. There's been a large security breach."

Kade thought about Alex and leaving him behind, bleeding somewhere. Maybe he needed to make a stand right now. He stood in place and put his hands on his hips.

"So what the hell am *I* supposed to do about it?"

"You're supposed to come with us right now," Constantino said.

Kade could tell Constantino and Lloyd were tense. He felt it with the same sensory clarity as when Hank accosted him with the knife. For a split second, he considered making a break for it, but he didn't like what he read in their faces. They were serious, with their weapons within reach. His Glock was tucked away next to his tailbone without a round in the chamber.

I'll get shot first.

He didn't like the thought of going back to the Chapter HQ. But at least he now had a weapon, and the chip in his head was out of commission. He still needed more evidence.

He clapped his hands together once and the two Guardians flinched.

"Okay, let's go home then," he said.

The two Guardians seemed relieved. Kade started walking toward the vehicle.

"Oh, and Guardian Constantino?"

Constantino looked at Kade and raised his eyebrows. "What?"

"Belated thanks for saving my life."

CHAPTER 28

Tuesday, June 25
1:17 p.m. (PDT)
AgriteX

Owens found Pierce in the hallway after making a quick call on the two-way radio. They both stepped into an empty AgriteX training room and sat down at two of the desks.

"What happened at the clinic?" Owens asked.

"We have one dead from a shooting," Pierce said. "Sentry Cummings died at Portland Emanuel. Three of our Associates were there when it happened."

"Who?"

"Lefear, Stanfield, and Sims," Pierce said.

"Where are they now?"

"On their way back here."

"How did this happen?" Owens asked.

"Lefear provided a rough phone report, but that's all we have for now. The shooter was one of a pair of Mexican men who came into the clinic for treatment and opened fire. Police on the scene suspect it's drug related."

"Less than twenty-four hours after Messia's visit. This can't be a coincidence," Owens said. "When can we get more details?"

"We're following up with our county and state police sources."

"Were there any other injuries?"

"Yeah, another person who was shot ran out of there on foot. Not one of ours. I'm trying to find out who it is."

Owens nodded. "Assuming this was Messia's design, we can't let him distract us from our main effort. Unless we find he's going to make a major move, I don't want to expend the resources. Just have a contingency plan ready."

"Agreed."

"And what's the status on finding our mole?" Owens asked.

"I'm sure we'll have resolution tomorrow," Pierce said. "We've narrowed it down after reviewing all of the access logs and surveillance. We're going to put several groups through the Verax and conduct some more interrogation to finalize our action."

There was a reflective stretch of silence before Pierce gave Owens a look of concern and asked, "Are you okay?"

"Yeah," Owens said and patted Pierce on the shoulder. "We knew we'd have some of these challenges as we got closer to launch," he said. "We've war-gamed this down to every conceivable obstacle. If we need to make adjustments, we'll make them."

"We're in the home stretch. Are you still having fun?"

Owens smiled. "Oh yeah. Now things are getting interesting."

CHAPTER 29

Tuesday, June 25
5:32 p.m. (PDT)
FBI field office, Portland, Oregon

Twenty minutes after leaving the field office and changing into workout clothes in a Subway, Zach Poole detached his Schwinn Paramount road bike from the rear rack, donned his helmet and sunglasses, and started cycling. The steep six-hundred-foot trail took him to the top of Rocky Butte State Park, built on an extinct volcanic cinder cone. He finished on one of the dirt paths, pulling up to the short wall of cut stone topped with vintage lanterns.

Catching his breath, he took in the spectacular view of Mount Hood and the Columbia River Gorge to the east and the view back toward the airport, across the river into Washington State, where he could see Vancouver and Camas. He'd broken a sweat during the ride and the slight breeze felt good.

Less than ten minutes later, another cyclist pulled up alongside him. A wiry man with black hair and large, flared nostrils.

"What's up, man?"

"Hey, Paul. Just another beautiful day, living the life," Zach said.

"Amen, brother. You've got some news for me today, I take it?"

"I do. And is this a day where I can expect a little extra?"

"Yeah. I know you're due."

"Okay." Zach took a quick unnoticeable scan of the area from underneath his sunglasses. The closest people nearby, a young couple, were more than fifty yards away.

"The op targeted against AgriteX is underway," Zach said. "It started no later than June tenth and is scheduled to be complete in mid-July."

Paul's own sunglasses couldn't hide his anxiousness. "Really? How can you be sure?"

"I noticed an operation activity listed on the staffing matrix to indicate resources being used, but it was left off the master project calendar for some reason. I knew from the staffing matrix that four agents were assigned to it. Recently, they assigned an analyst to the op, and I tracked her down today. She said she was assigned on the tenth and could expect to be off the op in mid-July."

"How do you know this op is targeting AgriteX?"

"I saw some of the analyst's notes. Just a five-second look. But I saw the name Marshall Owens, plus AgriteX and the Chapter, listed in the notes, right when she confirmed her participation in the unnamed op."

"You're positive?"

"No doubt in my mind," Zach said.

"Okay, thanks. This is going to sound some more alarm bells," Paul said.

"I figured."

"Are you getting low on water?" Paul asked.

"Yeah, can I borrow some of yours?"

The two swapped their identical bike water bottles. Zach knew that in the pocket of the outer shell of the water bottle he received would be a payment. This time, a roll of ten hundred-dollar bills.

"All right, I better be going," Paul said. "I'll check in with you next week."

"Okay, good luck," Zach said, and remounted his bike.

Now he was really looking forward to a no-strings-attached night of fun with a girl close to home *and* getting his wife a gift for putting up with his late nights at work.

CHAPTER 30

Wednesday, June 26
9:17 a.m. (PDT)
AgriteX

Kade had only slept for three hours during the night, tops, but now he was wide-awake, sitting on the floor near the window in the soft gray light of the sunless morning.

During the balance of hours lying awake with his eyes shut, he took a bathroom visit and transferred the Glock and ammo to the toilet tank. Hopefully, without observation or suspicion. His eyes moistened for a few seconds when he again thought of Alex's sacrifice during the drop.

Please, God, let him be okay.

Other than a breakfast bar tossed in his room, he hadn't eaten since returning the evening prior, and he felt like he was starving. Another headache gnawed at his temples and made his eyeballs hurt.

He swore to himself he'd try to escape at the next available opportunity. He'd wait until the security posture dropped and his room door was once again unlocked during the day. Stuff would calm back down again. He now knew the route to Lost Lake that Carol had shown him, and from there he could find his way to Kidders Butte by sight.

He would try to escape right after an evening meal, make it look like he was going to take a jog for exercise. There'd still be plenty of daylight left. If he got caught or confronted early on during the jog, he'd just say he felt great and had lost track of the distance on his route. This plan might give him an hour or two before they realized he was missing.

If he tried to get out by force, he'd most likely get killed, since there was no shortage of armed Sentries and Guardians who could be called at a moment's notice when an alarm was sounded.

He thought he had some information that could help prosecute the leadership of AgriteX. False imprisonment. Assault. Battery. But he knew he needed better evidence and more of it. All of the weapons and ammo he'd seen had to be stored somewhere, and where they stored the small arms, there might be more heavy-duty firepower nearby.

It seemed too convenient that Sentries did double duty as inmate mentors at the LLFC. Maybe that provided the right appearance of separation to cover militia activity.

He would try to find the weapons storage and get photos before slipping away. Maybe look for the cannabis seed if he had time. That was the best he could do at this point. He thought about the current risk combined with everything he'd been through already. The measure of danger was at a critical level, and his body had been through a lot of trauma. The FBI couldn't expect much more from him. They might want more, but he sure as hell didn't remember the risk of forced medical procedures being in his prep briefings.

He thought about the Verax machine, the announced review today, and whether he would be able to screw up the results like before. What would they do afterward? Beat him again? His body couldn't take much more of that. Another reason to get the hell out.

There were no other team members to carry on this mission without him.

I'm no good to anyone if I'm dead.

$\bullet \quad \bullet \quad \bullet$

About one hour later, while he continued to ruminate on his options, the door access reader beeped, and the automatic lock on his room clicked open. To Kade's surprise, Sentry Ignaty entered, bearing a tray of breakfast food.

"There you go, Sims." Ignaty set the tray down on the floor just inside the door. He looked up just enough to make eye contact and paused.

Kade gave him an incredulous look.

"What? You want a fucking tip for room service?"

Ignaty returned a crooked smile as he retreated out the door and it shut behind him. The breakfast was a cold, plain bagel with a square of butter, a strawberry yogurt, and a carton of orange juice. He scarfed down the bagel, scraped every drop out of the yogurt cup with the plastic spoon, and licked the interior. He thought about his pants getting looser and the increasing amount of slack in his belt.

Another hour later, Ignaty and Hill returned.

"Okay, Sims," Hill said. "Before you come along, the chief medical officer said you have to take this pill. She said you'd know what it is."

Hill produced a pink pill in a small crimped paper cup while Ignaty half filled Kade's water glass and handed it to him. Kade could tell from the color and markings it was carbamazepine.

Shit.

"I've got to make sure you swallow it," Hill said.

Kade took the glass of water and swallowed the pill, opening his mouth and lifting up his tongue.

"And we've got to cuff all of you Associates and take you to the holding room for the next couple of hours," Hill said. "Not going to be a pleasant day for you all, I'm afraid."

"Wonderful," Kade said, and held his hands out in front of him until Hill put the cuffs on.

Kade was happy they didn't put a hood on his head. It seemed like they were in too much of a hurry this time. They led him through the northwest quadrant, where he knew the other Associate rooms were located. He had no idea where the Sentries and Guardians lived. The southwest quadrant held the medical office, rec room, kitchen-and-cafeteria complex.

They approached a sizable secure door, currently wide open, as two Sentries passed through chatting. He got a glimpse of the enormous entrance atrium, but Ignaty and Hill guided him left and led him through a door to a small hallway that bypassed the lobby altogether. Once they entered the southeast quadrant, it was only a short walk to a room with an unlabeled four-foot-high door and a Sentry posted outside of it.

"Go ahead in," Hill said. "Sit down next to Slade. Eyes toward the door and no talking." The Sentry popped the door open and Kade ducked in.

Lin and Daniel and were already sitting on the concrete floor against the far wall of the windowless room. Both looked worried, but Daniel nodded, and Kade thought Lin mouthed "Hi" when he glanced at her. A pair of fluorescent tube lights shone through their wire enclosures from a ceiling mount, glaring off the glossy white painted cinder-block walls. The room smelled like there were too many nervous people in it.

Kade sat down, back against the wall, cross-legged. Across the room he saw a surveillance camera mounted above the door, and also noticed the door had no visible knob or lock on the inside. The movement of cool air through a one-foot-square ventilation grill was the only audible noise. Four Sentries stood facing them, two on each side of the door. Their pistols were holstered, but each person gripped a handheld stun gun with two metal prongs on the end.

The next person ducking through the door was Hank, followed by Walter and Carol. They were instructed to sit in sequence to Kade's left. Carol glared at Kade when she walked in, while Walter gazed about. Hank gave Kade a one-finger wave and seemed calm.

A Sentry with a blond flattop stepped into the room.

"We're waiting on the special assistant who's going to speak with you all. In the meantime, no talking. No looking at each other. No moving closer together. Remain sitting. If you don't follow instructions . . ." He held up a stun gun to reinforce the point. "Any questions?"

There were no questions, and Kade thought it best not to contribute a smart-aleck comment. The pill was helping him concentrate better, but the more he thought about Dr. Drakos forcing him to take it, the more he worried. He bet she'd deduced that his disorder was messing up the Verax system. Maybe he was overthinking, but the Chapter had gathered a ton of information on him and ransacked his apartment. They somehow were getting access to various government and private databases. Given the network of Chapter alumni, his military medical records and maybe even his private medical records could have been hacked.

Joshua Pierce ducked through the door and stood in front of them. His beard stubble seemed thicker than it had been the last time Kade saw him, and his eyes revealed some strain. He cleared his throat and put his hands on his hips.

"Good morning, Associates," he said. "I apologize for the handcuffs, but we have a significant security situation here. One of you has committed a serious violation of the Knowledge Tenet. Someone has been communicating with people outside of the Chapter and giving them information about our sensitive activities. This unauthorized communication has done damage and jeopardized ongoing operations. It's also resulted in a Sentry being killed. Does this turn of events sound familiar to anyone here?" Pierce paused and scanned the room. "Would anyone like to come clean with what they have done right now to avoid an additional Truth violation? This is your last opportunity."

Kade didn't look at any of the others.

They know about my communication to Alex. That whole incident at the clinic with Sentry Cummings somehow had to be related to me.

Cummings must have died.

He felt his heart beating faster and forced himself to take a slow, deep breath through his nostrils. No one in the room responded to Pierce.

"Yeah, I didn't think I'd have any volunteers," Pierce said after a couple of deep sniffs. "Here's what's going to happen. You're each going to be taken into the Verax room and given a series of questions. The violator will be identified when we're finished with the questioning, and then the Guardians will convene. They'll be shown the evidence, a decision will be made, and we'll discuss the penalty. Associate Soon, you're first."

Lin stood and walked to the door. Kade glanced down at his cuffed hands.

His shoes were still within reach.

It's time to send Alderville the signal.

Because if I don't, I think my time's run out.

CHAPTER 31

Lin returned and sat down, hunched with narrowed shoulders, knees pulled toward her chest like she was cold. Kade knew his turn was after Daniel's if they went in sequence.

How long would it take for the FBI to get me out of here? To bring the right number of people to do it? One hour? Two? If the Verax has problems and they decide to kill me this time, it'll already be too late. I need to act now.

Kade reached down and started playing with his shoes like he was fidgety when he felt no one was paying particular attention to him. He wedged a finger into the Velcro seam lining the boot tongue and widened it with two fingers until he could also slip his thumb inside. The tiny device clicked between his index finger and thumb when he squeezed it.

That click was just seconds before the metallic click sounded on the holding room door's autolock. All of the Associates looked toward the opening door and saw Daniel duck into the room and return to his spot. Daniel made eye contact with Kade and raised his eyebrows once before sitting.

The Sentry with the blond flattop poked his head in the open door.

"Sims, let's go."

Kade got up and felt a little woozy as he shuffled toward the door, crouching through the opening where a Guardian Stone put a hand on his back and directed him down the hall to his left.

Stone stepped to Kade's side when they reached a door marked "EVAL," motioning for him to enter first. It was the same ten-by-ten, white-walled room with the centerpiece reclining chair he remembered from his previous Verax session. Now from his unhooded and standing vantage point, he noticed the room had a tiny opaque window and the Verax chair was on wheels.

The lab technician, a man with thinning hair and psoriasis who was wearing a white lab coat over casual clothes, stood waiting for him.

"Let's get you strapped in and relaxed," the tech said.

"That's an oxymoron," Kade said.

The technician snorted. "Yeah, well, you know the drill now."

"I doubt it." He took his time climbing into the chair and situating his head in the U-shaped headrest.

After positioning the wired headband and the microphone, the technician disappeared from sight. Kade couldn't think of anything to calm himself. He wondered how the Chapter might euthanize him, whether it would come as a lethal injection or a bullet to the back of his head. At the same time, he imagined an FBI SWAT team mobilizing to pull him out of the building. That's when he heard Pierce's voice through the headrest speaker.

"Mr. Sims, are you ready?"

"I guess."

"Okay, the questions are coming from me this time. Let's get started with two. First, what is your full name?"

"Kinkade Alan Sims."

"And what is your date of birth?"

"November nine, nineteen-eighty-eight."

There was about a ten-second pause.

"Excellent. Now from this point forward, we need a simple yes or no answer. Nothing else. Do you understand?"

Fuck, the machine must be working now.

"Yes," Kade said.

"Mr. Sims, have you provided any unauthorized information to anyone outside of the Chapter since you have been initiated as a Chapter member?"

In the next second Kade thought: did his communication to Alex via the website count as unauthorized information? No. Maybe the communication was unauthorized, but he didn't disclose any Chapter knowledge.

"No."

"Have you attempted to harm the Chapter as an organization in any way since you have been initiated as a Chapter member?"

Not yet.

"No."

"Have you left or attempted to leave the grounds of the Chapter for any activity outside of authorized activity?"

"No."

"Have you ever had any known communication with a drug cartel?"

"No."

There was a pause for thirty seconds, giving him time to think.

Drug cartel? Why would they ask that? They had increasing tensions with their cartel relationships, but why?

Someone on the inside has been communicating with a cartel, and they think it could be me?

"Are you participating in or have you ever participated in a gang?"

"No."

"Three more questions for you, Mr. Sims. Are you an FBI agent?"

"No."

"Are you a member of any federal, state, or local law enforcement agency?"

"No."

"Are you working for any organization with the intent to collect information on AgriteX or the Chapter?"

"No."

"Perfect," Pierce said. "We're done here."

That's it. I'm probably screwed on that last question.

Two minutes later, the technician and Guardian Stone entered. The technician removed the headband, pulled the microphone to the side, and tore off the Velcro restraints.

"Let's go, Sims," Stone said.

Kade felt the wetness of his undershirt against his back as he slid out of the chair. Stone escorted him the thirty feet back down the hallway and activated the lock on the holding room, pushing the door open enough where he could slide through.

"Okay, go sit where you were before," Stone said.

Now Kade's heart started beating faster. Hank and Walter were next in line; if they were asked the right questions, he could be in jeopardy for what happened at the clinic. But maybe those weren't the kinds of questions they were asking. They hadn't asked him about his peers.

The room was again silent except for the occasional cough of someone in the room and the hum of the ventilation. Kade thought the four Sentry guards looked bored out of their minds as they stared across the room at them.

Another forty to forty-five minutes passed as each of the men completed their session and Stone returned.

"Associate Reese, you're up," he said.

As Carol passed, Kade met her glance. Her eyes held an intense look of bitterness while she gave the slightest smile. He could recognize that kind of smile anywhere.

You're fucked.

He started to sweat again. Had she sensed the uptick in problems after he'd joined the Associate group? Could she see right through his disguise?

Another thirty minutes elapsed—now it had to have been a couple of hours since he'd activated the transmitter. He was an idiot—he'd waited too long to activate the signal, and it was going to cost him his life.

No one was coming.

He should've sent the signal when he got back from the clinic, as soon as he heard the Associates were all going to be rounded up. He should've never let himself be handcuffed. Or he should've just taken off from the clinic when he first had the chance.

More time ticked by. Two bathroom requests, one from Lin and one from Daniel, were denied. One of the Sentries exchanged whispered words with the guy beside him. It looked like it was some kind of a joke. Carol had been gone a long time, maybe an hour. He thought about all of the nosy questions he'd asked her about the LLFC.

Then the door clicked open and Guardian Stone stepped inside. He whispered something to the first Sentry, who in turn passed the message on to the other three, and then Stone exited. Moments later, Pierce ducked into the room again and took a few steps toward Kade. When their eyes met, Kade felt a slight chill, but that was also when he felt the strange clarity kick in again. He read Pierce's face, his body language. It wasn't threatening; Pierce was not coming for *him* right now. And his thoughts were validated as Pierce turned around to face the door.

Something was being wheeled into the room through the opening. It was the Verax chair, reclined, with Carol still strapped into it. Black duct tape was wrapped twice around her mouth to the back of her neck. Stone pushed the chair to the center of the room and stood by it on the right. Dr. Drakos then stepped into the room. Pierce stood on the left and spoke in a voice that seemed too loud for the room.

"We have come to a resolution on our security concern. But before I continue, let me make something clear: the questions you were asked during your individual Verax reviews are not to be discussed with anyone.

"Now, it's been some time since we've had a transgression this serious. We can't provide you the details, but what I will say is that Associate Reese has betrayed the Chapter, AgriteX, and each one of you. We had clear evidence of her wrongdoing, and this was corroborated by findings from the Verax program. She had the opportunity to confess but chose not to. A council of Guardians met with the entire E-team a short time ago, and came to a unanimous agreement on the offense. The group recommended she be euthanized in a vote that well exceeded the seventy-five-percent threshold."

Kade looked at Carol struggling in her chair and trying to yell through the duct tape gag.

Do I get up and try to stop it?

I can't.

Pierce continued. "Having you all witness this event is to ensure you understand the serious consequences of your actions, and that penalties, along with Chapter rewards, are real. There are no final meals and no final words here, just final justice."

Pierce looked at Stone before pulling some kind of white card out from his pocket. At the same time, something Pierce said snapped Kade into focus.

Witness. Justice.

He fumbled at his shoe while looking around the room. Everyone, including the guards, was watching Pierce step in front of Carol while she thrashed with all of her might against the restraints.

He pulled the tiny camera/recorder from his other shoe. Slid the record switch on and brought the camera up on his kneecap between his fingers. Found the rough surface of the other raised button and began depressing it repeatedly, varying the angle he took the pictures. He would max out the number of pictures he could take, but that didn't matter now. He didn't stop.

"The Chapter Code has been broken," Pierce said. "The ultimate penalty has been decided."

Pierce held a white card in front of Carol's face as if he was offering it to read, and she stopped thrashing as it held her attention. She looked at the card, her eyes widening a bit as she read whatever was on it. She glanced up once at Pierce, and then stared forward again before convulsing in the chair. Within seconds, she slumped back in the restraints and lay still. Kade didn't see any kind of IV hooked up to her or any sort of injection administered. Maybe the chair was somehow electrified? He slid his camera/recorder back into the tongue of his boot and squeezed the Velcro back together.

Dr. Drakos stepped up to Carol and checked her with a stethoscope, then nodded to Pierce. Pierce put the white card back in his pocket.

"Associate Reese," he said, "or as she was known before joining us, Señorita Ries, is no longer a threat to the Chapter."

CHAPTER 32

Wednesday, June 26
1:13 p.m. (PDT)
FBI field office, Portland, Oregon

Morris knocked twice before opening the door to Velasquez's office space and leaning inside. Velasquez was in his usual form, standing and pacing in a circle while talking on his phone. His desk was covered by stacks of paperwork, with more paper spread on the floor or in piles, and paper overflowing from the trash can and from the bottom bin of his shredder.

Morris couldn't have cared less about the office's appearance, even though he joked that he could housebreak a puppy in it. Whatever methods Velasquez used to organize his casework, he delivered damn good results.

"Neal Graves is on the line for us—urgent," Morris said.

Velasquez nodded, said "I've got to go" into his phone, and ended his call. He scooped up an eight-page printout off his desk. "This just came in from Neal a minute ago."

"Yep, bring it."

He followed Morris down the hallway to the briefing room and shut the door behind them. Morris unmuted the speakerphone and both men stood leaning, palms down on the table, as if they were about to pounce.

"Neal?" Morris asked.

"Yeah, I'm here," Graves said.

"I have Chris Velasquez here with me now. What's going on?"

"A big flare-up in activity. Yesterday morning there was a drug-related shooting out on the coast with two fatalities. I received the initial police report and we're sending an investigator. I faxed that report to Chris ten minutes ago."

"Yeah, I got it," Velasquez said.

"The reason I'm calling," Graves continued, "is that there was a mention of an AgriteX employee fatality in the report—in one of the statements."

"What was the name?" Morris asked.

"Andrew Cummings," Graves said. "He was a shooting victim who died at Portland Emanuel Tuesday evening."

Morris shook his head, then looked at Velasquez to check his response, but Velasquez was already speed-reading the report.

"Where was the shooting?" Morris asked. He turned when he felt Velasquez grab his shoulder and point to a page on the conference table. Velasquez tapped on a line of text with his pen.

It was a statement made by Kinkade Sims. Velasquez pointed to Sims's signature.

Graves said, "It happened in Nehalem, not too far from Manzanita, at the Nehalem Clinic—a medical facility."

"Hold on, Neal," Morris said. "Give us a minute." Morris muted the phone.

"So Flash was a *patient* there?" Morris asked Velasquez.

"No. Here's the statement." Velasquez read aloud.

•   •   •

I was at the clinic as part of an internship observing medical treatment with Dr. Walter Lefear, Hank Stanfield, and a Mr. Cummings (don't know his first name). Cummings was supervising the three of us. We're all AgriteX employees. I was in the waiting room bathroom when the shooting started. I came out of the bathroom and helped Hank Stanfield subdue a young man with an injured arm. There was another man lying next to him dead and shot through the head. I had never seen either of these two men before.

• • •

"Was Flash the target? Or was it someone with him?" Morris asked.

Velasquez shrugged. "Maybe it was just a soft-target attack against a group of AgriteX employees away from their well-guarded corporate headquarters."

Morris unmuted the phone.

"Neal, who do you think was the intended target?"

"It's uncertain. A missing link is one of the shooting victims, a backpacker, who fled on foot and is now at Portland Emanuel. The doctors haven't cleared him for questioning yet."

"The shooter knew the AgriteX people would be there, meaning their surveillance is pretty good," Morris said.

"You'll find the deceased shooter, Esteban Morales, listed in the NGIC database as affiliated with Oeste-13," Graves said. "The shooter's assistant is being held for further questioning."

"So this could be the ordered hit we discussed before," Velasquez said.

"Yes, it could," Graves said. "It's another pencil line connecting AgriteX and drug activity. We'll be investigating further. A shooting like this has never happened in public on the North Coast, much less in a health-care facility."

"We'll want to reinterview some of these people," Morris said. "We'll coordinate with Tillamook County and the state police. Thanks for the call, Neal. Let us know if anything else trickles in."

"Will do."

"Okay, thanks, bye." Morris poked the big red "X" button on the phone and paused for a few breaths. "Flash called this an internship, but he has no medical background. It doesn't make sense."

"Maybe he didn't have a choice," Velasquez said. "Maybe it was an opportunity he decided to investigate, or an ad hoc escape plan if he thought our plan wouldn't work. The shooting couldn't have been anticipated."

Morris locked his hands together behind his neck.

"This isn't good. We've got a greater convergence of cartel and Chapter activity with our source in the middle. I think we need to get him out before we risk losing what he's already collected."

Velasquez knew when Morris phrased his thoughts like this he was asking for an opinion or even a debate. They had an unspoken, efficient rhythm used in many operations over six years. Velasquez ran over the options in his head for a full thirty seconds and consulted the calendar on his phone before he spoke.

"I agree," Velasquez said. "I'll call the Oregon police to notify them we are taking over the investigation. We'll send Alderville into AgriteX tomorrow during the business day to interview Flash and then bring him in for further questioning on the Nehalem Clinic shooting investigation. That'll be it. He'll have been inside AgriteX long enough, I think."

"On second thought," Morris said, "let's interview all three AgriteX employees who were at the scene and also see if Neal's available to link up with Alderville to go with them. It'll seem like the natural follow-up to have someone from DEA in the lead and questioning all three men."

Velasquez nodded. "Perfect."

CHAPTER 33

The first thing Kade noticed in the AgriteX café was the short supply of Sentries. Instead of seeing a herd of them seated together for dinner, he now only counted two black uniforms in the room. There was still one full table of Guardians about sixty feet away, at his ten o'clock, and the group seemed to be having an intense discussion, not regular, light dinner conversation. No arguments, but no smiles either.

He and the other four Associates at the table, Daniel, Walter, Hank, and Lin, sat in silence. No one else was eating the barbecue pork sandwiches. Across the table, Walter looked the same as he had since they'd left the clinic—scared shitless. Daniel stared at the table with his lips pursed. Hank looked calm and thoughtful. Lin had slid even closer to him on his right, grasping his knee like she was trying to move away from Carol's ghost still sitting beside her on the bench. That was okay with him.

A Sentry whose nametape read WHEELER approached the table.

"Hey, listen up," Wheeler said. "Mr. Owens and Mr. Pierce realize it's been a very tough day for you all. Following dinner you'll be released to your rooms until eight. From eight to ten, there will be an open bar in the rec room, and Mr. Pierce will join you around nine."

Kade tried to keep a blank look on his face.

Oh joy.

"And just a reminder," Wheeler said. "Please head directly back to your rooms following the meal. We're still under an enhanced surveillance order. Any deviation and you'll be cuffed and the whole nine yards. Thanks for your cooperation."

In the next five minutes, they all rose from the table and filed out the door, walking back to their rooms in a silent gaggle. Kade took a closer look at the door labels on each side of the hall during the walk back. First, the café, kitchen, and a storage room. After the first right turn, HVAC, the employee lounge, both employee health clinics, six training rooms, another four storage rooms, and a number of unlabeled doors in the mix.

After the final right turn, he passed five room doors before reaching his own. When he paused there, he saw Hank go to his room two doors down, across the hall. Daniel and Lin continued to theirs, across from each other, four doors down. Lin turned and looked at him before she went inside. With sixteen rooms in this hallway, it seemed there were a lot of empty rooms. He doubted they put Sentries and Guardians in the same area.

He let the door shut behind him, then turned the knob and opened it a crack to see if it had locked behind him, and it hadn't. He was again able to flip the dead-bolt lock, so he locked the door from the inside. Every second of early warning was important.

Surveillance up, but Chapter physical security posture has been lowered.

Two hours until mandatory reverse happy hour.

He paced for a bit before heading toward the desk computer station. He sat down and awoke the screen with the mouse. Even without logging in, a yellow inverted triangle containing a black exclamation point blinked on the screen, followed by a warning:

You are 1 day overdue in downloading the required Daily Update.

This was the first alert of this sort he'd received, and now, since the chipset in his head was no longer functional, he wasn't going to attempt a download. He wasn't sure how long it would be until another alert would trigger a human follow-up. Someone from AgriteX technical support would come and investigate why he was not taking the download.

He decided to log in so he'd seem at least halfway compliant. Then, if he needed to, he could come up with an excuse that there was something wrong with the system and he just couldn't process the download. Maybe that would buy him twenty-four to forty-eight hours. He didn't have much time before someone would want to run diagnostics on the computer, or perhaps on him.

Then there was the whole Verax test. They either knew he was lying and were deciding what to do with him next, or he beat the test again. Logic tilted toward believing he beat the test; otherwise they would've just killed him as they did Carol. It seemed he'd dodged another bullet.

It had been about eight hours since he'd activated the emergency transmitter. At this point he figured it didn't work, the battery had run out, or the signal couldn't penetrate the walls of the headquarters and reach the relay box. Otherwise, he would've expected the FBI to have moved in. There had to be a reason the technology was ineffective. He needed to believe that.

He thought about his escape plan again, went over the scenarios in his head. Making a move tonight was out of the question since there was now a planned after-dinner activity. He brainstormed anything he could do to further support his plan and create a better chance for success. Could he cause an additional disruption or distraction while he attempted to escape? He stared at the computer screen.

Yes, maybe I can do something.

Maybe some simple cyber warfare is in order.

He could create a simple computer virus in a more mainstream system, but it had been a number of years since he'd played around with viruses and hacks. This would be a challenge—the Chapter didn't run the typical operating systems, e-mail programs, or applications he could easily exploit. The Chapter OS didn't leave much available to him, and he'd only practiced coding a few simple programs in the test environment.

The remaining option appeared to be changing some personal preferences and settings, and he assumed everyone else had that option too. In those options you could do some simple things like changing defaults—word fonts, font size, brightness and contrast of text compared to the background in the field of vision.

Background brightness.

He logged into the main program and acknowledged the download reminder with a click to make it disappear. He then went to the Personal Settings menu, then to Background. Underneath that header, the default setting was No Color. There were two other possible selections: Black and White. The choices didn't make much sense.

Who would ever want their vision-screen to be all black or white? It has to be transparent for a person to see anything.

That gave him an idea: if he could change his own vision settings from No Color to Black or to White, then he would be blinded. It would be like having a blackout or a whiteout. He almost wished his program was still active to test it. With a little more time, he might be able to figure out how to impersonate an administrator and set a global default to either blackout or whiteout everyone on the program after their next download. But there was no way he was going to figure that out in the next thirty minutes. He logged out, found his way over to the easy chair, and flopped down in it again. Someone would come by to get him for the open bar, so he shut his eyes.

There was a knock on the door twenty minutes later and he got up to answer it, since a Sentry would have just come right in. Hank was standing there with the first-ever pleasant look on his face. A nice surprise.

"Hey, want to go have that drink?"

Kade gave him a fist bump. "Yeah, thanks."

They walked down to the rec room, Kade again observing no Sentries in the hallway. A janitor operating a noisy buffing machine on the hallway floor ignored them both.

"Where is everybody?" Kade asked. "The place seems deserted."

"I don't know. Maybe some kind of big outdoor project today."

"Yeah."

They could hear classical piano playing in the rec room as they came down the hall, and when they entered the room, Kade was impressed that Lin was the one seated at the piano bench. She looked up and he smiled at her, but she didn't smile back. She still appeared shaken.

Toward the back of the room, a stainless-steel cocktail bar on wheels had been rolled in and was staffed by a bulky man with a thin black beard, someone who he thought was a cook or server in the café. Daniel and Walter were playing pool near the back.

"Bar?" Hank prompted.

"Sure," Kade said, and followed Hank's lead.

Kade quickly judged that there wasn't going to be a critical turn of events this evening that would force him to try to break out. He'd made it through the Verax, and Pierce was just trying to calm the Associates down. It seemed all Sentries and maybe some Guardians were active outside, making it more dangerous to operate on the ground out there. So he'd have a few drinks to try to bond with the remaining Associates. Maybe a weak rationalization, but that's what his gut was telling him.

Hank ordered a scotch on the rocks, and Kade took two bottles of an IPA microbrew he'd never heard of. He followed Hank back to the pair of couches by the pool table where the men all exchanged terse hellos. Hank dropped onto the couch, while Kade walked over to Daniel with a sudden thought.

"Hey, can I talk to you for a sec?"

"Sure," Daniel said, and Hank took over his pool game.

"A few questions for ya," Kade said.

"Okay, but let's play some foosball." Daniel moved over to the adjacent game table.

After they started whacking the ball around, Kade asked, "You ever seen the inside of L-FAC?"

"Yeah."

"I was just wondering about the inmates firing guns and stuff. Like, wouldn't a state inspection fail the facility for safety?"

Daniel nodded. "Hard to believe, but with non-lethal rounds, it's legally permissible. The prison seems to do a careful dance around the semiannual inspections, and they always ace them. Fire drills, laundry, food service, whatever—they nail it."

"Okay, didn't mean to prod. Just seemed dangerous."

Daniel won two games while Kade's concentration was elsewhere.

"I'll be back," Kade said. "I think Lin needs some cheering up."

Daniel nodded like that was a good idea, but added, "Be careful with her."

He walked over to the piano and sat down on the bench to Lin's right.

"Just going to watch, if that's all right," he said.

She glanced back without saying anything. His brusque conversations must've permanently turned her off. He put his coaster and extra beer on the music rack and drank from the bottle in his hand.

The melody was gentle, a blend of melancholy and hope that perfectly fit the collective mood. He wasn't familiar with classical piano, but was enjoying the song and watching her delicate fingers. The first very cold beer slid down his throat within a few minutes and he started on his second.

"What are you playing?" he asked when she'd completed the piece.

"Chopin."

"That sounded really nice."

She turned to look at him and the expression in her eyes said thanks.

It happened like an involuntary response. He slid his hand from the bench across the small of her back to her opposite hip and kissed her for a few seconds. Her lips were soft and wet and tasted like the cold vodka cranberry she was drinking. He leaned in again and she seemed more into it this time. When she sat back, she drew her breath in and sighed.

"Yeah, okay . . . great timing, Sims." Her head turned back to the front, and she started playing again like she was exerting some kind of discipline upon herself. "I could've used some companionship before now. I was happy when you showed up. It made all this . . . different. I was hoping it might get even better."

"Sorry."

She played another piece, this one more somber, while he drained his second bottle. He went and got two more rounds of drinks for both of them over the next half hour. The music seeped into his bruised spirit and absorbed some of the stress he'd corralled in his mind. These were the first waking minutes since the mission started that he wasn't thinking about his predicament.

He was thinking about kissing her again when Joshua Pierce entered from his left into the room. Lin stopped playing and he got a feeling in the pit of his stomach like he was woken out of a wonderful sleep by a horrible-sounding alarm clock.

Pierce had one Sentry with him, a sturdy brunette. After a short private conversation, the two went to the bar together and ordered a drink. It looked as if Pierce had a whiskey drink and the Sentry ordered a club soda or Sprite.

After a couple of minutes, they motioned for everyone to gather around in the lounge area where four couches were positioned facing one another around a low center table. Lin joined Kade on one couch; Daniel and Walter took another; Hank sat alone; and Pierce took the one across from Kade. The female Sentry stood on the periphery of the room. Pierce looked around as if he was trying to get a read on everyone's temperament.

"I hope you've had some time to kick back and relax," Pierce said. "We try to do this when we know there's been a great challenge or we're celebrating a milestone."

Kade sat back and rubbed his eyes.

Celebrating survival—that's fucked up.

Pierce took a sip out of his cocktail glass and smacked his lips.

"We have another milestone to announce that'll be important to you. We're relocating you all to another one of our facilities. It'll either be in Montana or Nevada, but we haven't made the final decision yet. The two locations are identical as far as ongoing operations."

"Except for the climate," Kade said.

Pierce nodded with a sniff and shot him an annoyed look.

"Do you all have any questions?"

His mind was now back in high gear. If he was relocated, the FBI would have no idea where he was. There'd be no further chance for support. He also was reminded that Alex was wounded or dead, and the terrible feeling of guilt crept back.

"Why are we moving?" Daniel asked.

"We're running out of adequate space and we have security concerns," Pierce said.

"Is it because of what happened with Carol?" Walter asked.

"It was due to many factors," Pierce said. "We just want to make sure you all continue to develop in an environment with minimal disruption."

"When do we find out where we're going," Lin asked, "so we can let our personal contacts know where we'll be?"

"Relocation will be this Saturday at noon. We'll let you know our destination on that morning, and then you can make your phone calls. That applies to all but one of you."

The pause got everyone's attention.

"Hank—you won't be going with the rest of the Associates. You'll be going home Friday."

CHAPTER 34

Wednesday, June 26
11:17 p.m. (PDT)
AgriteX

Pierce arrived at the vault door of Owens's office five minutes after receiving an instant message on the Chapter internal network asking him to stop by. He stood in front of the surveillance camera and pulled the door open after he heard the whir of its motor disengage.

Pierce wasn't surprised he was being summoned at this late hour, given how close they were to launch, but when he smelled the smoke and saw Owens with a joint this late in the evening, he read it as unusual. Owens normally preferred a vaporizer pen in order to avoid the noxious smoke. Again, always one to use the latest and greatest technology.

"Hey, Marshall."

Owens sat behind his large cherry-toned pedestal desk. The office was windowless, but the illumination was comfortable and had the feel of natural light.

"Hi, Rick, could you please shut the door behind you?"

"Sure."

Pierce felt a split second of fear—first, from being shut in the most secure room in the headquarters, and second, from being called by his true first name. Owens was only one of two people who knew his real name at the Chapter. Dr. Heather Drakos was the other. This secrecy was kept so Pierce could operate completely off the grid. Everyone else knew him by his fake name, Joshua Pierce, which accompanied his AgriteX chief operating officer title and his special assistant title in the Chapter.

In his roles for both the legitimate and underground organizations, Pierce never signed any official document, never had his picture taken, and never made a public statement. He also hadn't spoken on a phone in the almost five years since Marshall had recruited him.

Pierce paused and stared, waiting for Owens to speak. *Is Marshall questioning my loyalty?*

Owens looked serious but pleasant. He took a drink from a mug of steaming tea with lemon in it.

"I've been meaning to have this conversation for many months," Owens said, "and I've put it off—for practical reasons and out of pride."

Pierce moved to the dark brown leather couch in Owens's work area and took a seat next to the front of the desk.

Owens took another slow drag on the joint.

"You already know the transition plan. I'm confident you can carry on the mission if something happens to me."

Pierce nodded like that was a no-brainer, and Owens continued.

"Well, something *is* happening to me now, or has been happening. I've kept information from you. Two things. First is my health. I learned that I have a brain tumor. It might be a result from the first protocol, from years ago. It's not clear."

Pierce exhaled in a whistle.

"Yes," Owens said. "A rare side effect in the older protocol. Mine may not even be related. I learned about it months ago and said nothing about it to anyone here at the Chapter, because I

216

wanted to see how it progressed. I wanted to make sure no one was concerned about their leadership. I've soldiered through. Figured I'd retire and disappear after Phase One. Then have this conversation. But the arc of my life isn't agreeing with me."

"I understand the need to show strength," Pierce said. "You've been our heart and our brain."

"The wake-up call came when I had a seizure two nights ago, late," Owens said. "The Sentry on my security detail that night got Heather. She was able to stabilize me."

"Thank goodness."

"So she knows everything. If I'm incapacitated with another seizure or my condition degenerates more before launch, I'll pass on full command of the Chapter to you. And I'm telling you right now that I'm officially retiring after Phase One. You'll head the Chapter when the dust settles. I'll move on and soon be gone. I'll be lucky if I get a couple of months on a quiet beach somewhere. Maybe Panama."

Pierce now looked floored. "I'm sorry, Marshall. You successfully fooled me."

"I've felt okay up to just a few days ago. On Monday, I felt *bad*."

"I remember—during the meeting with Messia. I thought you just had a headache. I didn't think twice about it. You seem to be handling this very well."

Owens smiled. "I can't explain why I feel calm. I feel happy. Happy about our mission. Happy about the many charitable contributions AgriteX has made since its inception."

Pierce had always thought the charitable work was a distraction, and it was hardly a focus at the moment. Maybe it was the pot talking.

"Anyway," Owens said, "about the second thing. I've kept contact with a handful of key intelligence operatives and I've always restricted their access to only me. They're all former Guardians. Some of the earliest, like you."

Pierce cleared his throat. "I suspected you had your own personal network. That never bothered me."

"But now it's also time I transition these contacts to you," Owens said, "including our routines and means of communicating. One of my key operatives needs to meet tomorrow evening to provide critical information, so that'll be your first priority. Then I'll communicate with each of the others. I'll tell them to expect you in my place from here on out. You already know how to reassemble all of the Guardians for Phase Two planning and execution as part of the transition plan."

Pierce nodded.

"Effective Monday, July eight," Owens continued, "C-E-C becomes part of its new holding company. All finances have been transferred except for a few weeks of cash on hand, and the corporate board that's only existed on paper has been dissolved. I'll give you more information on the various accounts over the next few days."

"So you're saying our transition has already begun," Pierce said.

"Yes. In my life I've been a start-up specialist, and people best suited for start-ups are often not best for the long-term. I take comfort in knowing you'll continue our mission with even greater skill and execution. You're a rare talent, and we wouldn't have come this far without you."

Pierce sighed and took a long pause before he spoke.

"If I can continue with half the leadership and energy you've given us, I've no doubt the Chapter will only continue to strengthen and expand."

Marshall got up and came around the desk to sit down next to him.

"Thank you for your steadfast service. You'll continue what I started here with much success. I'm sure of it."

Pierce now had a faraway but resolute look in his eyes.

"After the attack, people will think that it's the end. But I'll make sure we carry on this war to a new dimension. America will turn to us when we make everyone afraid."

Owens nodded. "*Mamook kwass.*"

CHAPTER 35

Four SUVs arrived within minutes of one another at the single-level green-sided house located twenty miles south of Portland and three miles west of I-5. The group surrendered their phones to David Cisneros and gathered inside the large detached garage. Cisneros made sure all of the phones were powered off.

A laminated topographical map lay on five square feet of the garage's concrete floor. Ten men, eight of them Mexican and two white, sat around the map in lawn chairs. While waiting for the start of the meeting, a few who had worked with one another on past jobs caught up on personal news. Cisneros returned with a case of water and tossed bottles around to everyone. Two oscillating fans tried to circulate the air, but the garage remained warm and stuffy and smelled like paint.

Juan Messia joined the group a few minutes later. He remained standing and pulled out some notes while he started the discussion in Spanish.

"Okay, friends," Messia said. "Leadership has called on us to strike a current supplier who isn't meeting their end of an agreement. The target is AgriteX, a company located out in the forest of the Coast Range. It's about twenty miles straight-line distance southeast of Cannon Beach. AgriteX has a large security team and I know their company's president, Marshall Owens. He's former Army Special Forces. I expect his force to be well trained and armed, but I'm confident our plan will offset any advantages they might have. We have solid information on their patrol routes and activities, and we know they have holes in their security."

The group paid even closer attention after Messia touched on the degree of difficulty.

"The primary mission," Messia said, "is to take possession of a large load of marijuana seed that's rightfully ours. It's been paid for already, but our leadership no longer believes that AgriteX will deliver it. So we have to be prepared to pick up a possible thirty thousand pounds of this seed. That means we'll need thirty trucks and maybe a couple extras."

Messia picked up a billiards cue stick leaning against the cinder block wall. He pointed to a small pile of cut-out cardboard squares that had been marked with a black Sharpie. There were five counters marked "A" through "E." Next to it was a similar pile of squares marked "SUV" and a pile of squares marked with "TR," for pickup truck. He placed these various counters down on the map while he spoke.

"To secure the seed, we need to neutralize their security force. While we stage this attack, we stay on the public lands as long as possible, since they won't be patrolling that area." Messia traced the border of the private land marked in red. "I'll provide maps and GPS before you leave today. All vehicles will be moved offroad on public land and covered with the A-TACS camouflage nets. Lead vehicles will need bolt cutters in case you run into locked pole gates. License plates will be swapped out with those in our inventory.

"Ramos, you're the Alpha Team leader, and Munoz is your assistant. Your team will take a position on this high ground southwest of their headquarters and be the main attacking force, following along Grassy Lake Creek toward the target.

"Garcia, you're Bravo Team leader. Harmon is your assistant. Your team is going to stage on the main AgriteX road approaching from the south, about a thousand meters short of the private land marker.

"Figueroa, you're Charlie Team leader, with Santos assisting. You will stage on the western approach road short of this ridgeline.

"Alvarado, you're the Delta Team leader, and your team will secure the entire northern route from Little Jack Creek to protect the convoy route as we move the seed out."

Alvarado looked disappointed he wasn't participating in the main attack, but Messia moved on, as he knew Alvarado was the least experienced of his team leaders.

"Teams Bravo and Charlie will move in to load the seed following the attack by Alpha, bringing vehicles from the west and south. We're going to use these Midland two-way radios for communications, channel thirteen.

"And Team Echo, led by Ramirez and Sandoval, will be with me during the attack."

Messia omitted his own team's location—on that small chance he might be betrayed, the other teams wouldn't know his position. His personal security team was comprised of those people he'd known the longest.

"So the night will begin with the attack by Team Alpha from the southwest," Messia said. "First objective is to locate and secure the seed. We are looking for black-and-white bags labeled "Erosion Control Seed" from the Hopkins Seed Company. At every opportunity, we kill their patrolling force while retrieving the seed, and damage or destroy their office. I want Marshall Owens taken alive if possible."

Messia split up the remainder of the TR and SUV markers between the Bravo, Charlie, and Delta teams.

"We're spreading out the load vehicles," he said. "In case we encounter difficulties, we'll be able to get the loading started or, worst case, still bring back part of the load. Your teams will ensure all weapons are test fired within the next three days and all vehicles inspected. We can't have any breakdowns. Once in position, don't turn on your vehicles until the attack starts. And no cigarettes, guys."

Messia pointed to several areas marked with a "PC" on the map.

"Once the attack begins, you will establish armed checkpoints at these locations so AgriteX can't get any vehicles out. Make sense?"

There were nods all around.

"Now, about the compensation," he said, twirling the cue stick. "The size of the cash payments you and your teams receive are contingent on bringing back the seed."

Messia pointed to another hand-drawn floor map on the other side of the garage.

"We have drawings of the headquarters and the surrounding area we'll get to later. We believe the person who got this key information for us is now dead, since they are no longer in contact."

Messia paused as he thought about the bravery of Carol Ries and the brief relationship they had. He needed more Carols and fewer gang mercenaries, but people like Carol were years in the making. Messia then thought of how the Nehalem hit had turned into a mess with one killed and one captured, and it reminded him of his next point.

"We need people on your teams we can trust. We're going to review the lists of all the people who you have assembled, and we want you to pick the best."

There were nods all around him. Messia then looked at Cisneros, which reminded him that maybe he should try to break the tension just a little bit.

"David won't be coming along on this attack due to the physical requirements of the strike." Messia pointed his thumb at Cisneros's belly. "We'd need an extra truck just for that."

Everyone laughed and Cisneros acted like he was offended.

"So my friends, any questions so far?" Messia asked.

"Yeah, when's the attack?" Garcia asked.

Messia paused, and his demeanor changed again to complete seriousness. He bounced the thick end of the stick on the cement.

"We attack on the Fourth of July. Oregon people love their fireworks, so no one will think twice about any faraway noise we'll be making in the forest. If anyone leaks the attack date, I will hold everyone in this room personally responsible. I will give you all a number to call if you are caught by the authorities. This will connect you with a lawyer I know, and you will say nothing to anyone else. But *do not* get caught. Am I clear?"

Messia made eye contact with everyone and they nodded in response.

"Any final questions before we dive deeper into the attack plan?"

"Yeah," Cisneros said, "the question I'm sure is on everyone's mind but they are too cowardly to ask."

Messia suddenly looked very concerned. "And what's that?"

"What are we doing for lunch?"

Everyone laughed.

Messia pointed at Cisneros with the stick. "I don't know," he said, "but since you've given it serious thought, you're now in charge!"

CHAPTER 36

A number of automated cameras alerted the guard to the vehicle's approach on the commercial route, and he immediately passed on the plate number for analysis. The make and model didn't match any vehicle on the appointment list for today, and visitors were required to provide that information to book an appointment. He then notified Joshua Pierce that three unidentified males were on their way to see him.

Special Agents Graves, Jenkins, and Stephenson walked through the entrance atrium, paused for a minute at the fountain to speak a few words to one another, then approached the security desk.

"Good morning, gentlemen," the guard said. "May I help you?"

Graves stepped in front and rested his hands on the security desk. He was short and middle-aged with a bad comb-over. His face, including his sizable jowl, was pink from a mild sunburn.

"Hi," he said, showing his credentials. "I'm Agent Neal Graves with the DEA. We need to speak to three of your employees: Walter Lefear, Hank Stanfield, and Kinkade Sims."

"I'm sure we can help. And what's this regarding?"

"Those three were witnesses to a shooting that occurred in Nehalem on Tuesday," Graves said.

"Okay, just one second." The guard spoke into his headset while typing on the keyboard in front of him. "We have three gentlemen here from the DEA who would like to speak to Walter Lefear, Hank Stanfield, and Kinkade Sims about a shooting in Nehalem."

Joshua Pierce's voice came through the guard's headset and told him what to say.

"Lefear and Stanfield are being notified," the guard said, "and HR will bring them out soon. But Kinkade Sims isn't here, because he's no longer an employee."

Graves looked like he was at a loss for words, so Jenkins stepped closer and spoke.

"Mr. Sims told the Tillamook County Sheriff on Tuesday that he was an employee of AgriteX."

"One moment," the guard said. "Our HR director will be out to speak with you. She'll explain the situation, if you could please have a seat over there." The guard pointed to a reception area.

The three men sat down in the nearby U-shaped nook and sent a few text messages to one another until a tall blond woman in her early forties emerged from the secure access door carrying a tablet computer and a clipped bundle of papers. The three agents stood up and introduced themselves with names only.

"Hi, I'm Kathie Lautermann," she said, and glanced down at her notes. "We'll have Walter Lefear and Hank Stanfield out shortly. The Kinkade Sims situation—I thought I'd come and give you the details about that myself."

"And where is he?" Stephenson asked.

"As of yesterday, we don't know any more," she said, "and here's why—on Tuesday we received the urinalysis results from Mr. Sims as part of a random drug test we conducted the previous week. Mr. Sims failed the test, so we terminated his employment immediately per company policy."

Jenkins felt a slight chill when she said *terminated*.

"So if he's not here, where can we find him now?" Jenkins asked.

"I have his mailing address for Herndon, Virginia," she said, "which is where he told us to send any subsequent paperwork. I assume that's where he'd be returning to."

"Wait—Sims was working here as recently as last week, but his address is Virginia?" Jenkins asked. "That doesn't make sense."

"Yes, he was part of our management training program, which includes free onsite boarding," she said.

"How long was he an employee?" Stephenson asked.

Lautermann referred to the printout in her hand.

"His employment agreement was signed on June tenth," she said, "so with the twenty-sixth being his last day of work, he was with us just a couple of weeks."

"So did you escort him out the door here and leave him in the parking lot?" Jenkins asked.

She gave Jenkins a look that showed she didn't appreciate his tone.

"No, as part of his termination outprocessing, we offered to cover the expense of a flight home and transportation to PDX, but he signed a waiver. He requested to be dropped off in downtown Portland, and so we did that late yesterday afternoon."

"And where was he dropped off?" Jenkins asked.

"Waterfront Park."

Lautermann watched Jenkins and Stephenson write notes. Graves didn't write any.

"Any idea why Sims was at the location of the shooting—the Nehalem Clinic?" Stephenson asked.

"Yes," she replied. "It was part of the management training program—volunteer work to instill in our new hires how important it is to give back to the community."

The security access door opened and Stanfield and Lefear emerged wearing jeans and AgriteX logo polo shirts. Lautermann waved them over and they sat down.

"I'll leave you gentlemen alone to talk. If you need to reach me again, let Ken know at the security desk, and after today, feel free to call me direct," she said, and handed out three business cards.

"Thank you, Kathie," Graves said.

Lautermann exited through the secure access door, walked down the hall, and stopped to look out into the entrance atrium through the one-way glass. A minute later, Joshua Pierce joined her there.

"Let me guess, they aren't satisfied," Pierce said.

"They probably won't be. They seem very interested in Kinkade Sims."

"Yeah, I heard the whole thing and agree with you. Thanks, you handled that beautifully."

"Thank you," she said. "I worked with PR on the statement for Cummings. Our condolences go out to his family. We are deeply saddened by the violence. All that good stuff."

"Great," Pierce said. "Let security know that when Lefear and Stanfield are done, we'll need a full debrief."

CHAPTER 37

There were no early-morning knocks at the door that disturbed him. It was the popping sound of gunfire outside that finally woke Kade up, and after a moment of panic, thinking it might be some kind of FBI rescue, he concluded it was more Chapter training. The firing was occurring in regular bursts of a minute or so. He looked toward the barred window and saw it was daylight, and then glanced at his computer and saw the time.

He sat up in his bed and cursed himself for sleeping in so ridiculously late, and for drinking the night prior, since he still felt fatigued. The computer screen had also changed again:

**You are 2 days overdue in downloading the
required Daily Update.**

The prompt was now red. He ignored it, rolled out of bed, and checked the door, finding it locked. He went to the dresser and pulled out the last clean AgriteX uniform with a T-shirt, pair of socks, and underwear while he formulated a number of excuses to get himself out of the room.

They've got us locked down until the relocation, forty-eight hours from now. I've got to do whatever it takes to get out of here now. Screw the attorney general's guidelines.

I've had enough sleep to last me three days. Time to get back to work.

He brought the clothes inside the bathroom with him. After a three-minute shower, he left the water running for the next five while he got dressed. This gave him time to retrieve the Glock and two extra clips from inside the toilet tank and remove them from their plastic bags.

The weapon still looked dry and clean when he inspected it. He slid it back in the rear of his pants, cinching the nylon belt tight and pulling the tail of his crinkly shirt down. He put each ammo clip inside a dirty sock and stuck one in each cargo pocket.

Another pile of his dirty clothes sat just outside his bathroom in the alcove. Someone must have washed a load for him after he'd arrived and restocked his drawer, but he suspected the laundry delivery service wasn't going to happen for him again. He bear-hugged the entire dirty clothes pile and dropped it in the middle of the room with a *whump*.

"Hey, Chapter Concierge," he said toward the cameras and speaker. "Where's the laundry room in this place?"

He waited ten seconds but there was no response.

"Hello up there? I need some clean clothes, stat. I'm on my last pair of clean underwear. Can't be freeballing here. We leave in two days."

The familiar soothing voice came back through the speaker.

"A Sentry will be there in a moment to take you to the laundry room."

"All right, thanks. And where'd the nice spa music go? My honeymoon's over?"

The spa music piped through the speaker again.

"There we go," he said.

Five minutes later, a few light knocks on the door preceded Sentry Hill entering. He held another paper cup with Kade's medication.

"Sims, I've got to watch you take another pill today, Dr. Drakos's orders."

"Yeah, I got it," Kade said. "Can you take me to lunch after the laundry?"

"Yes, I can."

Kade took his pill and then exited after Hill, walking beside him to the laundry room. Once Kade stuffed his laundry into one of the four large side-loading washers and ran it, Hill led him down to the café. During the walk, looking through the window to the entrance atrium, he could see two Sentries and a Guardian escorting a man in handcuffs and wearing a hood into the building. The man wore dirty jeans and a bloodstained white T-shirt.

"Who's that?" Kade asked.

"Probably another trespasser," Hill said.

"Like me?"

"I don't think so."

"You guys want me to wash those nasty hoods while I'm at it?"

Hill grunted a laugh. "No."

Inside the café, Kade saw two Sentries eating together and Hank sitting at a table by himself. He followed Hill through the lunch line and the server put spaghetti, garlic bread, and salad on their plates.

"Where's the lunch crowd?" Kade asked Hill.

"Out on duty or training."

Hill went and sat with the other two Sentries on the opposite side of the cafe. Hank waved, so Kade headed in his direction. He noticed Hank was wearing jeans and an AgriteX logo polo shirt. Hank also had a strange look on his face, which wasn't all that unusual.

But he looks nonthreatening. That's good.

"How do I get one of those cool shirts?" Kade asked.

"I can't believe you're here," Hank said.

"Oh yeah, why's that?" He sat down and saw Hank had already finished his lunch.

"Let's face this way so the cameras can't see our lips," Hank said. "And let's just keep smiles on our faces the whole time we're talking here, huh?"

"Uh, okay, sure, no problem."

Hank leaned back in his chair so he could scan the area without turning his head.

"So I was just interviewed by the Drug Enforcement Agency about the shootout at the clinic," Hank said.

"No shit?"

"Yeah, and when they were questioning me, one of them asked me if I had talked to you after the shooting, but before you were terminated."

"Terminated?"

"Yeah," Hank said. "The agents said the AgriteX Human Resources lady told them you failed a urinalysis and were let go. They asked me if I ever saw you taking drugs and I said no. When I was done, they told me I was forbidden to talk to you about it, so here I am disobeying that order. It looks like those Sentries over there didn't get the memo."

Kade felt an indescribable mix of fear and fury. He bit his tongue hard and tried to mentally regroup. He smiled and forced a fake laugh.

"That's very interesting," he said. "I don't remember any urinalysis. Sounds like their right hand ain't talking to the left. Thanks for sharing. Anything else they discussed I should know?"

"No, I just went through the shooting again, play-by-play. Nothing you don't know."

Kade nodded. "So are you happy to be going home?"

"Funny you should ask," Hank said. "I don't believe it. I don't think I'm going home at all."

"What? Why not?"

"Think about it. I have a death sentence that no one's bothered to tell me about."

Kade nodded and ate a few bites of food. "Yeah, that's true. So what are you going to do now?"

"I don't know, but I'm not waiting around for one of these thugs to put a bullet in me. That's not the way I'm going out. I'm going to leave and try and enjoy whatever little time I have left. My question to you is, are you coming with me?"

Kade couldn't think fast enough. The word *terminated* blazed in his mind. *Terminated* is what he and Hank now had in common, but he wasn't sure if he could depend on Hank either. He wanted his own plan on his own terms.

"I don't know, man," Kade said. "Maybe . . . I think they've got way too many guards with itchy fingers out on patrol right now. Why didn't you just skip town when we were down at the Nehalem Clinic or tell the DEA you were in danger?"

"'Cause I swore I'd give Heather Drakos a piece of my mind before I leave. She's responsible for my disease."

Kade nodded. "Yeah, she's done a lot of damage. How did you get caught up in this mess to begin with?"

"It sounded like a great idea way back," Hank said. "I was finishing my term as mayor, and the Chapter somehow took notice and recruited me so I could be better groomed for my next step—Congress. They accepted me after some interviews and a questionnaire, and they promised support and financing to accelerate my political career. There's already a good number of state and local politicians who've been through the program. I know some of them and they referred me. It was like a chance to be a part of a secret club."

"Couldn't you just run a campaign and raise money the old-fashioned way?"

"I believed this would give me an edge. Superior financing. Deep information on our opponents. That's what it takes to win campaigns these days. I'm not exactly sure how they're doing it, but the Chapter, AgriteX, or whoever, is funding the Domestic Strength Coalition—a nonpartisan super PAC with a platform focused on the environment and domestic security. It supports campaigns for over three hundred graduates of our program."

Kade contemplated why the Chapter would support greater domestic security when its militia would be considered a domestic security threat. That didn't seem to make sense.

"So you took a two-year break from politics for this?" Kade asked.

"No, the political action program, or P-A-P, is five months," Hank said, "and I was in one of many groups around the country that finished in May. Mine was based in a small temporary office in Chicago. They wanted to position a large number of us for the Congressional elections a year and a half from now. When I finished my last term as mayor, I'd already thought about taking two years to get ready for a run."

Groups around the country.

So this is a coordinated national operation.

"How'd you end up here in Oregon then?" Kade asked.

"While at the PAP, they approached me about a chance to participate in a new personalized training program, or protocol, they called it, one that would give me a bigger personal edge. They said it would require an extra ninety days at the headquarters. I didn't realize I had a botched surgical procedure as part of my stay. I thought I was undergoing some preliminary tests and that was all."

"But you went along with it because you wanted to win."

"Exactly."

As one of the Sentries passed by their table for a drink refill, Hank switched to talking about his interest in hockey. Kade played along until the Sentry returned to his own table. "How about all of the military drills outside?" Kade asked. "What's that all about?"

"I don't know. We were always told that as we helped to create an environment for political change, the Chapter could come under attack by those who want to maintain the status quo."

"Sounds like some of my downloads. But I might be a coin or two behind you."

"I'm just past silver on my program," Hank said.

"I guess by the time you hit gold, you're near the end of the Associate program and ready for the next step. A leap of faith."

"More like a leap from a ledge."

Kade saw Hill take a cell phone call and look over toward him.

"I think my time just ran out," Kade said. "Quick, what's your plan?"

"It starts tomorrow with a seven o'clock appointment with Heather."

"For what?" Kade asked while watching Hill get up from the table. Kade started to reach behind his back toward his Glock until he could see Hill didn't have a weapon in his hand.

"I'm having another medical exam," Hank said. "I pissed myself a few times on purpose as an excuse to get an exam, and that usually doesn't go with migraines."

"So how can I help y—?" Kade asked just as Hill shouted.

"Sims!" Hill was about twenty feet away, walking toward them. "Your lunchtime is over. I've got to get you back to your room."

The other two Sentries had also risen and were right behind him. Kade thought he could make a break for it on the walk back to his room if he'd only been escorted by Hill, but now with the additional two armed Sentries, he didn't like the odds.

"I can't finish my laundry?" Kade asked.

"We'll get it to you," Hill said. Kade watched Hill's eyes and face and read that Hill meant business.

"Okay, cool. You can't beat the service around here," Kade said. He stood up and Hank reached across the table to give him a fist bump.

"Be safe," Hank said.

CHAPTER 38

The energy of D8 Work Crew One was contagious, and the team's demonstrated readiness for the mission made Sentry Robertson even more confident. Robertson returned to his desk at the Camp Walpole inmate mentor staff office, satisfied after inspecting each of the soldiers assigned to him.

Fifty inmate-soldiers had been selected for two special "work crews" from the two hundred fifty-seven inmates in the camp. Work Crew One and Two had nothing to do with the regular work shifts and duties around the camp, but headquarters had given the attack teams nicknames to help keep communications secure.

As directed by headquarters, today Robertson made sure the crew member orders had been properly received in their program download. He quizzed each of the men to validate their understanding of the plan and the rules of engagement, and he answered their questions only within the permitted scope. Granted, the soldiers didn't know the full relevance of the district eight attack. They knew the risk and believed that success would bring them freedom and a cash bonus. Then they were "on their own" once the attack was over.

Robertson felt a little guilty about deceiving his troops, knowing they were disposable, but he knew the blend of security and discipline Marshall Owens instituted from the top was necessary to make this force effective. And he was not naïve enough to think that he was privy to the whole operation either. As part of the vanguard force, he wasn't sure about what would happen to him after the mission was over.

He finished filling out the mandatory checklist on the obscure and innocuous secure website created for this purpose and clicked "Submit." Minutes later, Sentry Wolf came into the staff room with an excited look on his face.

"I was told they're finished with the paint job," he said. "Want to go take a look?"

"Sure."

They exited the two-story red-brick administrative building and walked down the sidewalk until it connected to the main street running through the center of the camp.

"I drove the route to the target one more time," Wolf said.

"Good," Robertson said. "You've caught up fast since we lost Phillips. We'll review the grounds map and floor plan of the house a couple more times."

"Your local surveillance was good," Wolf said.

"Thanks."

They walked past the basketball courts, a pasture with several milking cows, and a two-acre vegetable garden with an elaborate barrier of eight-foot-high wire fencing to keep the deer out. They turned left and headed down the sidewalk, past the armory toward the camp motor pool.

"You were at headquarters for a good while," Robertson said. "Tell me—that had to be exciting, being at the nerve center of the revolution."

"*So* great," Wolf said. "But I'm glad I'm out in the field now for the action. To see the whole plan through."

"A chance to be a hero."

Wolf shook his head on that point.

"No, I don't think so. Most people outside the Chapter are going to think this is a cowardly act; they won't understand the importance. They'll call it a senseless attack on civilians when it's just a bold way to bring about change. Too many lives have been lost because of these spineless politicians and bureaucrats. They're cowards every day. Now it's finally payback time. We'll try to minimize collateral damage"

"You weren't around for the crew training we did with stun guns and firearms," Robertson said. "The crews know their rules of engagement—cold."

"Awesome."

They entered the motor pool area and went inside a covered garage and maintenance bay. The doors and windows had been left open to ventilate the fumes from the enamel spray paint. Two prison buses freshly repainted in school bus yellow were parked in the center.

"Brilliant," Robertson said.

"Oh yeah."

New black lettering on the side read "MILTON AREA SCHOOL DISTRICT." The windows, unlike those on a standard school bus, were moderately tinted.

Robertson pointed to the black SUV parked nearby.

"That's the escape vehicle," he said. "We're making final load preparations."

"I think SRV—Sentry Recovery Vehicle—is the name in the plan," Wolf said.

"Whatever, Mr. Acronym!"

Wolf laughed. He was happy he and Robertson had hit it off. He walked over to the SUV and opened the rear left door.

"So which side are you going to be on?" he asked.

"I'll be on the left," Robertson said, "the congressman on the right. Want to keep him away from the driver. If something happens to me, you move from shotgun to the backseat. We'll go through this again, don't worry."

"Good."

"My understanding is that our program will hibernate after mission complete?" Robertson asked. "Then somehow we'll be recontacted and reassembled? Did you learn any more about that at headquarters?"

"There's not much else," Wolf said. "Our last download is going to contain a message on how to recontact leadership, but for security reasons, the message isn't going to appear for months. So you're right. We maintain complete silence until that future date. The program will go dormant except for monitoring what we say, and at some point we'll be re-audited."

"Nothing you can tell me about the big picture though, huh?" Robertson asked.

"No," Wolf said. "There will be a gaping hole created in the nation's leadership, and my guess is the next stage is going to involve filling it. I'm sure Marshall Owens knows, but we're too low down the chain of command for him to tell us. Still, I trust him completely. He's always wanted the best for his people . . . before the Chapter even existed."

"You worked for him before?"

"Yeah, I ran the mail room back at his old company, NetStatz, after I left the Marines. He's a winner. That man always has every single detail worked out. Anyway, after this attack I'll be going back to Minnesota to do some fishing and hunting and just sit on my bonus for a while."

"Nice," Robertson said. "I've got two brothers in DC and I'm going to get some temp work as a private security guard. Otherwise I'll go crazy."

"Maybe we can plan on—"

Their cell phones chimed with text messages in unison. They both looked at each other and read the message.

TRAINING EXERCISE IS CONFIRMED FOR SAT, JUL 6.

Robertson and Wolf both looked up and slapped each other a high five.

"Shit yeah, that's next Saturday," Wolf said. "It's on!"

CHAPTER 39

Kade made it look like he was sleeping during the late evening, first in the easy chair, and then some more after moving to the bed around midnight, staying fully clothed. If someone came to *terminate* him during the night, he would be ready with his shoes and clothes on. He'd logged into the computer and dimmed the screen so he could keep track of the time. The overdue login warning now appeared in blinking red:

> **You are 3 days overdue in downloading the required Daily Update.**

He lay on his back with just the bed blanket covering him. His hand touched the grip of the Glock, which was now loaded and pressed against the side of his leg. Earlier, during a bathroom break, he'd quietly pulled the slide to chamber a round.

Escape options fell into two categories: either breaking out of the room or waiting until someone came in. He didn't like having zero control of the timing in the wait option. And the surveillance cameras made any action on his part to break out even more difficult. He really didn't like any of his options, but it was his own damn fault for missing earlier chances.

His conversation with Hank had been cut off, so they hadn't figured out a way they might coordinate a combined effort. He guessed Hank would go to one of the two employee health clinic suites for his appointment with Dr. Drakos, but which one?

It would take Kade less than a minute to get there in a sprint if he shot the lock off the door and broke out right after seven, but he'd be under surveillance the whole way, and the gunshot would attract instant attention. Sentries would most likely come with guns drawn and would shoot on sight. He wouldn't make it very far, probably not even out of the building.

While he felt he couldn't wait any longer, he wavered on strategy. Did it make sense to go help Hank or just go on his own? Hank wasn't in the best medical condition. Could Hank even make a run for it? His tumor had degraded his mental and emotional faculties. But Hank now had a nothing-to-lose mentality, which at least seemed to provide assurance of a fearless ally.

Kade rolled his head to the side and glanced toward the door. At the bottom of the door was a plastic cafeteria tray from when Hill had brought dinner at around six. Kade left it there with the water glass balanced on the doorknob above it to alert him if someone attempted to open the door quietly and he didn't hear the click of the automatic lock. And even though he'd flipped the dead bolt, he assumed that could be opened from the outside.

He traced the ceiling back from the door, past the ventilation grate he knew was too small and secured to be of use, when his eyes fixed on a common detail he'd overlooked. A smoke detector. He turned his head and scanned the rest of the ceiling and saw a single sprinkler head on the ceiling near the bed.

A fire. That would make them come to me. The sprinkler would help douse the fire if it gets too big and hot, but it might get big enough to help me.

Now the question was how the hell he could start a fire. After ruling out trying to create an electrical fire with one of the outlets, he recalled a few funny memories of Alex and him goofing around, starting fires in unusual ways while camping. In one instance they'd used a AA battery and a staple, following instructions from a YouTube video. Useful, of course, if only he had a battery and a staple.

But he *did* have both.

He slid his Glock under the pillow and prayed the person attending the surveillance monitors wouldn't be watching closely for the next few minutes. He rolled out of bed to take another fake bathroom break and on the way he opened his dresser drawer, grabbing some of the plastic packaging that he'd left in there. He also picked up the plastic trash can next to the easy chair, a dirty T-shirt, and the disposable razor. He shut the bathroom door behind him and turned on the light. There was no smoke detector or sprinkler head in the bathroom. This could work.

Taking a seat on the toilet, he took out the digital camera from the tongue of his boot and carefully removed the cylindrical miniature lithium battery from it. He was careful not to disturb the tiny memory card that now contained some key photos. He crushed the head of his disposable razor beneath the heel of his hiking shoe and separated the blade from the plastic.

He used the blade to scrape away some of the plastic around the negative pole of the battery and made a thin groove just under it. Removing one of the staples left on the discarded clothes packaging, he straightened it out and reformed it into a U shape. While holding the battery, he inserted one end of the U into the groove. When he was satisfied, he set it on the sink counter. He flushed the toilet for no good reason other to make it seem like he had other business going on.

He opened the cabinet below the sink and pulled out all of the toilet paper rolls and tissue boxes. He packed the trash can he'd brought inside and the one already in the bathroom tight with paper. He pulled the cardboard out of the one remaining toilet paper roll and put it on the tile floor, setting the rigged battery next to it.

When he was finished, he flushed the toilet again to hide the noise of his pulling the shower curtain rod off its mount and sliding the curtain off it. He turned off the light, exited the bathroom and shut the door behind him.

On his way back to the bed, he pulled the string on the window shade to flatten the slats. He'd try to keep the room dark as long as possible in the morning. He sat down on the bed facing the computer and saw that he'd spent about ten minutes in the bathroom. He coughed a few times, groaning and holding his belly like he had some gastric issues. After a minute, he lay down, curled in a fetal position, until eventually, he got under his blanket again and stretched out on his back. He slid the Glock down by his side and laid his hand on top of it.

He was ready. Now he'd lay and wait until just before seven.

CHAPTER 40

Pierce found Owens outside, a few hundred yards away from the headquarters building, at one of his favorite morning meditative spots, drinking tea from a travel mug. He was sitting on a comfortable all-weather bench overlooking a small stream with moss-covered rocks breaking the water's surface. Pierce thumped over the wooden footbridge and sat down next to him. Owens saw Pierce was holding a manila folder.

"Are you sure you don't want to go to your office?" Pierce asked.

"No, right here is secure enough. Hell, it might be safer than inside, given eighty percent of security is out on patrol."

"Well, you're not going to like this," Pierce said. "For starters, I spoke to Paul. He told me there's an FBI operation in play against us right now. He said it started no later than June tenth and is projected to run through mid-July."

Owens's demeanor darkened.

"That lines up with the timeline he projected months ago. If this is true, which I'll assume it is, given Paul's track record, they may know about the launch."

"No, I don't think they know yet. I thought about that on my drive back. I think if they knew our attack was imminent, given the size and scope, they would have already moved on us here at least, if not in other locations. No, I think they're just starting to collect information on us. Financial. Communications . . ."

Owens looked up at the sky through the forest canopy.

"I don't think they have drones up," Pierce said. "I've entertained the possibility there might be some collaboration between the FBI and Messia. With our increased patrols, we've found some Mexican nationals hiding in the area. Six to be exact. We interrogated two of them and they told us that they were paid to test our security, but they were unable to give us more than a first name for a contact. We're still holding them. I wonder how many we haven't detected. Maybe that whole visit by Messia was planned by the FBI."

"I'd think their collaboration isn't likely, but it's possible," Owens said. "Messia could be cooperating to avoid charges."

"Yes, he could. But here's what I do know, and it's more bad news: the FBI did penetrate us with a spy."

"You mean Carol Ries was working for them too?"

"No, Kade Sims *is* working for them."

Owens's mouth hung open for a few seconds and then he shook his head.

"No, I don't believe it."

"Believe it," Pierce said. "Let's begin with the timing. Paul's source said the start of the Bureau's operation against us was about June tenth. Sims showed up on June eighth."

Owens tilted his head to each side as if weighing that piece of information.

"Okay. So what?"

"Marshall, I'm just getting started. And forgive me for saying this, but I think you've suspended your better judgment here, because you developed a liking for the kid."

"I couldn't care less about him."

"No, I've seen it. You've treated him differently. Because he's a techie, and he has a military background. An army background."

"No, I haven't."

"Yes, you have, because he reminds you of Todd."

When he heard Pierce speak his son's name, Owens's eyes flashed with rage and he aimed a blow at Pierce's jaw right from where he sat. Pierce raised his forearm and easily deflected the punch upward. Owens attempted to connect on another swing, and the second time, Pierce grabbed Owens's wrist in a firm hold.

"Listen to me, damn it," Pierce said in a tense whisper. "I don't blame you for feeling that way. I've got to hand it to them. They picked a dysfunctional, bright-eyed kid. They somehow delivered him to us in a real car wreck complete with serious but not life-threatening injuries. His background story was almost flawless. He's the kind of guy anybody would like, including me, but particularly you. You wanted to take him under your wing. We went with the Verax as per procedure, but the Verax machine doesn't work on him because he's an anomaly. In fact, he is *the* anomaly documented in the old DARPA project. I went back and looked at your copy of the design specifications from the initial study and did some additional research. Look at this."

Owens already appeared shocked. Pierce pulled out two photocopied pages from the folder and handed them to him.

"This information came in an hour ago," Pierce said. "Look—they listed the last four digits of the Social Security number on the test subject, and the military unit on the study documentation. Here's the page from your copy of the study that you scanned into our database. Then I had a contact at the National Personnel Records Center pull Sims's army records. As you can see—same SSN and assigned unit on each."

Owens took the page and stared at it, dumbfounded. Then he handed it back to Pierce and set his face down inside his palm and pinched his temples.

"The FBI must have gambled on the flaw still being there," Owens said. "And it worked."

"So the Verax provided nonsensical results on Sims the first time. We learned from going through Sims's apartment and medicine cabinet that he had a prescription for a mood stabilizer. When we conveyed this information to Heather, she suggested we put him back on medication, thinking that otherwise he might not give accurate answers on the next test. When we realized that the cartel had someone inside, we put everyone through the Verax, including Sims. This time his responses made sense, but the machine didn't indicate he was lying. It looks like somehow he was able to beat the machine this time at will. We don't know how."

Pierce paused but Owens didn't comment, so he went on.

"I should've held firm to the other areas of his background check being completed and this wouldn't have occurred. We should've kept him in isolation. But we did finally complete the check. We cross-checked audio of his sister obtained from our surveillance team with that of the recorded conversations Sims had with his supposed sister when he phoned home. The voices didn't match. The number Sims called had to be an FBI line. Part of his cover."

Owens didn't respond; he just kept nodding.

Pierce said, "And finally, I got more information on the shooting at Nehalem Clinic. The name and address of the victim who was transferred to Emanuel. His name is Alex Pace, and his address in McLean, Virginia, matched that of Sims. When we went back to the notes from checking out Sims's apartment, it also confirmed that."

Owens displayed a look of confusion. "So Sims and this Pace guy are working for the Bureau, and Pace tried to collect information on the cartel? We missed something here."

"Or Sims was trying to pass intelligence to Pace. We know there's a linkage. I'm not sure the 'how' matters. I know you told me you were sure no one knew Todd was your son other than his mother when he died in Afghanistan. But maybe the Bureau or one of the other agencies made that connection. Maybe it was a weakness they somehow exploited."

Owens opened his mouth as if to speak, but returned to his thoughts for a minute. He reached and patted Pierce on the shoulder. Pierce flinched and then laughed.

"I thought you were going to try and hit me again," Pierce said.

"No, I'm too damn weak to hit you," Owens said, and sighed. "I accept all of your insights. I'm sorry I lost my temper. I'm sorry I haven't been . . . trusting enough. You're more than a partner and friend. You're like a brother. Your judgment has been impeccable and obviously mine has been flawed."

"Given your condition, I understand," Pierce said. "But we're still on track. Ours is the right mission, and with a few adjustments, we'll succeed. All preparations are in order. Since I believe we're now under surveillance here, I recommend we cancel the attack from L-FAC only. All others continue. The Bureau and the cartel are now too focused on our headquarters. I'll deploy the mobile command unit to guide and monitor the launch. All of our intellectual property will be removed from the headquarters ahead of schedule. All necessary relocation will occur and personnel redeployed prior to the launch ahead of schedule. A skeleton crew will remain at AgriteX and L-FAC during the actual attack."

"Great recommendations. I approve," Owens said. "Keep digging for more information on what Messia is up to."

"I will. I also think you should go forward with your own personal Phase Two."

"No, I think that's the only recommendation of yours I'll dis-agree with. I'll remain here for this battle. I think it'll be more fun than sitting on a beach somewhere, looking over my shoulder."

Pierce wasn't going to argue that point.

"Okay. And what about the final disposition of Sims?" Pierce asked.

"I wish we would've had the time to fully indoctrinate him. Make sure he's on lockdown in his room. Do a final reading on Verax and an interrogation to see if he turns up any information we can use. Let me know the result. Then kill him—quickly and in private. Tell the other Associates he was made a Guardian and sent on a mission. And deal with Alex Pace."

Pierce nodded as the vibrating ring from his two-way radio buzzed in his pocket. He pulled it out.

"Pierce," he responded. He listened to what security told him and his eyes began to dart around. "Okay, when the team gets the situation under control, take him straight to the Isolation Room."

Pierce turned toward Owens, shoved the radio back into his belt holder, and unholstered his Sig Sauer.

"There's a fire alarm reported from Sims's room," he said. "And we have a distress alarm from Heather's office."

CHAPTER 41

As soon as the smoke detector shrieked its ear-splitting tone, Kade clubbed the surveillance camera off the top of the wall with the shower curtain rod. He stomped on the camera with the heel of his boot and dashed back toward the bathroom, where the two trash cans in the bathroom were burning more fiercely by the second.

Holding a soaked bath towel, he grabbed each can in turn by its base and set them side by side in the seat of the easy chair and pushed the chair up against the door. The plastic was already melting on the trash cans and now smoke was clouding the front area of the room. Kade pushed the bed up against the back of the easy chair and tossed the bedspread on the burning pile.

He moved inside the bathroom and shut the door, first guzzling water from the faucet. He pulled a water-soaked T-shirt from inside the tub and tied it around his mouth, and then got down on the floor on his stomach, looking out under the crack in the door. The bathroom smoke stung his eyes, and he kept wiping tears away so he could see.

Less than a minute later, the room door opened inward with a forceful jolt, creating about a three-inch space.

"Get me the fuck out of here, man!" he screamed as loud as he could.

The second jolt of the door pushed it open a foot wide. There was a blast from a CO_2 fire extinguisher through the space, and then another heavy bump against the door that pushed the burning barricade back a few more inches. He could see there was now enough space for a person to get through. He stepped back into the tub and crouched down holding his Glock at the ready. The tiled front wall of the shower gave him a little cover.

The bathroom door flew open, inward, banged against the side of the tub, and he saw Sentry Hill step inside, bringing a cloud of smoke with him. Hill held a stun gun extended in his right hand and a can of pepper spray in his left. Kade had a split second as Hill looked straight forward, not seeing him low to his right.

"Drop it!" Kade yelled. "Both hands down!"

Hill turned, saw him, and froze—complete surprise on his face that Kade was leveling a gun at him.

"Drop it, now!" Kade yelled.

Hill's eyes met his, and Kade knew right then that Hill wasn't going to listen at all.

No, don't do it, man.

Hill's mouth opened and he began to yell.

"He's—"

Kade fired the Glock once, hitting Hill at an upward angle in the chest area, the sound deafening in the bathroom space. Hill fell to his knees and collapsed backward in one contorted motion, sprawling out just outside the door frame. Someone who had stepped in with an extinguisher withdrew, and the room door shut on its automatic hinge.

Kade scurried forward to Hill and could feel the fire's searing heat on his face while he tossed Hill's weapons toward the back of the room. Hill was still alive, but his breaths were short and raspy. He held the gun at Hill's chest, alternating hands as he pulled out the contents of Hill's pants pockets. In one he found what he was looking for, the silver badge with Hill's name on it. He shoved the badge and Hill's wallet in his front pockets. When he started to pull back, he saw a two-way radio on Hill's hip, so he also grabbed that and shoved it in his cargo pocket. That was all the pants space he had.

"Sorry, man," he said, right before the room door jolted open again and collided with the burning chair. He pivoted and fired into the opened space at the cloudy shape of a Sentry in the hall while he and Hill were showered with embers.

He dove to the right of the fire and began crawling on the floor in the direction of the window. Cold water started spraying on top of his head and body. The sprinkler must have engaged. The spray reached most of the bed, stopping the spread of fire toward the interior of the room, but the front of the easy chair was just out of its range and still engulfed in flame at the door. The amount of smoke seemed to intensify as some of the fire had been extinguished.

He pulled the bed back from the door outside the opening radius. As he stood up and turned to face the door, it started to push open again. He raised the Glock and fired three shots aimed right through the middle of the door frame. The door eased shut again.

I've got to get out of here.

Kade pulled the wet T-shirt off his face and wrapped it around his left hand, regripping the gun again in the right. He bolted around the left side of the bed, stepped over Hill, and reopened the scorched and perforated door with a single hard yank. Just as the door slammed into the easy chair bonfire again on the outswing, he dove out through the space in the direction of his right shoulder and tumbled into the terrazzo hallway floor.

Two Sentries were in the hallway, one dead within steps of his room door, the other slumped up against the opposite wall, blood running from a wound between his right shoulder and chest.

When the wounded Sentry saw him, he tried to fire but couldn't lift his arm. He fumbled as he tried to switch the gun to his other hand.

This bought Kade a fraction of a second. He pivoted on his hip, extended his arms in the direction of the Sentry, and as both of his elbows landed on the floor, he fired twice. The first shot sailed wide down the hall; the second hit the Sentry below the armpit through the ribs, and the gun dropped from his hand.

He swiveled to a knee and stood, breathing heavily and coughing. The other Associate rooms were close by. Should he try to get others out? Was there time? Would they care?

His decision was made when he heard the sound of the push bars clunking on the double doors far down the hallway, saw the doors opening, and spotted two more Sentries coming from behind them. He darted back in the opposite direction toward the hallway corner and made a left.

He didn't have time to process what he saw next.

Hank was a hundred feet down the hallway, running toward him with a stun gun in his left hand and a pistol in his right. There was also a Sentry down the hall on one knee with a firearm leveled in his direction.

"Get down, Hank!" Kade yelled and pressed his back to the wall to make himself a harder target.

Hank didn't get down; he instead started to look over his shoulder and run sideways. Before he could turn, a bullet tore into his lower back. He stumbled forward and fell to his knees, stopping as his two hands smacked down on the floor in front of him. Kade fired two shots and neutralized the Sentry with the first one.

"Come on, Hank, out the door—there!" Kade pointed to the steel door that Carol had walked him through once before. By the time Hank scrambled on all fours to the door, Kade had pushed the door open so Hank could go right in. Two more Sentries came around the corner from the direction of Kade's room, guns drawn, and he fired a lethal shot from behind the open door before his Glock clicked empty. He shut the door behind him and leaned against it, fished an extra clip out of his pocket and the sock container, and loaded it. Hank turned himself so he was sitting against the cinder block wall.

Hank had lost the stun gun but still had a Sig Sauer. Another gunshot wound in Hank's front, just below the collarbone, bled through his AgriteX top. Kade didn't waste time asking if he was okay, because he knew he wasn't.

"Let me see your gun. Can you fire it?" Kade asked. His hearing still felt muted and crackly from the shot he'd fired earlier in the bathroom.

"Yeah," Hank said.

"Okay, there's no safety on this thing." Kade made sure a round was chambered and handed it back. "I'm going to stop leaning on this door. Aim at the door frame there and shoot anyone who comes through if they're dumb enough to try."

"Okay," Hank said.

Kade stepped toward the outer door, pulled the silver badge from his pocket, and held it at the reader. The reader beeped, but the door didn't unlock.

"Shit, they locked everything down."

"Try this," Hank said, and tossed a gold badge on the floor toward Kade. After Kade raised it to the reader, it beeped and the lock clicked.

"There we go," he said. He opened the exterior door a hair and stuck the empty clip in the space to hold it open while he ran back to Hank. "Come on, let's go." When Kade went to pull him to his feet, Hank groaned in pain. He began to release him slowly.

"No, pull me up," Hank said. "Do it."

Kade struggled to bring him all the way to his feet and Hank took a few seconds standing to catch his breath while Kade leaned on the interior door again.

"This is where we've got to split up," Hank said. "I'm hit twice . . . the one in the back's bad. I'm not going to make it out of here."

"Come on, man."

"No, it's all right, I got what I wanted. I didn't think Heather would have an extra Sentry in her office. That bitch. So fuck it. I'll go out the door here to the left, toward the main entrance. You go right and head for the woods. I'll try and buy you a few minutes."

Kade's look said he wanted to debate it, but Hank yelled at him.

"Just fucking go! There's no time."

"Okay," Kade said. He took the gun and squeezed Hank's forearm. "Thanks, buddy."

"You got it."

Hank took a few deep breaths and Kade pushed the door open for him.

And they ran.

CHAPTER 42

Friday, June 28
7:15 a.m. (PDT)
AgriteX

Scanning in front of him for Sentries or Guardians, Kade sprinted on the dirt-and-gravel path to the circular turnaround where it joined the wider trail connecting AgriteX to the LLFC facility. The morning was cool and overcast, and he felt a spitting drizzle of rain on his face. As he reached the path, he heard the pops of gunshots from behind him. It was hard to tell how close with his hearing still screwed up.

He'd covered another forty yards when a chunk of dirt erupted upward a few yards down in front of him, accompanied by a louder and deeper-sounding gunshot. He jumped off the path to his left as another dirt clod exploded beside him, and he headed into the woods. Another dozen shots sounded in the distance far behind him, smaller pops.

Those two big shots—had to be a sniper.

He ran for another three or four minutes, keeping the path just within his view, until he heard some kind of siren back in the direction of the headquarters lasting for about a minute. Slowing to a walk and catching his breath, he remembered he had Hill's two-way radio in his cargo pocket and pulled it out. It was a bright yellow, ruggedized Motorola model. He pressed the "+" button to increase the volume and a radio conversation became audible.

". . . during the search, lethal force is authorized. Teams One through Five, you need to ensure you're looking inside the perimeter. Six through ten will continue roving sweeps until further orders are given. Acknowledge in sequence."

Kade listened as "Team One, roger," through "Team Ten, roger," sounded over the radio, and then he picked up the pace into a run again. So Hill wasn't a team leader, but they'd eventually figure out that he wasn't responding to his radio if they hadn't already.

What do they know about me?

They know I'm armed. They're thinking I'm going to make it to their perimeter in the next hour.

They've got ten teams in the hunt—probably like a hundred people. It'll take them a few minutes to get organized and moving, but not long.

No dogs, thank God.

Two minutes later, he slowed to a stop and started thinking about his footprints, which were sometimes visible behind him while he was running. The green growth and dead organic material on the forest floor helped his cause some, but his shoes had a deep tread. He ran toward the path again, right up to its edge, then stopped, took the shoes off, and tied the laces together. He walked back into the woods for five minutes, satisfied he was leaving no visible tracks. He heard another faint pop of a firearm in the distance, but couldn't tell the direction.

They'll send search teams through the woods to push me toward the perimeter teams. I can't play that game.

Since he was beginning to hear the background sounds of the forest, he knew his hearing was coming back to where it should be. After another few minutes of walking, he found a cluster of spruces with trunks about three feet in diameter and he stopped to put his shoes back on. The low branches on these trees were just moss-covered stubs a few feet long, but they were spaced close together near the bottom of the trunk.

He found an angular rock and placed it at the bottom of the tree he selected to climb, the rock pointing in the direction of the path he'd come from. Just in case he got disoriented later in the night. He put his pistol in his cargo pocket and began to step on the first few branches, realizing as soon as he was off the ground that the moss was going to make this a slippery ascent. It was a slow, tiring effort making sure he had good handholds.

When he'd climbed about twenty feet, he froze. In his peripheral vision, he saw six black uniforms moving through the forest at a speed walk. The uniforms made the Sentries easy to pick out, and he worried about his own navy-blue outfit being conspicuous. They approached from his two o'clock and passed behind him while he remained motionless and prayed. He turned his head after five minutes and saw they were nowhere in view.

He thought about climbing higher but then worried about the eventual descent. He decided to climb just another three feet to a spot where two solid branches were beside each other at a wide angle. With his back against the trunk, he situated himself, straddling one of the moss-covered branches. If needed, he could quickly shift to the other branch and be less visible from another direction.

The air carried the scent of fresh soil and evergreens, but the smell of his burned hair was stronger. His hair must have caught on fire before the sprinkler activated. His scalp and the left side of his face felt like they might have some light burns. He was hungry and thirsty, but he was going to have to just suck it up and sit here all day. Night would be more of an equalizer given the number of people who were out hunting for him.

Thinking about shooting Hill and looking right into his eyes while doing it made Kade shudder. He didn't know for sure, but between Hill and the other Sentries in the headquarters building, he'd killed at least one man, if not three to four. In the army, he'd worked on targeting insurgents in Iraq, whether through air support, unmanned drone strikes, or raids. But that was indirect responsibility, not up close and personal like this.

His dad had spoken a few times about killing two armed suspects on police duty, and said he'd killed a number of the enemy while part of his squad in Vietnam, but had never provided details. Now Kade knew how he must have felt, and that was not a new milestone he'd been striving for.

He pulled the gold badge from his pocket, which had DRAKOS etched on it, and wondered what act of violence Hank had carried out to obtain it. By now, Hank had to be dead. He thought about Lin, Daniel, and Walter, and what would become of them. He would've liked to have given them the chance to get out, but then again, that wasn't his mission. They may not have wanted to leave. Everything about his op had been so botched that he'd probably get charged with manslaughter or at least heavily reprimanded if he even made it back to safety.

As he replayed his final encounter with Hill again and again, breaking it down in mental slow motion, it validated something he'd felt over the last two weeks, now that he had hours to sort it out. It was what he'd discerned in Hill's eyes in those seconds before he pulled the trigger. What he'd been able to see in Hank and others' faces. He could feel a threatening intent if he was up close enough. He could see the signals and feel the level of intensity in their faces.

This had only started after the Chapter had put the chipset in his head. He knew it had been damaged enough to lose function, but something remained, or something had changed in his perception. His MRI had been cut short. Maybe these were symptoms of the kind of tumor that Hank was sporting, and he didn't have much time. Walter had mentioned some kind of neural growth stimulant used in part of the Guardian protocol. Kade really didn't know what to think.

He vowed that for whatever time he had left, he was going to make every minute count. The Chapter had authorized lethal force against him, so they were now more than an investigative target. He would have to adapt his mindset further and be prepared to kill again if necessary.

They are now the enemy.

CHAPTER 43

Friday, June 28
7:21 a.m. (PDT)
AgriteX

Pierce stood in the security room behind the technician as she started up the recorded digital surveillance video. It showed Hank Stanfield leave his room, arrive at the employee health clinic suite, and check in at the front desk. The female nurse assistant took Stanfield to a treatment room and told him the doctor would see him in a few minutes. Hank sat on the exam table with his eyes shut and arms crossed.

Pierce froze and listened to the audio as it began. He had ordered a Guardian to be present during this exam due to Stanfield's volatile temperament.

Heather Drakos and Guardian Emmett entered the room, and Emmett sat in the chair by the door.

"Hi, Mr. Stanfield," Drakos said. "How are you feeling?"

"Why is he in here?" Stanfield said and pointed to Emmett.

"We're on an enhanced security level, so having observers during exams is part of the deal," she said.

"Sounds like a violation of patient privacy," Hank said, followed by another inaudible grumble of words.

"So what can we help you with today?" she asked. "You complained of some incontinence and a rash?"

"Yeah, I'm starting to wet myself more, and now I got this rash right here all around my waist."

"Okay, let's see it," she said.

Hank slid off the table as if preparing to lift up his shirt or unbuckle his pants, but instead he lunged straight for Emmett. The Guardian reacted with remarkable quickness, reaching for his stun gun first, but Hank countered by grabbing Emmett's wrist with both hands, managing to pry the device free. Then Hank saw Emmett pull a handgun out of a holster on his right hip with his free hand, lightning fast.

Hank delivered a hard head butt to Emmett's nose, but as Emmett recoiled, he squeezed off a shot hitting Hank's left shoulder and spinning him sideways. The head butt made Emmett bring his hands to his face for a moment, but before he could see clearly enough again to aim another shot, Hank reached out and touched him with the prongs of the stun gun and pressed the button.

The shock immobilized Emmett for a few seconds, but by that time, Hank had removed Emmett's weapon and smashed him on the head with the barrel until he stopped moving. Hank turned his head and saw Drakos beside him at the sink counter filling a syringe, so he jumped over to stun her before she could finish.

He stunned her once more, causing her to fall and sprawl on the floor. After he grabbed the syringe from the counter, he got down on the floor and put his hands around her throat. The blood from his shoulder gunshot wound ran on to her neck and face.

"This is for everyone you ruined," Hank said as he choked her with one hand, and with the other, he stuck the syringe in the side of her neck and pushed the plunger.

After watching the segment, Pierce felt breathless. "Turn it off," he told the tech, and she stopped the video. He wished Heather had kept her weapon on her person as he'd always urged. While he was glad a group of Sentries had finally gunned down Stanfield, it was little satisfaction for what he'd just witnessed.

Pierce put his hand on the tech's shoulder.

"Begin deleting the surveillance file archives and discontinue recording," he said. "We'll use real-time surveillance only. Someone will come by later to collect the hardware."

"Okay," she said.

Pierce exited the security room, strode down the hall to the executive wing, and met four Guardians inside conference room 1.

"Start the Associate relocation now," he said. "Get them loaded up; we're going to ship them off early to Nevada. What's the status on the IP?"

"All of the servers are already on their way to Montana," Guardian St. John said.

"Great." Pierce turned to Guardian Latimore. "Make sure the mobile command unit is fully loaded."

"Roger," Latimore said.

"Status on Sims?" Pierce said to Guardian Haven.

"The perimeter is tight and we're conducting zone sweeps," Haven replied.

"Find him."

"What about Stanfield's body?" Guardian Ratcliff asked.

"Put it in cold storage."

CHAPTER 44

Friday, June 28
1:05 p.m. (PDT)
FBI field office, Portland, Oregon

Carla Singleton dialed out from the briefing room to Velasquez as he was driving back from a meeting with the Oregon State Police. Morris sat next to Singleton with an uneaten cheeseburger in front of him.

"This is Chris."

"Chris," Morris said, "I've got Jerry, Troy, and Jeff on the line, and Carla here with me. We've got big news: we just received information that Flash left the AgriteX corporate building, and he's been on the run since about seven thirty this morning."

"That's great," Velasquez said. "Wait, he's been on the run for over five hours and we're only finding out about it now?"

"Water under the bridge," Morris said. "The intel was an inter-agency gift, so I'm just happy we have it."

Velasquez nodded. "Okay. Do we know anything about the source?"

"It was picked up from some two-way radio chatter, which only lasted a few minutes," Morris said. "The AgriteX security team is now trying to track him down."

"Five hours," Velasquez said. "But we haven't received a sat-phone call from the cache site indicating he's there. No emergency signal relayed from his transmitter either."

"He wouldn't use the emergency transmitter," Lerner said. "He'd think we'd come looking for him at the headquarters building when he could be miles away."

"Good point," Velasquez said.

"We know Flash has been hurt," Morris said. "He might be in pretty bad shape. Jenkins, I want you to move to the cache site and see if he's there, or wait for him there until further direction. He may be moving slowly if he's injured. If AgriteX security is going after him, they could pursue him all the way to the cache site."

"Okay," Jenkins said.

"If we don't locate him by morning, we'll assemble and determine next options," Morris said. "Anything else?"

"Yeah, OSP just told me the Nehalem shooting victim has been stabilized," Velasquez said.

"You got a name?" Morris asked.

"Yeah, hold on a second." Velasquez flipped open his notebook on the passenger seat when he stopped at a red light. "Alex Pace."

"That name sounds familiar," Morris said.

"It's Flash's roommate," Lerner said. "If Pace has a Herndon, Virginia, address, that is."

"Yes, he does," Velasquez said.

"Oh my God," Morris said. "What the hell was Flash thinking?"

"It must've been an escape attempt at the clinic," Lerner said. "Improvised. But the cartel had surveillance on Pace, Flash, or both of them."

"I feel like my brain's going to blow a circuit on this one," Morris said.

There was silence.

"So how do we proceed with Pace?" Velasquez asked.

"Let me think about that until you get here," Morris said. "But we need to get Sims out first."

CHAPTER 45

Owens was seated by the fire in the outer area of his office, sipping a cup of tea. The receptionist, along with other standard employees, had now been sent home on paid temporary leave, so Pierce was escorted in by a Sentry who then stood outside the door.

"Hey, Marshall," Pierce said and sat down across from him. "Holding up okay?"

"Yeah, other than the headaches, nausea, and fatigue. More importantly, I'm so sorry about Heather. How are *you* holding up?"

Pierce sighed. "I'll make it. Sims is still out there and we're still looking."

"You now have authorization and access to all of the kill codes in your account, including Sims's code. Do you have your own succession plan in place?"

"Yes, I do."

"Great."

"I have another update on Messia's gang," Pierce said. "We found out from one of Cisneros's girlfriends that Cisneros told her yesterday he'd be gone for up to a week and that it was important. She bitched up a storm and Cisneros said, sorry, the boss was still in town. Then, one of our gang contacts said there were two people in his network picked for a "big job" this week—one that was going to pay well. Our contact tried to volunteer, but no dice. Also, I had all of the road surveillance reviewed and trail traffic counters checked. Not much difference in the road surveillance, but trail traffic is up forty-seven percent since Monday."

"Recon," Owens said. "Started after Messia's visit on Monday. Messia's an expert. I doubt anyone could teach a bunch of thugs recon better than Messia. So an attack is coming."

Pierce nodded. "We also reviewed the visit by the DEA agents as a follow-up. Two of the men were actually on our list as FBI agents out of Portland. We didn't find any surveillance devices left behind, but I'm concerned they may be looking to conduct their own raid."

"We need to move our launch forward," Owens said.

"Unless we think that's going to lower our impact and chance of success."

Owens finished the last of his tea and took a deep breath.

"What is mission success? It's causing enough damage in Phase One to create the right environment for Phase Two. The Fourth of July's symbolic value really isn't that important, and moving the launch forward to Sunday could be a great move—our targets may be out attending various events on the Fourth anyway. It couldn't change our target estimates more than a couple of percentage points. The more important question is, are you ready?"

"Absolutely," Pierce said. "I can deploy the mobile command unit. It's loaded. We'd just need to tweak the download and get it out ASAP."

"Okay, let's do it. I'll prepare our defenses for Messia and the FBI and reschedule the acquisition of CEC to occur on July one."

"I don't envy anyone trying to attack us here with you in command," Pierce said.

Owens smiled. "The more I think about it, a cartel attack could be a huge stroke of luck if we can encourage that first. It may just end up covering our tracks."

CHAPTER 46

It took Kade close to an hour to descend the tree at nightfall, knowing that a misstep and injury would most likely mean recapture and death.

There was the slightest bit of moon illumination through occasional breaks in the cloud layer, but it was now becoming harder to see. At least the night was cool and moist; it was keeping his tired mind alert.

When he reached the ground, he pulled out his pistol again and spent a few minutes stretching. His legs were cramped, his groin area and butt bruised from sitting in the tree in excess of twelve hours. His throat was dry and his stomach felt like a gigantic burning pit. Yet, he was thankful—he'd seen two other groups of Sentries during the day in the distance and remained unseen.

He got his bearings from his rock pointer and then moved in spurts from tree to tree. He didn't like the idea of being visible on the ground and imagined Sentry patrols might have night vision and thermal devices. Carol had said the LLFC was a mile and a half away from the headquarters via the path, and he estimated he couldn't have gone more than a mile yet.

He again walked parallel to the path but stayed as far away from it as he could without losing his way. In a few minutes, he felt the terrain slope downward and remembered the path would join the trail circling the edge of Lost Lake. Another path would run right by LLFC.

Remembering the training map of the terrain, Kade knew Kidders Butte was less than one mile away, but the base of the butte, on its west side, was also the boundary of the AgriteX private land. He thought about the FBI's escape plan and if it could've been compromised. Would Sentries have a dense patrol in that area or would they assume that he would avoid the steep grade of the butte? The private land boundary also ran between the butte and the lake with a much less rugged open space of a quarter mile. They would expect that to be his more probable route.

There was a third option that would add an extra mile and bring him uncomfortably close to LLFC. But it would be less risky if he could reach the outer boundary. In fact there'd be no risk at the perimeter at all.

He decided to go with it.

Moving to the forest edge and crossing the path to the opposite side, he stayed as low to the ground as possible. The down slope flattened out and he could see where the trees ended and the recreational fields began. He could also see the LLFC building lit up from its western edge. The fields weren't lighted, but there was zero cover out there.

In the next hour, he crawled on his stomach to traverse the fields until he reached a gravel road about ten feet wide. He paused and thought about his current position since the cloud cover had increased and the night had darkened. There was a shadow, something blocking a faraway light, down in the direction of the road, and he decided to take a short detour.

He crawled parallel to the path for another five minutes until he could discern two buses still parked in the road. They were the ones he'd seen before—they had a raised suspension and were equipped with oversized treaded tires. He continued until he was to the right of the first bus and stopped at the passenger door, which had a slight buckle in the middle. He pushed on it so the door folded all the way to the right, slipped inside, and slid the door shut behind him.

He stood up and walked down the aisle touching the seat backs of eleven rows, and realized he wasn't going to be able to see anything. He went back to the front and sat down in the driver's seat, pulled the Motorola radio out, and turned it back on. The small display window of the radio lit up with a soft orange glow. The radio also had a small white-light flashlight on it, but he didn't dare try that out and possibly reveal his position. First, he flipped through the channels to see if there was any security chatter, and there wasn't. They must have realized there was a radio missing.

He held the radio close to the steering column and in the faint orange light saw the bus had a Blue Bird logo in the middle of it, and to the left of the column were switches for four-wheel drive. There weren't any keys in the ignition and he couldn't find any. That eliminated the possibility of driving one of the buses out of here if he had to come back this way. He cupped his hand over the orange screen of the radio and stood up facing the back of the bus.

As he swung the light, the first unusual thing he discovered were rifle racks mounted above the windows on each side and a number of overhead storage bins. An interesting retrofit. He took a step forward and lowered the light below his waist level and saw two brown rectangles on the first row of seats. He reached down to the one to his right, and could feel it was an oversize plastic-coated envelope. Inside were six laminated sheets of white paper and two black grease pencils. He flipped through the pages and saw by the orange light that each page had a title at the top followed by blank lines, as if someone might write in those lines by hand:

Page 1: "Zulu Training Packet"
Page 2: "Target Diagram"
Page 3: "Target Known Security"
Page 4: "Target Evac Plan"
Page 5: "Target Photos"
Page 6: "Weapons Review"

He spread the pages out on the seat and stared at them.

This is an attack plan template. This is what they were training for. Only I don't know the target.

He wanted to take pictures, but remembered his camera no longer had a battery, and he'd maxed out the camera memory card.

A light flickered outside the bus. He turned off the radio, poked his head up, and through the rear exit window saw a pair of headlights in the distance, from the direction of the back of the bus.

Shit, they're coming—and coming on this trail.

He shoved the items back into the envelope, placed it back on the seat, then crouched on the stairs of the passenger door and slid the door open. The lights were coming too fast to run out in the open. He crawled flat onto the gravel from the door and slid the door shut with his outstretched arm. The vehicle was about fifty yards away.

He crept under the bus, and huddled next to the front right tire. The headlights were narrow and the only noise the vehicle made was the tires on gravel, so it had to be one of those electric ATVs. He slid his Glock out from his cargo pocket as the headlights came to a stop.

He angled his body forward, trying to keep his face and bare skin in the shadow. He couldn't see who was coming but heard more than one person walking on the gravel. Someone walked within three feet of him, pulled the door open, and went inside. Within seconds the ignition turned and the engine started. The headlights turned on. He assumed the other bus was doing the same.

He panicked. If he stayed where he was and dodged the bus's wheels as it pulled out, the ATV would see him in the headlight. Or run him over. If he ran for it, the ATV was going to see him in the field. He had to wait for the bus to pull away and take his chance with the ATV.

When the bus engine revved, he turned so he was facing rearward on his belly. The headlights from the ATV moved to the right, off the path, and he saw the ATV pass alongside the bus while the bus only moved forward a few feet. Once the ATV moved to the front of the other bus, both buses started to move. His heart thudded while he stayed pressed flat on the gravel, centered between the wheels on each side, as the bus passed over him. He felt a wave of relief when it was gone.

He crawled off the path into the field and watched the small convoy of headlights go about a hundred yards, veer right, then sweep left.

They're turning around and coming back. I'm going to be lit up.

He bounced to his feet and sprinted in the direction of the wood for five seconds, watching the headlights angle back toward him. He dove on the grass, landed on his stomach, and lay motionless about forty yards from the road while the headlights passed by. Now he'd check to see if there was some more radio traffic, if anyone was talking about him. All of a sudden, he got a feeling in his gut that something was wrong. He felt his cargo pocket.

I left the radio on the bus.

He got up and ran farther away from the road, reaching the edge of the field in less than a minute. There was a four-foot-high chain-link fence that he rolled over without a problem, and within seconds, he was inside the wood, bounding downhill. In less than a minute, he could see a slight shimmer from the water of Lost Lake in front of him.

He knew he wasn't a very good swimmer, but he sprinted harder when he reached the dirt banks, sloshing out into the cold water until he was up to his knees. He put his Glock back in his cargo pocket and buttoned it.

The dim light from the cloud-shrouded moon was as useful as a dying glow stick. He stood for thirty seconds with his hands on his hips, and when he'd caught his breath, he picked a direction toward a few points of light on the opposite side of the lake. He waded forward until the cold water enveloped his waist and he could begin a sidestroke.

He thought about what a disaster CLEARCUT had become. He thought about Alex, then about Janeen. There was no doubt he was responsible for putting them in danger. Were they victims of his own selfishness? Was this whole mission an attempt to prove his self-worth at their expense? His body began to feel heavier in the water but he told himself it was only in his mind.

Just focus—one stroke at a time.

CHAPTER 47

Sentry Robertson brought Yates and Russell, the last pair of Zulus from D8 Work Crew Two, into the inmate mentor training room of Camp Walpole and had them take a seat at one of the desks. Sentry Wolf was already seated in the first row. Russell leaned back in his chair, stretched, and yawned.

"Guys, we have a change in the plan," Robertson said. "Exact same mission plan, different date. We're moving out this time tomorrow. So we have to make an adjustment to your mission template."

"Wow, okay," Russell said. "Giddy up."

Yates shrugged. "Cool, let's do it."

"I love everyone's attitude," Wolf said.

Both Robertson and Wolf knew the update was necessary because the plan and the associated checklists would self-delete following the mission day, at 8:00 a.m. local time. It was an additional safeguard to ensure that even if any crew members were captured during or after the mission, no plans would be revealed.

"So we have a tiny download for you both to update the template," Robertson said, "and we needed to wake you up and keep you up until four this afternoon so we can adjust your sleep schedule. We want you all to be fresh and rested."

"Just keep the coffee comin' and we'll be good," Russell said.

"No problem, we'll have coffee and plenty of activities all day to try and keep you all from snoozing too much," Robertson said.

Yates and Russell took turns moving to the download station and sitting in front of the infrared beam for a few seconds.

"Okay, thanks, guys," Wolf said as the two Zulus got ready to leave with another IM escort.

"Just curious, why the pull-up in the date?" Yates asked.

"I can't tell you 'cause we don't know," Robertson said.

And even if we did, we couldn't tell you.

CHAPTER 48

Saturday, June 29
4:41 a.m. (PDT)
Lost Lake, Oregon

Kade reached a thick fluorescent orange rope stretching across the lake, supported by floats. When he passed under the rope and looked backward, he could see a sign on a nearby float and swam over to read it.

"PRIVATE PROPERTY OF LLFC—DO NOT CROSS"

This meant he was now in the recreational area of Lost Lake. Kade was elated at this small marker of progress even though he assumed Chapter thugs were still in pursuit. A small wave of energy came from nowhere, despite his extreme thirst and hunger. The hardest thing wasn't the swimming—it was making sure he didn't drink the lake water while he was so thirsty. It was nice and cold, and the numbing effect felt good on his body, but lake water had a ton of pathogens in it, and he wasn't going to take himself out with a double whammy of puking and diarrhea when he'd made it this far.

It took him between ten and fifteen minutes to finally reach the opposite bank. There were a few areas littered with fallen tree debris that were hard to navigate. A campfire burned in the distance and it looked like there were a few lights from either tents or RVs, so he avoided that direction. Most likely those were friendly people, but he couldn't take the chance. His feet touched bottom in another couple of minutes and he waded to where the water was at his waist.

Once again he put himself back on high alert. Sentries could be waiting for him down at the beach, in the park, or camping area. The Chapter would expect him to ask for help, for a ride, or to use someone's phone. He ignored the urge to stop and ask for food and water. No, his next finish line was Kidders Butte, and he knew there'd be survival supplies there. He could make it in another hour or two at the most.

Shivers coursed through his body as he emerged from the water and scrambled up the muddy, root-covered bank. A few more yards and he was enveloped again by the tall evergreen trees. After a few minutes' rest, he moved in a general eastward direction toward his next objective, the southeast corner of Kidders Butte. Without a compass, and still in darkness, he tried to stay moving in a gradual uphill direction. He had it in his mind to run, but his fatigued legs only allowed a walk.

It felt like about another hour had passed before the ground rose sharply. Now he turned a slight right to follow the base of the butte around to its south side, where its face wasn't so steep and two crude trails would run to the top. If the map he'd studied during training was correct, that is.

Moving was now more tedious due to the caution he was taking. He was afraid of accidentally losing the butte, so he came back to it at intervals, forcing him to do a blend of walking and climbing. He wanted to put some more distance between himself and the AgriteX private land boundary and didn't want to stray back north by accident in the darkness.

Once he reached the top of the butte, he'd move down the ridge to its north end to find the cache the FBI had left him. But he would need some light to find the cache there.

Shit, it's too dark right now.

He slowed to a stop and sat down at the base of a tree. Conserving energy until the start of daylight would be the smartest thing to do. Morning twilight couldn't be too far off.

I'll just take a quick nap.

In under a minute, his mind entered a state of light sleep.

He wasn't sure if it was five minutes or two hours later, but he awoke as if someone had shaken him. When he listened around him, he thought he heard movement nearby, so he stood up in place to make sure it wasn't delirium playing tricks on him. No, he definitely heard more than one person talking. Three or four words were exchanged between normal speaking voices several times, but he couldn't tell what was said.

He unbuttoned his cargo pocket and pulled out the Glock. He squatted at the tree's base, circled it, and probed around with his free hand until he found a fist-size rock poking out of the dirt. After wedging it out, he switched the Glock to his left hand and palmed the rock in his right. His nerves ratcheted up in readiness when he realized the sound of the movement had ceased. He was at a mental impasse. Maybe he'd wait five minutes and throw the rock as far as he could as a distraction for whoever was out there, then move out. Standing up against the tree, he calmed his breathing and kept still.

"*No te muevas,*" a male voice said from right behind him, just as he felt the barrel of a rifle press into the center his back. He felt an electric jolt of surprise and froze in place.

"*Suelte la arma,*" the man said. Kade knew *arma* was Spanish for a gun. His Glock was at shoulder level in his left hand. He pulled his finger outside the trigger guard and did a combination of dropping and flicking the gun away from himself. He heard it hit soft earth.

"*Manos arriba,*" the man said. Kade recognized *manos* as "hands" and so he figured he should raise his hands nice and slow. When his hands reached a level above his head, he felt the pressure of the rifle barrel on his back ease for a split second. And when he felt that tiny release, he did a quick pivot on his right hip and swung his right fist clockwise and downward like a hammer as hard as he could.

The rock in his palm connected with something hard and he let out a gasp as the tip of his middle finger got caught under the rock when it contacted. He also heard a cry of pain from the man who stood behind him. The momentum of the swing brought Kade around, facing backward as he swiveled on the ball of his foot. He pushed off that foot and dove with his arms outstretched, clasping the man in a sloppy bear hug as they fell down together in a heap.

He heard the rattle of a rifle as they hit the ground and felt the weapon lying sideways between him and the man underneath. A punch slammed into the left side of his face, but it didn't have much strength behind it. He realized he still had the rock in his hand and brought it down into the face area of the unseen man, but it hit against something hard. Again he swung and there was the sound of something metallic and plastic upon contact.

Night-vision goggles.

Kade absorbed another punch between his cheek and nose while he aimed toward the side of the man's head. The rock again connected and he pressed his left forearm into the man's neck while he continued hitting him. When the man stopped struggling, he let the rock fall out of his hand.

"Carlos!" a man shouted from what Kade thought was twenty or thirty yards away.

Kade slid his hands around the rifle stock and the barrel hand guard and pushed off the man below him to a standing position.

"Carlos!"

When Kade heard the voice, he turned and faced it. But he wouldn't be able to operate this rifle in the dark and there was no time to search for the Glock. He picked an angle to his front-right and dashed through the forest.

Automatic gunfire opened up—there were muzzle flashes to his left and behind. Now he just ran as fast as he could without slamming into trees. The smallest bit of morning light or moonlight now provided some contrast in the darkness.

He ran for what felt like fifteen minutes toward the emerging light, slowing or stopping only to climb hills or ease down ravines. He weaved sideways down one steep hill and saw a break in the forest in front of him. There was a field filled with stumps and forest debris, a clear-cut area of about ten acres. He slalomed through it and at its far end there was a dirt road with thick forest resuming on the opposite side. He stopped for a few minutes to catch his breath.

He decided to leave Kidders Butte behind, run down the road, and cover more distance versus reentering the forest. Running with an AK-47 in the middle of the road would attract attention if he were spotted, but he'd be able to hear and see approaching vehicles well enough to get off the road and out of sight.

He took a deep breath and started off at a jog again. Except for a mix of chirping birds in the forest and his coarse breathing, the morning was quiet. The sun peeked out a few times and let him know he was making his way toward the east despite the many bends in the road. If he continued east, he'd hit Route 57 sooner or later, and that was his ticket to safety. He'd have to try to hitch a ride.

After moving for about ten minutes, he heard the noise of heavy machinery in the distance. He slowed to a walk and stepped up the banked roadside into the tree line. His heart continued pounding longer than it should have and now a headache felt like it pressed in from every direction. He needed some water very soon. Food wasn't a bad idea either. When he neared the edge of a massive clearing, he stopped and rested again while standing behind a tree.

An additional dirt road split off from the one he'd been running on and snaked into the clearing in front of him. This had to be a forest logging operation. A number of yellow heavy machinery vehicles sat in the clearing—a backhoe, an excavator, and a large tracked vehicle with some sort of long hydraulic-powered arm.

Two semitrailers were lined up about seventy yards away. One had logs stacked high in its trailer's U-shaped holders. The other was in the process of being loaded. He could see three men with fluorescent-orange hard hats in the distance. Two were talking to each other and the other was walking away, moving out of sight.

Kade looked at the one fully loaded truck and then got an unexpected burst of energy.

There's another way to hitch a ride.

He leaned the AK-47 up behind the tree and sprinted back toward the road he was on before, past the road split for the work site and into the forest on the opposite side. From this direction, he got within thirty yards of the logging trucks while still in the tree line. The front truck was idling, but there was no one in the cab. No one was in the cab of the rear truck either.

He dashed in a crouch to the lead truck and jumped up on the rearmost double wheel, putting his hands on the nearest metal U-bracket and stepping up, using the space between the stacks of logs as footholds. Keeping his body profile as flat as possible, he pulled himself over the top, but barely, as his smashed finger screamed and reminded him of its sorry state. Once he slid over to the middle of the load, he stretched out flat on his stomach and lay still. The idling of the engine was loud but relaxing. His exhaustion was catching up with him and he had to fight to keep his eyes open.

Ten minutes later, he heard the door of the cab open and close. The truck shifted in gear and jerked forward at a crawl until it moved out on the main road. He took a gigantic breath.

Let's hope this thing is going in the right direction.

CHAPTER 49

Saturday, June 29
5:07 a.m. (PDT)
Kidders Butte, Oregon

Messia had been awake and waiting for a status report from his recon team since hearing the sound of gunfire. He sat in front of his camouflage dome tent chewing on a chocolate protein bar and sipping a bottle of water.

Behind his tent, shadowed in the evergreens, stood two guards from his security detail. The other ten guards were fanned out across Kidders Butte. All were dressed in digital-patterned camouflage fatigues and carried AK-47 rifles. Messia had stockpiled the equipment easiest to obtain through cartel channels.

Sandoval approached the tent looking frustrated. He sat down next to Messia and slung his rifle over his shoulder. The two guards moved closer and kept their eyes on Sandoval.

"*¿Qué pasó?*" Messia asked.

"Ramirez is dead," Sandoval said. "Killed by someone from AgriteX named Anthony Hill." Sandoval handed Messia a wallet and a pistol, and Messia flipped through the wallet's contents, pausing to look at Hill's Oregon driver's license.

"We already buried Ramirez," Sandoval said to fill the silence.

Messia examined the pistol, a Glock. He pulled out the clip and slammed it back in.

"So there was an AgriteX soldier over a mile outside their company's property," he said. "He kills one of ours and he's still out there wandering around. What am I to think about that?"

Sandoval knew to keep his mouth shut. Messia stood up and stared down into the valley.

Owens is trying to pick off my men. He may know we're coming, but he doesn't know when.

We need to get that seed now.

"We're going to attack tonight," Messia said. He turned to look at Sandoval. "And we're going to relocate our team northeast of here to Hill 2230. So get ready to move everything out."

"Okay," Sandoval said.

.   .   .

An hour passed as Team Echo gathered their gear and left the area. At the north end of the butte, Agent Jenkins sat huddled in the middle of a thick coyote bush, hidden from view. He clutched his Glock in one hand and turned on his phone with the other, putting it in silent mode.

When the armed group of men had moved into the area so fast, he'd shut it off in a panic. He was receiving a faint coverage signal, so he thumbed a message to Morris rather than going to the cache to use the satellite phone.

Jenkins: *Urgent situation*

Morris: *U ok?*

Jenkins: *Y right now*

Morris: *U got flash?*

Jenkins: *No flash...but armed soldiers were here...think they r gone*

Morris: *Where r u?*

Jenkins: *Hidden near cache in bush*
Morris: *What kind of soldiers?*
Jenkins: *They spoke Spanish*
Jenkins: *Camo uniforms*
Morris: *How far r u from cache and what direction?*
Jenkins: *Abt 30 yds SE*
Morris: *Hold on . . . must discuss*
Ten minutes passed.
Morris: *Do u have water?*
Jenkins: *Y*
Morris: *Stay put and out of sight...we'll come get you out...might take a few hours...stay safe...keep updates coming every 15 min*
Jenkins: *Ok...also think I saw a mortar tube*
Morris: *R u sure?*
Jenkins: *Think so...aiming sticks too*
Morris: *Ok...thx...stay safe*

CHAPTER 50

The logging truck descended the steep hill of the two-lane highway, slowing to about thirty miles per hour. Kade ached from head to toe, but riding on pavement was a gift after being bounced around on the rutted dirt roads. If his body had an energy reserve, it was now filled with the exhilaration of escaping and inserting plenty of distance between him and the Chapter.

To his right, there was a rocky mountain face several hundred feet high. To the left, he could see a fog-filled valley spanned by a long bridge with a city on the other side. The truck had to be crossing the Willamette or Columbia Rivers.

The older-looking bridge was a great latticework of steel trusses and rivets. As the truck crossed to the other side, he saw an overhead sign marked "SR433/432," which meant nothing to him except the route sign contained the profile of George Washington's head, like that on a quarter. They must have just crossed the Columbia River, moving north, and were now in Washington State.

When the truck stopped at the first intersection, he looked over the edge to see if he could jump off. It was over a ten-foot drop and the asphalt looked cracked and uneven. Not a good time to break an ankle. The light turned green before he could think about it more. The truck exhaled a breath of exhaust, accelerated, and turned right, veering into a parallel road that entered an industrial zone.

A complex of warehouse buildings formed a grid in the site. The truck passed gigantic stacks of both uncut logs and bundled lumber. He could see more stacks lying next to the river docks ready for cargo transport. The truck slowed and pulled into a well-lit central offloading area. There was a fair amount of activity—the sound of saw mills and heavy machinery moving between buildings. It had to be a twenty-four-hour operation, he thought.

The truck came to a halt. He spider-crawled left to the edge of the load and peeked over the side.

Oh God.

A heavy piece of machinery painted in bright yellow had advanced within feet of the truck. It looked like the offspring of a bulldozer mated with a giant forklift. The gigantic pincer-like jaws, including a massive overhead locking fork, were sliding forward to grab the entire load of logs at once.

He scrambled back to the other side of the load and let his body roll over the last log, both hands gripping its surface. He grit his teeth and struggled to hold on while leaving his smashed finger free. The load shifted as the machine closed its fork around the huge bundle, and right at that moment, he pushed off the log under his feet and released his hands from the top.

He grunted as he hit the blacktop hard and tumbled backward. Rolling up to his feet, he spotted the nearest woodpile and sprinted toward it for cover while orienting to the lights of the bridge he came from. He picked a point north, away from the river, and took off running again.

Someone shouted, but he couldn't tell if it was directed at him amidst the noise in the complex. He stayed close to the large piles of lumber, zigzagging between them, past large warehouses to the edge of the industrial area. There was a street leading up to a large fueling station island, and he could see trucks parked there. After a few minutes, he slowed to a walk as he got closer and stopped just short of the parking lot. It looked like a full-service truck stop.

He removed both his outer crinkly shirt and T-shirt, and sat down in the breeze catching his breath for a few minutes while picking some of the wood splinters out of his hands. He looked at his swollen and cut finger. He had an assortment of other cuts, bruises, and scrapes on his body, and a couple of the cuts would need a stitch or two. He thought he'd check to see if the wallet he'd taken from Sentry Hill had any money in it and felt a wave of guilt again after thinking about Hill's face. When he reached into his pocket, he found it had somehow fallen out. He had no money, only the gold badge of Heather Drakos.

That's just great.

When he stopped sweating, he got up, put the T-shirt back on, and walked across the parking lot, tossing the blood-speckled AgriteX shirt in the trash with Drakos's badge. He pushed open the door to the L-shaped building and paused by the cashier. The wing of the building to his left was set up as a convenience store and the other wing as a twenty-four-hour diner–style restaurant, with the cashier area at the juncture of the two wings. He looked at the stack of newspapers next to the cashier's desk. *The Daily News—Longview, Washington.*

He hesitated for a second, then strode into the restaurant area, down the aisle between the line of window booths and the stools of the front counter. There were four patrons at the counter and five of the ten window booths were occupied. The smell of cooked breakfast was overpowering and reminded him how hungry he was.

When he found the bathroom at the very back, he cupped his hands under the faucet and took the longest drink he could remember. Then he washed his hands and face in the sink with the pink liquid soap and let the cold water run on his hurt finger for a bit. He felt weak with hunger and knew he needed to get back into contact with the FBI.

What now? Hitch a ride? Try and call the TOC?

No, I need to call Janeen first.

He walked back out into the restaurant section and looked into the booths as he walked. One empty booth hadn't been cleared, and he scooped up a half-eaten sausage patty and two pieces of untouched toast with jelly packets from the plate and dropped them in his left cargo pocket. He thought the waitress behind the counter saw him, but he avoided eye contact and just kept walking until he was inside the convenience area.

At the refrigerated display cases, there were a few people selecting drinks. A thirtyish man with thinning black hair stood at the edge of the case playing with his phone.

"Hey, sir, can I make a phone call? It's an emergency call to my sister."

The guy looked him up and down.

"Sorry, buddy. I'm in a hurry."

"You can use mine," a guy said from behind another side counter. An employee. It looked like he was selling truck parts and accessories. He passed Kade a cordless handset.

"Thank you," Kade said. He dialed up Janeen's cell phone number, stepped a few feet away, and kept his voice low and calm. The call connected and he heard the voice of his sister.

"Hello?"

"Janeen, it's me."

"Kade! Are you okay? Where are you?"

"Janeen, listen to me. You're in danger. Where are *you*?"

"I'm in Portland with Alex at the hospital."

"What? Really?" Kade ran his hand through his hair. *Alex is alive, thank God.* He would leave the discussion on how the hell

Janeen made it out to Portland and found Alex for another time. "Is he okay?"

"Yeah, he's had three surgeries, but he's going to be okay. He's expected to be discharged in a few days. Alex made me stay here and not go looking for you. I did go get his truck and managed to convince Enterprise to pick up my rental."

Kade's heart sank. "Three surgeries . . . my God . . ."

Yes, it could be worse, but not much.

"Kade?"

He had to focus and not let his emotions take over.

"Kade?"

"Yeah, okay, listen. There're some very dangerous people who may be looking for you. I want you to be very careful while you're at the hospital."

"Kade, where are *you* right now? Can I come get you?"

Yeah, duh. His mind wasn't working as fast as it should. He was beyond exhaustion.

"Yeah, that sounds like a great idea. Come get me. I'm in Longview, Washington. At Clark's Truck Stop."

Kade heard some mumbling on the other side of the phone.

"That's a little more than an hour from here off I-5," Janeen said. "I just asked the nurse. I'll get more directions on the way. I'm going to leave in a couple of minutes."

"Okay, when you get here—stay in your car and just park near the car wash. No one's there, so I'll find you. I'm going to stay out of sight until then."

"I will," she said. "See you in a little while."

CHAPTER 51

The female nurse brought Kade and Janeen to Alex's hospital room on the second floor of Portland Emanuel. The room was comfortable and decorated in pastel colors with paintings donated from local artists. A male nurse assistant working at a computer station in the corner nook of the room turned and waved when they entered.

Alex was lying on his back with the bed inclined. A number of intravenous bags hung above him and multiple monitor clips gripped his fingers. His face looked listless and pale, but brightened when he saw the visitors.

"Kade . . . you made it," he said.

Kade's eyes began to fill with tears as he moved to the side of Alex's bed. He put his hand on top of Alex's and lightly squeezed it. *This is all my fault.*

"How ya doing, buddy?"

"Think I'm going to make it."

Kade shook his head. "I'm so sorry, so sorry, man."

"That's all right. I didn't need my spleen anyway."

Kade shut his eyes. "They took out your spleen?"

"Yeah. Bullet hit my bowel and spleen. I was lucky on the bowel. Suture repair, no resection. Not so lucky on the spleen."

"Are you in a lot of pain?"

"Some. I'm on oxycodone."

Kade sighed. Janeen slid a chair in behind him and he sat down in it. She sat down on the nearby sleeper sofa.

"Kade, you look like shit," Alex said.

Kade opened his eyes. "*I* look like shit?" He laughed once and wiped his eyes.

"Hell yeah, you do. But, hey, you're here. That's good news for you, huh? You must've done what you needed to do."

"I don't know. I hope so. I couldn't have done it without you."

"Bus twenty-six, brother."

Tears ran down Kade's cheeks. "Yeah."

"Your sister's been an angel to me."

"I'm sure she has."

"Alex," the female nurse from outside said, "the chaplain you requested is here to see you now."

Kade wasn't a regular churchgoer, but he knew Alex was a Pentecostal. They didn't talk much religion. "You want us both to step out?" Kade asked.

"No, stay, man," he said.

"Okay." Kade cranked his neck around to look behind him, and saw the tall, blond figure of the chaplain as he was shutting the door.

It was Guardian Constantino. He was dressed in khaki pants and a white polo shirt bearing an embroidered caduceus design in the pocket area with the word CHAPLAIN above it. He pulled a large pistol with a suppressor attachment out of a computer bag in his other hand.

Kade saw a smirk appear on Constantino's face as he aimed the gun toward him, and he remembered he didn't have his Glock anymore.

"Two-for-one deal today," Constantino said.

Kade dove sideways toward Janeen, and as the wide-armed chair tumbled with him, he heard the explosion of two gunshots. He heard Janeen scream, then realized somehow he *hadn't* been hit. He was now on the floor, turning on his hands and knees toward the door. Constantino was on the ground with blood soaking the chest area of his white polo shirt and his hand pressed against his bleeding neck. He glanced behind him and saw Janeen had crawled behind the sofa and looked okay.

Kade picked up Constantino's pistol off the floor, stood up, and backed up, keeping it aimed.

"Kade, can you move over to this side of the room and set that gun down next to me?"

Kade turned and saw the nurse assistant was still seated but now had a pistol aimed in a well-practiced double-handed grip. His muscles bulged through the short sleeves of his scrubs and his brown eyes couldn't have looked more intense. Kade lowered his pistol and stepped toward him.

"Is everyone okay?" the man said.

Janeen sat back up on the couch.

"Yeah, I'm fine."

"I'm good," Kade said. "Thank you."

"Wow . . . unbelievable," Alex said.

Kade laid the pistol down and then moved to the couch, sat down, and put his arm around Janeen.

The man removed one hand from his gun and spoke into a two-way radio, keeping his eye on the door. "Miller, it's Stephenson. We have one unknown assailant, badly wounded, here in two-fourteen. We're all fine. Not sure if there are any other hostiles. Okay, see you in a bit."

"We're okay. We're safe," Kade whispered to Janeen.

I've put my family and friends in danger. I should have never involved them.

Two minutes later, there were four solid knocks at the door.

"Come on in, slow," Stephenson said.

A disheveled-looking man in scrubs opened the door wide enough to squeeze through. He had a pistol drawn as he knelt down next to Constantino, who was now unconscious. Two uniformed security guards were behind him, along with an emergency medical team. They lifted Constantino on a gurney and wheeled him out.

The man in the corner stood up and holstered his weapon under his scrubs. "I'm Agent Jeff Stephenson. Janeen, we're going to move you to safer accommodations. Alex, you'll have Portland Police officers providing security for you now."

"That was fucking cool," Alex said with his eyes almost shut.

"Kade," Stephenson said, "we've got to get you treated and cleaned up. Then we need you over at the field office."

CHAPTER 52

Daniel, Lin, and Walter sat on a semicircular stone-aggregate bench near a small garden, talking quietly. Four sentries dressed in street clothes had loaded large duffel bags containing the Associates' belongings into a full-size van. Joshua Pierce appeared, looking freshly showered and dressed in jeans, a black T-shirt, and running shoes.

Pierce and a Sentry, Bernard, walked over to the bench.

"It's time to get going, folks," Pierce said. His eyes looked weary and distracted. "Sorry for the bumped-up schedule."

"Where are we going?" Daniel asked.

"Nevada," Pierce said. "A few hours east of Reno. I think you're all going to like it. Once you're situated, we're going to put you up in a nice resort in Tahoe for a week. I know everyone deserves a break."

There was no reaction to his statement.

"You'll also receive another cash bonus of forty thousand dollars," Pierce added. "You've all progressed through the program well."

"Where's Sims?" Walter asked.

"He's continuing his Guardian training," Pierce said. "You'll see him again soon."

"I thought he failed a drug test and was terminated," Walter said, looking at Lin and Daniel in turn. All three Associates intensified their stare at Pierce.

Before Pierce could respond, Lin added, "Guess it's getting harder to keep track of the lies, huh?"

"No, no, you're correct," Pierce stammered. "My mistake. Sims *was* terminated. We had to move some other people into Guardian training from other regions. It's a busy time. Look, I know you're all tired. I'm exhausted too. Let's try and stay positive. You've done well in the program."

"The problem is," Daniel said, "people in the program are dying. We're supposed to be taking your word for it, and it's not adding up."

Pierce clasped his hands and stooped over like he was speaking to a kindergarten class.

"This has nothing to do with you three. We have great plans for you all. Some people just aren't right for the program."

The three broke eye contact and looked unconvinced.

"You'll have Sentries Bernard, Maravar, Ash, and Patrick taking care of you. I'll see you all in a week or two from now."

"We still haven't been able to call anyone," Lin said.

"We have some cell phones we'll pass around on the drive," Bernard said. "You can make calls once we get going."

The group got up and filed into the van, Bernard taking the driver's seat and Ash sitting shotgun. Maravar and Patrick sat in the rearmost two seats while Lin, Walter, and Daniel spread out in the other two rows.

"Have a safe trip and see you soon," Pierce said. He slid the side door shut and patted the door panel with his hand. The van backed out and he waved in its direction as it turned and headed out of the parking lot.

Pierce pulled out a new Nabishi two-way radio from his belt clip. He'd ordered everyone make the switch to those radios because of their high level of encryption.

"Hey, Marshall, it's Josh," he said.

"What's up?" Owens responded.

"This is where we are. The Associates have been shipped off and the remaining Guardians are also gone. Sentries have been pulled back to the inner zones. L-FAC and the Zulus are ready to go."

"Perfect. Has Constantino reported in?"

"Not yet."

"I wouldn't give him more than an hour. Can't risk it this late in the game."

"I agree."

"And you need to get going now," Owens said.

"I'm leaving in ten minutes," Pierce said. "The mobile command unit is waiting for me out at Gale's Creek."

"Okay. Good luck to you and your team."

"*Klahowya sikhs*, Marshall," said Pierce. *Good-bye, my friend.*

"*Klahowya sikhs.* Tomorrow will be an unforgettable day."

CHAPTER 53

Saturday, June 29
12:37 p.m. (PDT)
Portland Emanuel Hospital

Morris crossed the sky bridge to the nearest hospital tower and paused before he entered the building to call Velasquez.

"Chris, good news. We have Joe's approval for the SWAT team and a THU bird to extract Jenkins from Kidders Butte."

Joe Caldwell was the special agent in charge, or SAC, of the FBI Portland field office. The tactical helicopter unit, or THU, was used to support FBI SWAT operations, and Morris knew Velasquez had previous experience working on a SWAT team.

"Great," Velasquez said. "I assume you want me going along?"

"Yeah, I'd like you to fly with them. Flight mission brief is at two. I'll be about a half hour late. This op is now a director's priority, and so we'll be briefing FBI HQ at two thirty."

"Where are you now?" Velasquez asked.

"Portland Emanuel. Flash is cleared for discharge but he's sleeping. I'm going to give him another hour of z's since he's going to have a long debrief later. I'll see if I can get any info out of Kevin Constantino in the meantime. Thanks for the backgrounder you e-mailed."

"Sure. Good luck with him," Velasquez said.

"Thanks. Talk to you later."

Morris took the elevator down to the main level. He found his way to the telemetry unit and checked in with Alondra, the nurse supervisor he'd spoken with earlier.

"Hi, Agent Morris. Follow me, please." Alondra led him down the hall past a number of room bays with sliding glass doors until they reached the one with a uniformed police officer posted outside of it. After the officer checked Morris's ID, Alondra brought Morris inside the bay and stayed there with him.

Morris left a bag of fresh clothing for Kade on the floor next to the door. As he stepped closer to the bed, he saw that Constantino looked horrendous, but his eyes were open and blinking.

"So, Kevin, looks like you're doing okay now," Morris said while leaning on the bed rails.

Alondra put her hand on Morris's shoulder and whispered, "Please sit down."

Constantino continued to gaze across the room while Morris pulled up a chair and sat facing the chair back.

"You want to share anything about why you were sent here to kill somebody?"

No reaction.

"We're on our way to arrest your boss and close down AgriteX right now," Morris said. "The party's over."

Constantino turned his head an inch and his eyes moved as if effort were required. But a trace of a smile manifested in his lower lip and chin.

"I don't think so," he whispered. "You're too late. It's already begun."

"What's already begun?"

"Impossible to stop. You lose."

Morris scooted the chair closer and grabbed Constantino's shoulder. "What's begun? What is the launch? I have a long memory if you do the right thing and help us. Otherwise . . ."

"Sir," Alondra said to Morris, "I'm going to have to ask you to stop now. This isn't the time or place for that kind of questioning."

"Okay, one more simple question," Morris said, and Alondra gave a reluctant nod. Morris pulled a cell phone out of his pocket and the plastic bag it was in. "You got a message about ten minutes ago. Any idea what it means?"

Morris held the phone in front of Constantino's face so he could see the text message.

84210994

Constantino's expression was quizzical while he looked at the number. He then blinked his eyes twice slowly and looked up at the ceiling. Morris leaned in closer, wondering if Constantino was going to respond.

Three seconds later, the electrocardiogram monitor sounded with an alarm.

CHAPTER 54

Saturday, June 29
2:13 p.m. (PDT)
FBI field office, Portland, Oregon

During their drive to the field office, Kade was surprised Morris didn't chew his ass out about Alex's involvement or Janeen showing up, and he wasn't sure how to read it except to conclude Morris was quite even-keeled and professional. Or that he was embarrassed the emergency transmitter didn't work.

Morris had first asked him why he didn't use the cache site sat-phone or transmitter as planned. Kade told him he tried activating the transmitter, and when there was no response, he then attempted to make it to the cache site, but ran into a hostile group of armed men he had to evade. Morris apologized and said he'd have the transmitter analyzed as part of the after-action report.

When Morris asked why Alex had come out to Oregon and was in the Nehalem Clinic, he said Alex brought his pickup and he had planned an extra backup opportunity for escape. Morris then asked him if he learned anything about Chapter drug cartel activity, and he explained what he could.

Kade asked what day it was—Morris told him Saturday, and joked that since his wife and three daughters were out shopping at the mall, it was better he wasn't around anyway. Kade sensed that

Morris was a dedicated family man and imagined what long-term life in the FBI must be like. Morris was steady and methodical, and those traits must have served him well in his career.

After they reached the briefing room, Kade recognized Agent Stephenson sitting nearest the door at the conference table and made a point to say "thank you" once more. A printed map of the CLEARCUT operational area was spread out on the table with the electronic version displayed on a wall flat-screen monitor.

Kade saw a woman in her early thirties walk over toward him from the other side of the table.

"Hi, I'm Carla. Nice to meet you, Flash," Singleton said. She was going to shake his hand but saw his bandages and bruised face. "You look like you've been to hell and back."

"Yeah, the burned hair is a good look for me, I know."

He now realized that the nickname the ball-busting personal trainer had given him weeks ago had somehow been officially assigned to him as the alias of their operational source. *Nice touch.*

A voice came over the speakerphone.

"Good to hear your voice, Flash. How are ya feeling?"

Kade recognized the voice and Texas accent. "Hey, Jerry," he said and sat down at the table. "I feel better, thanks." Kade was skittish about saying more than he had to. He still felt like he wasn't being told much about what was going on.

Morris shut the door. "Ready to get started?"

"Think so," Singleton said. "Waiting on Chris?"

"No," Morris said and then sat down. The new liter bottle of Diet Coke on the table in front of him hissed as he unscrewed the cap and took a large sip. "We're going to conduct a full, thorough operational debrief, but due to a current urgent situation, we need to skip out of sequence and ask a few targeted questions." Morris looked at Kade.

"So, Flash, let's review what you told me earlier for the team's benefit. You never reached the extraction point on Kidders Butte because you ran into a number of armed men in the forest."

"That's right, I think somewhere between eight to twelve men. I heard them speaking Spanish. Sounded like Mexican Spanish to me, but I couldn't swear to it."

"Where did you run into them?" Lerner asked over the speakerphone.

Kade found Kidders Butte on the map, traced it with his bandaged finger, and made an imaginary circle.

"Somewhere along the south side of the butte, around here, I think."

"And you think they were cartel?" Singleton asked.

"I assumed so. They uh—" Kade paused suddenly for five seconds.

"They what?" Morris prompted.

Kade shifted in his seat. What should he say? He'd most likely killed that guy in the forest. He stalled by coughing and drinking out of one of the two bottles of water he had with him. He drank it down halfway.

Attorney general's guidelines.

"Sorry," he said. "My throat's still messed up from the smoke and everything. These guys had decent equipment. And they had uniforms. At least one guy had night-vision goggles, and I assume his rifle was an AK. I saw the lead guy right at the slightest glimmer of morning light and made out the wood rifle stock and receiver piece. The group saw me moving out and opened fire on me. I got out of there quick. I didn't see any of them after that."

"They shot at you?" Carla asked.

"Yes." *Duh, isn't that what I just said?*

"Were they wearing body armor?" Morris asked.

Kade shook his head. "I don't think so." He remembered he had dropped his Glock at gunpoint in the forest and wondered if it would ever turn up.

"How about while you were inside AgriteX—anything related to cartel activity there?" Morris asked.

"Yeah, earlier this week there was a major incident. I think the Chapter was worried there was a cartel source inside. All of the people in my group, the Associates, were called in for questioning on the lie detector, and they asked me a few questions around my possible involvement. They concluded that one of the Associates, a Carol Ries, was some kind of cartel informant, and they killed her on the spot."

"How do you know?" Morris asked.

"I was there when they did it."

Kade remembered something—he reached down to his hiking boot and got out the camera/recorder device and set it on the table. "There should be some photos and some audio of it on here."

Morris looked at the tech.

"Greg, you want to process what he has on there?"

"I'll get started on it right now." Belmont scooped up the device and left the room.

Morris looked back at Kade.

"Nice work."

"Hopefully the pictures came out," Kade said.

"Do you know anything more about this Carol Ries?" Singleton asked.

"No, except that she was very smart," Kade said. "Chemistry background, she said. Seemed kind of cold. All business."

The room was silent, and he could sense all of the brains around him in overdrive. He just wasn't sure if they were driving in the right direction and on the shortest route.

"Look," Kade said. "I don't know what the cartel is up to with AgriteX. Seems like a turf war or something. But I think the

Chapter is up to something much bigger and more dangerous than that right now. They're planning something on a large scale. The whole environmental program is just their camouflage."

"Duly noted," Morris said and checked his watch. "But first things first. Okay, Marquart is going to be here in a few minutes. We'll reconvene when the debriefing is concluded. Questions?"

Everyone shook their heads.

"Okay, thanks everyone."

•   •   •

Morris left the room, strode through the hallway, and took the stairs down instead of waiting for the elevator. SAC Caldwell and he would brief the assistant director at FBI headquarters in Washington, DC, on the situation over a video link in ten minutes.

CLEARCUT was now elevated to twenty-four-hour watch operations at the Strategic Information and Operation Center, or SOIC, at FBI HQ, and the Critical Incident Response Group had been engaged. The team would now get additional analyst and intelligence resources, and could share information at the national level more effectively with the DEA and Department of Homeland Security.

And in a little more than an hour, the SWAT team would go pluck Agent Jenkins off the top of Kidders Butte.

CHAPTER 55

Looking through his high-power binoculars, Sentry Sheeley continued to scan the area for ground activity from the top of Chapter Hill, a magnificent spot and the highest point on AgriteX property, about a half mile north of the headquarters building. Thirty yards behind him, the towering three-bladed AgriteX wind turbine spun and hummed.

Sheeley had climbed Chapter Hill a number of times before, usually running as part of Sentry team training. Today he was alone, tasked to the hill as an observation post because it offered a panoramic view to the east.

He'd just given his eyes a short break from the binos when his ears picked up a noise—a vibration separate from the wind turbine, combined with a whirring, swishing sound. Seconds later, he saw a black helicopter emerge from the northeast and halt at a hover over Kidders Butte, a half mile due east of his position at about the same elevation. Sheeley raised the binos again and recognized the helicopter as a UH-60M Blackhawk, confirming it on the laminated identification sheet in the notebook next to him.

Sheeley had been given one of the new two-way radios with strong encryption prior to assuming his post, and he yanked it out of his cargo pocket.

"Base, this is Sheeley," he said.

"This is Base. What's up?"

"I've got a Blackhawk helicopter over Kidders Butte. Two people coming down on a rope. One already on the ground. Total of three on the ground now. You copy?"

"Roger."

Then the voice over the radio changed.

"Sheeley, I want you to take out the helicopter," Marshall Owens said. "Understood?"

"Roger that," Sheeley said. "Out."

Sheeley dropped the radio and leaned inside the pop tent right next to him. He picked up the SA-7 Grail, positioned it on his shoulder, and put the helicopter in the sight. After activating the launcher, he partially squeezed the trigger until he heard a buzzing sound. He tilted the tube back at a forty-five-degree angle into the sky, made sure his legs were in a firm stance, and squeezed the trigger the rest of the way.

The missile exploded out of the tube in a high arc, trailing gray smoke, then dropped toward the helicopter. Sheeley put down the launcher and picked up the binos again.

Five seconds later, he saw the missile impact. A small orange fireball erupted from the side of the craft and the helicopter careened and fell to the butte surface.

"Gotcha."

CHAPTER 56

Saturday, June 29
4:04 p.m. (PDT)
FBI field office, Portland, Oregon

Morris and SAC Caldwell sat facing the camera on the opposite wall of the thirty-by-thirty War Room, a dedicated meeting room in sub-basement two. Caldwell was in his midfifties, shorter than average, and his stack of forehead wrinkles compressed and expanded like an accordion depending on whether he was talking or listening. He was wearing a charcoal suit with the coat draped on the chair behind him.

Four monitors were positioned in front of them on a wide conference table, and at this moment, both agents were focused on the one farthest to the left, which displayed a link to the SWAT tactical operations center located at an annex adjacent to the PDX airfield.

On the other end of the link, Assistant Special Agent in Charge Bruce Warren had a grim look on his face.

"The aircraft crashed and we've lost communications with the pilots," Warren said. "The last transmission over the radio said they had an inbound rocket."

Morris thought of Velasquez and everyone else on board, made the sign of the cross, and said a silent prayer.

"Oh God," Caldwell said. "How bad is it?"

"We have a Shadowhawk over the wreckage area now. The two SWAT agents who roped in, Pickney and Creviston, are okay and are with Agent Jenkins. Creviston managed to call in a report from his phone. They were getting Jenkins into his harness when the craft was hit, and the three of them were able to get out of the way as it came down. They ran back to the wreckage and managed to pull one person out—Agent Marrone."

Warren paused and another video came up on the third monitor.

"Okay," he said, "you can see them on the drone feed right now, zoomed in. Marrone is backed up against the tree and has a serious leg injury. They're going to have to move again soon—the fire's spreading."

Caldwell and Morris could see the group of four now sitting about one hundred yards away from the burning helicopter.

"And the others?" Caldwell asked.

"It doesn't look good," Warren said. "It looks like the three agents on the ground tried to get the others out of the wreckage, but they could only pull out Marrone due to the intense fire."

"Jesus," Morris said, and took a deep breath. "How are we getting these four out now?"

"We have a second SAR mission underway," Warren said. "A Blackhawk from the Oregon National Guard aviation company out of Salem is picking up another SWAT team and will be en route. We couldn't get another aircraft here quick enough. We're lucky to have a good relationship with that Guard team—their Blackhawk has flare countermeasures, unlike the one that went down."

"I thought the butte area was clear of any hostiles," Caldwell said.

"It is, as far as we can see," Warren said. "There's no visible activity on the ground except for our four agents. Once we have those four clear, Joe, we'll look to you and headquarters for guidance on recovery. We'll plan on continuing the drone surveillance support through the evening."

"We need to be patient and observe the situation before further action," Caldwell said in coarse monotone. "I don't want agents caught in the crossfire between these cartel soldiers and the AgriteX militia if they're gearing up for a battle. If they're going to slug it out, it's in the middle of the forest, and we can contain it there."

Caldwell turned to Morris. "There'll be a few others from the CIRG showing up here to support us. An agent from the Communications Exploitation Section and another behavioral analyst should be here shortly."

The Critical Incident Response Group (CIRG) was an on-call FBI team used to support the Bureau during a national crisis. Morris knew he was losing control of his operation, but the way things were going, he was happy to have the national-level support.

"Okay, we'll get them up to speed," Morris said.

"We'll need to work with Oregon state and local police on providing security for the closest residential areas," Caldwell said. "Try to find out from your source how many employees were at AgriteX round the clock at the time he left. Having to evacuate people from that AgriteX building is the scenario I'm most worried about."

Morris nodded. "Okay." Caldwell's plan wasn't aggressive, but after losing four agents in the crash, the ongoing safety of agents would be in the spotlight.

And knowing that Chris Velasquez was one of the four dead made Morris feel like his guts were getting ripped out.

CHAPTER 57

Saturday, June 29
7:29 p.m. (PDT)
Tillamook State Forest

Except for Messia and Sandoval, who sat next to each other inside their tent, the members of Team Echo were spread out on Hill 2230, northeast of Kidders Butte, with digital camouflage space blankets draped over their heads to reduce their infrared signature from aerial detection. A light rain had started ten minutes ago, and that made Messia feel a little more comfortable.

At Messia's direction, Sandoval called the teams over the radio in sequence and finished with Team Delta.

"Hey, the guys are hungry so we're moving up dinnertime," Sandoval said to Alvarado. "We need you to pick up the pizza at eight. Any problems with that?"

"No, that's cool," Alvarado said.

"Okay, we'll see you later tonight," Sandoval said.

Sandoval listened to the rain patter on the tent's fabric above his head. He wished he was with one of the lead teams, but Messia had become accustomed to having him close. He turned to Messia and said, "They'll do better with a bit more daylight left. They haven't had enough training in the dark."

"I was thinking the same thing," Messia said. "And now we've got some rain, which will make it harder for drones. We'll be done before we need to use any vehicle headlights. It's going to take the feds some time to get their shit together, but they'll be back."

When Messia, Sandoval, and several members of Team Echo saw the Blackhawk crash on Kidders Butte, Messia concluded it had to be a DEA or FBI bird. His teams all responded that they hadn't fired at the aircraft, thank God. To his surprise, there was no swarm of local law enforcement following the incident that his teams could see. Another helicopter appeared on the east edge of the butte for about twenty minutes and then departed. There was still a fire burning on the butte, but it had gotten smaller.

This whole event, in Messia's mind, ended his worry that AgriteX was collaborating with the feds. Owens was now trying to scare him off. Shooting down the helicopter seemed suicidal, but then again, Marshall always seemed to have a death wish. Messia thought he was right to trust his instincts and move his command and control off Kidders Butte. Marshall had to have known Messia's team was on the butte and wanted him to get bogged down there.

Sandoval received a text message and turned to Messia.

"Ramos says his observer is now in position. And I already checked on the mortar team. They're ready to go."

Messia nodded. He was confident in the targeting data since he'd personally taken the GPS reading in the AgriteX lobby last Monday during his visit.

"Great, let's walk the mortars right through their front door."

CHAPTER 58

Saturday, June 29
7:49 p.m. (PDT)
AgriteX

Positioned in the center of the 120,000-square-foot AgriteX build-ing roof, Owens and Guardian Stone heard the message come over one of Owens's radios. It was barely audible above the rooftop hum of ventilation units and their large fans. The drizzle had also picked up in the last few minutes, creating more background noise.

"This is Branson, Team Two. We've got some movement. Five or six people out there. Movin' real slow and wearin' camouflage. Got another eight hotspots on the thermal."

Owens's ten Sentry teams were regrouped into five teams of double the size, and they were fanned out around the outside of the headquarters, about three hundred yards into the forest. Owens looked at his ruggedized Samsung tablet PC, which showed views from the exterior cameras. He toggled between the camera views but couldn't pick out any movement from his perspective.

"Any other teams see anything?" Owens asked.

"This is Osterweis, Team Four. I've got people out there too. Think I can pick out two more on the thermal."

"Okay, everyone start drawing back to your headquarters posi-tions, nice and slow," Owens ordered. "We'll start taking 'em out from up here." He picked up the other radio to speak on the rooftop team's channel. "Okay, guys, we're giving our ground teams a few minutes to bring it back in. Get ready. I'll give the word, and then start dropping 'em."

There were eight Sentries on the rooftop, two per side. One Sentry per pair was set up with an M24 bolt-action sniper rifle and lay in position at the edge of the wall on a perch built out of two-by-four lumber with cushioned mats draped over the top. The other Sentry acted as a spotter and had an M240 machine gun ready for engaging targets closer to the building.

"So are these FBI or cartel targets out there?" Stone asked Owens. Stone was now the lone Guardian remaining at AgriteX, and Owens had picked him because of his strong performance and top Knowledge and Loyalty Index scores.

"I'm almost certain they're cartel," Owens said. "The FBI wouldn't be coming in this quick. We don't have hostages, and even though we took down one of their birds, they'd take more time to plan before coming in. I'm sure they're watching us at this point, but that's okay. If their attention is here with us, that's a good thing."

Stone nodded. "I'll give the L-FAC a heads-up that—"

At that second, a deafening crack-thump thundered thirty yards away. Owens and Stone collapsed into a ball and tried to cover their heads. There was a three-second pause. Owens grabbed the roof channel radio. He knew what that sound was.

"Take cover, we've got mortars inbound!"

In the next two minutes, which felt like fifteen, explosions ripped through the building around them. Stone dragged Owens inside the roof exit and shut the thick steel door behind them. Owens wasn't counting, but the building violently shook from around twenty explosions. Then, at once, they stopped.

"I've got to get you down to the vault before there's more," Stone said.

"There won't be any more. Messia was just softening us up. Wouldn't have thought he'd bring fucking mortars. Goddamn! Okay, let's get back out there."

They pushed the door back open and crawled onto the roof. Dust and smoke clouded the air. Owens regripped the radio. "This is Roof Base. Is everyone okay?"

"This is North. We're okay."

"West is okay."

"This is East. We're all right, but Lowry checked on South. They're gone. That part of the building is caved in."

"Damn," Owens said. "Okay, hold on."

Owens picked up the other radio and spoke into both at the same time as the sound of sporadic gunfire began from the fringes of the forest. The drizzling rain continued, and the gray sky created an early nightfall.

"Sentry teams," Owens said, "give me status in sequence."

Teams One through Five replied they were all inside the building and using the first-floor barred windows for defensive positions, tapping out those panes that hadn't shattered already. Team Three reported they had four killed from the mortar impacts while retreating back through the main entrance. The rest of the team ran to an alternate fortified service door to get inside.

"Okay, all teams, this is Base. Listen up," Owens said. "We've got some casualties up here on the roof and the building's damaged in front from what looks like a mortar attack, but we're hanging tough. This is our sacred land. Our home. And we're going to defend it. Now let's light 'em up!"

All of the Chapter teams opened fire with a combination of measured shots and automatic bursts. The roof snipers started hitting targets as fast as they could. When their adversaries in the forest realized they were being shot at long range, they responded with a ferocious barrage from their AK-47s.

"They're in digital camo," Team One said. "Kind of hard to see 'em."

Owens tapped on his tablet and turned on the building floodlights, then activated the additional floodlights out in the tree line.

"Here they come," the Team Four leader said.

"Fuck," the West sniper team said in unison.

"They're running right at us!" Team Two said.

The force assembled at the forest's edge emerged in a full assault. Owens and Stone crawled up behind the West roof sniper team. Owens didn't have to look over the wall to see the flood of Messia's men rushing toward them, as they were now showing up on camera and on his tablet's wireless video.

Owens nodded and clenched his fist while watching Messia's men get cut down. His teams were doing a great job, but Messia had many more people, and those people would be well trained in raid tactics. It was only a matter of time.

"They're at the walls, starting to fire in the windows," someone from Team One said.

"Roof team, we've got enemy at the wall," Owens said. "Hit them with the two-forties."

The Sentries who had been spotting for their sniper partners grabbed their M240 machine guns, leaned over the walls, and fired down on Messia's men.

"There's another big group moving to the east in the forest toward the storage facility," the closer member of the North sniper team said.

"West and North, let's move the twenty-fours to the north wall and try to take out as many of that group as you can." Owens then spoke into the other radio. "Sentry teams, move to reinforce the main entrance if you can."

They'll go through the front. Messia already knows the way to the executive area from the front.

We'll give them a good fight, then let them all in.

Sentry Conrad of Roof Team West slid off his sniper perch, pivoted, and began to move across the roof in a crouch. There was a dull thud of something bouncing twice on the roof beside him. He craned his neck to the right and saw the green sphere roll and come to rest, and as his mind registered what it was, he dove to the ground in the opposite direction and yelled, "Grenade!"

CHAPTER 59

Owens and Stone both felt like they'd been stabbed in the back by a burning pitchfork as the shrapnel from the exploding M67 fragmentation grenade sank into their flesh. They rolled forward and huddled next to each other.

"I'm hit!" Owens said.

"Same here," Stone said in an agonized grunt. "Get inside. I'll check on Conrad."

Owens ignored Stone's suggestion. Instead, he refocused and found his radios.

"Roof Team: Stone and I are hit. We're moving down to the executive wing. You're welcome to come and join us."

"This is Team North. We're engaging targets near the storage area," Sentry Stewart said. "There's also a convoy of enemy vehicles moving in—mostly pickups. We're going to stay and keep shooting."

"Okay," Owens said. "Watch out for more grenades." Owens switched to the radio in his other hand. "This is Base. Team Leaders, give me a status in sequence of how many men you've got, and where you are."

The Team Leaders responded as they'd been trained to do.

Team One had been cut down to four men at the entrance atrium.

There was no response from Team Two.

Team Three was on the run with six left.

And Team Four and Team Five had linked up for eleven men total.

"Okay," Owens said, "the enemy has a foothold in the atrium so you guys need to fall back. Teams Four and Five, move through the north side of the building and come south into the executive wing. Team One, withdraw to the executive wing and let me know when you're behind the access door."

Owens saw Stone crawling back toward him, shaking his head.

"Conrad's gone," Stone said. "We've got to leave him."

Owens nodded. Most of his own strength had left him, and now being both weak and wounded, he knew he was becoming useless. He shoved the radios in his cargo pockets. Together, Owens and Stone crawled on all fours over to the roof door again, and helped each other to get on their feet and slip inside the door to the stairwell.

They caught their breath and staggered down the steps, clutching the rail until they reached the second-floor landing. Owens paused next to another narrow door inside the stairwell marked "FIRE EQUIPMENT," and deactivated the lock by placing his thumb on the access pad. Stone had never been inside the four-foot-wide hallway or known about this secret door.

The passage curled to their right and ended at a black steel spiral staircase. With Stone behind him, Owens descended to ground level, where a door opened into the sitting room of Owens's office. When Stone shut it behind him, the door blended into the foggy lake wall mural.

"Come on, let's go inside the vault," Owens said. They both limped into the room and Owens pointed to a matted area of the floor. "We can sit down here and bleed together."

Stone knelt on the mat with a tortured look on his face while he unbuttoned his shirt top.

"How bad is it?" he asked.

Owens looked at Stone's black undershirt, which was soaked with blood in the back and shredded in several spots where the shrapnel had penetrated. There were four deep wounds. He sighed. "All of our docs are gone, and I'm afraid my first-aid kit in here isn't going to help. I don't even think I can get up again to fetch it."

"That's all right. I knew the deal," Stone said. "I noticed you didn't shut the vault."

Owens nodded. A voice came over his radio.

"Base, this is Team Four!"

"This is Base," Owens said.

"We're getting overrun—they've got too many."

"If you're able to get out of the building now, get the hell out," Owens said. He pulled the second radio out of his pocket.

"Roof Team, are you there?"

"Your roof team is fucking dead," a voice with a Mexican accent said on the other end.

Owens turned off the radio and set it on the glass cocktail table. Within arm's reach was a compact refrigerator, and he pulled out two bottles of water and set one in front of Stone. They both guzzled some water down, listening to the sound of gunfire outside of the executive wing.

Owens opened a small bamboo box from the coffee table and retrieved two joints, handing one to Stone and then lighting them both with a silver Zippo lighter.

"You fought with your men to the end, Marshall. That says it all. It's been fun working with you."

"Likewise," Owens said. "This whole thing is going to work out beautifully. We're just not going to be around to see the end. But I'll see you again."

"The only punishment is here on Earth."

"Amen."

Five minutes later, the nearby sound of gunfire stopped. Owens hit a button on a remote control from the coffee table and soft flute music began to play around them. They could hear shouting in Spanish out in the reception area.

His teams had fought with honor to the last man. They fought with the belief they could win and the Chapter would grow and prosper as a people. The spirit of the Chapter was unbroken.

Now his *cultus tilikum*, his Sentry warriors, would soon attack. His *tilikum*, or Guardians, would continue his important work. And his *elitah*, his Zulu slaves, would continue to serve him in the afterlife.

His time as *tyee*, the chief of a company and of a people, was coming to an end.

He picked up his radio and flipped to another channel.

"Team L-FAC, you there?"

"This is L-FAC," Sentry Judge said on the other end.

"Get ready to launch the Zulus' attack in about two minutes," Owens said. "You'll hear the signal, loud and clear. Anyone in a digital camo pattern is a target."

"Roger," Judge said.

A team of six cartel soldiers moved into the room, their AK-47s at the ready.

"How are you guys doing?" Owens asked.

The leader looked at Stone, at Owens, then back at Stone, and squeezed the trigger of his weapon. From fewer than ten feet away, the short burst of gunfire ripped into Stone's chest, killing him as he fell backward on the mat.

The leader swung the barrel of his AK-47 toward Owens and motioned with it.

"Get up. You're coming with us."

"No, I'm not going anywhere now," Owens said, and inhaled deeply on his joint. With the fist of his other hand, he wiped away the drops of Stone's blood that had landed on the right side of his face. "And you can tell Messia that his seed shipment was sold to other buyers months ago. He can give Tesar our personal thanks for financing us with the advance payment. So you have all fought for nothing. But I suppose you're not going to be around to tell him that. Well, don't worry, I'm sure he'll figure it out."

"Get him," the leader said and motioned to the pair of his men closest to Owens. The men reached under Owens's armpits to yank him up to his feet.

Owens shut his eyes and clicked the detonator inside his fist, and the 115 one-pound blocks of C-4 lining the walls of the vault exploded around him.

CHAPTER 60

Saturday, June 29
9:17 p.m. (PDT)
Tillamook State Forest

On top of Hill 2230, Team Echo was packed up and getting ready to hike back to its vehicles when a thundering boom echoed west of them in the valley.

"What the fuck was that?" Messia asked no one. He turned to Sandoval. "Have Alpha and Delta Teams check in." Messia stepped closer so he could listen to the radio.

"Ramos, what are you seeing?" Sandoval asked. "You hear that explosion?"

There was no response.

"Ramos, you hear me? Munoz?" Sandoval looked at Messia. "That's strange."

Now Messia was worried. He'd ordered Team Delta to peel off some men to support Alpha when Alpha encountered fierce fighting. That had chewed up another precious twenty minutes. And Ramos had just reported that most of Owens's men were dead and Ramos's men were flushing out the executive area of the building.

"Echo, this is Garcia!" Garcia's voice over the radio shouted. "The whole side of AgriteX exploded. Like, half the building is gone!"

Messia said to Sandoval, "What about the seed?"

"Have you gotten the seed?" Sandoval relayed.

"We haven't found it yet. We checked the bins in the storage facility, the storage units outside. We checked some other bags in the warehouse and there's just mulch and bark dust. Nothing in the composting area. Charlie is checking the other side—maybe they've had better luck."

"Keep looking. We're running out of time," Sandoval said. He didn't need Messia to tell him to say that.

"This is Charlie!" Figueroa yelled over the radio. "We're under attack!"

"You're under attack? From what?" Sandoval asked.

"They've got hundreds more soldiers with rifles, coming out of nowhere. Screaming like a bunch of fucking crazy people."

Sandoval looked at Messia, who showed no reaction to the news.

"What do you want me to say?" Sandoval asked.

Messia thought through every possible permutation of a plan during the next thirty seconds.

"Tell them to keep looking for the seed and that Bravo will come reinforce. Then call Garcia and tell him to go support."

Messia walked a few steps away while Sandoval relayed the messages. He couldn't tell Sandoval or anyone else, but from this point forward he knew they had failed. Marshall must have moved the seed inside the building, rigged it into whatever explosives he'd wired the AgriteX building with, and now the seed was just part of a massive dust cloud.

At this point, not only would every federal agency be looking for him, Tesar would hold him responsible for the seed and the failed attack—which almost assured a painful execution.

His best hope at this point would be to negotiate a deal for turning himself in to the feds through his attorney. He still had time to do this with a shred of planning.

Messia walked back to Sandoval and put his hand on his back. "Come on, Victor. We're getting out of here."

CHAPTER 61

Saturday, June 29
9:23 p.m. (PDT)
FBI field office, Portland, Oregon

The recorded debriefing dragged on for more than four hours in the briefing room. Morris had stopped by early on and informed the group that four agents were dead, and his disclosure added a tense weight to the air.

An agent named Cody Marquart led the questioning, which documented all of Kade's activities hour by hour during the entire operation to the best of his recollection. When Kade became impatient and tried to leap ahead to his opinions and conclusions, Marquart reeled him right back to the current discussion. Carla Singleton, Greg Belmont, and behavioral analyst Erica Norcross sat around the conference room table. Jerry Lerner continued listening in over the speakerphone.

When Kade spoke of the Chapter's technology and the medical procedures he'd undergone, the tone of the team's follow-up questions and their looks suggested they had some skepticism. There were suggestions he'd been hypnotized or otherwise brainwashed, which he didn't believe but couldn't effectively deny either.

Did he have tangible proof there was a chip inside his head? No, it was only what he'd been told and what he could see in his visual overlay before the MRI. There was nothing he could "show" anybody.

Marquart said he would suggest Kade receive a more thorough physical exam in the coming weeks.

Brilliant suggestion, buddy.

So Kade decided, until he was examined again, he would pull back from sharing everything, including the odd residual effects of the procedures. The facial recognition. His ability to pick up on and analyze micro-expressions in more detail if he could see them up close. If this team thought he'd lost his marbles now, they wouldn't believe the information he needed them to understand.

He also omitted some key incidents, such as shooting Sentry Hill and others inside AgriteX, and his fight with a presumed cartel member in the forest.

I'm not letting myself get arrested for doing whatever it took to get out of there.

No one would understand.

Other than short bathroom breaks and delivery pizza, there were no distractions. Before Marquart departed, he called Morris to let him know the debriefing was complete. Kade leaned toward the speakerphone and broke the ensuing silence.

"It's after midnight, your time, Jerry," he said. "Way past your bedtime."

"Yeah," Jerry said. "Sorry, you're stuck with me, pal. Hanging in there?"

"I don't have much of a choice."

Kade popped the lid on the ibuprofen bottle the hospital had given him and shook out a large pill, downing it with a sip of water. He then took an antibiotic pill from the bottle next to it.

Morris returned with stress and fatigue showing on his face. SAC Caldwell entered behind him, walking with a slight natural limp.

Morris waved to the group and then said to Kade, "I know that was a long time to sit, but we needed all the debriefing information first as evidence for warrants in case you got hit by a bus tomorrow."

"You look like you already got hit by the bus," Caldwell added. "Thanks for your efforts—I understand you've been through quite an ordeal."

Kade nodded and looked down.

Caldwell sat down in the center chair and was silent for a moment.

"Let me give you all an update on our current situation," he said. "We rescued our four agents near the crash site, so now our operational focus turns to preventing any immediate threat to the public from Chapter elements or cartel forces, and to stop the spread of any violence from their conflict.

"We also need to update our assessment of the Chapter's capability of conducting a terror attack within days. I'm speaking with the director and assistant director of the Counterterrorism Division in a few minutes, and want to make sure we're providing the best analysis we can."

Kade nodded. *About fucking time.*

"So we're asking all our resources," Caldwell continued, "what larger attack threat could be imminent? And so we pose that question to all of you in this room as well." Caldwell looked at Morris, who was still standing next to the door.

Morris nodded. "Before Constantino died in the hospital, I tried to dig into that question and got a troubling answer. He said it had already begun. And he said it was impossible to stop. Impossible to stop what? Do they have a pile of SA-7s and Owens is planning on using them around the country?"

"From what we already know," Singleton said, "and what Flash told us, they've trained their militia for an attack, not just defense. They just used an SA-7 on one of our helicopters to defend their headquarters against a perceived threat. So it seems they'll use the missiles opportunistically or in defense, but missiles aren't the thrust of their attack plan."

"General terror among the American public doesn't appear to be the goal," Norcross said. "They're looking at a government target, like government buildings. I would get all federal buildings on alert."

Morris looked at Kade. "You agree?"

"I saw an attack training template. I think we're talking multiple targets. So, yeah, government buildings would be likely. They fed me a diet of antigovernment propaganda daily. I imagine it would've only gotten more radical the longer I stayed. I think you can rule out military bases. Everything I heard was supportive of the military."

"So what kind of attack force are we looking at?" Morris asked.

"I tallied up the manpower while Flash was talking," Lerner said. "Confirmed, they've got a few hundred of these Sentries, which sound like well-trained small-unit leaders. Then there are over two hundred Guardians, graduates of their elite program, involved with some kind of government service or working at AgriteX. Another three hundred–plus people are graduates of a so-called political action program. And then they have a number of standard employees."

"You're not counting the prisoner-soldiers I talked about," Kade said. "They're a threat."

"If we're counting them," Morris said, "we probably don't have too much to worry about. From watching the situation at AgriteX from the Shadowhawks, it looks like someone released the prisoners at the Lost Lake Forest Camp, and they fought with the cartel gangs who attacked AgriteX. Both sides look like they got chewed up pretty bad. Seems like it would be hard to reconstitute a force to attack anything. We're working with Oregon State Police right now on rounding up the prisoners."

"So the Sonora cartel messed up the Chapter's attack before it got started," Caldwell said. "And now, worst case, we have a few hundred well-trained Chapter operatives who could lead various sleeper cells and hit targets. Multiple attacks, more like Oklahoma City. But no evidence that the Chapter has WMDs."

"No, the worst case is the Chapter has a much larger force," Singleton interjected. She had been quietly punching figures into her computer. "Several thousand by my quick-and-dirty math."

Morris gestured "hold on" with his hand.

"Thousands? How could they have anywhere near that?"

"Flash told us AgriteX and Lost Lake Forest Camp had some sort of partnership," Singleton said. "The inmates work on AgriteX-contracted projects, and it seemed like the AgriteX employees or Sentries worked at LLFC as inmate mentors."

"Okay," Morris said.

Singleton continued. "I asked Financial Crimes to check out that business structure for us. Turns out LLFC is one of one hundred ninety-one minimum-security prisons managed by Correctional Enterprises Corporation, or C-E-C, which is owned by Correctional Enterprises Group, or C-E-G. CEG is a holding company registered in Belize that also owns forty-nine percent of AgriteX, so there is an ownership relationship. CEG is then owned by a private-interest foundation registered in Panama."

"One hundred ninety-one prisons?" Caldwell asked in disbelief.

"Yes, one hundred ninety-one privately owned facilities nationwide," Singleton said. "Between a hundred fifty to two hundred fifty inmates at each."

"This is a national threat," Morris said.

"That's a damn sleeper *army*," Caldwell said.

"LLFC must be like a beta site," Kade said. "It's located right next to AgriteX and they've been spending months doing all of this training—training all of these other sites. Maybe years."

Norcross asked, "How could they keep discipline, silence, in a group of prisoners like this? It's hard enough in a small sleeper cell."

"You don't get it," Kade said. "They're Zulus. It's more than a little indoctrination. It's a protocol, or program. They're optimized for obedience and security."

Singleton said, "The transcript of our interview with Wade Rooker, the guy who escaped from the Chapter, indicated that when you're at the bottom of the organization, you're under constant surveillance and threatened. Or as he said, 'They're inside your head.'"

"Exactly," Kade said.

Morris waved his hand. "Okay, so let's assume a federal building target. Any way to prioritize locations?"

Kade shook his head. "Wait a sec. Doing multiple Oklahoma City–style attacks would kill thousands of low-level civilians. That doesn't sound like Owens."

"Why not? He's a dying megalomaniac," Norcross said. "He doesn't care about people."

"Nah, not quite," Kade said. "Yeah, he thinks he's invincible. Supremely confident, possibly delusional. But he knows he's on his way out. That changed things. Now he wants to make sure he takes his enemies with him. *Mamook sollecks.*"

"What?" Caldwell asked.

"It's Chinook," Kade said. "It means 'to make anger.' To make war against those you're angry with. He's not angry at your regular federal building employees."

"Who's he angry with?" Morris asked.

"The buck stops at the top," Kade said. "It's got to be the president or Congress. Owens isn't antiwar, even though he's angry at American abuse of power. It's about how he sees America's approach to war. Soldiers are pawns in a broken system. The government isn't decisive or effective. It's filled with cowards who don't use troops carefully, and when troops are deployed, they're hamstrung. Technology isn't benefitting soldiers on the ground. Veterans aren't taken care of."

Caldwell asked, "If they have prisoner-militia members at all these other facilities, how do they coordinate and move this army?"

"Buses," Kade said. "I mentioned that in the debrief I saw a couple of them at LLFC that were retrofitted to carry weapons and ammo. So they load these buses up for a basic but massive ground attack. Stealth and surprise. That sounds like Marshall's style to me."

"A fleet of buses wouldn't be a great way to go after the president," Singleton said. "Congress would be more likely."

Lerner said, "I have Owens's statement 'we need to clean house' from my debriefing notes. Is it too simple to think he's going after *the* House?"

Caldwell turned toward the phone "That's it. He means it literally. My God, he's going after Congress."

Kade could start to visualize it. "Yeah, thousands of armed soldiers bused in to attack the Capitol. That seems unbelievable . . . it would overwhelm the Capitol Police. If Marshall has that kind of manpower at his disposal, I think he'd order it. He hates Congress that bad. He said Congress has our soldiers' blood on its hands."

"It's plausible," Caldwell said. "But they'd have to position these buses within striking distance."

Morris didn't look convinced. "That's a long drive from western U.S. facilities. Buses would have to be on the road for days. Seems like it would attract a lot of attention."

"We need to set up checkpoints into the District for bus traffic," Caldwell said. "And have our assets looking for groups of buses and bus movement."

"The director should also task the National Counterterrorism Center with surveillance on the current activity inside and around as many CEC prisons as possible," Kade said.

"What are you thinking?" Caldwell said.

"It's almost one in the morning. It's lights-out for any of these prisons. If the lights are on, and prisoners are up and about, that's a big red flag something's going on right now. There are plenty of video assets that could be exploited quickly—surveillance systems, computer web cams, you name it."

Caldwell nodded. "Okay. Rob, let's go make the update call. Thank you, everyone."

"Hold on," Singleton said, looking at her laptop computer screen. "I looked it up while we were sitting here. Congress is in recess, now through July fifth. So the Chapter must be targeting the president or something else."

The room was silent, and then all of a sudden Kade stood up.

"No, Carla, that's it."

He's hitting them at home.

At night.

CHAPTER 62

Saturday, June 29
10:01 p.m. (PDT)
Portland, Oregon

Fox Five News's Amy Michalek reported it first. "We have breaking news tonight from Tillamook County. An FBI helicopter is downed in the Tillamook State Forest by armed gang members backed by the Sonora drug cartel. And a Tillamook County company gets caught in the crossfire.

"Now the details. Confidential sources have reported to Fox Five that an FBI and DEA operation against Oeste-13 gang members, who are supported by the Sonora drug cartel, culminated in a battle earlier this evening at about eight o'clock. The sound of gunfire and explosions were reported for several hours in the Tillamook State Forest by a hiker in the area. Fox Five was not permitted to fly Chopper Five into the airspace surrounding the reported operation.

"The conflict has reportedly spread to the private land of the AgriteX Corporation, an agricultural technology company located near Alderville. Reports of multiple fatalities of gang members and AgriteX employees have been confirmed by Oregon State Police sources. There are also unconfirmed reports of several federal agent deaths during the operation.

"Fox Five has also received a recorded video statement from AgriteX CEO Marshall Owens. Owens appears to have been very aware of the growing threat of gang violence to his business and the community."

Owens's face appeared on screen above the caption "Statement by Marshall Owens, CEO, AgriteX Corporation."

"The Sonora Cartel has declared war on our citizens, and no one in Washington seems to care about defending America. The cartel has repeatedly encroached upon our land and tree farms in an attempt to cultivate and harvest marijuana to sell in America. This has put our employees and the citizens of our local communities in danger. We've repeatedly asked state and federal authorities for assistance, but they have ignored us. Today, we said enough is enough. We spent many months training our employees to defend themselves against these gang members, and there's a good chance that a number of us may get hurt in expelling them. But we have to take a stand on our land, and we are taking that stand today."

Amy Michalek's face returned to the screen. "Obviously this is a very important developing story, and we will bring you continuing updates as we learn more."

CHAPTER 63

Saturday, June 29
10:21 p.m. (PDT)
FBI field office, Portland, Oregon

The FBI Strategic Information and Operations Center (SOIC) set up two colocated units inside FBI headquarters, SOIC-4 and SOIC-5, to coordinate communications between the Portland field office, the NCTC, and the White House Situation Room. SOIC-4 picked up the current FBI Criminal Investigative Division's operations in the vicinity of AgriteX, and SOIC-5 was assigned as the operational hub for the Counterterrorism Division's efforts to thwart the Chapter's presumed attack.

Agent Sean Lockwood, in SOIC-5, was connected via phone to the Portland field office briefing room, and another SOIC-5 connection went to the field office War Room in sub-basement two.

The seats around the briefing room's conference table had shuffled between breaks as some new faces had rotated in and out. Kade now sat between Norcross and Singleton, who both seemed concerned about how he was holding up. Morris had returned for a few minutes while Caldwell remained down in the War Room. Lerner was still on the phone making occasional comments. Another counterterrorism analyst, Raj Badesha, had been added to the group in the briefing room and sat next to Greg Belmont.

"Will killing Owens stop the attack?" Morris asked. "Assuming this is a simultaneous attack on our Congress members' homes?"

"It's not clear if Marshall Owens is still in charge or even alive, right?" Lockwood asked.

"It's not," Morris said.

"There was a big explosion at the headquarters we observed," Lockwood said. "That wasn't from any ground operation?"

"No, and we didn't fire any Shadowhawk munitions," Morris said. "They wouldn't have done that kind of damage anyway. A good portion of the building is demolished."

"We haven't picked up Owens in any two-way radio or phone chatter," Lockwood said. "We're now dealing with monitoring encrypted comms, so we can't review traffic in real time."

"So Pierce would be in charge with Owens gone?" Norcross asked.

"Yeah," Kade said.

The room was silent for a few collective breaths. Then Kade said, "I think it's too late to cut off the head of the snake and expect this thing to stop. Maybe you could get Marshall or Pierce to order the attack called off, but that sounds like a long shot."

Belmont pulled off his headphones and set them on the desk. "Check this out." He pulled up some new video on the wall screen. There was a recorded statement from Owens that the news networks were now showing. Everyone in the room watched it.

"He's blaming the cartels," Badesha said.

"And the authorities for not responding," Kade added.

"It's a complete lie . . . designed to sound convincing," Singleton said.

Morris grumbled a few cuss words.

Lockwood said, "We're now getting a directive to acquire targeting information on their leadership. Do we have any idea where Pierce is?"

"No," Morris said.

Kade said, "The other Associates like me were supposedly being moved to either Nevada or Montana, so Pierce could be on the road or in a number of different states."

"Can't you try and pick up his communications like you're doing for Owens?" Morris asked.

"We have no known voiceprint for Pierce," Lockwood said.

"Damn," Morris said.

"No, we *do* have a voiceprint," Belmont said. "Flash recorded Pierce talking during what he described as an execution." He clicked on a thumbnail picture to enlarge it on the screen, showing Carol Ries strapped into the Verax chair and Pierce standing beside her.

"Okay, can you get that audio to us now?" Lockwood asked.

"Yeah, the file will be coming in a few seconds," Belmont said.

"Good, good," Morris said.

Kade shook his head. *It's progress, but we're going to run out of time.*

CHAPTER 64

Saturday, June 29
11:00 p.m. (PDT)
Gale's Creek, Oregon

In the small campground area, Pierce keyed *GREEN LIGHT* into the cell phone Owens had provided him and hit "Send to All." The final chance to abort the mission had passed. The teams were all loaded onto vehicles and a few of them were already on the move, timing their own attacks for 3:00 a.m. Eastern. All had planned, rehearsed, and timed their route.

Pierce next went to the contact list in the phone, searched for "Paul Courson," and dialed the number.

"Hello?" Paul responded.

"Our renegade Associate I spoke to you about was never recovered. On the chance he's taken refuge in the field office, I'd like you to task our asset with delivering the Associate his code."

"That's not going to be easy," Paul said. "His access level in the field office is still low."

"I know," Pierce said. He read Paul the code number and then gave him a few ideas. When he was done, he said, "If none of that works, he'll have to improvise."

"Okay. This risks exposing him, so should I direct him to get out afterward and await further orders?"

"Yes, and I'll get him a large bonus if he's successful," Pierce said. "You can tell him that."

"Okay, good luck."

"Thanks, and good luck to you," Pierce said, and disconnected.

Pierce now dialed the number of a cell phone lying in the dashboard cubby of the mobile command unit RV and set his own phone beside it. He muted both phones.

Sentry Luciani was sitting next to him in the driver's seat. "Not much time now," Luciani said.

"Yes, not much time," Pierce said. He got out of the RV, walked over to the adjacent SUV, and popped the hatchback.

He leaned inside and attached the suppressor to his pistol.

CHAPTER 65

Saturday, June 29
11:12 p.m. (PDT)
FBI field office, Portland, Oregon

Zach Poole returned to the field office by way of the parking structure entrance, passing through the security/duty officer section.

"Late night for you too?" the duty officer, Agent Montez, asked. The security guard next to Montez guided Poole through the metal detector and inspected his Targus backpack.

"Yeah," Poole said with a frustrated look. "Forgot a few details on a deadline."

"Have fun," Montez said.

Poole took the elevator to the third floor and walked the hall to where his cubicle was located. He could see a handful of people working in the first bay so he took a route around it through the break room. When he reached his own area, the lights were dimmed in energy-saving mode, and he didn't bother to hit the switch to wake the lights back up.

He sat down at his desk and turned on his laptop. If Associate Sims was in sub-basement two, Poole would never be able to get to him. He'd have to try to draw Sims out with a phone call. But maybe he was elsewhere in the building. Poole would try to rule that out first.

He went to his Microsoft Outlook scheduling program and started searching through the rooms that were booked for meetings. He looked for rooms that were reserved for continuous use at the present time, and scribbled down the numbers CR 2C, CR 3F, BR 4B. He then shut down his laptop again.

Conference room 3F was not too far away. After he walked up and stood outside the door, he didn't hear any activity. He knocked lightly before opening the door and confirming no one was inside.

Poole walked out from the cubicle bays back to the elevator and took it down to the second floor. When he found CR 2C, he could see a band of light under the door, and heard active discussion inside. He rapped on the door with his knuckle and opened it a crack. He saw four people inside, and recognized one of the two women from Public Relations. They all looked at him a little funny.

"Sorry, wrong room," he said with a smile and shut the door.

He was now left with BR 4B, which posed a challenge similar to that of the War Room down on SB-2. His badge didn't allow entry through the door on the fourth floor. Maybe he could knock on the door and someone would let him in. He took the elevator to the fourth floor and stepped out into the foyer, which had two break couches side by side on the carpet and a pair of restrooms. He decided to go and wait inside the men's bathroom until he heard someone come out the main door.

Instead, six minutes later, the elevator sounded with a *bing* and Poole heard its door open. He waited until he heard the beep of an access card and came out of the bathroom. The man on his way into the office held the door open for him. Poole recognized the face but couldn't remember a name.

"Thanks," Poole said.

He slowed his pace and let the man get a good distance away before he started scanning the rooms. At the end of the hall, he made a right turn and then spotted the placard for BR 4B. There was quiet discussion going on inside, and he could also hear the sound from a speakerphone. He took a few seconds to get his thoughts together before he knocked and pushed on the door, which he found was locked.

Shit.

He knocked again.

CHAPTER 66

President Darryl Greer took the call from Hugh Conroy, director of National Intelligence, with Stanley Hassett, director of the FBI, on the same line. Greer, a Democrat from Missouri, had turned fifty last month and was six months into his first term. He sat on the couch of the anteroom in his boxers and a white T-shirt. His thick gray hair was in a jumble, and his face now had a light salt-and-pepper beard growth.

"Mr. President," Hassett said, "we have an emergency situation, credible intelligence leading us to believe an attack on Congress, a simultaneous attack on the members' homes while they're now in recess, is imminent."

"Oh my God," Greer said, his brown eyes snapping into instant focus. He paused, then asked, "Do we know who's being threatened?"

"No," Hassett said, "but it's conceivable that most, if not all of them, could be under threat."

"*Every* member?"

"Yes, sir," Hassett said. "The group leading this is the same one responsible for the deaths of our four agents yesterday."

"The Chapter," Greer said.

"Yes, sir."

Greer had received a few notes on AgriteX and the Chapter from Conroy over the last two mornings as part of the Daily Intelligence Briefing, and Greer had received an additional update on the slain FBI agents at about seven o'clock the prior evening.

"Hugh and I are already en route. Should be there in ten minutes," Hassett said.

"Okay, I'll meet you in the Situation Room," Greer said.

Greer disconnected and took a deep breath. He looked back toward the bedroom and decided to let his wife, Sylvia, sleep for a few more hours. An aide had left some clothes in the bathroom. *I don't think we can move quick enough to stop this. This is going to be absolutely devastating.*

He went to the pink marble sink to splash water on his face and wet down and comb his hair.

How could we not have known about this?

CHAPTER 67

Saturday, June 29
11:27 p.m. (PDT)
FBI field office, Portland, Oregon

The briefing room became silent when SOIC-5's Agent Lockwood said over the speakerphone, "We're getting word that it appears the prisons are ramping up for an attack."

"What if their goal is hostages?" Singleton asked. "Have there been any kind of demands communicated?"

"No demands we are aware of, but all hostage rescue teams have been alerted to that possibility," Lockwood said. "And that's not going to help much in the next hour. Notifications are being blasted out now, so the early warning can help everyone get to safety or add security quickly."

"I remember Pierce saying hostages were a waste of time," Kade said. "I don't think I mentioned that in my debrief."

"We're assuming they have the worst intentions," Lockwood said. "If we can get Owens on the phone, what could make him call off the attack?"

"There's not much," Norcross said. "He's dying—it's his last hurrah."

"He had a son die in Afghanistan," Singleton said. "Mortally wounded from an IED, and they couldn't medevac him fast enough. Maybe we lie and say we have additional information he'd want to know."

Kade looked at Singleton, surprised and disappointed she hadn't shared that information before, but Kade told himself to get over it. That's how intel sometimes worked.

"That's a creative angle," he said. "You know, Marshall asked me about Afghanistan, and I didn't have any idea why. But it's probably too late for him to call this thing off."

"Can we jam communications from Pierce?" Badesha asked. "Cut off any orders?"

"There're still trying to get a fix on his position," Lockwood said.

"I think the attack is on autopilot now," Kade said.

A wall phone rang in the room, which Belmont answered.

"Okay, we'll all come down," he said, then hung up and turned toward the team. "Agent Morris wants us all down in the War Room, Flash included. The director is verbally granting everyone in this group temporary access." Belmont stepped over to the speakerphone. "Sean, it looks like we'll add a line for you down in the War Room, but we're shutting down here."

"Okay," Lockwood said. "Talk to you again in a little bit."

At that moment, there was a light knock at the door as everyone at the table started to talk among themselves and gather their belongings. Belmont stepped over to the door and opened it.

The man standing there scanned the inside of the room and stopped when he saw the person he was looking for. He then leaned in and spoke to Belmont.

"I have a note from the duty officer—a message from a Janeen Sims for Kade Sims? Some new contact information for her."

Belmont looked puzzled, but Kade overheard and turned around.

"Yeah . . . that must be for me, thanks." Kade stood up and came over. "So much for confidentiality," he mumbled to himself.

He took the folded message out of Belmont's hand and got a glimpse of the man's face in the door as he turned and left. He wasn't sure if he imagined it, but for a split second, he saw a name flash in his vision. It was so quick he couldn't make it out, and Kade thought it was his exhausted mind playing tricks with him.

He looked at the paper form and the word *PHONE* was circled with the number *84379513* handwritten below it. He thought there had to be a mistake since Janeen's number had a 351 prefix, but when he read the number anyway, the digits seemed like they leapt off the paper at him, enlarged somewhere in his consciousness to an enormous font size, and he instantly felt as if he had the worst case of flu in history.

He became dizzy and collapsed on the floor, his muscles weak and stomach nauseous. His head pounded and even the feeling of his shirt against his skin was painful.

"Flash, are you okay?" Singleton said. Her voice sounded warbly and he saw her face and Belmont's in the edge of what was becoming tunnel vision.

"No, I'm not." He started to shake with chills and his teeth began to chatter.

Belmont and Badesha stretched him out flat on the floor. Singleton's cool hand touched his forehead. Other people were speaking, but it was as if he could only hear and see right in front of his face.

"You feel hot," she said.

"I'll call an ambulance," Belmont said.

Kade rolled sideways and threw up water and pepperoni pizza. He wasn't sure what happened for the next five minutes, but he saw Morris's distorted face peering over him.

"Hang in there, Flash. You'll be okay," Morris said.

"I know. If I wasn't, I'm sure I'd be dead already."

"Who brought this?" Morris said to the room while holding the message.

"I don't know who it was," Belmont said.

"I think it was Zach Poole," Singleton said. She wiped Kade's eyes and mouth with a wet towel.

Morris looked at Belmont. "Call the duty officer. See if we can stop everyone from leaving the building." He leaned over Kade. "Flash, when I talked to Constantino, he received a message before having a stroke." Morris pulled out a business card with the number written on the back. "Can you see this?"

Kade tried to not think about the number still burning in his mind. He looked at the new number Morris had. He didn't read the number, just counted eight digits.

"Yeah, I see it. You should have told me about that earlier."

"Why, do you know the number?"

He coughed, forced himself to sit up, and then took a few deep breaths to make sure he wasn't going to vomit again. He thought about Carol Ries and glanced over at the picture Belmont still had up on the screen.

"No, but that doesn't matter. Forget the ambulance and get me to the War Room."

CHAPTER 68

Sunday, June 30
2:36 a.m. (EDT)
Walpole, Massachusetts

The D8 Crew bus idled at the front gate of Camp Walpole, with the Crew One and Crew Two Zulus respectively filling the twenty seats on the left and right sides of the aisle. Between their legs, resting on the seat, were AR-15 semiautomatic rifles with the muzzles pointed upward. On their hips were stun guns fixed to their belts.

Sentry Wolf sat in the driver's seat and Sentry Robertson stood behind the front right seat next to the door with the intercom microphone in his hand. They each carried a Sig Sauer P226 pistol with eight extra clips slid into pouches on their custom belts.

"Listen up," Sentry Robertson announced to the crews on the D8 bus. "We've got two minutes until we roll out of Walpole. Twenty minutes to reach the house in North Hills, one minute for offload, and ten minutes to get our business done. Roger?"

"Roger!" everyone repeated.

"Remember, you have sixty rounds total once you leave the bus. But we're going to try to use the stun guns inside the house first, roger?"

"Roger!"

"We'll do our best to not harm family members. We've reviewed the photos. We separate their twelve-year-old son, Colin; eight-year-old son, Matthew; and six-year-old daughter, Lily, to the southwest side of the home to one of the three bedrooms. Loren Seale remains near the front of the home in the dining room. We bring Congressman Seale out the garage exit and to the gate. If he can't open it for us, then we have Mrs. Seale do it at gunpoint. You have the plan's checklist on your home screens. Listen to the commands from Wolf and me, roger?" ·

"Roger!"

Behind the bus, in the idling black SUV, Sentry Severa flashed the brights and the front gate of the facility began to open. Severa looked in his rearview mirror and saw the D4 Crew bus ready to follow them out of the gate to go on their own route.

"Okay, it's time, gentlemen!" Robertson said. "You're about an hour away from the end of your contract and the beginning of your freedom. Let's get it done!"

CHAPTER 69

The national security team had been summoned, but other than Directors Conroy and Hassett, only General (retired) Reid McAlister, the national security advisor; Fredrick Bivens, the assistant to the president for homeland security and counterterrorism; and General Trent Ridder, vice chairman of the Joint Chiefs of Staff, had arrived and were seated at the conference table.

The five men were transfixed by updates from their notebook computers, phones, and live video displayed on wall-mounted monitors. Two aides assisted with the room technology. President Greer joined the group, sitting at his preferred chair in the center of the table.

"Do we know the when and how of this attack yet?" Greer asked.

"Yes, sir," Bivens said. "The attack's already underway. Up on the screen here, as I advance through some of the pictures and the live video streaming from a handful of these CEC prisons, you can see that buses are leaving or waiting to leave the facilities."

Greer looked back and forth between the pictures and video. "*School* buses?"

"Yes, sir," Bivens said. "It looks like they've painted their prison buses to look like school buses."

"Bastards," Greer said. The screen flashed between surveillance video photos of buses departing, grainy pictures of soldiers armed with semiautomatic rifles loading buses, and prisoners getting dressed in uniforms—those time stamped at just after eleven o'clock Eastern time.

An aide set down a mug of coffee in front of Greer and he pushed it aside.

"What are we doing to stop this?" he said.

"We've sent NTAS alerts to all subscribers," Bivens said, "contacted all of the governors, and alerted every FBI office. The FBI is sending alerts out to every state and local law enforcement organization they have emergency procedures established with. We've also notified Congress, alerting them of an imminent threat and directing them to seek refuge in a place of safety."

"Only problem is it's the middle of the night," Greer said. "And they may feel safest in their homes."

"Every available intelligence resource and asset is tasked on this," Conroy said.

"We're targeting the Chapter's command and control," Hassett said, "and believe we'll have a target in minutes. But engaging the target this rapidly leaves us with only a few options."

"And what are they?" Greer asked.

General Ridder said, "Sir, we can't scramble aircraft or launch drones fast enough to engage the target once we acquire it. The only way we can hit it immediately is with a Block Four Tomahawk fired from one of our subs in the Puget Sound. We alerted the USS *Michigan* and they are ready. It would be thirteen minutes from launch to target impact in the Portland area. But we'd need to launch now, before we have the target acquired."

"A Tomahawk fired into greater Portland?" Greer said, thinking of the horrible consequences of this "option."

"Yes, sir," Ridder said. "Assuming the target is correct, it will be dead accurate. Even if the target moves, we can still hit it."

"And what if it's not the right target?" Greer asked. "Or it's near people?"

"We can retask the missile in flight to splash in the Pacific," Ridder said.

Greer looked at the large digital wall clock. Ten seconds elapsed while he watched it and the time changed to 2:41 a.m. Eastern. He looked back at Ridder.

"Fire the Tomahawk."

"Yes, sir." Ridder moved to the other side of the room to talk on a different communications line.

"But this doesn't stop the militia force on the move right now," Greer said. "What else can we do about that?"

"There are too many potential targets," Conroy said, "and we can't get a fix on them fast enough. We can only send the alerts."

Hassett had been on the phone and his voice suddenly grew louder and more animated with information he'd just received.

"Mr. President, we may have another way to hinder the attack, but we'll need you to authorize it."

"Okay, let's hear it."

CHAPTER 70

Saturday, June 29
11:47 p.m. (PDT)
FBI field office, Portland, Oregon

The field office leadership, CLEARCUT team members, and new additions were now crammed into the War Room, except for Jerry Lerner, who was no longer permitted to dial in on an unsecured line.

The room was hot, and Kade took sips of cold water to take his mind off his discomfort. The number 84379513 had faded to a watermark in his mind and he tried to forget it.

Agent Lockwood from SOIC-5 came on the line. "The EOC for GETS is now asking us for clarification on what we need. Go ahead, EOC," he said.

The Government Emergency Telecommunications Service (GETS) was a network set up to bypass regular traffic in the case of national emergencies, and the Emergency Operations Center (EOC) was a group of technicians from all major phone carriers in partnership with the National Security Agency that could be called on 24/7 in a national emergency to serve on order of the president.

President Greer had just ordered it activated.

"Okay, Joshua Pierce's phone has an active signal and is stationary," the female EOC technician said. "You are requesting additional information from the phone?"

"Yes," Kade said. "First, we need the contact lists."

"Okay," EOC said.

On the videoconferencing monitor, the EOC technician's shared computer view let the team in the War Room see her clicking through various screens. The system seemed sluggish.

"We're out of time," Morris said. "Why is this taking so long?"

"Poor signal strength," EOC said. "The model of phone that Pierce is using doesn't store the contacts or other information in the cloud where we can grab it. We're having to go to the actual phone, and the phone has 128-bit encryption on it, which we're now finally through."

After a minute, a diagram of folders appeared on the phone.

"Okay, where from here?" EOC asked.

Kade looked at the folder list—five folders titled with the single letters A, E, G, S, and Z.

"Upload the contacts from G, S, and Z," he said.

"Any particular order?" EOC said. "It's going to be one at a time on the upload, and the phone is almost out of power."

"And you need to hurry—that location has been targeted," Lockwood said.

Zulus won't have phones. Sentries are leading the attack.

"Okay," Kade said. "Upload S, then G, then Z. Can you look into a contact record while they are uploading?"

"Yes, I can do that," EOC said. "Here's the first one in the S folder."

A contact record screen popped up for a Barry Adams.

"Scroll down, please," Kade said.

Kade watched as the screen moved down through the name, phone number, and personal e-mail address fields to a field labeled PIN#.

"Stop," Kade said.

In that field was an eight-digit number.

"Okay, here's what you're going to do," Kade said. "You're going to send a high-priority text message to every contact you're uploading, and that message is going to be the contact's own PIN number."

"I don't think we have time to do that," EOC said.

"You have to figure it out," Kade said.

"You've got less than ten minutes," Lockwood said.

"Find a way!" Morris yelled.

CHAPTER 71

The Camp Walpole D8 Crew bus had avoided I-95, taking secondary roads northeast past Canton to Route 138 and following it north through the Blue Hills Reservation. Five minutes later, the bus turned off the highway and entered a residential neighborhood next to the Blue Hills Golf Club. After weaving through the quiet streets, the bus made a final left turn and headed straight down a row of houses toward a cul-de-sac.

At four hundred yards out, Robertson and Wolf could see two royal-blue-and-white police cars illuminated under the streetlights, parked in front of the gated residence at 15 Laurel Place. Wolf slowed the bus to less than five miles per hour. After a quick conversation with Wolf, Robertson got on the intercom.

"Listen up, Crews! We've got two Milton police cars at the target, standing between justice and your freedom. So we have a slight change in plan. Crew One, as we come to a halt, your side will be facing the two cars. The team member closest to the window will target both police cars with a full clip of ammo and then stop. Your buddy will secure you an extra clip from the storage bin.

"Crew Two, when we stop and Crew One is finished targeting the cars, rows one to ten will exit out the front with me, and neutralize the car on the right. Rows eleven to twenty out the rear to neutralize the car on the left. Then proceed as planned at the front gate. Roger?"

"Roger!"

"Crew One, when Crew Two is off-loaded, your entire crew will exit out the rear to the lower section of the western wall, with ladders and smoke grenades, and proceed as planned. Roger?"

"Roger!"

"Okay, Crew One, drop your windows and wait for my command. I need everyone to be silent."

Amidst the clatter of the bus windows sliding down, Robertson picked up the two-way radio on the channel Sentry Severa was monitoring in the trailing SUV.

"Severa, we've got two police cars we're gonna take out now. Watch our backs in case they've called backup."

Severa did a slow U-turn and stopped.

"Roger, I've got your back."

CHAPTER 72

Sunday, June 30
2:57 a.m. (EDT)
The White House Situation Room

Everyone's attention was focused on two screens—a video feed showing a bird's-eye view of the solitary RV target in the forested park area and a live feed being streamed by the Tomahawk's own camera in flight.

"Sir, our Tomahawk operator has one minute remaining to redirect it," Ridder said.

"Why would we redirect it?" Greer asked. "We're looking at the target now, right?"

"Yes, we are," Director Hassett said. "But we're still uploading data from the target area—data that can help us kill or capture more Chapter members. A phone contact list."

"How much data do we have?" Greer asked.

"About half of the directory," Hassett said.

"Any idea on how accurate the list is?" Greer asked.

"No, we can't say for sure," Hassett said. "But we'll have the names to go after."

"Assuming it's accurate, you'll have to locate all of these people," Greer said. "And that may take days or weeks, right?"

"Yes, sir," Hassett said.

Greer folded his hands and rested his chin on top of them while looking at the screen showing the RV.

"Quick recommendations—hit the target or redirect?" Greer asked, and went around the room for responses. McAlister, Bivens, and Ridder recommended hitting the target. Conroy and Hassett recommended redirecting.

"Keep the missile on target," Greer ordered.

Twenty seconds later, the black-and-white video of the missile showed its precise route threaded through a small clearing of trees right up until impact with the RV.

The other overhead video feed displayed a billowing dust cloud and shock wave that split, uprooted, and shook all of the trees within several hundred feet of where the target used to be.

CHAPTER 73

At fifty yards from Congressman Seale's home, Robertson thought he could make out that each police car only had one officer seated inside.

"I think they've got one officer posted outside and their partner posted inside," Robertson said to Wolf. "I like the odds. This shouldn't be a problem if we get it done quick."

"Yeah, all right, here we go." Wolf began to ease the bus to a stop.

Robertson unholstered one of his Sig Sauers. As he reached for the intercom microphone, his cell phone chimed and buzzed with an inbound text message. He could hear the same from Wolf's phone, sitting somewhere on the console. At this hour, it had to be from headquarters.

A final message?

He glanced at the text for a split second, saw it was a number, and ignored it. Wolf also did a quick check of his phone, shrugged, and gave Robertson an annoyed look.

"Now!" Robertson said over the intercom while pointing toward the police cars.

Crew One opened an enormous volley of fire on the two cars from the windows. In less than ten seconds, the firing was complete and the cars were pocked full of holes. There was no return fire. Robertson felt an ordinary level of nervousness, but suddenly he felt weird. For some reason, the text message he'd glanced at remained in his mind, like he'd looked at a bright light and the impression was still there.

"Crew Two, let's go!" he yelled without the intercom and signaled with his hand for everyone to get up. He opened the bus door and began to head down the stairs, but then staggered out onto the pavement. The eight-digit number still burned in his mind, grew larger, and now he could see it.

39804772

He shook his head, but he couldn't get rid of it. Then the stoplight graphic on the side of his vision turned red and started to blink.

There was a sharp pain inside his head, and he felt his body hitting the asphalt.

What's going on? Did I just get shot in the head?

Robertson saw his crew members gathering around him in confusion as his consciousness began to slip away.

CHAPTER 74

Over the fourteen-hour drive, the relocation van containing the four Sentries and three Associates traveled from AgriteX through Salem, over the Cascade Range to Bend, continuing southeast into Nevada using small two-lane highways. Bathroom and stretch breaks were no longer than ten minutes every three hours and were chosen in remote pull-off areas. The Sentries seemed to be familiar with the route.

When night fell at about nine o'clock, Lin and Daniel slept while Walter stayed awake as long as he could. What would this next stage in Nevada mean? What would the Associate program become?

Everyone had their individual hopes for advancement and reward, but promises had been broken. He was supposed to join a small, elite group of physicians on the headquarters staff, or be positioned for a leadership role at the National Institutes of Health. Daniel would climb the law enforcement ladder. Lin would be a star in American-Chinese business development.

But Carol had been executed, Hank was probably dead, and if Kade was alive, his days were numbered once he got back on the network.

And now he was complicit in Kade's disloyalty. He was trapped.

The road signs showed their route had merged into I-80 east of Reno and continued for about thirty minutes before exiting and heading south on a Lincoln Highway, Route 50. It looked like Sentry Patrick, seated behind him, was the only Sentry who was awake other than the driver, Bernard.

Walter had shut his eyes for a few minutes when he heard an almost simultaneous chime of the Sentry phones. This had occurred twice during the drive, and the Sentries had seemed highly interested in the messages. Bernard and Maravar proceeded to check their messages while the other two slept. And that's when Walter noticed something was wrong with Bernard. Bernard grabbed his head with both hands and cried out in pain.

The van drifted left, across the center lane stripe to the other side. Walter could feel the vehicle hitting coarse gravel on the road shoulder. He considered unbuckling his seat belt and scrambling to the front to grab the wheel, but it all happened too fast. The van left the road and veered into the desert, bouncing and smashing through brush and running over small boulders.

"What's going on?" Sentry Ash yelled from the front passenger seat as he woke up, but got no answer from Bernard. Ash tried to steady the wheel, but there was nowhere to steer at this point.

Ten seconds later, the van plunged into a shallow wash and everyone was thrown forward as it came to a sudden halt.

A struggle broke out in the rear seats. Daniel pulled Maravar's Sig Sauer out of the holster while Maravar looked unconscious, and then Daniel pistol-whipped Patrick with two hard whacks.

"Run!" Daniel said to Lin as he slid the side door of the van open and jumped out, pulling Lin with him. Walter followed her and they both ran into the darkness while Daniel yanked open the front passenger door. Both of the front-seat airbags had deployed, and Daniel had a gun pressed against Ash's temple before the stunned Ash could think to draw his own weapon. Daniel saw Bernard was motionless in a tangle of seat belt with his eyes open and glazed.

"Get out and down on your knees," he yelled.

Ash slid out looking stunned, and then stood and turned toward him. "Come on, man, you're not really gonna—"

Daniel lowered the pistol and fired a shot through Ash's knee. Ash crumpled to the ground in agony.

"I've fucking *had* it," Daniel said. He checked Ash for any other weapons and found a small hunting knife. Out of his peripheral vision, he saw Patrick stepping up to the second row of seats to come out the side door, so he pivoted and fired two shots into the door area.

"Get out and down on the ground! Now! Hands on your head!"

Patrick stumbled out and onto the ground. His hand was bleeding from a bullet ricochet.

"What happened?" Patrick asked.

"Shut up," Daniel said. He pressed the gun barrel against Patrick's knee and squeezed the trigger. Patrick screamed out in pain and never stopped moaning after that. Daniel stood in the glow of the van's interior light and caught his breath.

"Need any help?" Walter asked.

Daniel swung around and pointed the gun at Walter's head for a split second before lowering it. "Sorry," Daniel said. He could see Lin now standing at the fringe of the light. "I didn't see you guys come back."

"Should we call somebody?" Walter asked.

"I don't know about you," Daniel said, "but I don't want to be found for a while. Who knows if the van or their phones are being tracked. We can get some food and water from the van, and we can just walk or flag down a car if we need to. Tie these guys up and leave them with some water. See if they have any cash and ditch the weapons. Then we'll call in a tip to someone where they are later today."

"I saw we're in Eureka County," Walter said.

"We can go call the Eureka County sheriff, then," Daniel said. "Let's destroy all of their phones."

Lin picked up Ash's phone from the front seat and gave him a hard kick to the ribs. She looked at the illuminated phone screen.

"It's just after one o'clock." She set the phone down on a large rock and smashed it with another.

"You both feel good enough to walk?" Daniel asked.

Walter nodded and looked at Lin, and she nodded and said, "Yeah."

"No one's watching us anymore," Daniel said. "No more cameras or microphones."

Walter's eyes filled with tears. "I don't believe it. We're free."

"Oh my God," Lin said, "this is going to be the best sunrise ever."

CHAPTER 75

President Darryl M. Greer looked steadily into the camera as his address broadcast live. "Earlier this morning our country suffered one of the most ruthless and despicable terror attacks since 9/11. An American-based organization calling itself the Chapter launched hundreds of attacks in an attempt to assassinate our members of Congress in their home states.

"At this time we know that three of our members, Senator Jared Scheider of Kentucky, Congressman Steve Gramling of Minnesota, and Congressman Carl Lasker of Louisiana were killed in this unspeakable atrocity and act of evil. Our prayers are with their families.

"We know that ten more members were seriously wounded. We are withholding names today as we are in discussion with their families. I ask for your prayers in their recovery.

"We know that four family members of our Congress members were killed and seventeen were wounded. We know that thirty-one law-enforcement personnel have been killed and fifty-seven wounded in doing their utmost to protect and defend our members and their families.

"As this horrible attack was directed against hundreds of members of our Congress, it was the heroic actions and, for some, the ultimate sacrifice, of our FBI agents, state and local law enforcement officials, and emergency responders that prevented many more fatalities and casualties. Your country has the highest gratitude for your heroic efforts.

"We will have further details on this attack, the Chapter, and its members as this day and week progress, and we will give you the most accurate information possible. We have already conducted aggressive counterterror operations against the Chapter to dismantle its ability to cause harm.

"Our citizens and the families of our elected officials can be assured that I will do everything in my power to bring these murderers to justice and ensure that this threat is eliminated.

"I ask for your prayers today for our Congress, our courageous public officials, and for their families."

CHAPTER 76

Kade left this particular visit for last and decided he'd just show up unannounced. It was worth a shot to see if he was here.

He walked to the front door and rang the doorbell. A minute later, Jerry Lerner opened the door with a happy, surprised look on his face.

"Well, if it ain't Flash in the flesh." He came out on the stoop with a big smile and lowered his voice. "Took me a sec with the cap and mustache. How the hell are ya?"

"Good!"

Kade gave him a hug when Lerner offered a handshake, and the older man seemed to appreciate it.

"I honestly thought I'd never see you again," Lerner said. "How did ya get my address?"

"I talked to Rob after the funeral for Chris Velasquez and he gave it to me."

Lerner's smile faded, and he gave a solemn nod. "Come on in."

"I should have called. I'm sorry," Kade said. "But with everything that happened, I'm pretty skittish about being on the phone."

"Not a problem. The missus is out for a coupla hours, so I can suspend my honey-do list. I was fixin' to have a beer. Want one?" he asked as they passed through the kitchen.

"Yeah, thanks."

Lerner twisted the tops off two bottles of Rolling Rock and handed him one. "What brings ya back in town? I thought you were going back to Boston after you testified."

"Not quite. I have to appear before the House Intelligence Subcommittee on Terrorism."

Lerner gave him a fake look of pain. "Sounds like fun." He picked up a jar of peanuts. "So, are you goin' in witness protection?"

"Yeah. Next time you hear from me, I'll be going by the name Kyle Smith."

Lerner nodded. "Kyle Smith . . . That sounds all right. Let's head out back."

They went out the sliding glass door to the deck overlooking a small yard and vegetable garden. Next to it was a spot for a basketball hoop where the driveway curled around the side of the house and stopped. A picnic table was centered in the deck, and they took seats on the benches facing each other.

"Well, three months gone, and Speaker Bostwick is still throwing blame-bombs at the president on the attack," Lerner said.

"And at the intel community," Kade said. "But they're always the convenient punching bag. It never matters who's in office."

"The investigation sounds like a mess. That Marshall Owens really muddied the waters with those videos he left behind, huh?"

Kade nodded with a mouthful of peanuts.

"It's like a PR campaign from the grave, I swear. Hard to believe polls show Americans think the cartels are partially responsible for the prison problems and attack. The cartel money link to AgriteX was exposed. And since we're not being told everything about the Chapter, disinformation and rumor are ruling the day. "

"Well, that Owens was nuttier than squirrel shit."

"Maybe he had good intentions a decade ago, but somewhere along the way he lost himself. Then his son died. I think he really believed the right technology, leadership, or policy could have prevented it. He thought *he* should have prevented it."

"So how are *you* feelin' these days?" Lerner asked.

"Good, thanks. My symptoms from the Chapter protocols have gone away, hopefully for good. And my hypomania's improved some too. I'm using less medication, maybe because now I have more focus than I've had in years." He smiled big and said, "See, I'm no longer the mess you thought I was."

"That's great," Lerner said and gave Kade a funny look. "I haven't heard anything emerge in the press about the Chapter's technology since your debriefing either. Another reason people feel like they're not gettin' the full story. How could thousands be radicalized for an attack under the radar?"

"Yeah, I know. A lot of details around the recovery of Sentry bodies by the CDC and the AgriteX technology have been classified. Since some of the Chapter technology came from DARPA, and Owens had that involvement with DARPA years ago, there are some major internal investigations going on."

"You wonder where they're puttin' the Zulu prisoners they've found."

"Not back in private prisons, I bet," Kade said.

"I hope not. One piece of good news I heard was that one Zachary Poole was found dead in his car on the side of the highway," Lerner said.

"Yes, Sentry Poole was an FBI employee, and I imagine that caused some huge security reviews."

Lerner took a large swig to finish his beer.

"Everyone in the administration sounds confident this won't happen again."

"Yeah, they're confident they got Joshua Pierce too. I've kept my mouth shut, but I'm not so sure about that."

"Why's that?"

"They reviewed some thermal imagery of the RV that was targeted from his voiceprint, and the person in the passenger seat looks about twenty degrees cooler than the other one."

Lerner paused to take this in, and then said, "You mean, already buzzard bait."

"Yeah, and I doubt Pierce was in the driver's seat either. Plus, there were fresh tire tracks from another vehicle visible next to the RV before missile impact."

"Interesting," Lerner said. "I imagine they're still tryin' to track people down."

"All of the AgriteX contacts were erased from the cloud," Kade said. "And the employee electronic and paper records couldn't be found or went up in smoke. I guess they'll have to work backward from W-2 forms to try and locate more suspects that way."

"And what about the other people you mentioned—Guardians and whatnot?"

"Who knows if they'll regroup? They said they had two other facilities in Montana and Nevada, but it was hard to know what lies we were told. The FBI only has limited data to work from at the moment."

"How about your peers who were in there with ya?"

"I haven't heard anything, but they wouldn't know how to contact me anyway. I hope they got out, at least the three who had a chance."

"Well, you made it out of there. I heard there was some talk of recognition for you. An intelligence award or something?"

Kade shrugged. "It was nice talk, but we contractors aren't employees of the government and aren't eligible for anything. Hey, I got some nice thank-yous from Directors Conroy and Hassett. A nice bonus and some follow-up medical care. They've taken care of me. I can't complain."

"You should be very proud of what you did, and I have to give kudos to Rob for finding you."

"Thanks for your guidance and standing behind me. We all did the best we could, ramping up in such a short time. Would it be okay if I called you for some advice here and there?"

"Ha, I'll take a call from Kyle Smith any time. Or just show up at my doorstep again. It was an honor to work with ya."

"Thanks."

"Oh, that reminds me, I have something for ya. Hold on." Lerner got up and walked inside for a moment like he was excited.

Kade watched a handsome cardinal land on a nearby pine tree, look around for a few seconds, and fly away. It had been Lerner's job to train Kade for the operation, but Lerner had done more than that—he'd helped restore Kade's confidence and bring his self-awareness to a new level. He wished he had trusted Lerner and the team more from the beginning, but at that time he hadn't been ready.

Alex had been a casualty of that mistrust, that weakness. When Kade had visited him last week in Worcester, he was surprised how a fully recovered Alex had followed the news and pieced together his involvement in helping stop the attacks. When Kade apologized again for getting him involved and the near-fatal result, Alex said he would've done it all over again.

The thought made him damp-eyed and he took a deep breath.

He again imagined what the toll of the Chapter's attack could've been if CLEARCUT hadn't provided some warning. He'd never say anything in public, but it could have been so much worse.

Lerner reappeared, holding a piece of paper and two more beers.

"Someone you know was reassigned to FBI headquarters, and asked me to give this to ya."

Kade hesitated. "Jerry, the last time someone handed me a note it was *really* bad news."

Lerner laughed. "No, this won't make ya sick. These digits were to be delivered if I ran into you again and you wanted to catch up, that's all."

Kade opened the note and smiled. It was Carla Singleton's phone number.

"Good deal, thanks. I'll give her a call later."

"She's smarter than shit," Lerner said.

"And I know that's a very high standard for you."

"So what's next?"

"I'm not completely sure," Kade said. "While I'd like to move near my aunt and sister to make sure they're never threatened again, that may not be practical now. I may still have to come back and testify more. And it may be a good idea for me to stay somewhere in reach of the Beltway."

"Why's that?"

"I've gotten more inquiries from different agencies. I'm hearing the Bureau might need some more help in strategy—they want to make sure these guys don't try to reorganize. They've asked if I can be available for questions or discussion."

"And what did you say?"

"I told them it was an honor to work on CLEARCUT, but my contract was done. If they needed more help, I might be willing to start another one."

Lerner laughed and raised his beer in salutation.

"What?" Kade asked.

"Congratulations, you're now a consultant."

ACKNOWLEDGMENTS

A small group of fantastic people provided reviews and suggestions through many drafts, helping to make this project a fun and memorable adventure. Some may not want recognition by name, so I used initials for everyone.

My sincerest thanks to: WG, BK, SR, ES, NK, ND, SK, DH, JB, MP, and TM.

Many thanks to the Thomas & Mercer team! Kjersti Egerdahl, for discovering my story, and Jacque Ben-Zekry, Tiffany Pokorny, and Dan Byrne for their support. I would also like to thank Nancy Brandwein, Dara Kaye, Monique Vescia, and Amy Eye for their editing expertise.

My choice of Chinook heritage for the villain of the novel only reflects my respect for the Native American tribes of the Pacific Northwest. The Chinook words I included were pulled from the *Dictionary of Chinook Jargon* by George Gibbs (2005). Any misuse of the language is entirely my own doing. While working on this novel, I learned that Ambassador John Christopher Stevens, who died in the line of duty on September 12, 2012, in Benghazi, Libya, was of Chinook ancestry. As the United States continues to defend itself against the global terror threat, there couldn't be a better example of bravery and service than Chris Stevens. May we never forget his sacrifice.

I would also like to apologize if my characterization of any military branch or government agency was perceived in a negative light while creating this story. I had the honor of serving with wonderful people in the military, and many of my friends continue to serve. I'm proud of you all.

•　　•　　•

If you've enjoyed this book, I'd greatly appreciate an Amazon review (you have to log in to Amazon to write one) and a Goodreads review if you use that service. These reviews are treasured for helping readers find new authors like me.

My author website is www.jklages.com. I also have a Facebook author page and would welcome a "Like" and any feedback comments you're willing to share on a post, message, or e-mail. If you give me a shout, I promise to write back!

Thank you for spreading the word, and I look forward to sharing the next Kade Sims adventure with you all as soon as I can.

—JK

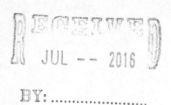

ABOUT THE AUTHOR

Jay Klages is a former military intelligence officer and West Point graduate. He attended the MBA program at Arizona State University, where he successfully deprogrammed himself for service in corporate America. He currently lives in Gilbert, Arizona.